PORTRAI...

After a tip from a reporter, Lieutenant Eve Dallas finds the body of a young woman in a Dumpster on Delancey Street. Just hours before, the news station had mysteriously received a portfolio of professional portraits of the woman. The photos seemed to be nothing out of the ordinary for any pretty young woman starting a modeling career. Except she wasn't a model. And the photos were taken after she had been murdered.

Now Eve is on the trail of a killer who's a perfectionist and an artist. He carefully observes and records his victims' every move...

"A well-paced and expertly rendered series."

—*Publishers Weekly*

"Edgy and raw." —*Booklist*

Please turn to the back of this book
for a special excerpt from J. D. Robb's

IMITATION IN DEATH

Available from Berkley Books!

JAN 2019

SF

Anthologies

SILENT NIGHT
(with Susan Plunkett, Dee Holmes, and Claire Cross)

OUT OF THIS WORLD
(with Laurell K. Hamilton, Susan Krinard, and Maggie Shayne)

REMEMBER WHEN
(with Nora Roberts)

BUMP IN THE NIGHT
(with Mary Blayney, Ruth Ryan Langan, and Mary Kay McComas)

DEAD OF NIGHT
(with Mary Blayney, Ruth Ryan Langan, and Mary Kay McComas)

THREE IN DEATH

SUITE 606
(with Mary Blayney, Ruth Ryan Langan, and Mary Kay McComas)

IN DEATH

THE LOST
(with Patricia Gaffney, Mary Blayney, and Ruth Ryan Langan)

THE OTHER SIDE
*(with Mary Blayney, Patricia Gaffney, Ruth Ryan Langan, and
Mary Kay McComas)*

TIME OF DEATH

THE UNQUIET
*(with Mary Blayney, Patricia Gaffney, Ruth Ryan Langan, and
Mary Kay McComas)*

MIRROR, MIRROR
(with Mary Blayney, Elaine Fox, Mary Kay McComas, and R. C. Ryan)

DOWN THE RABBIT HOLE
(with Mary Blayney, Elaine Fox, Mary Kay McComas, and R. C. Ryan)

PORTRAIT
IN
DEATH

J. D. Robb

BERKLEY
New York

BERKLEY
An imprint of Penguin Random House LLC
375 Hudson Street, New York, New York 10014

Copyright © 2003 by Nora Roberts
Excerpt from *Imitation in Death* by J. D. Robb copyright © 2003 by Nora Roberts
Penguin Random House supports copyright. Copyright fuels creativity, encourages
diverse voices, promotes free speech, and creates a vibrant culture. Thank you for buying
an authorized edition of this book and for complying with copyright laws by not
reproducing, scanning, or distributing any part of it in any form without permission.
You are supporting writers and allowing Penguin Random House to continue to
publish books for every reader.

BERKLEY is a registered trademark and the B colophon
is a trademark of Penguin Random House LLC.

ISBN: 9780425189030

Berkley mass-market edition / March 2003

Printed in the United States of America
21 23 25 27 29 30 28 26 24 22

Cover art by Oyster Pond Press
Cover design by G-Force Design

The light of the body is in the eye.

—New Testament

A mother is a mother still,
The holiest thing alive.

—Samuel Coleridge

PORTRAIT
IN
DEATH

Prologue

We begin to die with our first breath. Death is inside us, ticking closer, closer, with every beat of our heart. It is the end no man can escape. Yet we cling to life, we worship it despite its transience. Or perhaps, because of it.

But all the while, we wonder of death. We build monuments to it, revere it with our rituals. What will our death be? we ask ourselves. Will it be sudden and swift, long and lingering? Will there be pain? Will it come after a long, full life, or will we be cut off—violently, inexplicably—in our prime?

When is our time? For death is for all time.

We create an afterlife because we cannot rush through our days chased by the specter of an end. We make gods who guide us, who will greet us at golden gates to lead us into an eternal land of milk and honey.

We are children, bound hand and foot by the chains of good with its eternal reward, and evil with its eternal punishment. And so, most never truly live, not freely.

I have studied life and death.

There is only one purpose. To live. To live free. To

become. To know, with each breath, you are more than the shadows. You are the light, and the light must be fed, absorbed from any and all sources. Then, the end is not death. In the end we become *the light.*

They will say I am mad, but I have found sanity. I have found Truth and Salvation. When I have become, what I am, what I do, what I have created will be magnificent.

And we will all live forever.

Chapter 1

Life didn't get much better. Eve knocked back her first cup of coffee as she grabbed a shirt out of the closet. She went for thin and sleeveless as the summer of 2059 was currently choking New York, and the rest of the Eastern seaboard, in a tight, sweaty grip.

But hey, she'd rather be hot than cold.

Nothing was going to spoil her day. Absolutely nothing.

She pulled on the shirt, then with a quick glance at the door to make certain she was alone, did a fast, hip-shaking boogie to the AutoChef for another hit of coffee. A glance at her wrist unit told her she had plenty of time if she wanted breakfast, so what the hell, she programmed it for a couple of blueberry pancakes.

She went back to the closet for her boots. She was a tall, lean woman, currently wearing khaki-colored pants and a blue tank. Her hair was short, choppy in style, and brown, with lighter streaks teased out by that mean and brilliant sun. It suited her angular face, with its wide brown eyes and generous mouth. There was a shallow dent in her chin—a feature her husband, Roarke, liked to trace with a fingertip.

Despite the heat she'd face when she stepped outside the big, blissfully cool bedroom, outside the big, blissfully cool house, she pulled out a lightweight jacket. And tossed it over the weapon harness she had draped over the back of the sofa in the sitting area.

Her badge was already in her pocket.

Lieutenant Eve Dallas grabbed her coffee and pancakes out of the AutoChef, plopped down on the sofa, and prepared to enjoy a luxurious breakfast before clocking in for a day as a murder cop.

With a feline's psychic sense when food was involved, the fat cat Galahad appeared out of nowhere to leap on the sofa beside her and stare at her plate with his dual-colored eyes.

"Mine." She forked up pancakes, and stared back at the cat. "Roarke may be an easy mark, pal, but I'm not. Probably already been fed, too," she added as she propped her feet on the table and continued to plow through her breakfast. "Bet you were down in the kitchen at dawn sidling around Summerset."

She leaned down until they were nose to nose. "Well, there won't be any of that for three beautiful, wonderful, mag-ass weeks. And do you know why? Do you know *why*?"

Overcome with joy, she caved and gave the cat a bite of pancake. "Because the skinny, tight-assed son of a bitch is going on vacation! Far, far away." She almost sang it, riding on the bliss of knowing Roarke's majordomo, her personal nemesis, wouldn't be there to irritate her that night, or for many nights to come.

"I have twenty-one Summerset-free days ahead of me, and I rejoice."

"I'm not sure the cat shares your jubilation." Roarke spoke from the doorway where he was currently leaning on the jamb watching his wife.

"Sure he does." She scooped up more of the pancakes before Galahad could nose his way onto the plate. "He's just playing it cool. I thought you had some interstellar honcho transmission to take care of this morning."

"Done."

He strolled in, and Eve added to her considerable pleasure

by watching him move. Smooth, long-legged, graceful in a way that was pure and dangerous male.

He could give the cat lessons, she mused. Grinning at him, she decided there wasn't a woman alive who wouldn't be thrilled to have that face next to hers over breakfast.

As faces went, it was a masterpiece, carved on one of God's more generous days. Lean, with edgy cheekbones, with a firm, full mouth that could make her own water. All this was framed by a sweep of glossy black hair, and high-lighted by Celtic blue eyes.

The rest of him wasn't bad either, she thought. All long and rangy and tough.

"Come here, pretty boy." She fisted a hand in his shirt, gave him a yank. Then sank her teeth, with some enthusiasm, in his bottom lip. She gave it a lazy flick of her tongue before settling back again. "You're better than pancakes any day."

"You're certainly chipper this morning."

"Damn straight. Chipper's my middle name. I'm going out to spread joy and laughter to all of mankind."

"What a nice change of pace." There was amusement rid-ing along with the Irish in his voice. "Perhaps you'll start now by going down with me to see Summerset off."

She grimaced. "That might spoil my appetite." Testing, she polished off the pancakes. "No, no, it doesn't. I can do that. I can go down and wave bye-bye."

Brow lifted, he gave her hair a quick tug. "Nicely."

"I won't do the happy dance until he's out of sight. Three weeks." After a joyful shudder, she rose and foiled the cat by putting the plate out of reach. "I won't see his ugly face or hear the squeaky sound of his voice for three orgasmic weeks."

"Why do I think he's probably thinking something very similar about you?" Sighing, Roarke pushed to his feet. "I'm as sure about that as I am that both of you will miss sniping at each other."

"Will not." She picked up her harness, strapped on her weapon. "Tonight, to celebrate—and make no mistake, I'm going to celebrate—I'm going to lounge around the living room and eat pizza. Naked."

Roarke's eyebrows winged up. "I'll certainly enjoy that."

"Get your own pizza." She shrugged into her jacket. "I have to wave bye-bye now. I'm due at Central."

"Practice this first." He laid his hands on her shoulders. "Have a good trip. Enjoy your vacation."

"You didn't say I had to speak to him." She blew out a breath at Roarke's calm stare. "All right, all right, it's worth it. Have a good trip." She stretched her lips into a smile. "Enjoy your vacation. Asshole. I'll leave off the asshole, I just wanted to say it now."

"Understood." He ran his hands down her arms, then took her hand. The cat darted out of the room ahead of them. "He's looking forward to this. He hasn't taken much time for himself in the last couple of years."

"Didn't want to take his beady eyes off me long enough. But that's okay, that's all right," she said in a cheerful voice. "Because he's going, and that's what's important."

She heard the cat screech, the curse that followed, then a series of thuds. Eve was fast on her feet, but Roarke beat her to the stairs, and was already sprinting down there to where Summerset lay in a heap along with scattered piles of linen.

She took one look at the scene at the bottom of the stairs and said, "Oh, shit."

"Don't move. Don't try to move," Roarke murmured as he checked Summerset for injuries.

Reaching the bottom of the stairs, Eve crouched. Summerset's always pale face was bone-white and already going clammy. She read shock in his eyes, along with considerable pain.

"It's my leg," he managed in a voice gone reedy. "I'm afraid it's broken."

She could see that for herself by the awkward angle it took below the knee. "Go get a blanket," she told Roarke as she pulled out her pocket-link. "He's shocky. I'll get the MTs."

"Keep him still." Moving fast, Roarke whipped one of the tangled sheets over Summerset, then dashed upstairs. "He could have other injuries."

"It's just my leg. And my shoulder." He closed his eyes

as Eve called for medical assistance. "I tripped over the bloody cat." Gritting his teeth, he opened his eyes and did his best to smirk at Eve though the heat of the fall was rapidly turning to a cold that made his teeth chatter. "I imagine you think it's a pity I didn't break my neck."

"Thought crossed by mind." Lucid, she thought with some relief. Didn't lose consciousness. Eyes a little glassy. She glanced over as Roarke came back with a blanket. "They're on their way. He's coherent, and pissy. I don't think there's any head injury. Take more than a spill down the stairs to crack that stone anyway. Tripped over the cat."

"For Christ's sake."

Eve watched Roarke take Summerset's hand, hold it. However she and the skinny baboon dealt with each other, she understood the man was more Roarke's father than his own blood had been.

"I'll get the gates, clear the MTs through."

She headed to the security panel to open the gates that closed off the house, the expansive lawns, the personal world Roarke had built, from the city. Of Galahad there was no sign, nor Eve thought sourly, would there likely be for a while.

Damn cat had probably done it on purpose to spoil her good time because she hadn't given him enough pancakes.

So they would hear the sirens, she opened the front door, and nearly staggered against the wall of heat. Barely eight, and hot enough to fry brains. The sky was the color of sour milk, the air the consistency of the syrup she'd so cheerfully consumed when there'd been joy in her heart and a spring in her step.

Have a nice trip, she thought. Son of a bitch.

Her 'link beeped just as she heard the sirens. "Here they come," she called to Roarke, then stepped aside to take the transmission. "Dallas. Shit, Nadine," she said the minute she saw the image of Channel 75's top reporter on screen. "This isn't a good time."

"I got a tip. Seems like a serious tip. Meet me at Delancey and Avenue D. I'm leaving now."

"Hold on, hold on, I'm not going down to the Lower East Side because you—"

"I think somebody's dead." She shifted so Eve could see the images on the printouts she'd spread over her desk. "I think she's dead."

It was a young brunette in various poses, some candid from the looks of them, others staged.

"Why do you think she's dead?"

"I'll fill you in when I see you. We're wasting time."

Eve motioned in the MTs as she scowled at the 'link. "I'll send a black-and-white—"

"I didn't give you a heads-up so you could fob this, and me, off on uniforms. I've got something here, Dallas, and it's hot. Meet me, or I check it out alone. Then I go on the air with what I've got, and what I find."

"Fucking A, what a day this is turning into. All right. Stand on the corner, get a bagel or something. Don't do anything until I get there. I've got a mess to clean up here first." Blowing out a breath she looked over to where the MTs examined Summerset. "Then I'm on my way."

She clicked off, jammed the 'link back in her pocket. She walked back to Roarke, and couldn't think of anything to do but pat his arm while he watched the medicals. "I've got a thing I've got to check out."

"I can't remember how old he is. I can't quite remember."

"Hey." This time she gave his arm a squeeze. "He's too mean to be down for long. Look, I'll ditch this thing if you want me to stay around."

"No, you go on." He shook himself. "Tripped over the goddamn cat. Could've killed himself." He turned, pressed his lips to her forehead. "Life's full of nasty surprises. Take care, Lieutenant, I'd as soon not have another one today."

Traffic was mean, but that suited the ruination of her mood. A maxibus breakdown on Lex had everything snarled from 75th, as far south as she could see. Horns blasted. Above, traffic copters clipped and hummed among the air traffic to keep the rubberneckers from jamming the sky as well.

Tired of sitting in the sea of commuters, she flipped her

siren, then punched into a quick vertical. She cut east, then headed south again when she found some clear road.

She'd called Dispatch and informed them she was taking an hour personal. No point in reporting in that she was following the crooked finger of an on-air reporter, without authorization or any clear reason.

But she trusted Nadine's instincts—the woman's nose for a story was like a beagle's for a rabbit—and had tagged Peabody, her aide, with orders to detour to Delancey.

There was plenty of business being done on the street. The area was a hive of delis, coffee shops, and specialty stores that crowded along on sidewalk level and served the inhabitants of the apartments above them. The bakery sold to the guy who ran the fix-it shop next door, and he'd diddle with the AutoChef for the woman who ran the clothes store on the other side, while she ran across the street to buy fruit from the stand.

It was a tidy system, Eve imagined. Old and established, and though it still bore some scars from the Urban Wars, it had rebuilt itself.

It wasn't a sector where you'd want to take a stroll late at night, and a couple of blocks south or west you'd find the not-so-tidy communities of sidewalk sleepers and chemi-heads, but on a sweltering summer morning, this slice of Delancey was all business.

She pulled up behind a double-parked delivery truck, flipped up her On Duty light.

With some reluctance, she left the cool cocoon of her vehicle and stepped into the hot, wet wall of summer. The smells hit her first—brine and coffee and sweat. The more appealing hint of melon from the fruit vendor was overpowered by the rush of steam gushing out of a glide-cart. It carried the distinct odor of egg substitute and onions.

She did her best not to breathe it in—who *ate* that shit—as she stood on the corner scanning.

She didn't spot Nadine, or Peabody, but she did see a trio of what she took to be shopkeepers and a City Maintenance drone having an argument in front of a green recycle bin.

She kept an eye on them while she considered calling

Roarke to check on Summerset. Maybe there'd been a miracle and the medical techs had glued his bone back together and he was, even now, on his way to transport. As a result of the morning trauma, he wasn't taking three weeks vacation. But four.

And while he was gone, he'd fall madly in love with a licensed companion—who would have sex with that freak unless she was paid for it—and decide to settle down with her in Europe.

No, not Europe. It wasn't far away enough. They'd relocate in the Alpha Colony on Taurus I, and never again return to this planet called Earth.

As long as she didn't call, she could hold on to the silver threads of that little fantasy.

But she remembered the pain in Summerset's eyes and the way Roarke had held his hand.

With a mighty sigh, she pulled out her pocket-link. Before she could use it one of the shopkeepers shoved City Maintenance. Maintenance shoved back. Eve saw the first punch coming even if Maintenance didn't, and he ended up on his ass. She shoved the 'link back in her pocket and headed down the sidewalk to break it up.

She was still three feet away when she smelled it. She'd walked with death too many times to mistake it.

The living were currently rolling around on the sidewalk, being cheered on or berated by the people who popped out of storefronts or stopped their hike to work to watch the show.

Eve didn't bother with her badge, but simply hauled the guy on top up by his shirt, and planted her foot on the chest of the one still on the ground.

"Knock it off."

The shopkeeper was a little guy, and wiry with it. He jerked away, leaving Eve with a handful of sweaty shirt. The blood in his eye was from temper, but his lip was sporting the real thing. "This is none of your business, lady, so just move before you get hurt."

"That's Lieutenant Lady." The guy on the ground seemed content to stay there. He was paunchy, he was winded, and his left eye was already swelling shut. But as she didn't have any love for anyone in any sector of maintenance, she kept her boot weighted on his chest as she flipped out her badge.

The smile she sent the shopkeeper showed a lot of teeth. "You want to take bets on who's going to get hurt here? Now back off, and shut it down."

"A cop. Good. You ought to throw his sorry ass in a cage. I pay my taxes." Shopkeeper threw up his hands, turning to the crowd for support like a boxer circling the ring between rounds. "We pay out the wazoo, and dickheads like this screw us over."

"He assaulted me. I want to file charges."

Eve spared a glance at the man under her foot. "Shut up. Name," she demanded, pointing at the shopkeeper.

"Remke. Waldo Remke." He fisted his bruised hands on his narrow hips. "*I* want to file charges."

"Yeah, yeah. This your place?" She gestured toward the deli behind her.

"Been mine for eighteen years, and my father's place before that. We pay taxes—"

"I heard that part. This your bin?"

"We paid for that bin twenty times over. Me, Costello, and Mintz." While sweat ran down his face, he jerked a thumb toward two men standing behind him. "And half the time it's broken. You smell that? You fucking smell that? Who's gonna come in our places to do business with that stink out here? This is the third time one of us has called for repair in the last six weeks. They never do shit."

There were mutters and murmurs of agreement from the crowd, and some joker called out: Death to fascists!

With the heat, the stink, and the blood already spilled, Eve knew the harmless neighborhood crowd could turn into a mob on a dime.

"Mr. Remke, I want you, Mr. Costello, and Mr. Mintz to step back. The rest of you people, get busy somewhere else."

She heard the rapid clop behind her that could only be cop shoes on pavement. "Peabody," she said without turning, "move this crowd along before they find a rope and lynch this guy."

A little breathless, Peabody jogged up beside Eve. "Yes, sir. We need you people to disperse. Please go about your business."

The sight of the uniform, even though it was already wilting in the heat, had most of the crowd sidling away. Peabody adjusted her sunshades and her hat, both of which had tipped during her jog up the sidewalk.

Her square face was a bit shiny with perspiration, but behind the tinted lenses, her dark eyes were steady. She shifted them to the bin, then to Eve. "Lieutenant?"

"Yeah. Name," she said and tapped her boot on the city worker's chest.

"Larry Poole. Look, Lieutenant, I'm just doing my job. I come out here in response to a repair call, and this guy's up my ass."

"When did you get here?"

"I ain't been here ten minutes. Son of a bitch didn't even give me a chance to look at the bin before he's in my face."

"You're going to look at it now. I don't want any trouble from you," she said to Remke.

"I want to file a complaint." He folded his arms, and curled his lip when Eve helped Poole up.

"They dump all kinda shit in here," Poole began. "That's the problem, see? They don't use the proper slots. If you dump organic in the nonorganic side, it stinks up the whole business."

He limped to the bin, then took his time strapping on his filter mask. "All they gotta do is follow directions, but no, they'd rather complain every five fricking minutes."

"How's the lock work?"

"Got a code. See they rent it from the city, and the city keeps the codes. My scanner reads the code, then . . . Crap, this one's busted."

"I told you it was busted."

With some dignity, Poole straightened, and stared at Remke with his blackened eyes. "The lock and seal's busted. Kids do that sometimes. It ain't my damn fault. Who the hell knows why kids do the shit they do? Probably busted it last night, dumped some dead cat inside from the smell of it."

"I'm not paying because your locks are defective," Remke began.

"Mr. Remke," Eve warned. "Save it. It's unlocked, unsealed?" she asked Poole.

"Yeah. Now I'm gonna have to call a crew down here for cleanup. Damn kids." He started to pry up the lid, but Eve slapped a hand down on his.

"Would you step back, please. Peabody?"

The smell was already making her queasy, but Peabody knew it was about to get worse. "Wish I hadn't had that egg pocket on the way here."

Eve got a grip on the lid, shook her head at her aide. "You eat that crap? What's wrong with you?"

"They're pretty good, really. And it's a quick fix." She sucked in a breath, held it. Nodded. Together they pushed up the heavy lid.

The stench of death poured out.

She'd been crammed into the organic side of the bin. Only half her face showed. Eve could see her eyes had been green—a sharp, bottle green. And she'd been young, probably pretty.

Death, spurred on by the heat, had bloated her obscenely.

"What the hell did they put in there?" Poole pushed up, looked inside. Then immediately stumbled away to retch.

"Call it in, Peabody. Nadine's on her way. She got hung up in traffic, or she'd be here by now. I want you to keep her and her camera back. She'll give you lip, but you keep this block clear."

"Somebody's in there." All the anger had drained from Remke's face. He simply stared at Eve with horrified eyes. "A person."

"I'm going to need you to go inside, Mr. Remke. All of you. I'll be in to speak with you shortly."

"I'll look." He had to clear his throat. "I might—if it's someone from the neighborhood, I might know . . . If it'll help, I'll look."

"It's hard," she told him, but gestured him over.

His face was pale, but he stepped up. He kept his eyes closed for a moment, then set his teeth, opened them. Even the faint hint of color drained out of his cheeks.

"Rachel." He fought not to gag, and stumbled back. "Oh God. Oh God. It's Rachel—I don't know her last name. She, Jesus, Jesus, she worked at the 24/7 across the street. She was a kid." Tears began to track down his white face, and he turned away to cover it. "Twenty, twenty-one, tops. College student. She was always studying."

"Go inside, Mr. Remke. I'll take care of her now."

"She was just a kid." He swiped at his face. "What kind of an animal does that to a kid?"

She could have told him there were all sorts of animals, animals more vicious, more deadly than anything in nature. But she said nothing as he walked to Poole.

"Come on inside." He laid a hand on Poole's shoulder. "Come inside where it's cool. I'll get you some water."

"Peabody, field kit's in the car."

Turning back to the body, she clipped the recorder onto her lapel. "All right, Rachel," she murmured. "Let's get to work. Record on. Victim is female, Caucasian, approximately twenty years of age."

She had the barricades up, and the uniforms who responded keeping the curious behind them. Once she had the body, the bin, the surrounding area on record, she sealed up and prepared to climb into the bin.

She spotted the Channel 75 van at the end of the block. Nadine would be steaming, Eve thought, from more than the humidity. She'd just have to wait her turn.

The next twenty minutes was grisly.

"Sir." Peabody offered a bottle of water as Eve climbed out.

"Thanks." She glugged down ten ounces before taking a breath, but couldn't quite wash the taste out of her mouth. She used a second bottle on her hands. "Keep those guys on ice." She nodded toward the deli. "I'm going to deal with Nadine first."

"Did you get an ID?"

"Her prints popped. Rachel Howard, part-time student at Columbia." She swiped at the sweat on her face. "Remke was right on the age. Twenty. Bag and tag," she added. "I can't get cause of death, hell I can't get a gauge on time of death the way she's been baking in there."

She looked back at the bin. "We'll see what the sweepers find, then let the ME have her."

"You want to start the knock-on-doors?"

"Hold off until I talk to Nadine." Tossing the empty bottle back to Peabody, she headed down the sidewalk. One of the gawkers started to call out to her, then shrunk back at the look on her face.

Nadine stepped out of the van, looking camera fresh and mad as a cat. "Damn you, Dallas, just how long do you think you can keep me blocked?"

"As long as it takes. I need to see those printouts. Then I need you down at Central for questioning."

"You need? You think I give a rat's ass about what you need?"

It had been an ugly morning. She was viciously hot, she stank, and the breakfast she'd so gleefully consumed was no longer settling well. The steam from the glide-cart where the operator was doing double his usual business thanks to the people who hovered, hoping to get a closer look at somebody else's death, added another greasy layer to the heavy air.

It didn't even occur to her to reign in her temper as she stared at Nadine, looking fresh as a spring morning, with a cup of iced coffee in her pretty, manicured hand.

"Fine. You have the right to remain silent—"

"What the hell is this?"

"This is your Revised Miranda warning. You're a material witness in a homicide. You." She jabbed her finger at a uniform. "Read Ms. Furst her rights, and escort her to Central. She's to be held for questioning."

"Why you stone bitch."

"Got it in one." Eve turned on her heel and walked back to confer with the ME.

Chapter 2

Inside the deli, the air was cool and smelled of coffee, of lox, of warm bread. She drank the water Remke offered her. He no longer looked like the human rocket about to launch. He looked exhausted.

People often did, in her experience, after violence.

"When's the last time you used the bin?" she asked him.

"About seven last night, right after I closed. My nephew usually closes, but he's on vacation this week. Took the wife and kids to Planet Disney—Christ knows why."

With his elbows on the counter, he rested his head in his hands, pressed his fingers to his temple. "I can't get that girl's face out of my head."

And you never will, Eve thought. Not completely. "What time did you get in this morning?"

"Six." He let out a long sigh, dropped his hands. "I noticed the . . . the smell right off. I kicked the bin. God almighty, I kicked it, and she was in there."

"You couldn't have helped her, but you can help her now. What did you do?"

"I called it in. Reamed the operator. Costello and Mintz, they got here, I don't know, about six-thirty, and we had a bitch session over it. I called back about seven 'cause nobody'd showed up. Called I don't know how many times, worked myself up good, too, until Poole got here. That was about ten minutes, I guess, before I punched him."

"You live upstairs?"

"Yeah. Me and my wife, our youngest daughter. She's sixteen." His breath shortened. "It could've been her in there. She was out last night until ten. That's curfew. She was out with a couple of her friends. I don't know what I'd do if . . . I don't know what I'd do." His voice cracked. "What does anybody do?"

"I know this is hard. Do you remember hearing anything, seeing anyone, last night? Anything that comes to mind?"

"Shelley got in right on time. We're strict about curfew, so she walked in at ten. I was watching the game on-screen— mostly waiting up for her, though. We were all in bed by eleven. I had to open, so I turned in early. I never heard a damn thing."

"Okay, tell me about Rachel. What do you know about her?"

"Not a lot. She's been working at the 24/7 for about a year, I guess. Mostly days. Some nights, but mostly days. You'd go in, and if she wasn't busy, she'd be studying. She was going to be a teacher. She had the sweetest smile." His voice cracked again. "Just made you feel good to look at her. I don't know how anybody could treat her like that."

He looked back outside, to the bin. "I don't know how anybody could do that to her."

With Peabody at her side, Eve walked across to the 24/7. "I need you to get in touch with Roarke, find out how Summerset's doing."

"He went on vacation today. You had it set on your calendar, with a trumpet fanfare and shooting stars."

"He broke his leg."

"What? When? How? Jeez."

"Fell down the damn steps this morning. I think he did it to spite me. I really do. Just check. Tell Roarke I'll be in touch as soon as I sort through some of this."

"And send your concern and support." Peabody kept her face admirably sober when Eve shifted her eyes and pinned her. "He'll know it's bogus, but it's what people do."

"Whatever."

She stepped inside. Some sensible person had killed the chirpy music that played in every 24/7, on or off planet. The place was a tomb, filled with grab-it-and-go food, overpriced staples of everyday living, and a wall of AutoChefs. A uniform loitered at the entertainment disc display while a young male clerk sat behind the counter. His eyes were red and raw.

Another young one, Eve thought. Clerks at 24/7's tended to be kids or seniors who would work ridiculous hours for stingy pay.

This one was skinny and black, with a shock of orange hair standing straight up off his head. He sported a silver lip ring, and a cheap knockoff of one of the more popular wrist units.

He took one look at Eve and began to cry again, silently.

"They said I couldn't call anybody. They said I had to stay here. I don't want to stay here."

"You can go soon." She jerked her head to send the uniform outside.

"They said Rachel's dead."

"Yes, she is. Were you friends with her?"

"I think there's a mistake. I think there's been a mistake." He swiped a hand under his nose. "If you'd let me call her, you'd see there's been a mistake."

"I'm sorry. What's your name?"

"Madinga. Madinga Jones."

"There's no mistake, Madinga, and I'm sorry because I can see you were friends. How long had you known her?"

"I just don't think this is right. I just don't think this is real." He scrubbed at his face. "She came to work here last summer, early last summer. She's going to college, she needed the job. We hang out sometimes."

"You were close. Were you involved, personally involved?"

"We were buds, that's all. I got a girl. We'd go clubbing sometimes maybe, or catch a new vid."

"Did she have a boy?"

"Not especially. She kept it loose, because she needed to study. She dug on school."

"Did she ever mention that somebody was hassling her? Maybe somebody who didn't want to keep it loose?"

"I don't . . . well, there was this guy we met at a club, and she went out with him once after, to like some restaurant he owns or something. But she said he was too grabby, and she shook him off. He didn't like it much, and kept after her for a while. But that was like months ago. Before Christmas."

"Got a name?"

"Diego." He shrugged. "I don't know the rest. Slick looking, fancy threads. Told her he was a cruiser, but he could dance, and she liked to dance."

"The club?"

"Make The Scene. Up by Union Square on Fourteenth. He—did he mess with her before he put her in there?"

"I can't tell you."

"She was a virgin." His lips trembled. "She said how she didn't want to just do it to do it. I used to rag on her about it, just for fun, you know, because we were buds. If he messed with her." The tears dried up, and his eyes went marble hard. "You gotta hurt him. You gotta hurt him the way he hurt her."

Outside, Eve dragged a hand through her hair and wished for her sunshades. Wherever the hell they were.

"Broken leg," Peabody informed her. "Jammed shoulder and some damage to the rotator cuff."

"What?"

"Summerset. Roarke said they're going to keep him overnight, and he's making arrangements for in-home care as soon as he can be released. He racked the knee of the unbroken leg, so it'll be a while before he's on his feet."

"Shit."

"Oh, and Roarke says he appreciates your concern, and will communicate same to the patient."

"Shit," she repeated.

"And just to add to your joy, a communication came through, from Nadine's representative. You have an hour to request and complete an interview, or a formal complaint will be filed by Channel 75 on behalf of Ms. Furst."

"She'll have to stew." Eve plucked Peabody's shades out of her uniform pocket, and put them on. "We need to notify Rachel Howard's next of kin."

The single thing Eve wanted when she reached Central was a shower. It was just one more thing that would have to wait. She headed straight to what the cops called The Lounge, a waiting area for interviewees, family members, potential witnesses who weren't active suspects in an investigation.

There were chairs, tables, vending machines, a couple of screens to keep those who waited occupied. Nadine, her crew, and a sharp-looking suit Eve assumed was the rep were the only current residents.

Nadine surged to her feet immediately. "Oh, we're going to go a round."

The suit, tall, slim, male, with a waving mass of brown hair and cool blue eyes, tapped her arm. "Nadine. Let me handle this. Lieutenant Dallas, I'm Carter Swan, attorney for Channel 75, and here as representative for Ms. Furst and her associates. Let me start out by saying that your treatment of my client, a respected member of the media, is unacceptable. A complaint will be made to your superiors."

"Yeah." Eve turned away to one of the vending machines. The coffee here was crap, but she needed something. "Ms. Furst," she began as she coded in her ID, then cursed under her breath when she was informed her credit was at zero. "Ms. Furst is a material witness in a criminal investigation. She was asked to come voluntarily for questioning, and was not cooperative."

She dug in her pockets for coins or tokens, came up empty. "I was within my rights, and my authority, to have your client brought in, just as it was within her rights to bring your fancy ass in here to annoy me. I need the printouts, Nadine."

Nadine sat again, crossed her long legs. She fluffed her streaky blonde hair, smiled thinly. "You'll have to show your warrant to my representative, and when he's verified its authenticity, we'll discuss the printouts."

"You don't want to play hardball with me on this."

Nadine's eyes, a feline green, sparkled with temper. "Oh, don't I?"

"Under state and federal law," Carter began, "Ms. Furst is under no obligation to turn over any property, personal or professional, without a court order."

"I called you." Nadine spoke in a quiet voice. "I didn't have to. I could have gone straight to Delancey, filed my story. But I called you, out of respect, out of friendship. And because you got there first . . ." She paused long enough to aim a hot glare at one of her crew. He seemed to shrink under it. "You shut me out. This is my story."

"You'll get your goddamn story. I just spent the last half hour in a pretty little row house in Brooklyn with the parents of a twenty-year-old girl, parents I watched fall to pieces, bit by bit when I told them their daughter was dead, when I had to tell them where she'd been all fucking night."

Nadine got slowly back to her feet as Eve strode across the room. They stood now, toe to toe.

"You wouldn't have found her if it wasn't for me."

"You're wrong. It might not have been me, but somebody would've found her. Five, six hours in a recycle bin, ninety degree temps outside, a good one-twenty inside that box, somebody would've found her pretty quick."

"Look, Dallas," Nadine began, but Eve was on a roll.

"He probably thought of that when he shoved her in there, when he sent you the images. Maybe he got a kick out of thinking about the poor son of a bitch who found her, about the cop who'd have to wade around in there with her. You know what happens to a body after a few hours in that kind of heat, Nadine?"

"That's not the point."

"No? Well, let me show you what the point is." She yanked the recorder out of her pocket, then marched over to plug it into the unit. Seconds later, the image of Rachel Howard, as Eve had found her, shot on-screen.

"She was twenty years old, studying to be a teacher, working at a 24/7. She liked to dance and collected bears. Teddy bears." Eve's voice slashed like a razor as she stared at what had become of Rachel Howard. "She has a younger sister named Melissa. Her family thought she was at the dorm where she had friends, pulling an all-nighter as she did once or twice a week, so they weren't concerned. Until I knocked on their door."

She turned away, looked at Nadine now. "Her mother went right down on her knees, collapsed like all the air had gone out of her body. You'll have to run over there with your crew when we're done. I'm sure you'll get some good image for your story. That kind of thing, all that suffering, it really pumps the ratings."

"This is uncalled for." Carter snapped the words out. "This is intolerable. My client—"

"Be quiet, Carter." Nadine reached down for her leather portfolio bag. "I want to speak with you in private, Lieutenant."

"Nadine, I strongly advise—"

"Shut up, Carter. In private, Dallas."

"All right." She unplugged her recorder. "My office."

She didn't speak as they walked out, said nothing as they moved to the glide that would take them up to her division.

They moved into the bullpen, and the initial calls of greeting trickled into silence as both women moved straight through.

Eve's office was small and spare, with a single narrow window. She shut the door, took the chair at her desk, and left the other, badly sprung chair, for Nadine.

But Nadine didn't sit. What she'd seen, what she felt was clearly printed on her face. "You know me better. You know me better, and I didn't deserve to be treated this way, didn't deserve the things you said in there."

"Maybe not, but you're the one who pulled in a rep, you're the one who jumped down my throat because I blocked you from a story."

"Fuck it, Dallas, you arrested me."

"I did not arrest you. I remanded you into custody for questioning. You've got no sheet out of this."

"I don't give a damn about the sheet." Sick and furious, she shoved at the chair. It was a gesture Eve understood and respected, even as the flying seat caught her on the shin.

"I called you," Nadine spat out. "I notified you when I was under no obligation to do so. Then you cut me out, you haul me in, and you treat me like a ghoul."

"I didn't cut you out, I did my job. I hauled you in because you have information I need, and you were being pissy."

"*I* was being pissy?"

"Yeah, you were. Christ, I need coffee." She pushed up and bumped past Nadine to her AutoChef. "And I was feeling pissy, so I didn't take time for our usual dance. But for treating you like a ghoul, I'll apologize, because I do know better. You want a hit of this?"

Nadine opened her mouth, closed it again. Then let out a puff of steam. "Yes. If you respected me—"

"Nadine." Coffee in hand, Eve turned. "If I didn't respect you, I'd have had a warrant in hand when I came into The Lounge." She waited a beat. "Are you making it with that suit?"

Nadine sipped coffee. "As a matter of fact. I made copies of the printouts for you before I headed to Delancey—where I would have been considerably earlier if Red hadn't nipped the fender of another car." She drew them out of her bag.

"EDD's going to need your 'link."

"Yeah. I figured." The battle was over, and they stood facing each other. Two women scraped raw by the job.

"She was a pretty girl," Nadine commented. "Great smile."

"So everyone says. This was taken while she was at work. You can just see the candy display. This one . . . subway, maybe. And this, I don't know. A park somewhere. They're not posed. Just as likely she didn't know they were being taken."

"He stalked her."

"Could be. Now this. This is posed."

She held up the last printout. Rachel was in a chair set against a white wall. Her legs were crossed, her hands neatly folded just above the knee. The lighting was soft, flattering. She wore the blue shirt and jeans she'd been found in. Her face was young and pretty, lips and cheeks rosy. And her eyes, that strong green, were empty.

"She's dead, isn't she? In this picture, she's already dead."

"Probably." Eve shifted the image aside, and read the text of the transmission.

SHE WAS THE FIRST, AND HER LIGHT WAS PURE. IT WILL SHINE ON FOREVER. IT LIVES IN ME NOW. SHE LIVES IN ME. TO RETRIEVE THE RECEPTACLE, GO TO DELANCEY AND AVENUE D. TELL THE WORLD, THIS IS ONLY THE BEGINNING. A BEGINNING FOR ALL.

"I'm going to tag Feeney, have him send somebody from EDD to pick up your 'link. Since we're so full of respect here, I don't have to tell you that certain details, such as the contents of this transmission, need to be kept out of the story entirely or played down during the investigation."

"You don't. And bulging with that respect, I don't have to ask you to keep me in the loop, or for the series of one-on-ones we'll conduct throughout this investigation."

"Guess not. Don't ask me for one now, Nadine. I've got to move on this."

"A statement then. Something I can tag on that will show viewers the NYPSD is pushing forward."

"You can say that the primary on this investigation is pursuing any and all possible leads, and that neither she, nor this department will stand by when a young woman is treated like garbage."

Alone, she sat back down at her desk. She did need to get moving, and her first stop would be the ME. But right now she had another duty to perform.

She called Roarke's private 'link, got the bland message he was unavailable at this location, and was bounced to his admin before she could cut the transmission.

"Oh. Hi, Caro. I guess he's busy."

"Hello, Lieutenant." The pleasant face smiled. "He was just finishing a meeting. Ah, he should be free now. Just let me transfer you."

"I don't want to bother—damn." She was bouncing again.

She shifted uncomfortably as she heard the quick series of beeps. Then it was Roarke's face on-screen. Though he, too, smiled, she could see he was distracted.

"Lieutenant. You just caught me."

"Sorry I didn't call in earlier. I haven't had much breathing room. Is he, um, doing okay?"

"It's a bad break, and he's irritable. The shoulder and knee—and other assorted bumps and bruises—complicate it. He took a hard fall."

"Yeah. Look, I'm sorry. Really."

"Mmm. They'll keep him until tomorrow. If he's recovered enough to be released, I'm bringing him home. He won't be able to get around on his own initially, so he'll need care. I've arranged it."

"Should I, you know, do something?"

This time the smile seemed more at ease. "Such as?"

"I have absolutely no idea. You okay?"

"Shook me up, considerably. I tend to overreact when someone I care for is injured. Or so I'm told. He's almost as annoyed with me for dumping him in the hospital—as he called it—as you are under similar circumstances."

"He'll get over it." She wanted to touch him, brush those lines of worry away that were haunting his eyes. "I mostly do."

"He's been the only constant in my life, until you. Scared me brainless to see him hurt that way."

"He's too mean to stay down for long. I've got to go. I don't know when I'll be home."

"That makes two of us. Thanks for calling."

She ended the transmission, and after one more pass, loaded the printouts in her bag. Heading out, she swung by Peabody's cube. "Peabody, we're moving."

"I got the victim's class schedule." Peabody jogged to keep up with Eve's ground-eating stride. "And a list of her instructors. Also the names of her coworkers at the 24/7. I haven't started to run them yet."

"Do it on the way to the morgue. Plug in photography and imaging. See if any of them have an interest."

"I can tell you that straight off. One of her electives was

Imaging. She was acing it, too. Hell, she was acing everything. She was really smart." She dragged out her PPC as
they headed down to the garage. "She had the Imaging
course Tuesday evenings."

"Last evening."

"Yes, sir. Her instructor was Leeanne Browning."

"Run her first." She sniffed the air as they crossed the
garage. "What's that smell?"

"As your aide and boon companion, I must inform you,
that smell is you."

"Oh hell."

"Here." Digging in her bag, Peabody came out with a
little spray bottle.

Instinctively Eve stepped back. "What is that? Keep it
away from me."

"Dallas, when we get in our vehicle, even with the air on
full, it's going to be tough to breathe. You are rank. You're
probably going to have to burn that jacket, and it's too bad,
because it's mag."

Before Eve could dodge, she aimed and fired, and kept
firing even as her courageous lieutenant yelped.

"It smells like . . . rotten flowers."

"The rotten part is you." Peabody leaned closer, sniffed.
"But it's much better. You'll hardly notice it from ten, fifteen
feet away. They probably have really strong disinfectant at
the morgue," Peabody said cheerfully. "You could wash up,
and maybe they've got something for your clothes."

"Just button it, Peabody."

"Buttoning, sir." Peabody scooted into the car and began
her run on Leeanne Browning. "Professor Browning is fifty-
six. Affiliated with Columbia for twenty-three years. Married, same-sex style, to Angela Brightstar, fifty-four. Upper
West Side address. No criminal record. Also second residence, the Hamptons. One sib, brother, Upper East Side, also
married, one child, son. Twenty-eight years of age. Parents
still living, retired, with residences Upper East Side and Flor-
ida."

"Run criminals on Brightstar and the family."

"Brightstar's got a little pop," Peabody said after a moment. "Illegals possession twelve years back. Personal stash of Exotica. Pled guilty, did three months community service. Brightstar is a freelance artist, with a studio in residence. Brother's clean, so are the parents, but the nephew's got two tags. One illegals possession at age twenty-three, and one assault last spring. His current residence is Boston."

"He may be worth talking to. Bump him up on the list, and we'll see if he's been visiting our fair city. Get Professor Browning's class schedule. I want to work her in today."

In the morgue, Eve strode down the white corridor. Yeah, they used strong disinfectant, she thought. But you could never quite hide it. The business of the place snuck into all the cracks and crept into the air.

As directed, she found Rachel Howard already on a slab, and ME Morris working on her. He wore a long green cover over his lemon yellow suit. His hair was pulled into a trio of ponytails that waterfalled, one over the other down his back. And somehow didn't look ridiculous spilling out from his protective cap.

Eve stepped up to the body. She could see Morris's work, and she could see the cause of death. The autopsy wouldn't have put the tiny, neat puncture through the skin and into the heart.

"What can you tell me?"

"That the toast will always fall jelly-side down."

"I'll put that in my file. The heart wound do the trick?"

"It did indeed. Very quick, very neat. A stiletto, an old-fashioned ice pick or similar weapon. He wanted no muss, no fuss."

"He? Was she sexually assaulted?"

"Using he in the general sense. No sexual assault. A few minor bruises, which may have been caused during transport. No muss, no fuss," he repeated. "He bandaged the wound. I've got traces of adhesive around it. A nice, neat circle. Probably NuSkin, which he removed when he was done. And this." He turned Rachel's hand, palm up. "Small round abrasion. Most likely from a pressure syringe."

"She doesn't look like the sort to pop illegals, and that'd

be a strange place to skin pop. He injected her with something. Tranq, maybe."

"We'll see when we get the tox screen. No violence to the body but for the puncture. There are, however, very mild ligatures at the wrists, at the left knee, on the right elbow. See here."

He picked up a second pair of microgoggles.

"Restraints?" she asked as she took the goggles. "It's a funny way to restrain someone."

"We'll discuss the fun and games of bondage another time. Take a look first."

She fit on the goggles, bent over the body. She could see them now, the faint and thin lines that showed blue through the light.

"Wires of some kind," Morris said. "Not rope."

"To pose her. He used the wires to pose her. You can see the way the wire wrapped over one wrist, under the other. He folded her hands on her knee. Yeah, crossed her legs, wired her to the chair. You can't see them in the photograph, but he'd have taken that out during imaging."

She straightened, took one of the printouts from her bag. "This jibe for you with that theory?"

Morris pushed up his goggles, scanned the image. "The positioning works. So he takes pictures of the dead. That was a custom a couple of centuries ago, and it came back into fashion early this century."

"What kind of custom?"

"To pose the dead in an attitude of peace, then take their picture. People kept them in books designed for the purpose."

"It never fails to amaze me just how sick people are."

"Oh, I don't know. It was meant to comfort and remember."

"Maybe he wants to remember her," Eve mused, "but I think more, he wants to be remembered. I want her tox screen."

"Soon, my pretty. Soon."

"She didn't fight, or wasn't able to fight. So she knew him and trusted him, or she was incapacitated. Then he transported her to wherever he took this." She slid the image back in her bag. "She was either dead already, or he killed her there—I'm betting he did it there—bandaged her so she didn't bleed through the shirt, then he posed her, took his shots. He transports her again and dumps her in a recycler across the street from where she worked."

She began to pace. "So maybe her killer's from the neighborhood. Somebody who sees her every day, develops an obsession. Not sexual, but an obsession. He takes pictures of her, follows her around. He comes into the store, and she doesn't think anything of it. She's friendly. Probably knows him by name. Either that or someone from college. Familiar face, trusted face. Maybe he offers her a ride home, or a ride to school. Either way, he's got her.

"She knew his face," she murmured, looking down at Rachel, "just as well as he knew hers."

Mildly refreshed by a spin in the detox tube at the morgue, Eve pulled up at the curb in front of Professor Browning's high-dollar building.

"I thought teachers got paid worse than cops," she commented.

"I can do a standard run on her financials."

Eve stepped out of the car, then cocked her head and her hip as the doorman rushed over.

"I'm afraid you can't leave . . . that here."

"That is an official vehicle. This," she added, flipping it out, "is a badge. Since I'm going in there, on police business, that stays out here."

"There's a parking facility very nearby. I'd be happy to direct you."

"What you're going to do is open the door, go inside with me, and inform Professor Browning that Lieutenant Dallas, NYPSD, is here to speak with her. After that, you can come out here and direct people to Morocco for all I care. Clear?"

It appeared to be as he scuttled to the door, coded through security. "If Professor Browning was expecting you, I should've been informed."

He was so prim and pompous about it Eve gave him a

fierce grin. "You know, I've got one just like you at home. Do you guys have a club?"

He merely sniffed, and danced his fingers over a keyboard. "It's Monty, Professor. I'm sorry to disturb you, but there's a Lieutenant Dallas at the desk. She'd like clearance to come up. Yes, ma'am," he said into his earpiece. "I've seen her identification. She is accompanied by a uniformed officer. Of course, Professor."

He turned to Eve, lips so thin they could have sliced paper. "Professor Browning will you see. Please take the elevator to the fifteenth floor. You will be met."

"Thanks, Monty. How come doormen always hate me?" she asked Peabody as they moved to the elevator.

"I think they sense your disdain, like pheromones. Of course, if you told them you were married to Roarke, they'd immediately fall to their knees and worship you."

"I'd rather be feared and hated." She stepped inside. "Fifteenth floor," she ordered.

Chapter 3

The elevator opened on fifteen where a domestic droid was waiting. He had black hair slicked back over a round head, and a thin mustache over his top lip. He was dressed in a formal suit, the kind Eve had seen characters wear in some of Roarke's old videos. It had a jacket with a short front and long tails at the back, and the shirt beneath looked stiff and impossibly white.

"Lieutenant Dallas, Officer," he said in a fruity voice, heavy on the Brit. "Might I trouble you for identification?"

"Sure." Eve pulled out her badge, watched a thin red line shoot through the droid's eyes as he scanned it. "You're top-line security?"

"I am a multifunction unit, Lieutenant." With a slight bow, he offered the badge back to her. "Please follow me."

He stepped back to let them exit the elevator. There was a kind of lobby, or entrance area with white marble floor tiles, glossy antiques topped with urns that were elegant with flowers.

There was a tall white statue of a nude woman, with her head tipped back and her hands in her hair as if she were washing it. There were artfully arranged flowers at her feet.

On the walls were framed images—photographic and

multi-media. Additional nudes, Eve noticed, that were more romantic than erotic. Lights of filmy draper and diffused light.

He opened another set of doors and bowed them into the apartment.

Though *apartment*, Eve mused, was a poor word for it. The living area was enormous, full of color and flowers and soft, soft fabrics. More art decorated the walls here as well.

She noted wide doorways right and left, another leading down the side of the room and calculated that Browning and Brightstar didn't live on the fifteenth floor. They *were* the fifteenth floor.

"Please be seated," the droid told them. "Professor Browning will be right with you. And might I offer you some refreshment?"

"We're fine, thanks."

"Family money," Peabody said out of the side of her mouth when they were left alone. "Both of them, but Brightstar's seriously loaded. Not Roarke loaded, but she can roll naked in it without worrying. Angela Brightstar's *the* Brightstar of Brightstar Gallery on Madison. Swank artsy joint. I went to a showing there once with Charles."

Eve stepped up to a painting that was slashes of color, lumps of texture. "How come people don't paint houses or something? You know, stuff that's real?"

"Reality is all perception."

Leeanne Browning entered. You couldn't say she came in, Eve thought. When a woman was a good six feet tall, lushly built, and draped in a glistening robe of silver, she entered.

Her hair was a long fall of sunlight to her waist, her face equally striking with its wide mouth and deeply indented top lip. Her long nose tipped up at the end, and her wide eyes were a vivid shade of purple.

Eve recognized her as the model for the white statue in the entrance area.

"Excuse my appearance." She smiled in the way a woman smiled when she knew she made an impression. "I was posing for my companion. Why don't we sit, have something cool, and you can tell me what brings the police to my door."

"You have a student. Rachel Howard?"

"I have a number of students." She arranged herself on a poppy colored sofa, as cannily, Eve thought, as the art was arranged on the wall. And for the same purpose. Look at me, and admire. "But yes," she continued, "I know Rachel. She's the sort of student who is easily remembered. Such a bright young thing, and eager to learn. Though she's only taking my course as a filler, she does good work."

Her smile was lazy. "I hope she's not in any trouble—though I must admit, I think it's a pity if young girls don't get in some trouble now and then."

"She's in a great deal of trouble, Professor Browning. She's dead."

The smile vanished as Leeanne pushed herself straight. "Dead? But how did this happen? She's just a child. Was there an accident?"

"No. When did you see her last?"

"At class, last night. God, I can't quite think." She pressed her fingers to her temple. "Rodney! Rodney, bring us something . . . something cold. I'm sorry, I'm so very sorry to hear this."

The flirtation, the smug female arrogance was gone now. Her hand dropped into her lap, then lifted helplessly. "I can't believe it. I honestly can't believe it. You're certain it's Rachel Howard?"

"Yes. What was your relationship with her?"

"She was a student. I saw her once a week, and she attended a workshop I give the second Saturday of each month. I liked her. She was, as I said, bright and eager. A pretty young thing with her life ahead of her. The sort you see on campus year after year, but she was just a little brighter, just a bit more eager and appealing. God, this is horrible. Was it a mugging? A boyfriend?"

"Did she have a boyfriend?"

"I don't know. I really didn't know very much about her personal life. A young man picked her up after class once, I recall. She was often in a clutch of young people—she was the sort who was. But I did notice her with another boy on campus a couple of times—that struck me because they looked so striking together. The Young American Hope. Thank you, Rodney," she said as the droid set a tray with three glasses of frothy pink liquid on the table.

"Is there anything else, madam?"

"Yes, would you tell Ms. Brightstar I need her."

"Of course."

"Do you remember her mentioning anyone named Diego?"

"No. Honestly, we were not confidantes. She was a student, one I noticed particularly because of her looks and her vitality. But I don't know what she did outside of class."

"Professor, can you tell me what you did last night, after class?"

There was a hesitation, and a sigh. "I suppose that's the sort of thing you need to ask." She picked up her glass. "I came straight home, so I'd have gotten here about nine-twenty. Angie and I had a late supper, talked about work. I had no classes today, so we stayed up until nearly one. We listened to music, we made love, we went to sleep. We didn't get up this morning until after ten. Neither of us has been out today. It's so bloody hot, and she's working in the studio."

She shifted, held out a hand as Angela Brightstar came into the room. She wore a blue smock that fell to mid-calf and was a rainbow of paint splotches. Her hair was a curling mass, the color of port wine, and currently bundled on top of her head and anchored with a trailing scarf.

Her face was delicate, fine-boned with a pink, doll-like mouth and vague gray eyes. Her body seemed very small and lost inside the baggy smock.

"Angie, one of my students was killed."

"Oh, sweetheart." Angie took her hand, and despite the paint splotches, sat beside her. "Who was it? How did it happen?"

"A young girl, I'm sure I mentioned her to you. Rachel Howard."

"I don't know. I'm so bad with names." She brought

Leeanne's hand to her cheek, rubbed it there. "You're the police?" she asked Eve.

"Yes. Lieutenant Dallas."

"Now see, I know that name. I've been puzzling over it since Monty called up, but I can't put it in the right slot. Do you paint?"

"No. Ms. Brightstar, would you verify what time Professor Browning got home last night?"

"I'm not very good with time either. Nine-thirty?" she looked at Leeanne for confirmation. "Somewhere around there."

There was no motive here, Eve thought, no vibe—at least not yet. Curious, she opened her bag, selected one of the candid shots of Rachel.

"What do you think of this, Professor Browning?"

"It's Rachel."

"Oh, what a pretty girl," Angie said. "What a nice smile. So young and fresh."

"Could you give me your opinion on the image itself. Professionally."

"Oh." Leeanne took a deep breath, angled her head. "It's quite good, actually. An excellent use of light, and color. Nice angles. Clean and uncluttered. It shows the subject's youth and vitality, centers that so the eye is drawn, as Angie's was, to the smile, to how fresh she is. Is that what you mean?"

"Yes. Could you set up a shot like that without the subject being aware?"

"Of course, if you have good instincts." She lowered the image. "Did the killer take this?"

"Possibly."

"She was murdered?" Angie wrapped an arm around Leeanne. "Oh, this is awful. How could anyone hurt a young, sweet girl like that?"

"Sweet?" Eve echoed.

"Just look at her face—look at her eyes." Angie shook her head. "You can tell. You can look at her face and see the innocence."

As they rode back down in the elevator, Eve brought the

images of Rachel into her head. As she'd been, and as he'd left her. "Maybe that's what he wanted," she murmured. "Her innocence."

"He didn't rape her."

"It wasn't sexual. It was . . . spiritual. Her light was pure," she remembered. "It might mean her soul. Isn't there some deal, some superstition about the camera stealing the soul?"

"I've heard that. Where are we headed now, Lieutenant?" Peabody asked.

"We're going to college."

"Icy. A lot of college guys are totally hot." She hunched her shoulders when Eve sent her a bland stare. "Just because McNab and I are in a committed, mature relationship—"

"I don't want to hear about your committed, mature anything with McNab. It gives me the creeps."

"Just because," Peabody continued, undaunted as they crossed the lobby, "doesn't mean I can't look at other guys. Any woman with eyes looks at other guys. Okay, maybe you don't because, hey, what would be the point?"

"Perhaps I should point out that we're investigating a homicide, not going off on a man-ogling spree."

"I like to multitask whenever possible. Speaking of which, maybe we could get some actual food. That way, we could investigate, feed the body, and ogle."

"There will be no ogling. Henceforth, ogling is forbidden at any and all junctures of active investigations."

Peabody pursed her lips. "You're really mean today."

"Yes. Yes, I am." Eve took a deep gulp of hideous air, and smiled. "I feel good about that."

The announcement of sudden, violent death drew many reactions. Tears were just one of them. By the time Eve had spoken to a half dozen of Rachel's friends and instructors at Columbia, she thought she might wash away on the sea of tears.

She sat on the side of a bed in a dorm room. The space was tight, she thought. A closet jammed with two beds, two desks, two dressers. Every flat surface was covered with what Eve thought of as mysterious girl stuff. The walls were plastered with posters and drawings, the desks with disc boxes and girl toys. The bedspreads were candy pink, the walls mint green. In fact, the whole place smelled like candy somehow and made her stomach rumble.

She should've taken Peabody's advice on the food.

Two girls sat directly across from her, locked in each other's arms like lovers as they wept, copiously.

"It can't be *true*. It can't be *true*."

She couldn't tell which one of them was wailing the words, but she did note that the longer they howled, the more dramatic their grief. She began to think they were enjoying it.

"I know this is hard, but I have to ask you some questions."

"I can't. I just *can't!*"

Eve pressed the bridge of her nose to relieve some of the pressure. "Peabody, see if there's something to drink in the fridge over there."

Obediently, Peabody crouched down in front of the mini-coldbox and found several tubes of Diet Coke. She opened two, brought them over. "Here you go. Take a drink, and some deep breaths. If you want to help Rachel, you have to talk to the lieutenant. Rachel would do that for you, wouldn't she?"

"She *would*." The little blonde didn't cry well. Her face was blotchy, her nose runny. She slurped at the soft drink. "Rach would do *anything* for a friend."

The brunette, Randa, was still blubbering, but she had the presence of mind to get some tissues and stuff them in her roommate's hand. "We wanted her to room with us next term. She was saving up for it. She wanted the whole, you know, college experience. And it's not so bad when you split a triple."

"She'll *never* come *back*." The blonde buried her face in the tissue.

"Okay, Charlene, right?"

The girl lifted her gaze to Eve. "Charlie. Everybody calls me Charlie."

"Charlie, you need to pull it together, help us out. When did you see Rachel last?"

"We had some dinner at the cafeteria, before her Imaging class last night. I'm on the food plan, and you never eat enough to use all the credits, so I treated her."

"What time was that?"

"About six. I had a date with this guy I'm seeing, and we were hooking up at eight. So Rach and I had dinner, and she went to class. I came back here to change. And I'll never, never see her again."

"Peabody." Eve nodded toward the door.

"Okay, Charlie." Peabody patted the girl on the arm. "Why don't we go for a walk? You'll feel better if you get some air."

"I'll never feel better again. Never, never."

But she let Peabody guide her away.

When the door closed behind them, Randa blew her nose. "She can't help it. They were really tight. And Charlie's a drama major."

"Is that what she's studying, or is it just her personality?"

As Eve hoped, Randa's lips trembled into a smile. "Both. But, I don't feel like I'll ever get over this either. I don't feel like I'll ever think about anything else."

"You will. You won't forget it, but you'll get through it. I know you and Charlie, and a lot of the other people I've talked to, liked Rachel."

"You just had to." Randa sniffed. "She was just the kind of person who lights things up. You know?"

"Yes," Eve agreed. "Sometimes people are jealous of someone like that. Or they dislike them because of what they are inside. Can you think of anyone who felt that way about Rachel?"

"I really can't. I mean, she only went here part-time, but she made a lot of friends. She was smart. Really smart, but she didn't geek."

"Anybody who wanted to be a better friend than she did?"

"Oh, like a guy?" Randa drew a breath now. The tears were drying up as her mind became occupied. "She dated around. She didn't sleep around. She was really firm about not giving it out until she was good and ready. If a guy pushed, she'd turn it around into a joke until they got to be friends, or if that didn't work, she'd walk away."

"She ever mention somebody named Diego?"

"Oh, him." Randa wrinkled her nose. "God's gift, Latino type, hooked onto her at the club. She went to dinner with him once, some Mex restaurant he *said* he owned. He tried to put the moves on her, wasn't too happy when she deflected. Came by campus once and got a little hot because she laughed him off. That was a few months ago, I guess."

"Got a last name for him?"

"No. Um, short guy, too much hair, soul patch. Always wearing those cow-kicker boots with little heels. But he could dance."

"Anybody else try to put the moves on her?"

"Well, there was Hoop. Jackson Hooper. He's a TA, ah teacher assistant—English Lit. Another one of those God's gifts, but whitebread style. He racks girls up like pool balls, and Rachel wouldn't play. He came on pretty strong, following her around. Not stalking her," Randa qualified. "Just being where she was a lot, and making plays. We all figured it was because she was the first girl to turn him down in his life, and he didn't want to spoil his streak."

"Did he end up where she was just on campus, or did it happen elsewhere?"

"She said he came into the store where she works a couple times. Just hanging around and being charming. She got a kick out of it, actually."

"When did you see her last, Randa?"

"I didn't make dinner, had to study. She was talking about bunking here after class. She did that sometimes on her evening classes. She's not really supposed to, but nobody cared. Everyone liked having her around. But when she didn't show, we just figured she'd gone home. I didn't even think about it."

Two fresh tears trickled down her cheeks. "I didn't think about her at all. Charlie was out, and I had the room to myself. All I thought was, how nice and quiet it was so I could study. And when I was thinking that, somebody killed Rachel."

They tracked down Jackson Hooper at another dorm. The minute he opened the door, Eve knew word had spread. His face was a bit pale, and his lips trembled once before he firmed them into a thin line.

"You're the cops."

"Jackson Hooper? We'd like to come in and speak with you for a few minutes."

"Yeah." He dragged his hand through a tousled mop of sun-streaked hair as he stepped back.

He was tall, and he was built. The kind of body created through regular workouts or through stiff fees for body sculpting treatments. Since he was a teaching assistant, his quarters were even smaller than the ones she'd just come from, and he was probably strapped for cash, she opted for workouts.

That meant he was strong, disciplined, and motivated.

He had chiseled looks—the All-American boy—clear skin, blue eyes, firm jaw. It was easy enough to see why he'd rack up available coeds.

He dropped into the spindly chair at his desk, and gestured vaguely toward the bed. "I just heard about ten minutes ago. I was heading to class and somebody told me. I couldn't go to class."

"You dated Rachel."

"We went out a couple times." He hesitated, then rubbed his face as if coming out of a long sleep. "Somebody's already told you. Somebody's always hot to talk. I wanted to go out with her again, and yeah, I wanted her in the sack. She wasn't having any."

"That must've irritated you," Eve commented and wandered over to the framed photographs grouped on his wall. They were all of him, in various poses. A nice little pile of vanity, she thought.

"Yeah, it did. I don't have any trouble getting girls in bed. I'm good at it," he said with a shrug. "So I was a little steamed when she wouldn't go for it, then kept turning me down when I asked her out. More, I was like, well, baffled. Hey." He flashed a white, straight-toothed smile as he gestured toward the photographs. "Prime merchandise."

"But Rachel wasn't buying it."

"Nope. So I was steamed, and I was baffled. But then, you know, I was interested. Like, what was it going to take. And what was it with this girl anyway? So I got hooked." He lowered his head into his hands. "Fuck."

"You followed her around."

"Like a pet droid. I'd find out she was going to a club, or heading to the library, whatever, and I'd be there. I trotted over to the place she worked just to talk to her. Borrowed my roommate's scooter so I could talk her into letting me take her home a couple times. She'd let me. I didn't worry her one damn bit."

"Did you fight with her?"

"I shot off my mouth a few times. She'd just laugh, then what could you do? Another girl would've told me to screw myself, but she'd just laugh. I think maybe I was in love with her." He dropped his hands. "I think maybe I was. How do you know?"

"Where were you last night, Hoop?"

"I was going to catch her after her class, see if I could talk her into a cup of coffee, or some pizza. Something. But I got hung up. A couple of the guys got into a shoving match, and I had to break it up. She was gone when I got over there. I beat it to the subway, figuring maybe I could catch her there, and when I didn't I took it over to her place in Brooklyn. But the light wasn't on in her room. She always turns the light on in her room when she gets home. I hung around maybe an hour—I don't know. Went and had a beer, walked back, still didn't see her light. Then I said what the fuck, and came back here."

"What time did you get back?"

"I don't know, close to midnight, I guess."

"Anybody see you?"

"I don't know. I was irritated and feeling sorry for myself. I didn't talk to anybody."

"What about your roommate?"

"He's banging a girl off campus. He's there more than here. He wasn't around when I got in. I didn't hurt Rachel. I didn't hurt her."

"Where'd you have the beer?"

"Some bar—a couple blocks up from the subway over there." He gestured vaguely to indicate Brooklyn. "I don't know the name."

"These pictures look professional," Eve commented.

"What? Oh yeah. I do some modeling. It's good money. I'm writing a play. That's what I want to be—a playwright. You have to live pretty lean to make it. So I pick up coin where I can. TA, dorm monitor, modeling. I got certified as an LC last year, but it's not what I thought it would be. I never figured sex could be work—and boring."

"Got a camera?"

"Yeah, somewhere. Why?"

"I wondered if you liked to take pictures, too."

"I don't see why . . . oh Rachel, her Imaging class." He smiled a little. "I should've thought of that one. As TA I could've monitored that class, hung out with her." The smile faded. "I'd've been there last night when class ended. I'd've been with her."

"Keep him on the short list," Eve told Peabody as they headed back to the car. "He had motive, means, and opportunity. We'll run him a little deeper, see if anything pops."

"He seemed really torn up about it."

"Yeah, really torn up over a girl who laughed at him, who wouldn't fall at his feet begging for his pretty penis, and who let her friends know she'd turned him down."

She slid into the car. "He's got an ego the size of Saturn, and as a model potential knowledge of photography, and access to the necessary equipment. He knew where she lived, where she worked, he knew her movements and habits. She trusted him because she believed she could handle him. So we'll take a good, long look at him."

She headed back to Central to tie up loose ends. The tox report on Rachel Howard was waiting for her. At least she hadn't known what was done to her, Eve thought as she scanned it. Not with all those opiates in her system.

So he'd tranq'd her, she thought, leaning back in her desk chair. Before transport, or during? Either way, he had a vehicle. Or he'd lured her somewhere. An apartment, a studio. Had to be private. Then he'd slipped her the drugs.

If it was the last scenario, she'd known him. She was too smart to be lured by a stranger.

She was his first, he'd said. But he'd been well prepared. Step by step. Selecting, observing, recording. Youth and vitality, she thought. He'd wanted to own them. And her innocence.

She'd walked out of class at nine. Had he waited for her? She spotted him, flashed that smile. Maybe he offered her a ride home, but she turned him down. *Going to study with pals, but thanks.* A couple of her classmates had verified that. She told them she was going to stay on campus, study with some friends.

He couldn't afford to be seen, so how had he lured her?

Staged the run-in, she decided. He was good at staging. Maybe he's on foot. Easy to meld and blend. But he has to make her take a detour, has to get her into his vehicle. Can't take a chance on public transportation.

He wants her face in the media—his image—so he knows she could be recognized after the murder. And he could be described. So, no subway, no buses, no cabs. Private vehicle.

But why did she go with him?

She began to write her report, hoping that some of the facts she put in would trip over into theory.

Her desk 'link beeped.

"Dallas." Captain Feeney's hangdog face slid onto the screen. Noting the crumbs at the corner of his mouth, she leaned closer to the 'link.

"You got danishes up there?"

"No." He swiped the back of his hand over his mouth. "Not anymore."

"How come EDD always rates pastries and stuff? Murder cops need sugar substitute the same as the rest."

"We are the elite, what can I say. We're finished with Nadine's 'link."

"And?"

"Nothing that's going to help much. He transmitted the images and text from a public comp at one of those dance, drink, and data joints. Transmitted it just after six hundred hours, but he shot it out earlier, with a hold. Shot it out about two. Straight job—he didn't bounce it around. Either he doesn't know how, or he didn't give two shits. Those places are crawling that time of night. Nobody's going to remember some guy who popped in for a brew and used a 'link."

"We'll check it out anyway. Location?"

"Place called Make The Scene."

"Pop."

"Mean something?"

"It's a club she frequented. Thanks. Quick work."

"That's why we're the elite, and get danishes."

"Bite me," she muttered and cut him off.

She swung into the bullpen. There were no danishes, she noted. There weren't even crumbs. She'd have to settle for a Power Bar from vending or take a chance on the food at the data club.

Surely it couldn't be worse than a Power Bar.

"Peabody, we're in the field."

"I was just about to have this sandwich." She held up a wrapped lump.

"Then you should be thrilled to be able to demonstrate those multitasking skills. Eat and roll."

"This is bad for the digestion," Peabody replied, but she stuffed the sandwich in her bag, grabbed her tube of OrangeAde.

"EDD's got the location of the transmission to Nadine."

"I know. McNab told me."

Eve pushed through the crowd on the elevator and studied her aide's face. "I just got off the 'link with Feeney, his superior—as I am yours. So why is it my aide and his detective are chatting about the information in my investigation?"

"It just happened to come up—between kissy noises." She smiled, pleased when Eve's eye twitched. "And sexual innuendos."

"As soon as this case is closed, I'm putting in for a new aide—one who has no sexual drive whatsoever—and transferring you to Files."

"Aw. Now that you've hurt my feelings, I'm not inclined to share my sandwich."

Eve held out for ten seconds. "What kind is it?"

"Mine."

It was also some sort of fake ham drowned in fake mayo. Eve was forced to shift to auto on the trip, then grab Peabody's tube of OrangeAde to try to wash down the two bites she scrounged. "Christ, how do you drink this crap?"

"I happen to think it's refreshing, and find it goes very well with the shortbread cookies I have for dessert." She took the tiny package out of her bag and made a production out of opening it.

"Give me a goddamn cookie, or I'll hurt you. You know I can."

"My fear is almost as great as my love for you, Lieutenant."

Eve found a slot on the second level, curbside, and zipped up the ramp at a speed and angle that had Peabody's lunch lurching dangerously in her belly.

Delicately, Eve brushed cookie crumbs off her shirt. "Smartasses always pay."

"You never do," Peabody said under her breath.

Chapter 4

In the daylight hours, the action at data clubs whittled down to the geeks and nerds who thought they were living on the edge by hanging in a joint that offered a holoband and sports screens.

The stations were silver, and so small, so crammed together that even the shyest nerd was virtually guaranteed a free feel of a neighboring butt during peak hours.

The holoband was in mellow mode, with soft guitars and whispering keyboard with the vocals going for plaintive croon. The girl singer was dressed in black to match her glossy skin. The only spot of color was her stoplight red hair that fell over most of her face while she murmured something about broken hearts and minds.

The clientele was primarily male, primarily solo, and since no one looked distressed or interested in Peabody's uniform, Eve figured a sweep of the place wouldn't net an Illegals hound enough of a cache to fill a dwarf's pocket.

She made her way to the sluggishly circling central bar.

There were two servers, a human male and a female droid. Eve opted for the one that breathed.

His dress was trendy—the loose shirt in sunset colors, the small army of multicolored loops riding up the curve of his left ear, the crop of spikes in the crown of his ordinary brown hair.

His shoulders were wide, his arms long. There was a sturdiness about him that told her he had a few years on the afternoon clientele. His face was white, edging toward pasty.

She pegged him at mid- to late twenties, probably a grad student, a shaky step up from geekdom, earning his tuition by manning the stick and chatting up the patrons.

He stopped playing with the small computer set on the bar and offered her an absent smile. "What can I do for you?"

Eve set her badge and the smiling image of Rachel Howard on the bar. "You recognize her?"

He used a fingertip to nudge the image closer and gave it the earnest study that told her he was fairly new at the job. "Well, sure. That's, ah, shoot. Rebecca, Roseanne, no . . . Rachel? I'm pretty good with names. I think it's Rachel. She's in here most every week. Likes, ah, whatzit?" He closed his eyes. "Toreadors—orange juice, lime juice, a shot of grenadine. She's not in trouble, is she?"

"Yeah, she's in trouble. You remember the names and the drinks of all the patrons here?"

"The regulars, sure. Well, especially the pretty girl regulars. She's got a great face, and she's friendly."

"When was the last time she was here?"

"I don't know, exactly. This is one of my part-time jobs. But the last time I remember being here and seeing her was maybe last Friday? I work the six to midnight on Friday. Hey, look, she never caused any trouble in here. She just comes in now and then with some friends. They grab a station, listen to tunes, dance, keyboard. She's a nice girl."

"You ever notice anyone hassling her?"

"Not so much. Like I said, she's a pretty girl. Sometimes guys would hit on her. Sometimes she'd hit back, sometimes she'd blow them off. But nice. Things get zipping in here after nine, especially weekends. You get the cruisers, but this one always came in with a friend, or a group. She wasn't looking for a one-nighter. You can tell."

"Uh-huh. You know a guy named Diego?"

"Ah . . ." He looked blank for a moment, then drew his

eyebrows together in concentration. "I think I know who you mean. Little guy, cruiser. Likes to strut around. Got some good moves on the dance floor and he's always flush, so he didn't leave alone very often."

"Did he ever leave with Rachel?"

"Shit." He winced. "Sorry. Not her type. She flicked him off. Danced with him. She'd dance with anybody, but she wasn't after that kind of action. Maybe he tried to put the squeeze on her a few times, now that you mention it, but it wasn't a big deal. No more than Joe College."

"Joe?"

"Big, good-looking college guy used to shadow her in here sometimes. All-American looking guy. Got kinda broody when she'd be up there dancing with somebody else."

"You gotta name?"

"Sure." He looked more baffled than nervous. "Steve. Steve Audrey."

"You're an observant sort, aren't you, Steve?"

"Well, yeah. You work the bar, you see everything once. Probably twice. It's sort of like watching a play or something every day, but you get paid for it."

Oh yeah, he was new at this, Eve thought. "You got security cams?"

"Sure." He glanced up. "When they're working. Not that they show much once the place gets jumping. Light show hits at nine, when the music changes, and everything starts flashing and rolling. But we don't have much trouble here anyway. It's mostly college kids and data freaks. They come in to hang, to dance, keyboard, do some imaging."

"Imaging."

"Sure we got six imaging booths. You know, where you can cram in with your pals and take goofy shots, then mug them up on a comp. We don't have an X license, so it's got to be clean. No privacy rooms either. What I'm saying is, the place gets busy, but it's still low-key. Tips suck, but it's pretty easy work."

"I'm going to need to see the discs for the last twenty-four hours."

"Gee. I don't know if I can do that. I mean, I just work

here. I think you have to talk to the manager or something, and he's not here until seven. Um . . . Officer—"

"Lieutenant."

"Lieutenant, I just work the bar, mostly days, maybe twenty hours a week. I talk up the customers, give them a hand if they have trouble with the stations or booths. I don't have any authority."

"I do." She tapped her badge. "I can get a warrant, and we can call in your manager. Or you can give me the discs, for which I'll give you an official NYPSD receipt. All that will take time, and I don't like wasting time when I'm on a murder investigation."

"Murder?" His white face lost even the hint of color. "Somebody's dead? Who? Oh man, oh man, not Rachel." His fingers inched away from the picture that remained on the bar, and crawled up to his throat. "She's *dead*?"

"You ever have anything but sports on-screen here?"

"What? Ah, music vids after nine."

"I guess you don't watch much news."

"Hardly ever. It's depressing."

"You got that right. Rachel's body was found early this morning. She was killed last night." Eve leaned companionably on the bar. "Where were you last night, Steve?"

"Me? *Me*?" Terror rippled across his face. "I wasn't anywhere. I mean, sure, I was somewhere. Everybody's somewhere. I was here until about nine, and just went on home— got a pizza on the way, then watched some screen. I'd put in eight on the stick, and just wanted to flake, you know? I'll get you the discs, you'll see I was here."

He dashed off.

"Pizza and screen doesn't alibi him for Rachel Howard," Peabody pointed out.

"No. But it's getting me the discs."

It was only two hours past end of shift when Eve drove through the gates toward home. She considered it a major accomplishment. Of course, she calculated she had at least two more hours to put in before she called it a day, but she'd be putting in the time from her home office.

The house looked its best in summer, she thought, then immediately shook her head. Hell, it looked its best at every season, at any time of the day or night. But there was something to be said about the way that rambling elegance of stone showed itself off against a summer blue sky. With the rolling sea of green grass surrounding it, the splashes and pools of color from the gardens, the lush shade spilling along the ground from the trees, it was a miracle of privacy and comfort in the middle of the urban landscape.

A far cry from a downtown recycle bin.

She parked, as was her habit, in front of the house, then simply sat, drumming her fingers on the wheel. Summerset wouldn't be lurking in the foyer, ready with some sarcastic observation about her being late. She wouldn't be able to jab back at him, which was just a little annoying now that she thought about it.

And he wasn't there to be irritated by her leaving her car in front instead of stowing it in the garage. It almost compelled her to put it away herself.

But there was no need to get crazy.

She left it where it was, trudged through the smothering heat, and into the glorious cool of home.

She'd nearly turned to the monitor to ask Roarke's location when she caught the faint drift of music. Following it, she found him in the parlor.

He sat in one of the plush antique chairs he favored, a glass of wine in his hand, his eyes closed. It was so rare to see him completely shut down, she felt a little twist under her heart. Then his eyes opened, that shock of blue, and when he smiled the pressure released again.

"Hello, Lieutenant."

"How's it going?"

"Better than it was. Wine?"

"Sure. I'll get it." She crossed over to the bottle he'd left on the table, poured a glass for herself. "Been home long?"

"I haven't, no. A few minutes."

"Did you eat?"

His eyebrows arched, the eyes beneath warming with humor. "I did, if one considers what's available at the hospital edible. And you?"

"I caught something, and yours couldn't have been worse than what I can get at Central. So you went by to see Mr. Grace and Agility?"

"He sends you equally fond thoughts." Roarke sipped his wine, watched her over the rim. Waited.

"Okay, okay." She dropped into a chair. "How's he doing?"

"Well enough for someone who fell down a flight of steps this morning. Which he wouldn't have done if he'd use the flaming elevator. Snapped his fucking leg like a twig, ripped bloody hell out of his shoulder. Well."

He closed his eyes again, tapped his fingers on the arm of his chair. Opened his eyes again. And made her wonder if he went through that same routine when he was settling down after dealing with what he liked to call one of her "snits."

"Well. They've got the leg in a skin cast and brace, and tell me it'll fuse like new. A clean break. The shoulder's likely to trouble him longer. He's sixty-eight. I couldn't remember that this morning. You'd think he'd use the elevator when he's got an armload of something or other. And why he'd bother with linens when he should've been getting himself out the door for holiday is another that's beyond me."

"Because he's a stubborn, tight-assed son of a bitch who has to do everything himself, and his way?"

Roarke let out a half-laugh and drank more wine. "Well, so he is."

And you love him, Eve thought. *He's your father in every way that counts.*

"So, you're bringing him home tomorrow."

"I am. My ears are still ringing from his annoyance that he isn't home tonight. You'd think I'd locked him in a snake pit rather than seeing he's in a private suite at the best medical facility in the goddamn city. Fuck me, I should be used to that sort of thing."

She pursed her lips when he shoved out of the chair and headed back to the wine bottle. "I guess you bitch to him about how I complain when you dump me in a health center. Maybe the two of us can arrange for you to have some hospital time. Then Summerset and I will finally bond."

"What a happy day that'll be."

"Had a crappy day, haven't you, ace?" She set her glass aside and rose.

"Tomorrow promises to be just as delightful. He's not happy with the idea of having a medical aide in-house here for the next week or so."

"Can't blame him. He's feeling stupid, uncomfortable, and pissed off. So he kicks at you, because he loves you best." She took the glass from Roarke's hand, set it down. "That's what I do."

"From the bruises on my ass, both of you must love me desperately."

"I guess I do." She linked her arms around his neck, fit her body to his. "Why don't I show you?"

"Are you taking my mind off my poor mood?"

"I don't know." She rubbed her lips over his. "Am I?"

"Well." He gripped her hips, pressed her closer. "Things are looking up."

She snickered, and bit him. "We're all alone. What should we do first?"

"Let's try something we haven't before."

She eased back to study him. "If we haven't done it yet, it must not be anatomically possible."

"You've such a gutter mind." He kissed the top of her nose. "I love that about you." He drew her back to him. "I was thinking of dancing in the parlor."

"Hmm," she decided as she swayed with him. "It's not bad. For starters. Of course, in my earlier fantasy, we were naked while we were dancing."

"We'll get there." Relaxing, making the effort to relax, he brushed his cheek over her hair. This was what he needed, he thought. She was what he needed. To hold onto. To sink into. "I haven't asked about your day."

She was drifting now, on the music, on the moves. "About as crappy as yours."

She'd wanted to ask him about Browning and Brightstar.

He probably knew them, or of them. They were the sort he'd know, and in a way that might give her an edge on them. But it could wait. She'd just let it wait until she didn't feel all this tension balled inside him.

"I'll tell you later."

She rubbed her cheek to his, then skimmed her lips there, teasing her way to his mouth. With a long, low sound of pleasure, she trailed her fingers into his hair and used her lips, her teeth, her tongue, to seduce.

The worries of the day slid away as she filled him. The warmth with its promise of heat, the lazy desire that was sure to turn to urgency. While he guided her in small circles, she led him in this more intimate dance with kisses that drugged the mind, with hands that aroused the body.

As her mouth became more demanding, she tugged the jacket off his shoulders, then raked her short nails up the back of his shirt.

He could feel the music, a kind of rising pulse inside him as he tasted the flesh of her throat. What beat inside him beat for her, and always would. Her fingers were busy now with the buttons of his shirt even as he shoved her own jacket down her arms.

She shook herself free of it before clamping her teeth, small, nibbling bites, on his bare shoulder.

"You're getting ahead of me," he managed.

"Keep up." Nimble and quick, she unhooked his trousers and closed her hand over him.

His blood surged, stealing his breath so that he fumbled with her weapon harness. Though he hit the release, the strap tangled with her half-open shirt. "Bloody hell."

Her laugh was muffled against his mouth, and her hands were ruthless.

She could feel his heart raging against hers now, just as she could feel his struggle for control. But she'd make him lose control this time, until he thought of nothing but her, felt nothing but that burn in the blood.

She knew how the need would build in him—in her— gathering fast and hot, as painful as a fresh bruise, spreading until the system screamed for release.

That was what he brought her, what they brought each other.

They dragged each other to the floor, rolling over the rug as they pulled and tugged at clothes, as hands rushed over damp flesh and mouth sought mouth.

She wanted him wild, mindless, raging, and knew his body—its weaknesses, its strength—well enough to exploit both. She waged power against power and felt a fresh spurt of excitement when his breath caught on her name.

His hands were rough, she wanted them rough, as they raced over her. His mouth was hot, voracious when it closed over her breast.

Feeding, he fed her so that even as she flew over that first whippy edge, she could crave more.

When he clamped his hands over her wrists to still her hands, she didn't struggle. She would let him believe he had the control, let him take and take until he thought them both sated. She arched, offering herself to that greedy mouth, and absorbed every shattering thrill.

And when she felt him brace to plunge inside her, she rolled—quick as a snake—and reversed their positions. Now her hands cuffed his wrists, and her body pinned his.

"What's your hurry?"

His eyes were madly blue, his breath in tatters. "Christ, Eve."

"You'll just have to wait till I'm done with you."

Her mouth crushed down on his.

His system was one raw nerve, and she scraped pleasure over it without mercy. His skin was slick with sweat, his heart a painful hammer blow against his ribs, his blood already screaming in his ears. And still she used him.

He heard himself say her name again, again, then lost his own words in a frantic spate of Gaelic that might have been prayers, might have been curses.

When she rose over him, her skin gleaming in the last red lights of the dying sun, he was beyond any speech.

Now her fingers linked with his, and she took him in.

She bowed back, her body a slim and lovely arch of energy, and it shuddered, shuddered, as his did. Then she shifted her gaze, fixed her eyes on his. And rode.

He lost his senses, lost his mind as she drove him. Sensations pounded him, too hard, too fast for any defense. As his vision dimmed, he could see her face, and those dark eyes focused so intently on him.

Then he went blind as the pleasure shot through him, a hot bullet, and he emptied himself into her.

They were both still quivering when she slid down to collapse in a sweaty heap beside him on the floor. He could hear, as the roaring in his ears began to subside, her wheezing gasps for air.

It was good to know he wasn't the only one who'd been knocked breathless.

"It's gone dark," he managed.

"Your eyes are closed."

He blinked, just to make sure. "No. It's dark."

She grunted, and still wheezing, flipped to her back. "Oh yeah, it is."

"Funny, with all the beds in this house how often we end up on the floor."

"It's more spontaneous, and primitive." She shifted to rub her butt. "And harder."

"It's all of that. Should I thank you for doing your wifely duty?"

"I object to any term that contains the word 'wifely,' but you can thank me for fucking your brains out."

"Yes, indeed." His heart was still knocking, but he nearly had his wind back. "Thanks for that."

"No problem." She stretched, luxuriously. "I've got to go grab a shower, and put in some time on the case I caught today." She waited two full beats. "Maybe you'd like to give me a hand."

He said nothing for a moment, just continued to contemplate the ceiling. "I must have looked fairly pitiful when you came home. I get sweaty, burn up the carpet sex, and now you voluntarily decide to ask me for help on a case. What would be another word for 'wifely'?"

"Just watch it, pal."

When she sat up, he ran a hand affectionately up her back.

"Darling Eve. I'd be happy to give you a hand in the shower, but then I've got some work of my own to see to. This business today's put me behind. But maybe you could tell me about it before we go our separate ways for the next couple hours."

"College girl, part-time clerk at a 24/7," she began as she rose to gather up scattered clothes. "Somebody killed her with a single stab to the heart late last night, and crammed her body into a recycle bin on Delancey, across from where she worked."

"Cold."

"It gets colder."

She told him of the images, the tip to Nadine, as they went upstairs to shower. It helped, she'd discovered, to run through the steps and stages of a case out loud, particularly with an audience who picked up on the nuances.

Roarke never missed a nuance.

"Someone she knew, and trusted," he said.

"Almost has to be. She didn't put up a fight."

"Someone who blends at the college," he added, grabbing a towel. "So if he or she was seen loitering, nothing would be thought of it."

"He—or she—is careful." Out of habit, she stepped into the drying tube and let the warm air swirl. "Methodical," she added, raising her voice. "Tidy. A planner. Mira's going to tell me, when she profiles, that the killer probably holds a job, pays bills in a timely fashion, doesn't make trouble. Has a knack with imaging, so I'm betting it's either a serious hobby or a profession."

"There's something you haven't said," he added as Eve stepped out of the tube. "You haven't said he's already looking for his second."

"Because he's not." She scooped a hand through her hair as she walked into the bedroom. "He's already picked number two. He's already got the first images locked."

She chose ancient gray pants and a sleeveless tank. "The data club might be a trolling spot. I'll see what I find on the security discs and the employee files." She glanced over her shoulders. "You don't happen to own Make The Scene."

"Doesn't ring," he said easily as he put on a fresh shirt. "I've a few data clubs around the city, but most of mine are close to schools or on campus. More traffic, i.e., more profit."

"Hmm. Did you ever go to college?"

"No. School and I had a poor relationship."

"Neither did I. I can't relate. It's like another planet. I'm worried I'll miss something there, if there's anything there, because I can't relate. I mean, take this professor. Why is she teaching Imaging classes? She doesn't need the money, and if she wants to work in Imaging, why not just do that?"

"Those who can't, teach. Isn't there some saying along those lines?"

She gave him a blank look. "If you can't do something, how the hell can you teach somebody else to do it?"

"I haven't the vaguest idea. It may be she enjoys teaching. People do."

"God knows why. People asking questions all the time, looking at you for the answers, for approval, whatever. Dealing with fuck-ups and smartasses and pompous jerks. And all so they can go off and get jobs that pay more than you make to teach them how to get the jobs in the first place."

"Some might say very similar things about cops." He gave the dent in her chin a quick flick with his fingertip. "If you're still at it when I'm done, I'll give you a hand."

She fixed a smirk on her face. "If you're still at it when I'm done, I'll give you a hand."

"That's a very nasty threat."

In her office, Eve headed straight to the kitchen and the AutoChef to order up coffee. At her desk, she loaded the discs from the data club, then absently picked up the statue of the goddess Peabody's mother had given her.

Maybe it would bring her luck, she thought, and setting it down again, ordered the disc images on screen.

She spent the first hour threading her way though the disc, studying the crowd, the movement. The lighting was poor, dim in corners, harsh and jerky on the dance floor. If she needed to ID anyone specifically, she'd probably need the EDD magicians to clean it up. But for now what she saw was a young crowd, mixing, mingling, cruising.

As advertised Steve Audrey was at the bar until nine when the light show burst into being and the music went from merely loud to eardrum damage. He did his job competently enough, spending a lot of time chatting with the customers, but managing to fill their orders without delays.

Most of the cruisers, male or female, traveled in pairs or packs, she noted. There weren't many solos. The killer, Eve figured, would be alone. He didn't troll with a friend.

She plucked out the few singles she noted, marked the section of the disc.

And there, zeroing in, was Diego. She'd bet the bank on it. Swaggering little guy, slicked up in a red silk shirt and pegged trousers. Heeled boots. Oh yeah, thinks he's a god.

She watched him scan the crowd, pick his marks for the night's hustle.

"Computer, freeze image. Magnify section twenty-five through thirty." She pursed her lips as she studied the face. Dark, handsome, if you went for the macho-slick, pretty-boy type. "Computer, run standard ID program on this image. Get me a full name," she murmured.

It would take time, so she shifted to other work.

Somebody in that club had transmitted those images to Nadine. Someone who'd walked through those lights, those shadows, had plugged that data into one of the units, coded in Nadine's number at 75 and sent it on.

While EDD went over the stations, picked their way through the drives until they found the echoes, whoever had killed Rachel Howard was preparing for the next portrait.

I am so full of energy. It can't be an exaggeration to say I've been transformed. Even reborn. She is in me now, and I can feel her life *inside me. The way a woman must feel with a child in her womb. And yet, more than that. More. For this is not something that needs me to live, that needs to grow and develop. She is whole and complete in me.*

When I move, she moves. When I breathe, she breathes. We are one now, and we are forever.

I have given her immortality. Is there any greater love?

How amazing it was, with her eyes locked on mine in that moment when I stopped her heart. I could see in them that all at once she knew. She understood. And how she rejoiced when I drew her essence inside me so her heart would beat again.

Forever.

See how she looks in the images I created of her, one after another in the gallery I've given her. She will never grow old now, or suffer, or know pain. She will always be a pretty young girl with a sweet smile. This is my gift to her, in exchange for hers to me.

There must be more. I must feel that flood of light again, and give my gift to one who deserves it.

Soon. Very soon, other images will grace my personal gallery. We will join together, Rachel and I, and the next.

One day, when the time is right, I will share the whole of this journal with the world instead of short passages. Many will condemn or question, even curse me. But by then, it will be too late.

I will be legion.

Chapter 5

Eve woke from a dream of being pinned under a train wreck to find the cat sitting on her chest. Purring ferociously, he stared. When she only stared back, he shifted his considerable weight and bumped his head against hers.

"Feeling pretty lousy, huh?" She lifted a hand to scratch under his chin where he liked it best. "You didn't mean to do it, and he'll be home today. Then you can sit on him."

Still stroking the cat, she sat up. She and Galahad were alone in bed. It was still shy of seven, she noted, and Roarke was already up. He'd still been working when she'd climbed into bed at one.

"Man or machine?" she asked the cat. "You be the judge. But either way, he's mine."

She frowned at the sitting area. He was often awake before her, and the first thing she'd see in the morning was Roarke having coffee and checking the stock reports onscreen, with the sound muted. It was a kind of routine she'd become accustomed to.

But not today.

Hefting Galahad, she rolled out of bed and headed to Roarke's office.

She could hear his voice, cool and Irish, before she

reached the doorway. The content was another matter, and seemed to have something to do with cost analysis, projections, and outlay. She peeked in and saw him standing in front of his desk, already dressed for business in a dark suit. Three of his wall screens were running, filled with numbers, schematics, diagrams. God knew.

There were holo-images of two men and a woman seated in chairs, and another, just off to the side, of Roarke's admin, Caro.

Curious, Eve stifled a yawn, and leaned against the door-jamb with the cat in her arms. She didn't often see him in full Roarke the Magnate mode. If she was following the topic—and some of it was in, she thought, German—they were discussing the design and manufacture of some sort of all-surface vehicle.

He was using a human translator rather than a program. More personal, she imagined. And he was very much in charge.

The discussion moved into the nitty-gritty of thrusters and aerodynamics, hydroponics, so she tuned it out.

How the hell did he keep it all straight? she wondered. When she'd glanced in before she'd gone to bed, he'd been hip deep in some high-end resort complex he was opening in Tahiti. Or maybe Fiji. Now it was road to air to water vehicles for the sports enthusiast.

And before oh seven hundred.

She clicked back in as he wound the meeting to a close. "I'll need reports from each department by Thursday noon. I expect to start production within the month. Thank you."

The holograms winked away, but for Caro.

"Leave a disc of this business on my desk," he told her. "And I'll need you to handle the Tibbons's matter."

"Of course. You have an eight-fifteen, EDT, with the Ritelink Group, and a 'link conference at ten with Barrow, Forst, and Kline regarding the Dystar Project. I also have your afternoon schedule."

"We'll deal with that later. Set Ritelink up for holo, here, and the 'link as well. I need to be clear from noon till three, and expect anything else that needs doing will have to be done from here today. Possibly tomorrow as well."

"Certainly. I'm sure Summerset will be glad to be home. You'll let us know how he's doing?"

"I will, yes. Though I don't know how glad he'll be when he's told he'll have round-the-clock care for the next few days. He'll kick at me for it, even if he breaks the other leg doing it."

"Well, you should be used to that." She smiled, turned her head. "Good morning, Lieutenant."

"Caro." Galahad leaped out of Eve's arms, pranced over to ribbon himself through Roarke's legs. The admin's tidily perfect suit, the beautifully coiffed white hair, had Eve realizing she was standing there in the sloppy gray sweats she'd slept in. "Early start for you today."

"Not if you're in Frankfurt." She glanced down, laughed a little as the cat sidled over to sniff at her image and poked his head through her calf. "So this is the culprit." She crouched, cocked her head as Galahad stared at her. "A big one, aren't you?"

"He eats like a draft horse," Roarke said. "I'm grateful, Caro, for you coming in at such an ungodly hour."

"I stopped noticing the time working for you years ago." She straightened. "I'll take care of Tibbons. Give my best to Summerset."

"I will."

"Have a good day, Lieutenant."

"Yeah. Bye." Eve shook her head when the holo vanished. "Does she ever look messed up? Hair out of place, coffee stain on the jacket?"

"Not that I recall."

"I didn't think so. What are you calling it?"

"What would that be?"

"The vehicle. You were talking about a vehicle, right? With the German guys."

"Ah, well, we're still kicking that about. Coffee?"

"Yeah," she said as he moved to the AutoChef. "Did you get any sleep?"

"A couple hours." He glanced back as he retrieved the

cups. "Are you worried about me, Lieutenant? That's very sweet."

"You've got a lot on your plate. You've always got a lot on your plate," she added as he brought her the coffee. "I just don't usually notice."

"Once you've been hungry, you prefer a full plate to an empty one." He leaned down to kiss her. "How's your plate doing?"

"I've got plenty of portions left. Listen, if I can manage it, I'll try to swing home this afternoon for a bit. To—I don't know—help you out or something."

His smile was warm and gorgeous. "See there. You're acting like a wife."

"Shut up."

"I like it," he said, backing her against the door. "Quite a bit. Next thing I know you'll be down in the kitchen, baking."

"Next thing you know I'll be kicking your ass, and you'll be the one who needs round-the-clock care."

"Can we play doctor?"

She lifted her cup to hide a reluctant smile. "I don't have time for your perverted fantasies. I'm going to grab a swim before I leave." But she grabbed his chin, planted a hard kiss on his mouth. "Feed the cat," she told him, and walked away.

To save time, Eve swung by to pick up Peabody and headed straight for the lab. It was easier to squeeze results out of lab-tech king Dickhead Berenski in person.

Stopped in traffic, Eve studied her aide. The rosy cheeks and sparkling eyes didn't quite blend with the spit and polish of the uniform and hard, black cop shoes.

"Why are you smiling all the time? It's starting to make me nervous."

"Am I?" Peabody kept on grinning. "I guess I had a really enjoyable wake-up call this morning. That's a euphemism for—"

"I know what it's a euphemism for. Christ." Eve punched through a gap in traffic, then braked a breath away from the bumper of a Rapid Cab. "Just get your mind out of bed with the rest of you."

"But it really likes it there. It's all warm and soft and . . ." She trailed off at Eve's fulminating look, and studied the roof of the vehicle. "Somebody didn't get their enjoyable wake-up call this morning."

"You know, Peabody, when you started to have regular sex, if such a term can be used to describe whatever it is that goes on with you and McNab, I figured you'd stop thinking and talking about sex all the damn time."

"Isn't it nice to be surprised? But since it's making you grouchy we'll talk about something else. How's Summerset doing?"

"I'm not grouchy," Eve muttered. "Old men who hang out in the park and shake their fists at small children are grouchy. Summerset's all right. Well enough to give Roarke a shitload of grief about being in the hospital in the first place."

"Well, Roarke should be used to that."

Eve sucked air through her nose. "The next person, the very next person, who says that is going to know my wrath."

"I'm on a first-name basis with your wrath, sir. I guess this isn't the best time to tell you that McNab and I are thinking of cohabitating."

"Oh my God. My eye." Desperate, Eve pressed her fist to the twitch. "Not while I'm driving."

"We're going to start to look for a place because both of our apartments are too small." Peabody spoke in a rush, wanting to get it all out before her lieutenant imploded. "So I was wondering, after things calm down at your place, maybe you could ask Roarke if he has any units available downtown. Anything within, say, a ten-block radius of Central would be great."

"My ears are ringing. I can't hear you because there's this strange ringing in my ears."

"Dallas," Peabody said, pitifully.

"Don't look at me like that. I *hate* when you look at me like that. Like a damn cocker spaniel. I'll ask, I'll ask. Just don't, in the name of all that's holy, talk about it anymore."

"No, sir. Thank you, sir." Though she pressed her lips together, Peabody couldn't quite defeat the smug grin.

"Wipe that smile off your face." Eve wrenched the wheel and managed a full block before traffic slowed down again. "Maybe you'd be mildly interested in some pesky investigative work I've been toying with in my free time."

"Yes, sir. I'm all nonringing ears."

"Diego Feliciano. Works in a family-owned Mex eatery called Hola. Off Broadway at 125th. Between City College and Columbia. Lots of college trade. Diego's a bit of an entrepreneur and has, allegedly, picked up extra credit supplying some of the coeds, and their dedicated teachers, with Zoner and Push along with their burritos. Several arrests, but no convictions on that score."

"Does this mean tacos for lunch?"

"I like a good taco. Get Feeney on the 'link. I want to know what EDD's got on the transmission to Nadine."

"They'd eliminated thirty percent of the stations by twenty-two hundred last night, and were resuming the search and scan through Make The Scene at oh eight hundred this morning. They expect to have the unit tagged by midday."

"And how does my aide come by this information before I do?"

"Well, you know . . . pillow talk. See, sex—in this case—is an advantage to you. McNab said they'd get through faster, but at data clubs like that, the units are totally clogged. But he's on it and it's his top priority."

She cleared her throat when Eve made no comment. "Should I still contact Captain Feeney?"

"Oh, Feeney and I appear to be superfluous at this point. You and McPecker can fill us in whenever you feel it's appropriate."

"McPecker." Peabody snorted. "That's a good one. I'm going to use it on him."

"Happy to help." She shot Peabody a deceptively friendly look. "Perhaps I'm wasting my time going to the lab. Have you and Dickie also had a liaison?"

"Eeeuw."

"My faith in you is, at least, partially restored."

• • •

Dickie Berenski wore his white lab coat over a yellow shirt with blue polka dots. His thin, dark hair was slicked back over his egg-shaped head. His attention was focused on one of his many screens while he munched on what was left of a strawberry bagel.

He nodded when Eve came in. "Finally, she walks into my joint again. Can't stay away from me, can you, sunshine?"

"I had to get my inoculations first. Spill."

"Aren't you going to ask where I got this fine, tropical tan?"

"No. Rachel Howard, Dickie."

"I just got back two days ago from a fun-filled week at The Swingers' Palace, that elegant all-nude resort on Vegas II."

"You walked around without anything covering up that body, and no one died or went mad?"

"Hey, I'm built under my clothes. Any time you want to check it out—"

"Stop now, before things get ugly. Tell me about Rachel, Dickie."

"Work, work, work." Shaking his head, he scooted on his stool to another screen. "Morris gave you the lowdown on time of death, cause, and blah-de-blah-blah. Opes in the system, last meal, no sexual contact. Kid was driven snow. Got some fibers off her clothes and shoes."

He played his long, spider fingers over a keyboard until the image popped. "Off the bottom of the shoes I got carpet fibers. Vehicle carpet. Bagged the brand for you. Trouble is it's way common. Find this type, this color, in lots of lower-end vehicles. Mostly vans, SUVs, trucks manufactured between '52 and '57. Newer stuff's been ungraded, but you can still buy this carpet for replacement. See, it's a brown, beige, black mix."

He tapped the screen where a sample of the fiber was magnified so it looked like a frayed hunk of rope. "Pretty much a horseshit color. You get the carpet, we can match it, but it's not a lot of help unless you do."

"Give me something better."

"A little patience, a little respect." He stuffed the rest of the bagel in his mouth and talked over it. "Fibers on her clothes from the chair he had her in. Colors match the image he shot, and are again typical of low-end upholstery fabric. Our guy doesn't spend a lot of money on vehicles and furniture if these are representative. But . . ."

He moved to another image. "He doesn't stint on the enhancements. Look, here are shots of her taken before. The shot of her taken post-mortem. He made up her face for the portrait."

"Yeah, I got that already."

"None of these products used match anything she had at home. Fact is, you can see from the candids she didn't wear much face paint. Didn't need it. Got a fresh look about her. But he polished her up for this shot. Samples taken from the body are top-drawer, professional enhancements. The sort of stuff models and actors use. This brand of lip dye—counter name Barrymore, shade First Blush? It goes for a hundred-fifty smackeroos retail."

"I'll need the list of all identified products."

"Yeah, yeah." He flipped her a disc. "And we got another interesting tidbit. Traces of NuSkin bandage on her chest."

"Yeah, so Morris said."

"The unmedicated kind. He bandaged the wound, but no point in medication because, hey, dead girl. But he didn't want her bleeding on her shirt." He brought up a close-up image of the wound on-screen. "No corresponding hole in the shirt she was wearing. He didn't stab her through the shirt or the bra."

"He took them off her first," Eve murmured. "Maybe not off, maybe just loosened them. Stabbed her. Pressure bandage to stop the bleeding so it didn't get on her clothes for the shot. Buttoned her back up, posed her. But when he's done, he takes the bandage off again. Why?"

She paced away to think. "Because he was done. He's finished with her and she's just garbage now. Maybe he worries about fingerprints on the bandage, or that it can somehow be traced back to him. Or maybe he doesn't think or worry about that, and just kept it back as a fucking souvenir." She dragged a hand through her hair.

"I've seen sicker," Dickie commented.

"Yeah, there's always sicker."

"Trina'd be a good source on the enhancements," Peabody said as they got back into the car. "She'd know all the local and online sources for the products."

"Yeah." Eve had already thought of that. And of what would happen if she contacted the stylist. She'd be trapped into some sort of horrifying and sadistic session that involved haircuts and facials and body treatments.

She shuddered.

"You talk to her."

"Coward."

"That's right. Want to make something of it?"

Peabody studied Eve's hair. "You could probably use a little trim."

"Maybe you could use a good colonic."

Peabody hunched her shoulders. "Just saying."

"Contact her when you're back in your cube. I don't want to be anywhere in the vicinity. If she asks, tell her I'm on a top-secret investigation off planet. I may not be back for weeks. No, years."

"Check. Meanwhile?"

"Diego."

"It's not lunchtime."

"You can have a breakfast burrito."

But Peabody knew she was doomed to go hungry within five minutes of entering the pretty cantina. It smelled great. All spicy and exotic. Kids were chomping down their morning meals in booths and four-tops, giving the place a buzzy chatter while the waitstaff moved along efficiently, topping off mugs of fancy coffees.

Diego didn't work the breakfast shift they were told by one of the busy waitresses. Nobody saw him until noon when he surfaced from his apartment above the cantina.

"Works the lunch and dinner shifts," Eve said as they

headed up to the apartment. "Better tips, more action. Comes from having an uncle as a boss. See if he's got a vehicle registered under his name, Peabody. Then check the uncle, or the business for a van."

"On it."

Peabody started the search as Eve knocked on the door. There was silence, so she used her fist. Moments later there was a spate of Spanish. From the tone, she took it to be curses. She pounded again, and held her badge up to the Judas hole.

"Open up, Diego."

"Nothing under his name," Peabody said under her breath. "Uncle's got a late-model sedan, and a service van."

She broke off when Diego opened the door and she was treated to a blast of color from a pair of electric blue pajamas.

McNab, she thought, would totally dig on them.

"What's this about?" His eyes were dark and slumberous, his stance both lazy and cocky. As he scanned Eve, his full lips set in a leering smile while he lifted a finger to run it over the dot of beard on his receding chin.

"Questions. Want me to ask them out here, or inside?"

He shrugged, using one shoulder, then swept his hand in what was supposed to be a courtly gesture as he stepped back. "I always welcome ladies into my home. Coffee?"

"No. Night before last. You know the drill."

"I'm sorry?"

"Where were you night before last, Diego? Who were you with, what were you doing?"

She got a look at the room while she spoke. Small, furnished in sex-god style of red and black. Overly warm and smelling too strongly of some musky male cologne.

"I was with a lady, of course." He flashed brilliantly white teeth. "And we were making sweet, sweet love all night long."

"Lady got a name?"

He cast his heavily lashed eyes downward. "I'm too much of a gentleman to say."

"Then I'll give you one. Rachel Howard."

He continued to smile, and lifted his hands, palms up.

Eve gestured to Peabody, and took the picture of Rachel, held it out. "Refreshed?"

"Ah, yes. Pretty Rachel of the dancing feet. We had a brief and beautiful romance, but I had to end it." He laid a dramatic hand on his heart, and a gold ring winked on his pinky. "She wanted too much of me. I have to give myself to all the ladies, not just one."

"You ended it? By stabbing her in the heart and tossing her in a recycler?"

The smirk vanished as his jaw dropped, and his expression went bright with fear. "What is this?"

"She was killed night before last. Word is you were hassling her, Diego."

"No. No way." The slight Spanish accent disappeared, and his voice was all New York. "We danced a few times, that's all, in that data club a lot of the college crowd hangs in. I hit on her, okay, no crime in that."

"You came by her place of employment."

"So what? So the hell what? Wanted a taste, that's all."

"What about your brief and beautiful romance?"

He sat now, looking slightly ill. "We never got down to it. I took her to dinner, showed her a nice time, then she brushed me off. Challenged me, so I put the squeeze on. Figured she was playing me, wanted a pursuit."

"Want to give me that lady's name now?"

"I don't know it. Jesus. I was on the bounce, club to club. Got a little action with some girl at her place. On the East Side. Shit. Second Avenue. Halley, Heather, Hester. Fuck if I know. Just some blonde *chica* who wanted a bang."

"You're going to want to do better."

"Look." He put his head in his hands a moment, then scooped them through all the glossy black. "We were wasted, okay? Scored a little Zoner, dipped a little Erotica. Went to her place. Second, I know it was Second, maybe in the Thirties. Near a subway, 'cause I caught a train home at three, maybe four in the morning. It was just a one-night bang. Who pays attention?"

Eve nodded toward the pictures of naked and scantily clad

woman that graced his walls. "You like to take pictures, Diego?"

"Huh? Oh. Man, what *is* this? I download them from the Net, frame 'em up. I like looking at women, so what? I *like* women, and they like me. I don't go around killing them."

"Slimy," was Peabody's opinion when they walked back to the car.

"Yeah, slimy's an offense, but it's not a crime. We'll get a search for the uncle's vehicles, see if we get a fiber match. But I can't see him planning this out. Popping her in the heat of the moment, maybe, but putting all the parts in play? He's a petty operator. Still, he'd be able to score the opiates, had contact with the victim, a reason to be annoyed with her, played in the club where the transmission was sent, and has access to a vehicle that fits the general type we suspect was used for transport. We'll keep him on the short list."

"What now?"

"We're going shopping."

"Sir, have you had a blow to the head recently?"

"Cameras, Peabody. We're going to take a look at cameras."

She'd run a list the night before of the top outlets for cameras and imaging supplies in the city. This was someone who considered himself a professional, even an artist, and who took pride in his work. To Eve, that meant he'd take pride in his tools.

A good investigator had to understand the murder weapon. A camera had killed Rachel, every bit as much as the knife through her heart.

She stepped into Image Makers on Fifth.

Businesslike, she noted, scanning the shelves and counters. Organized. In addition to products there were two wall screens that ran various still photos, all very colorful and artsy.

A small, dark-haired man in a limp white shirt hustled right over to her. "Something I can show you?"

"Depends." She flipped her jacket to show the badge she'd hooked to her belt. "I got some questions."

"Christ on a crutch I *paid* those traffic citations. I got a receipt."

"Good to know. This isn't about traffic citations. I have some questions about cameras. About photographs, imaging." She drew out the candid shot of Rachel at work. "What do you think of this?"

He took it—fingertips and thumb—at the corners. Then immediately huffed out a breath. "I saw this. On the news. This is that girl they found downtown. It's a dirty shame. A damn, dirty shame."

"Yeah, it is. What about the photograph. Is it any good? Artistically speaking."

"I sell cameras. I don't know dick about art. It's good resolution. Wasn't taken with a throwaway. Hold on."

He hustled away again, signalled to a woman behind the counter. "Nella. Take a look at this."

The woman was thin as a stick with magenta hair that rose up in a six-inch loop that curled back into the crown of her head. Beneath the arrangement, her face was a triangle of absolute white relieved by magenta lips and eyes.

She studied the photo, then Eve.

"This is the dead girl." Her voice was nasal Queens. "I saw her on the news. The sick fuck who killed her take this?"

"That's the theory. How's the sick fuck as an imager?"

Nella laid the photo on the counter, examined it. Held it up to the light, put it down again, and looked at it through a hand-held magnifier.

"Good. Pro or talented amateur. It's got excellent resolution—good texture, light, shadows, angles. Shows a connection with the subject."

"What do you mean, connection?"

Nella opened a drawer, took out a pack of gum. She continued to study the print as she unwrapped a stick. "He's not just snapping shots of the family dog or the Grand fucking Canyon. This shows an affection and understanding of the subject. An appreciation for her personality. It's a good candid portrait done with a good eye and a steady hand."

"What kind of camera did he use?"

"What am I? Sherlock fucking Holmes?" She cackled at

her own wit and folded the gum into her mouth.

"What would you use, if you took yourself seriously? If you wanted to document a subject without her knowledge?"

"Bornaze 6000 or the Rizeri 5M, if I had bags of money. The Hiserman DigiKing, if I didn't." She pulled a camera the size of her palm out of the display. "This here's the Rizeri. Top-of-the-line pocket model. You want candid, you need small. But you want art, you probably don't go for the lapel or spy size, so if you're any good, this is your baby. Especially for serious work. This interfaces with any comp."

"How many of these do you sell in a month's time?"

"Hell, we maybe sell a dozen of these in a year. The good news is they are damn near indestructible. And that's the bad news, too. You buy one, you got it for life unless you upgrade. And at this point, there's nowhere to upgrade."

"Got a client list for the three models you mentioned?"

Nella snapped her gum. "You think that sick fuck bought something here?"

"Gotta start somewhere."

"We'll run the three brands," Eve told Peabody when they walked out. "Start citywide, see if anyone pops. I'll do a probability on them, but I'm betting top-of-the-line. We cross the cameras with the enhancements, and maybe we'll get lucky."

"What if he rented the equipment?"

"Don't burst my bubble." But she leaned on the car before opening the door. "Yeah, I thought of that, but we go with purchase first. How many professional photographers do you figure are in the city?"

"Can this be a multiple choice question?"

"We're going to find out. We'll start with four sectors. Crime scene, victim's residence, college, data club. He had to see her to want her. She had to know him, at least by sight, to go with him. Once we get that, we go back to interviews. People who knew her, taught her, worked with her. Area photographers, imaging artists."

Her dash 'link beeped as she merged with traffic, and McNab's pretty face popped on.

He had his long blond hair pulled back to show off the trio of silver hoops in his earlobe.

"Lieutenant . . . Officer. I've pegged your unit. If you want to swing by and—haha—make the scene, I'm—"

"Get it to Central," Eve told him. "The transmission to Nadine was sent at one-twenty with a hold. Run the security disc. I want to see who was using that station at that time. I want that individual ID'd asap. I'm on my way in."

"Yes, sir. But it might take me a little while to—"

"Status meeting at eleven hundred. I'm booking a conference room now." She shot a look at Peabody who obediently pulled out her communicator to do so. "Be there, with the data." She waited a beat. "Fast work, Detective."

His face brightened again before she cut him off.

"Conference room A, Lieutenant," Peabody told her.

"Fine. Contact Feeney and ask him to join us."

She had time to organize her own data, to run probabilities, to study both the lab and ME reports before updating her own. Then guilt had her contacting Nadine.

"I wanted to bring you up to speed, but there isn't a hell of a lot I can tell you."

"*Will* tell me," Nadine corrected.

"Can or will. I've got angles I'm working, and a lead I'm about to look at more closely."

"What lead?"

"If anything breaks out of it, I'll tell you. You have my word. I'm not cutting you out, I just don't have anything to give you."

"There's always something. Give me something."

Eve hesitated, then blew out a breath. "You can say that a source at Cop Central confirmed that there was no sexual assault, and investigators believe that the victim knew her killer. The primary is unavailable for comment at this time."

"Slick. See, there's always something. Has the body been released to the family?"

"The Medical Examiner will release the body to the victim's family tomorrow. I've got to go, Nadine. I've got a meeting."

"One more thing. Will you confirm that the primary, and the investigative team, believe Rachel Howard's killer will kill again?"

"No, I will not. Don't play that card, Nadine. Don't play that card until it falls."

She broke transmission, rubbed her hands over her face. Because, she thought, it was going to fall soon enough.

She was the first to arrive in the conference room, so she settled down, took out her notebook, and began to write and review.

Images, youth, pure, portrait, light.

Her light was pure.

Virginity?

How the hell would the killer know her sexual status?

Had the killer been a confidant? A potential lover? Counselor, authority figure?

Who did Rachel trust? Eve wondered and brought the pretty, smiling face back into her mind.

Every damn body.

Had she herself ever trusted people so completely, so simply? Hardly, Eve thought. But then again, she hadn't come from a nice, stable home, with nice, stable parents and a perky kid sister. Everything had been almost preternaturally *normal* in Rachel's life. Up until the last hours of it. Family, friends, school, a shitty part-time job, a settled neighborhood.

At Rachel's age Eve had already graduated from the Academy, had already donned a cop's uniform. Had already seen death. Had already caused it.

And she hadn't been a virgin, not since she'd been six. Seven? How old had she been the first time her father had raped her?

What difference did it make? Her light had sure as hell never been pure.

That's what had drawn him to her. What he'd wanted from her. Her simplicity, her innocence. He'd killed her for them.

She looked over as McNab came in, carting the bulky unit from the data club.

She couldn't stop herself from checking the rhythm of his walk. The previous month he'd taken a direct hit with a police issue, and it had taken several worry-filled days until the feeling had started to come back in his left side.

He wasn't quite back to prancing again, Eve noted. But there was no limp, no drag in the step. And the stringy muscles in both arms were bulging satisfactorily at the effort of carrying the unit.

"Sorry, Lieutenant." He puffed a bit, and his cheeks were already red from hauling the weight. "Just take me a minute to set up."

"You're not late yet." She watched him as he worked.

He wore summer-weight pants in grass green with a skin top that had green-and-white stripes. The vest over it was hot pink, like his gel sandals.

Rachel had been wearing jeans and a blue shirt. Slip-on canvas shoes. Two little pinprick studs, silver, in each ear.

Victim and cop, she thought, might have come from different planets.

So why did a conservative young girl frequent a data club? She wasn't a geek or a freak, a nerd or a cruiser. What was the draw?

"You hit the data clubs on your off-time, McNab?"

"Nah, not so much. Boredom city. I did some when I was a kid, and fresh into the city. Figured I'd find action, and skirts who'd be impressed with my magical skills with the comps."

"And you found them? Action and skirts?"

"Sure." He sent her a quick and wicked grin. "All pre–She-Body era."

"What was she doing there, McNab?"

"Huh? Peabody?"

"Rachel." She scooted the picture down the table toward where he was working. "What was she looking for in that club?"

He angled his head to study the picture. "It's a big draw for students, especially under drinking age. You can go in and play grownup. Nonalcoholic drinks with snappy names, hot music. You got the comps so you can do homework, break, take a spin on the dance floor, talk about classes, flirt. Whatever. It's like, I don't know, a bridge between being a kid and being an adult. That's why you don't see many over-thirties in those places."

"Okay. I get that." She stood, heading for coffee as Peabody hurried in a few steps ahead of Feeney.

"Looks like the gang's all here." Feeney dropped down at the table. "How about a hit of that shit, kid?"

Eve got a second mug. Kid, she thought. Feeney was the only one who ever—had ever—called her that. Odd that she'd just noticed it.

If she'd had a bridge, Eve realized, it had been Feeney.

She set the mug down in front of him. "Okay, this is what I've got."

Once they were briefed, she gestured to McNab. "Over to you, hotshot."

"The transmission was sent from this unit to Nadine Furst's station at 75. We have the time stamp on Nadine's machine, and the correlating stamp on this. When reviewing the security disc for the time in question, we see . . . a lot of flashing lights, bodies, and mass. On-screen," he ordered.

"This unit is—wait." He dug in several of his many pockets until it came up with a laser pointer. "Here." He circled a section of the screen. "It's blocked by people moving around, back and forth, crowding in. But here, yeah, pause disc. Here you get a glimpse of the operator. Split screen, display enhanced image. Didn't take much, just bumping out the light show, magnifying."

"Female." Eyes cool, Eve rose to step closer to the screen. "Mid-twenties, tops, mixed race. She weighs a hundred pounds if she's hauling a full field pack and wearing jump boots. No way this girl killed Howard, and hauled her up and into that bin. She's a fucking toothpick."

"Data junkie," McNab said.

"A what?"

"Data junkie. They get off on data. Can't get enough of the machine. Some of them hole up in some little room and have little to no actual contact with human beings. It's all the machine. Others like to be around people, or have people around. They pick up some change sending and receiving, or doing reports—business, school, whatever. Anything that gives them a reason to deal with data."

"Like EDD geeks," Eve commented.

"Hey." But Feeney's lips twitched. "Data junkies rarely hold actual jobs. Or don't keep them." He drummed his fingers as he watched the screen. "Yeah, there you go. There's a drop. See, the waitress dropped off a stack of discs. Waitress probably takes a cut—club might, too—of what the dj charges per transmission or per job."

"It's not illegal," McNab added. "It's like I say to you, hey, Dallas, can you send these transmissions for me—my unit's down, or I'm squeezed for time, and I give you ten bucks for the time and trouble."

"Or if you're an illegals dealer, for instance, you dump discs on a junkie, transmissions are sent from any number of locations that can't be traced back to you."

McNab lifted his shoulders. "Yeah, there's that. But who's going to trust a junkie for serious business?"

Eve hissed out a breath. "The killer did. Let's get her ID'd. We'll still need to talk to her. Peabody, call the data club, see if anyone there can give us a name on their resident dj. Does she look at what she's sending?"

"Sometimes they do, part of the thrill," Feeney said. "You get peeks into other people's lives or thoughts without having to deal with people."

"I can get behind that part," Eve grumbled.

"You can block the data from the sender," McNab added. "If you want to keep something private. Still, a good dj could hack through a block. She's not hacking though. She's going through the disc stack too fast for that."

"What happens to the discs when she's done?"

"Waitress will pick them back up and give her a fresh supply if there is one. Done discs would go back on the bar, or a table specified for it. You pick it back up if you want it, or the club recycles. You're supposed to label them," he added. "If you want data generated or written, that request goes on a disc, and is set in another location. Fee's higher for that. She's just doing sends now."

"He could've come in any time, dropped the disc off. Hung around for a drink, watched her send it off. Bides his time," Eve said quietly. "Makes sure he stays in the crowd so he doesn't show up on the security. A drink, a dance— might even be trolling for the next one—and he picks up the disc, puts it in his pocket, and strolls on out. Goes home, gets himself a good night's sleep. I bet he slept just fine. And watches some screen so he can hear all about his fine work over morning coffee."

"It was easy for him," Feeney agreed. "It was all easy, straight down the line. He'll be looking forward to doing it again."

"We run the cameras, the enhancements, and the photographers in the three designated sectors. Check through any discarded discs the club hasn't already cycled in case he didn't pick it up. McNab, you hunt down the data junkie. You'd speak her language."

"I'm on it."

"I'm going back to the college, take a look at the Imaging class, try to reconstruct her last few hours. Then I need to take an hour's personal time. Peabody, you're with Feeney."

Eve picked up the photographs. She wasn't ready, not quite, to pin Rachel Howard to the dead board.

"I'll be back by fourteen hundred."

Chapter 6

It would've been different for Rachel, Eve thought as she stood in the back of the imaging lab and watched the workshop. It had been night, and there wouldn't have been so many students. Still Rachel would have been at a work station, like many of these young people, refining, defining, adjusting, admiring, the images she'd transferred from reality to camera, from camera to screen.

What had she been thinking as she'd taken that last class? Had her mind been on her work, or had it wandered toward spending the night with her friends? Had she listened to Professor Browning, as some of the students were now? Or had she focused on her own work, her own world?

Maybe she'd flirted with one of the boys who worked nearby. There were mild flirtations going on—the body language, the eye contact, the occasional intimate whisper that made up the mating dance.

She'd liked to date, she'd liked to dance. She'd enjoyed being twenty. And she'd never be a day older.

She listened while Browning wrapped things up, outlined assignments, and she made sure the professor saw and acknowledged her as the class began to disperse.

They coupled up, Eve noted. Or grouped up, with a few

solos winding through the cliques. That sort of thing hadn't changed since her school days, she mused.

God, she'd hated school.

She'd been a solo, by personal choice. No point in getting close to anyone, she thought now. Just passing through here, just marking time until I'm out of the goddamn system and making my own choices.

Which had been the Academy. The department. And another system.

"Lieutenant Dallas." Browning gestured Eve forward. She'd tamed her hair somewhat by pulling it back, pinning it up, but she still looked lush and exotic. Hardly Eve's internal vision of a college professor.

"Is there news?" she asked. "News on Rachel?"

"The investigation's ongoing" was all Eve would say. "I have a few questions. What would Rachel have been working on in here?"

"Wait." Leeanne drew out a memo book. "That's an introductory course, summer semester. We have a number of part-time students, like Rachel, and a good portion of full-timers on a fast track during summer session," she continued as she flipped through the book. "Not quite as big a load as during the fall and spring semesters, but . . . Ah yes, Faces. Portraits in the City. The connection between image and imager."

"Would you have any of her recent work?"

"Yes, I should have some samples and finished assignments in my files. Hold on just a minute."

She went to her computer, keyed in a password, gave a series of commands. "As I told you, Rachel was a conscientious student. More, she was having fun with this course. It wasn't a make or break for her, simply a filler, but she put effort into her assignments, and wasn't just warming a seat. Here. Take a look."

She stepped back so Eve could see the screen.

"Remke. It's the guy who runs the deli across from the 24/7 where she worked."

"You can see she captured a certain toughness by the

angle of his head, the jut of his chin. He's a bulldog from the look of him."

Eve remembered the way he'd clocked City Maintenance. "That's on target."

"Yet there's a kindness in his eyes that she catches as well. There's the staging, the sheen of perspiration on his face, and the coolness of the tubs of salads in the chill box behind him for a good contrast and sense of place. It's a nice portrait. There are a few more, but this was the best of them."

"I'd like a copy of anything she turned in."

"All right. Computer, copy and print all imaging documents from Rachel Howard's class file." She angled toward Eve as the computer went to work. "I don't understand how these will help you find her killer."

"I want to see what she saw, and maybe I'll see what her killer saw. The students who just left this class, most of them had bags. Disc bags or portfolios."

"Education requires a lot of baggage. A student will need a notebook, a PPC, discs, probably a recorder, and for this course, a camera. That doesn't touch the enhancements, the refreshments, the 'links, the completed assignments, the personal items they haul around campus."

"What kind of bag did Rachel carry?"

Browning blinked, looked blank. "I don't know. I'm sorry, I can't say I noticed."

"But she carried one?"

"Well, they all do." Browning reached behind her desk, held up a large briefcase. "So do I."

The killer had kept her bag, or disposed of it, Eve decided. He hadn't dumped it with the body. Why? What use was it to him?

She made her own notes as she walked down the hall, as Rachel had done.

There wouldn't have been as many people wandering through that night. Just a handful here and there from evening classes—summer evening, Eve thought. Campus isn't as full.

She'd walked out with a group. Laughter, talking. Let's go have pizza, a beer, coffee.

She declines. Heading over to the dorm to hang out with some pals. See you later.

Eve stepped out of the building, as Rachel had done, loitered a moment on the steps, as she imagined Rachel had done. Then stepped down, turned left on the walkway.

There may have been a few other students walking the same path, heading to dorms or toward public transpo. Quiet, she imagined, it would've been fairly quiet. The street and traffic noises buffered back, the bulk of the students in dorms or at their clubs and coffeehouses.

Others heading to apartments or action off campus. Breezing off to the subway, the bus stop. To the parking facilities. Older students, too, adults who'd decided to expand their horizons with an evening class.

Anyone might wander on campus. Columbia was part of the city, merged with it. The way it sprawled over Morningside Heights made security a joke. Rachel wouldn't have worried about it. She was a city girl, and she'd have thought of the campus as a kind of haven.

Had he walked behind her? Had he crossed that open area between buildings? Or had he walked toward her?

She paused, judging the distance to the dorm, the parking facilities, the buildings. He'd wait, Eve decided. Why be seen with her if he could avoid it, so watch and wait while she turned again, started moving on the walkway toward the dorms. Still a good, solid five-minute walk, and heading into more secluded areas.

She wasn't in a hurry, not with the whole night ahead of her. *Dark by this time, but the paths are lit, and she knows her way. She's young and invulnerable.*

It's a hot summer night, and she's enjoying it.

Rachel! Hi.

Very friendly, very easy. Just happened to spot her. And she'd stop, recognize the face. Flash that pretty smile.

But the killer doesn't want to loiter on the path. Someone could come by. Maybe fall into step with her to keep moving, talk about school. What are you working on, how's it going?

Want me to carry that bag for you, it looks heavy.

Can't take her out here, got to get her to the vehicle, and that means parking facility.

Something to show her, or give her. Something in the van/ car/truck. Parked right over on Broadway. Just take a minute. Lead her along a little, keep up the chatter.

Not too many people heading on or off the campus now. And there has to be some risk, or there's less thrill.

Eve detoured toward the four-level vehicle port on Broadway used for college parking. Students and faculty bought a holo-stamp, fixed it to the window. They could come and go as they pleased. Visitors bought an hourly or daily. She made a note to get the data on how many vehicles left the facility between nine and ten on the night of the murder.

Of course, he could have parked elsewhere, could have lucked out and found something on the street, but this was the closest point between dorm and the classroom. And the port was more secluded, less likely to have people nearby than a spot on the street.

It was jammed now, but it wouldn't have been that evening. Nobody would have paid any attention to two people heading toward a vehicle.

Top level would have been the smartest because there would be fewer cars, less traffic at the top. *Get her in the elevator if it's empty, the glide if it's not. Elevator would be lucky.* Inside, a quick move with a pressure syringe full of opiates, a little hand squeeze, and she's floating.

By the time you step out, Eve mused as she rode up to level four, she's light-headed. *Not to worry, I'll drop you off close to the dorm. No trouble at all to drive you down. Gee, you look a little pale, let's get you in the car.*

Eve stepped out on the level, scanned the area. They had security droids do a run-through every thirty minutes or so, but the killer would know, would have it timed. Get her in the car, and it's over for her.

She'd be groggy, maybe unconscious by the time they were down to street level. Drive down Broadway and take her to the place you've prepared. Have to help her inside, so it's got to be fairly private. No lobby to go through, no security to record the moment. A house, a small downtown loft, a business closed for the night, an old building set for renovation.

A business maybe, with an apartment over it. All the conveniences in one place. Nobody to question what goes on inside when the doors are locked.

She stepped over to the rail, looked down over the campus, out over the city.

It could have been done in under fifteen minutes. Add the transportation time and there'd been plenty of time left to take that final portrait.

Back in her car, Eve contacted Peabody at Central. "Get me a list of businesses in or around the college that supply students. Clothes, food, recreation, study guides, whatever. And the photography studios and galleries in the same area. Flag anything that includes private residence. Toss out anything with families. The killer doesn't have a spouse and kiddies running around. I'm taking personal time," she added, "but tag me if you find anything that rings."

She clicked off, and headed toward home.

She hated taking personal time. Hated knowing she'd feel guilty and small if she didn't take it. Marriage was a big enough mass to negotiate, but it had so damn many offshoots. Who could navigate all that?

She should be heading back down to Central, doing the run she'd just dumped on Peabody herself. Letting the data circle around in her head without this outside interference.

Why did people say a busy personal life made you a well-rounded individual? What it did was make you insane more than half the time. Things had been simpler when her edges had been squared off.

She'd done the job, she'd gone home. Maybe, if she'd been up for it, she'd have hung out with Mavis. Now and again, she might catch a post-shift beer with Feeney.

But there hadn't been all these people in her life to worry about. To care about, she admitted. And now there was no going back.

For better or worse, she thought as she swung through the gates. There was plenty of better with Roarke in her life. She couldn't begin to measure it. And if the worst was a skinny, sour-faced snake, well, she was stuck with him.

But when the hour was up, she thought as she jogged up the steps to the front door, she was back on the clock and Roarke would just have to deal with the patient on his own.

The house was cool and quiet. Her first thought was that there'd been complications, or some holdup at the hospital and she'd beaten Roarke home. She turned to the monitor in the foyer.

"Where is Roarke?"

DARLING EVE, WELCOME HOME . . .

The endearment, in the computer's polite tones, had her rolling her eyes. Roarke had some weird-ass sense of humor.

ROARKE IS IN SUMMERSET'S QUARTERS. WOULD YOU LIKE TO SPEAK WITH HIM?

"No. Hell." Did this mean she had to go back there? Into the snake's pit? She *never* went into Summerset's private quarters. Jamming her hands in her pockets, she paced in a circle. She didn't want to go back there. He might be in bed. Would she ever be able to erase the horror of Summerset in bed from her vision once seen?

She didn't think so.

But her only choice was to sneak out of the house again, and feel like an idiot for the rest of the day.

Stupidity or nightmare, she wondered, then hissed out a breath. She'd go back, but she was *not* going in the bedroom. She'd stay in the living area, consider it a courtesy to both herself and the patient. She'd see if Roarke needed any-thing—though what that might be she couldn't imagine—and get the hell out.

Duty done, life goes on.

She wasn't often in this section of the house. Why would she need to go to the kitchen when there were AutoChefs in virtually every other room? Summerset's private habitat was off the kitchen, with access via elevator and stair to the rest of the house. She knew he sometimes used some of the other rooms for music, for entertainment, and she liked to think for secret rituals.

The door to his suite was open, and the laughter that poured out put Eve in a better frame of mind. There was no mistaking Mavis Freestone's happy cackle.

Eve looked in and saw her oldest friend, still in mid-laugh as she stood in the center of the room. Mavis was made for the center, Eve thought.

She was such a little thing, almost fairylike. If you imagined your fairies in skin-baring sunsuits and neon gel sandals.

Mavis's hair was summer blonde today, a conservative color until you got to the pink and blue tips, and noted those curling tips were topped by tiny silver bells that rang cheerfully with every movement. The sunsuit was short and backless with a complex series of crisscrossing strips of that same pink and blue over each breast, to a bare midriff and a pair of micro-shorts.

Though the belly was flat as a board, Eve was reminded— with a sharp jolt—that Mavis had a baby cooking in there.

It was, probably, some sort of high-fashion, I'm pregnant getup, Eve mused, designed by Mavis's one true love, Leonardo, who was currently looking down from his great height on the stylish mother-to-be with such adoration Eve was surprised his pupils weren't shaped like little hearts.

Looking on from a mobile chair, his sour face wreathed in smiles, was Summerset.

She felt a stir of pity as she saw the stiff angle of his supported leg, wrapped in the skin cast, and the sling support on his shoulder. She knew what it was to break bones and tear muscles—and how much worse the cure could seem to anyone used to doing for himself.

She might have said something consolatory, even marginally friendly, but he shifted his head, spotted her. She saw surprise flicker an instant before his face shut down into an icy sneer.

"Lieutenant. Is there something you need?"

"Dallas!" Mavis gave a shout of greeting and threw out her arms. "Come on in, join the party."

Eve followed the direction of Mavis's hands and saw the colorful banner that shouted: WELCOME HOME, SUMMERSET, hanging between the elegant draperies on his windows.

Only Mavis, Eve thought.

"Want a drink? We got fizzy ices." Mavis spun over to an antique server that currently held a carnival setup of crushed ices, sparkling water, and syrups. "Nonalcoholic," she added, "because, you know. Hitchhiker in here's too young to drink." She patted her belly, wiggled her hips.

"How's it going?"

"I'm totally mag. Absolutely ult. Leonardo and I got the word on what happened to Summerset. Poor sweetie pie," she murmured, and whirled back to kiss the top of his head.

Eve felt her gag reflex engage at the thought of Summerset and sweetie pie in the same sentence.

"So we gathered up some fun stuff, and zipped right over to keep him company."

"We were at the doctor's this morning, too." Leonardo continued to beam at Mavis. He was draped in white, long, loose pants, long, loose shirt that flowed around his impressive body and gleamed against the gold-dust tone of his skin. He had a single pigtail draped down one side of his face, and like Mavis, had it tipped in pink and blue, and belled.

"Are you sick?" Eve demanded, forgetting her aversion to the room and moving quickly to Mavis. "Is the baby sick or something?"

"No, we're RRA—rolling right along," she explained. "We just had a checkup deal. And guess! We got pictures."

"Of what?"

"Of the *baby*!" Mavis rolled her baby blue eyes. "Wanna see?"

"Oh, well, I don't really have—"

"I've got them right here." Leonardo pulled a portfolio from some canny split in the shirt. "We only took the ones that don't show the baby's personal area. Because we haven't decided if we want to know."

"Isn't the whole . . ." Eve gestured vaguely toward Mavis's belly. ". . . place its personal area?"

"He means any of the shots that would show if the baby has a penis or a vulva."

"Oh." She actually felt blood draining out of her face. "God."

"Come on, come on, look at your godbaby." Mavis took the portfolio from Leonardo, flipped it open. "Aww, can you believe that? Is that too cute for words?

Eve saw something that looked, sort of, like an underdeveloped, hairless monkey with a really big head. "Wow."

"See, you can even count the tiny, little fingers."

Which, to Eve's mind, made it all creepier. What did it *do* with those fingers inside there?

"Leonardo's going to print the best ones on fabric and make me some tops." Mavis pursed her pink lips to blow Leonardo a kiss.

"Great. That'll be great. Um." Since they made her nervous, Eve looked over the top of the pictures to Summerset. "I just stopped by to see how everything was going."

"Let me make you a cold drink." Leonardo patted Eve's shoulder.

"Yeah, good, okay. Where's Roarke?"

"He's in the bedroom with the physician assistant, making sure everything's set up. Mavis and I will stay awhile."

"Sure we will." To prove it, Mavis perched on the arm of Summerset's chair. "We're going to be in town for the next couple weeks, so we'll come by every day if you want. And you only have to give me a buzz if you're lonely or feeling out of sorts. I'll come right over." She took Summerset's good hand, patted it.

Eve slurped up the flavored ice Leonardo passed her. "Well, I'll just see if Roarke . . . needs anything, then get going. I've got work to—" She let that hang, grateful when Roarke stepped in from the next room.

"Hello, Lieutenant. I wasn't sure you'd make it by."

"I was in the neighborhood." He looked harried, she thought. You wouldn't notice it, not unless you knew every inch of that fabulous face. And she did. "I had an hour to spare, so I thought I'd swing in, see if you needed any help."

"I think we're under control here. PA Spence is satisfied with the arrangements."

There was a quick, and audible sniff from Summerset. "I'm sure she's more than satisfied at the prospect of sitting around doing nothing but annoying me for the next several days, while you pay her an exorbitant salary."

"That's all right," Roarke said pleasantly, "I'll dock it out of yours."

"I don't want that woman hovering over me every minute of the day and night. I'm perfectly capable of seeing to my own needs."

"It's her, or it's the hospital." The pleasant tone had taken on the faintest edge, one Eve recognized very well.

"And I'm just as capable about making my own decisions regarding my medical care."

"I guess they didn't get to do that anal probe while you were in the hospital," Eve said before Roarke could speak. "And extract that stick from your ass."

"Eve." Roarke pinched the bridge of his nose. "Don't start."

"Here now." The woman who came out from the bedroom was perhaps fifty, with a long white coat over pale pink shirt and pants. She had what seemed to be cushy, round breasts to go with a cushy, round butt. They suited her face, also cushy and round. She wore her hair in ginger-colored curls pulled back into a bouncing tail.

Her voice had that peppy, behave yourself tone used by child-care workers and novice parole officers.

"Isn't it nice to have company? But it's time for our nap."

"Madam." Summerset's tone was barbed wire. "*WE* do not nap."

"We do today," she said, unfailingly pert. "A nice hour's rest, then an hour of therapy."

"Eve, this is PA Spence. She'll be seeing to Summerset's at-home care for the next several days. Ms. Spence, my wife, Lieutenant Dallas."

"Oh yes, a policewoman, how exciting." She marched to Eve, grabbed her hand and pumped. The skin might have been soft, Eve thought, but the woman had the grip of a wrestler. "Don't you worry about a thing, not a thing. Mr. Summerset's in good hands."

"Yeah, I bet. I guess we should clear out."

"I am *not* going to be put to bed like a toddler. Or spoon-fed, or clucked over by this—this person." Summerset snarled out the words. "If I can't be left in peace in my own quarters, then I'll go somewhere I can be left in peace."

"Now, Summerset." Still on the arm of his chair, Mavis, stroked his head. "It's just for a few days."

"I've made my feelings on this matter abundantly clear." Summerset folded his lips and stared holes in Roarke.

"As I have mine," Roarke returned. "And as long as you're living under my roof and in my employ, you'll—"

"That, too, can be rectified."

"Oh, you bet your ass."

It wasn't Roarke's response—one that was music to Eve's ears—that had her stepping forward. It was the tone, thick with Ireland that warned her he was about to snap.

"Okay, everybody out. You—" She pointed at Spence. "Take five."

"I don't believe—".

"Take five," Eve repeated in a tone that made even seasoned officers tremble. "Now. Mavis, Leonardo, give me a minute here."

"Sure." Mavis leaned over, kissed Summerset's cheek. "It's going to be okay, honeybunch."

"You, too." She jerked a thumb at Roarke. "Out."

Those blue eyes narrowed. "I beg your pardon?"

"I said clear out. Go down to the gym and beat up a workout droid, or up to your office and buy Greenland. You'll feel better. Take off," she said and gave him a good, solid nudge.

"Fine." He bit the word off. "I'll just go and let the two of you snipe each other to death. At least that'll put paid to the bickering around here."

He strode out, slammed the door.

Summerset remained, arms folded, face set. And trapped in his chair. "I have nothing to say to you."

"Good." Eve nodded, slurped a little more flavored ice.

"Keep your mouth shut. Personally, I don't care if you roll yourself out of here in that chair, and get mowed down by a maxibus, but he does. He's spent the last, what is it?" She checked her wrist unit. "Oh, thirty hours or so worried sick about you, arranging things, re-arranging things so you'd be comfortable, and as happy as your demon soul allows you to be. You scared him, and he doesn't scare easily."

"I hardly think—"

"Shut up. You don't want to be in the hospital. Okay, there we've got a point of agreement. You don't want the PA—"

"She smiles too goddamn much."

"You'll take care of that in no time. I wouldn't want her either, and I'd kick about it some. But if I came out of my own little bitch-world long enough to see how miserable it was making him, I'd put a plug in it. And that's what you're going to do, or I'll put one in for you."

"He needn't worry about me."

"Maybe not, but he will, and you know it. He loves you. And it rips him when someone he loves is hurt."

Summerset opened his mouth, shut it again. Sighed. "You're right. It burns my tongue to say it, but you are. I hate this." He rapped his fist on the arm of the chair. "I don't like being tended."

"Can't blame you for that. Got any alcohol in here? The drinking kind?"

"Perhaps." Suspicion covered his face. "Why?"

"I figure Spence is going to poo-poo any alcoholic beverage, and if I was stuck with her, I'd need a belt now and then to counteract the bouncy smile and chirpy voice. Plus, if it became absolutely necessary, I could bash her over the head with the bottle and put her down for a while."

Eve tucked her thumbs in her front pockets, eyeing Summerset closely as she heard him emit some sound that might have been a laugh. "Anyway, you might want to take this opportunity to stash a bottle somewhere close to the bed, where she won't find it."

Amusement loosened the tightness around his mouth. "That's an excellent idea. Thank you."

"No problem. Now I'll go get Smiley, so you guys can have your nap."

"Lieutenant," he said as she walked to the door.

"What?"

"She won't let me have the cat."

She glanced back, and saw a tinge of embarrassed color run into his cheeks. Since it embarrassed her, too, she studied a point on the wall six inches above his head. "You want him?"

"I just fail to see why he should be banned from my quarters."

"I'll fix it. You want to get that bottle now," she told him. "I'll hold her off a few minutes, but then you're on your own."

She heard the quiet purr of the chair as she slipped out the door.

She wound her way through to the kitchen and found Roarke placating Spence. The woman was still smiling, but there was something maniacal about it.

"Just give him a moment or two to compose himself," Eve said, and headed for coffee. "He wants the cat."

"I'd prefer keeping the area sterile," Spence began.

"He wants the cat," Eve said flatly, and turned her own smile—the one she used to loosen the bladders of suspects and rookies—on Spence. "He gets the cat. And you might want to tone down the cheer meter. He was a medic during the Urban Wars, and will respond better to direct, clear orders than cooing. You're going to have your hands full, Spence. I pity you." She gestured with the mug. "So just let us know if you need a break to go bang your head against the wall."

"All right then." Spence squared her shoulders. "I'll go tend to my patient now."

Roarke stepped over, took the mug from Eve and drained it as Spence left the room. "You handled that with a great deal more skill than I."

"I didn't have to hassle with the prep work. I was just cleanup. Mavis and Leonardo?"

"I suggested they have a swim. They're going to stay,

cheer him on during the physical therapy. I'm so grateful, if they weren't having a child, I believe I'd see if I could buy them one." He rubbed the ache at the back of his neck. "Are you going to tell me what went on in there between you?"

"No."

"Is he?"

"No. I'm going back to work. You ought to do the same, and let the dust settle around here without you. Oh, and take a blocker for the headache." She grinned. "I can't tell you how much I enjoy saying that to you."

He leaned down, kissed her forehead, her cheeks, her lips. "Despite that remark, I love you. I will, indeed, take a blocker—though it doesn't appear I'll need the tanker load I wanted ten minutes ago—and get back to work. I've a meeting scheduled at Dochas," he said, referring to the abuse shelter he'd financed. "It looks like I'll make it."

"Later then." She started out, stopped. "Oh, where'd you dig up Smiley?"

"Who? Oh." He managed a half laugh. "PA Spence? Louise recommended her."

"I guess she had a reason."

"I'll be seeing her shortly." Roarke opened a cupboard, took out a bottle of blockers. "Be sure I'll ask her what it was."

Chapter 7

Eve headed straight to her office, hunkered down at her desk, and called up the Howard file to see if Peabody had added the requested data.

As the list of businesses with attached residences streamed on-screen, she sat back. Okay, this was going to take time. She culled out any that dealt with photography or imaging, and focused on a more workable list of nine.

With them, she ran down the list of possible suspects looking for another link.

Diego Feliciano. Knew the vic, hustled and hassled her. Spent time and money on her, and didn't get the bang for his buck. Several possession with intent arrests. Access to illegals. Alibi runs like a sieve. Access to data club and to a vehicle. Little guy, not much brawn; more hot-headed than cold-blooded. No known imaging skills.

Jackson Hooper. Knew the vic, desired her. Knew place of employment and home residence. Attended Columbia. Would know campus setup and vic's class schedule. Alibi won't hold. Access to data club. Vehicle? Big, athletic. Good brain. Knowledge of photography at least from modeling gigs.

Professor Leeanne Browning. Knew vic. One of the last

to see victim alive. Teaches imaging. Frustrated photographer? Alibied by spouse and security discs. Technical knowledge to doctor discs? Tall woman, well-built. Strong. Knowledge of campus and vic's class schedule.

Other possibles: Angela Brightstar, Browning's spouse. Steve Audrey, bartender data club. Disc junkie at club yet to be ID'd. Fellow students at Imaging class. Neighbors. Teachers.

The killer had a camera, a good one, and imaging equipment, she thought. She'd go back to the tools.

"Okay, let's just see here. Computer, split screen. Display map, ten square block radius around Columbia University, highlight listed addresses."

WORKING . . .

When the map flashed on, she sat back, considered. "Computer, highlight Broadway parking port, Columbia. Calculate most direct routes from that location to marked addresses."

WORKING . . .

"Yeah, you do that," Eve mumbled, and rubbed her empty stomach. Why the hell hadn't she thought to grab something besides coffee when she'd been home, in a fully stocked kitchen?

She glanced toward her open door. Through it, she could hear the buzz and beeps from the detective's bullpen. Easing away from the desk, she walked to her door, poked her head out, scanned.

Satisfied, she closed the door, quietly. Locked it. She climbed onto her desk, stretched up and worked one of the ceiling tiles out of its slot. Playing her fingers over the back of its neighbor, she reached her goal, and laughed softly, almost evilly as she pulled down the candy.

"I have beaten you, Candy Thief. You sneaking bastard." With as much pride as avarice she stroked the wrapper.

It was the real thing, genuine chocolate, rich and pricey as gold. And hers. All hers.

She replaced the tile, studying it from all angles to make certain it was exactly positioned, then hopped down. She unlocked her door, sat back down, then began to slowly peel away the wrapper with all the attention, the affection, the anticipation a woman might use to undress her beloved.

She sighed deeply, and savored the first bite. And tasted both chocolate and victory.

"Okay, let's get serious."

Straightening in her chair, she nibbled candy and studied the information on-screen.

Browning and Brightstar had a big-ass apartment close to the university. Rachel would have trusted her instructor, her instructor's spouse. She'd have gone with either one of them, or both of them into the parking port, even to their apartment if the play had been good enough.

Of course, there was the sticky part, getting Rachel past the doorman, past security. But nothing was impossible.

Motive? Jealousy—pretty young girl. Art? Notoriety?

She input data, and ordered a probability scan.

WITH CURRENT DATA, the computer informed her, PROBABILITY BROWNING AND/OR BRIGHTSTAR MURDERED RACHEL HOWARD IS THIRTY-NINE POINT SIX.

"Not so hot," Eve said aloud. "But we're just getting started."

"Lieutenant, I found something I think—" Peabody stopped her forward march into the office and stared at the small chunk of candy still in Eve's hand. "What's that? Is that chocolate? *Real* chocolate?"

"What?" Panicked, Eve shoved the hand behind her back. "I don't know what you're talking about. I'm working here."

"I can smell it." To prove it, Peabody sniffed the air like a wolf. "That's not chocolate substitute, that's not soy. That's real goods."

"Maybe. And it's mine."

"Just let me have a little—" Peabody's gasp was shocked

and heartfelt as Eve stuffed the remaining chunk in her mouth. "Oh, Dallas." She swallowed hard. "That was very childish."

"Uh-uh. And delicious," Eve added with her mouth full. "What've you got?"

"I don't have chocolate breath, that's for damn sure." At Eve's arch look, she pokered up. "While others, who will remain nameless, were stuffing their face with candy, I diligently pursued an angle in the investigation that I believe might be of some interest to the incredibly selfish candy-hog primary."

"It was dark chocolate."

"You're a mean person and will probably go to hell."

"I can live with that. What angle did you diligently pursue, Officer Peabody?"

"It occurred to me that one or more of the individuals attached to businesses around the college might have a sheet. It seemed prudent to do a run on said individuals to determine any and all criminal records."

"Not bad." And exactly what Eve had in mind to do next. "You can sniff the wrapper," she offered, and held it out.

Peabody grimaced, but she took it.

"And the results?"

"There's good news and bad news. Bad news is the city's full of criminals."

"My God. How could this be?"

"Which leads to the good news that our jobs are secure. Most of what I got was petty stuff, but I did get a couple of nice pops. An assault with illegals possession, and a multiple stalking."

"What's your pick?"

"Oh, well." Suddenly nervous, Peabody puffed out her cheeks. "We'd have to check out both, because . . . the assault doesn't ring so much since the kill was careful, and he didn't rough her up any. But the illegals does, because of the tranq used. But the stalking's more in line with the MO, so I guess I'd start with the stalker."

"You're coming right along, Peabody. Got the name and address?"

"Yes, sir. Dirk Hastings, Portography, on West 115th."

"Dirk's a really stupid name. Let's take a ride."

With Dr. Louise Dimatto as his guide, Roarke took a tour of the newly completed common rooms of the abuse shelter. He approved the soothing colors, the simple furniture, and the privacy shields on the windows.

He'd wanted to establish this . . . sanctuary, he supposed, as a kind of symbol of what both he and Eve had ultimately escaped. And to provide a safe haven for the victims.

He wouldn't have taken advantage of such a place, he thought. No matter how hungry, bruised, battered, he wouldn't have bolted to a shelter.

Too proud, he supposed. Or too bloody mean.

He might have hated his father, but he hadn't trusted the social workers, the cops, the do-gooders, and had figured better the devil you know. There'd been no system for him, as there had been for Eve once she was found broken and bloody in that alley in Dallas.

She'd learned to work her way through the system, while he'd spent most of his life working around it. And somehow he'd become part of it and a do-gooder himself.

It was baffling.

He stood at the wide doorway leading to the recreation area. There were children playing a bit too quietly, but playing. Women with babies on their hips, and bruises on their faces. He caught the looks aimed his way—panic, suspicion, dislike, and outright fear.

Men were a rarity within these walls, and were usually the reason others huddled inside them.

"I'll only interrupt for a minute." Louise spoke in an easy tone as she looked around the room. "This is Roarke. There'd be no Dochas without him. We're pleased he could make the time today to visit, and see the results of his vision and generosity."

"As much your vision, Louise, if not more. It's a nice room, feels like a home." He, too, looked around, at the faces. He felt the weight of their waiting, and their discomfort.

"I hope you're finding what you need here," he said, and started to step out again.

"How come it's got such a funny name?"

"Livvy." A thin woman, no more than twenty-five, by Roarke's gauge, and with faded bruises covering most of her face rushed over. She scooped up the little girl who'd spoken. "I'm sorry. She didn't mean anything."

"It's a good question. It's always smart to ask a good question. Livvy, is it," he continued, addressing the child now.

"Uh-huh. It's really 'livia."

"Olivia. That's a lovely name. It's important, don't you think, what something's called? People, places. Your mum picked a special name for you, and see how well it fits you."

Livvy watched Roarke and leaned closer to whisper in her mother's ear, loud enough for half the room to hear. "He talks pretty."

"She's only three." The woman managed a nervous laugh. "I never know what she's going to say next."

"What an adventure that must be." As the tension lines around the woman's eyes relaxed, Roarke lifted a hand, smoothed a finger over Livvy's brown curls. "But you had a question about the name of this place. It's a Gaelic word, *Dochas*. That's an old, old language people spoke—and still do here and there—in the place I was born. In English it means *hope*."

"Like I hope we can have ice cream again tonight?"

He flashed a grin. They hadn't broken this child yet, he thought. And God willing, they never would. "Why not?" He looked back at the mother. "Are you finding what you need here?"

She nodded.

"That's good then. It was nice to meet you, Livvy."

He stepped out, and made certain they were out of earshot before he spoke again. "How long have they been here?" he asked Louise.

"I'd have to ask one of the staff. I don't remember seeing them when I was here earlier in the week.

"We're helping them, Roarke. Not every one, not every

time, but enough. I know how hard it is, from my clinic, to have some slip away, and how hard it is not to get involved with every one, on a personal level." Though she'd been brought up in wealth and privilege Louise knew the needs, the fears, the despair of the disadvantaged. "I can't give more than a few hours a week here myself. I wish it could be more, but the clinic—"

"We're lucky to have you," Roarke interrupted. "For whatever time you can manage."

"The staff—the counselors and crisis workers—are wonderful. I can promise you that. You've met most of them."

"And am grateful to you for finding the right people. I don't know my way around this sort of thing, Louise. We'd never have pulled this off without you."

"Oh, I think you would have, but not half as well," she added with a grin. "Speaking of the right people," she said, pausing by the steps leading up to the second floor. "How is PA Spence working out for you?"

He let out a long breath, knowing there would be more hell to pay when he got home again. "When I left, she hadn't yet smothered Summerset in his sleep."

"That's a plus. I'll try to stop by and take a look at him myself." She glanced up the steps, broke into a huge smile. "Moira, just who I wanted to see. Have you got a free minute? I'd like you to meet our benefactor."

"That makes me sound like an old man with a beard and a belly."

"And that you're surely not."

Roarke lifted a brow when he heard the Irish in her voice. He could see it in her face, as well. The soft white skin, the pug nose and rounded cheeks. She wore her dark blonde hair in a short wedge to frame them. Her eyes, he noted, were misty blue and clever. The sort that warned him she would see what she intended to see and keep her thoughts to herself.

"Roarke, this is Moira O'Bannion, our head crisis counselor. You two have something in common. Moira's originally from Dublin, too."

"Yes," Roarke said easily. "So I can hear."

"It does stick with you, doesn't it?" Moira offered a hand.

"I've lived in America for thirty years, and never have shaken it. *Dia dhuit. Conas ta tu?*"

"*Maith, go raibh maith agat.*"

"So, you do speak the old tongue," she noted.

"A bit."

"I said hello, and asked how he was," Moira told Louise. "Tell me, Roarke, have you family yet in Ireland?"

"No."

If she noticed the flat, and very cool tone of the single syllable, she gave no sign. "Ah well. New York's your home now, isn't it? I moved here with my husband, he's a Yank himself, when I was twenty-six, so I suppose it's mine as well."

"We're lucky it is." Louise touched her arm as she turned to Roarke. "I stole Moira for us from Carnegie Health Center. Their loss is very much our gain."

"I think it was the right choice, all around," Moira commented. "This is a fine thing you've done with this place, Roarke. It's the finest of its kind I've seen, and I'm pleased to be a part of it."

"High praise from Moira," Louise said with a laugh. "She's a very tough sell."

"No point in saying what you don't mean. Have you seen the roof garden as yet?"

"I was hoping I'd have time to take him up." Wincing, Louise glanced at her wrist unit. "But I'm running behind. You really should take a look before you go, Roarke."

"I'd be pleased to show you," Moira said. "Would you mind if we use the elevator? There are a number of groups and classes in session on the upper levels. The sight of you might make some of the residents uneasy."

"That's fine."

"You're in good and capable hands." Louise rose to her toes to kiss Roarke's cheek. "Give my best to Dallas. I'll drop by and see Summerset the very first chance I get."

"He'll look forward to it."

"Thanks, Moira. I'll see you in a few days. If you need anything—"

"Yes, yes, go on now. Not to worry." She shooed Louise,

then gestured. "She never walks when she can run," Moira added as Louise dashed toward the doors. "A bundle of energy and dedication, all wrapped up in brains and heart. Thirty minutes with her, and I was agreeing to resigning my position at the center and taking one here—and at quite a significant cut in salary."

"A difficult woman to resist."

"Oh aye. And you're married to one I'm told." She led the way through another living area and to a narrow elevator. "A woman of energy and dedication."

"I am."

"I've seen the two of you on the news reports, from time to time. Or read of you." She stepped inside. "Roof please," she ordered. "Do you get back to Dublin often?"

"Occasionally." He knew when he was being studied and measured, and so studied and measured in turn. "I have some business interests there."

"And no personal ones?"

He met those eyes, those clever eyes, straight on. He also knew when he was being pumped. "A friend or two. But I've a friend or two in a number of places, and no more ties to Dublin than anywhere else."

"My father was a solicitor there, and my mother a doctor. Both still are, come to that. But life gets so busy, I'm lucky to get back every second year for a few weeks. It's come back well from the Urban Wars."

"For the most part." He had a flash of the tenements where he'd grown up. The war hadn't been kind to them.

"And here we are." She stepped out when the doors opened. "Isn't this something? A little bit of country, high up here in the middle of the city."

He saw the dwarf trees, the flowering beds, the tidy squares of vegetables with straight paths lined between. A faint mist from the perpetual sprinkler system kept everything lush and watered in the blazing heat.

"It's something they could plant and that they can maintain themselves. For pleasure, for practicality, for beauty." There was a quietness about her now, as if the gardens brought her peace. "We work here early mornings and evenings when it's a bit cooler. I like to get my hands in the dirt, always did. Still, I swear to you, all these years, I've never got used to the bloody heat of this place."

"Louise mentioned something about a garden." Impressed, intrigued, he walked through. "I had no idea she meant something like this. It's beautiful. And it says something, doesn't it?"

"What does it say?"

He ran his fingers over the glossy leaves of some flowering vine. "You beat the hell out of me, you kicked me down. But I got back up, didn't I? I got back up and I planted flowers. So bugger you," he murmured, then shook himself back. "Sorry."

"No need." A faint smile ghosted around her mouth. "I thought pretty much the same myself. I think Louise might be right about you, with all her praise."

"She's prejudiced. I give her a great deal of money. I appreciate you showing me this, Ms. O'Bannion. I hate to leave it, but I've other appointments."

"You must be the busiest of men. Not what I expected altogether, to see the powerful Roarke charmed by a rooftop garden. A plot of wax beans and turnips."

"I'm impressed by resilience. It was good to meet you, Ms. O'Bannion." He offered his hand, and she took it. Held it.

"I knew your mother."

Because she was watching, very closely, she saw his eyes go to chips of blue ice before he drew his hand free. "Did you? That's more than I can say myself."

"You don't remember her then? Well, why should you? I met you before, in Dublin. You weren't much more than six months old."

"My memory doesn't stretch quite that far." There was nothing of the simple pleasure of the rooftop garden in his tone now, but the edge of the Dublin alley. "What do you want?"

"Not your money, or some favor, or whatever it is people must try to wheedle out of you. Not every blessed soul's on the take, you know," she said with some impatience. "But

I'd like a few minutes of your time." She mopped at her face. "Out of this bloody heat. In my office? We could be private there, and I think you'll have an interest in what I have to tell you."

"If it's about her, I've no interest whatsoever." He called for the elevator, fully intending to go all the way down, and straight outside. "I don't give a damn where she is, how she is, who she is."

"That's a hard line, and from an Irishman, too. The Irish men, they love their mam."

He flashed her a look that had her taking a full step back before she realized it. "I've managed fine without one since she walked out the door. I've neither the time nor inclination to discuss her, or any personal business with you. Louise may believe you're a valuable asset to this facility, but push the wrong button, and you'll be out on your ear."

She lifted her chin. She squared her shoulders. "Ten minutes in my office, and if you're so inclined, I'll resign. I feel I have a debt to pay, and I begin to think I've left the paying too long. I don't want anything from you, lad, but a bit of your time."

"Ten minutes." He snapped it out.

She led the way to an office, past a series of session rooms and a small library. It was cool inside, and orderly, with a trim little desk, a small sofa, two comfortable chairs.

Without asking, she went to a small friggie and took out two bottles of lemonade.

"I worked on a crisis line in Dublin," she began. "I was fresh out of university, working on my advanced degree, and thought I knew everything I needed to know. I intended to go into private practice as a counselor, and make myself a tidy pile of money. The hours on the crisis line were part of my training."

She handed him one of the bottles. "It happened I was working the lines when your mother called. I could tell she was young. I could hear that. Even younger than me, and hurt, and scared to death."

"From what I know of her, that's unlikely."

"What do you know of her?" Moira shot back. "You were a baby."

"A bit older when she walked."

"Walked, my arse. Siobahn wouldn't have left you if there'd been a knife at her throat."

"Her name was Meg, and she dusted her hands of me before my sixth birthday." Finished with this nonsense, he set the bottle down. "What's your game?"

"Her name was Siobahn Brody, whatever the bastard told you. She was eighteen when she came to Dublin from Clare, looking for the adventure and excitement of the city. Well, the poor thing got more than her share. Bloody hell, sit down for five minutes."

She ran the cold bottle over her brow. "I didn't know this would be so hard," she murmured. "I always thought you knew, and after this place, was sure of it. Though the fact you built it changed my opinion of you entirely. I figured you for another Patrick Roarke."

A good act, he thought. The sudden distress and weariness of tone. "What you think, what you figure, means nothing to me. Nor does he. Or she."

She set the bottle down, as he had. "Does it matter to you that I know, as sure as I'm standing here, that Patrick Roarke murdered your mother?"

His skin flashed hot, then cold again. But he never flinched. "She left."

"Dead was the only way she'd have left you. She loved you with every beat of her heart. Her *aingeal*, she called you. Her angel, and when she did, she all but sang it."

"Your time's moving quickly, Ms. O'Bannion, and you're not selling anything I'm buying."

"So, you can be hard, too." She nodded, picked up the bottle and sipped as if she needed something to do with her hands. "Well, I expect you can be, and have been. I'm not selling anything here. I'm telling you. Patrick Roarke killed Siobahn Brody. It couldn't be proved. Why should the cops have listened to me if I'd had the courage to go to them? He had cops in his pocket back then, and enough of the scum he ran with would've sworn to it when he said she'd run off. But it's a lie."

"That he killed is no news to me. And that he had pocket cops to cover his murdering ass isn't a bulletin either." He lifted a shoulder. "If you're toying with blackmailing me for his sins—"

"Oh, bloody hell. Money doesn't drive every train."

"Most of them."

"She was your mother."

He angled his head as if mildly interested, but something hot was roiling in his belly. "Why should I believe you?"

"Because it's true. And I've nothing to gain by telling you. Not even, I'm afraid, a lightening of my conscience. I did everything wrong, you see. With all good intentions, but I handled it wrong because I thought I was so wise. And because I cared about her. I got wrapped up in it all."

She drew a deep breath, and set her lemonade aside again. "The night she called the crisis line, I told her where she could go. I soothed and I listened, and I told her what she could do, just as I was trained, just as I'd done too many times before. But she was hysterical, and terrified, and I could hear the baby crying. So I broke the rules, and went to get her myself."

"I might believe you went to get someone, but you're mistaken if you think she was connected to me."

She looked up at him again, and this time her eyes weren't so canny, but swamped with emotion. "You were the most beautiful child I'd seen in my life. Breathtaking little boy, dressed in blue pajamas. She'd run out, you see, snatching you right out of your crib, and not bringing anything along. Nothing but you."

Her voice broke on the end, as if she saw it all again. Then she drew in, went on. "She held you so close, so tight, though three of the fingers of her right hand were broken, and her left eye was swollen shut. He'd given her a few good kicks, too, before he'd stumbled off, already half-pissed, to get more whiskey. That's when she'd grabbed you up and run out. She wouldn't go to the hospital or a clinic, because she was afraid he'd find her there. Afraid he'd hurt her so bad she wouldn't be able to take care of you. I took her to a shelter, and they got her a doctor. She wouldn't take the drugs. She wouldn't have been able to tend to you. So she talked to me, talked through the pain of it, and through the long night."

Though Roarke continued to stand, Moira sat now, gave a long sigh. "She got work in a pub when first she came to Dublin. She was a pretty thing and fresh with it. That's where he found her, her only eighteen and innocent, naive, wanting romance and adventure. He was a handsome man, and it's said charming when he wanted to be. She fell in love, girls do with men they should run from. He seduced her, promised to marry her, pledged his true love, and whatever it took."

She gestured, then walked to stare out of the window while Roarke waited. While he said nothing. "When she came up pregnant, he took her in. He said he'd marry her by and by. She said she'd told her family she was married as she was ashamed to tell them the truth of it. That she was married and happy and all was well, and she'd come home for a visit when she could. Foolish girl," she said quietly. "Well, she had the baby, and he was pleased it was a boy, and still said by and by for marriage. She pushed for it, as she wanted her child to have a true father. And that's when he began to beat her, or knock her about."

She turned back, facing him now. "It wasn't so bad at first—that's what she said to me. A lot of them say that. Or it was her fault, you see, for nagging or annoying him. That's part of the cycle this sort of thing takes."

"I know the cycle, the statistics. The pathology."

"You would, wouldn't you? Wouldn't have done what you've done here without taking the time to know. But it's different, entirely, when it's personal."

"I don't know the girl you're speaking of." A stranger, he told himself. A fantasy, more like. A tale this woman wove with some cagey endgame in mind. It had to be.

"I knew her," Moira said simply.

And her quiet voice shook something inside him. "So you say."

"I do say. The night she called the crisis line, he'd brought another woman into the house, right under her nose, and when she'd objected, he broke her fingers and blackened her eye."

His throat was dry now, burning dry. But his voice stayed cool. "And you have proof of all this?"

"I have proof of nothing. I'm telling you what I *know*. And what you do with it is your business. Maybe you're as hard as him after all. But I'll finish it out. She stayed a week at the shelter. I saw her every day. I'd decided she was my mission. God help us both. I lectured her, and used my fine education on her. She had family back in Clare—parents, two brothers, a sister—a twin she told me. I convinced her to write to them, for she refused to call. Said she couldn't bear the shame of speaking it all out loud. So I pressured her to write, to tell her family she was coming home and bringing her son. I posted the letter for her myself."

Her desk 'link rang, and she started like a woman coming out of a dream. After a quick, trembling breath, she ignored it, and went on.   •

"I pushed her into this, Roarke. Pushed her too hard and too fast because I was so flaming smart. I was so right. And the next day she was gone from the shelter, leaving a note for me that she couldn't run off and take a man's son away from him without giving him the chance to do what was right. Her son should have a father."

She shook her head. "I was so angry. All my time, my precious time and my efforts wasted because this girl was clinging to her romantic foolishness. I stewed about it for days, and the more I stewed the madder I got. I decided I'd break more rules, and go to the flat where she'd been living with him and talk to her again. I'd save her, you see, and that beautiful little boy, in spite of herself. So I took my self-righteousness and my high-flown principles to the slum where he'd kept her and knocked on the door."

He had a flash, the sights and smells of his childhood. The beer vomit and piss in the alleyways, the crack of a hand across a cheek. The air of mean despair. "If you knocked on his door in your social worker's suit, you were either brave or stupid."

"I was both. Back then, I was both. I could've been sacked for what I was doing, should've been. But I didn't care, for my pride was on the line here. *My* pride."

"Is that what you were after saving, Mrs. O'Bannion?"

His cool, and lightly amused voice made her wince. "I wanted to save her, and you, but aye, I wanted my pride with it. I wanted the package."

"Few were saved in that time and place. And pride was a bit dear for most of us to afford on a daily basis."

"I learned the truth of that, and Siobahn was my first lesson. A hard lesson. I had with me the letter that had come from her parents, and I fully intended to scoop the two of you up and send you off to Clare."

There was a bright burst of laughter, a child's laughter, outside the office, then the sound of feet running down the hall. A rush of female voices followed, and then there was silence.

She sat again, folded her hands on her lap like a school girl. "He answered the door himself. I could see right away why she'd fallen for him. Handsome as two devils. He looked me up and down, bold as brass, and I jutted my chin right up and said I'd come to speak to Siobhan."

She closed her eyes a moment, brought it back. "He leaned on the doorjamb there, and smirked at me. She'd run off, he said, and good riddance to her. Stolen fifty pounds of his hard-earned money and taken herself off. If I saw her, I was to tell her to keep right on going.

"He lied so smooth, I believed him. I thought she'd come to her senses after all, and gone home to Clare. Then I heard the baby crying. I heard you crying. I pushed my way inside. I must've taken him by surprise or I'd never have gotten past him. 'She'd never leave her baby,' I said, 'so where is she? What have you done with Siobhan?' "

Her hands unlinked, and one of them curled into a fist to pound on her knee. "A woman came out of the bedroom carrying you with as much care as you carry a cabbage. Your nappie was dripping, your face was dirty. Siobhan, she tended to you like you were a little prince. She'd never have let you get into such a state. But the woman was a bit worse for drink, a florid-looking thing wearing nothing but a wrapper gaping open in the front. 'That's my wife,' he said to me. 'That's Meg Roarke, and that's our brat there.' And he slipped a knife from his belt, watching me as he flicked a thumb over the point. 'Any who says different,' he said, 'will find it hard to say anything after.' "

More than three decades later, in the cool haven of her office, Moira shuddered. "He called me by name. Siobahn must've told him my name. Never in my life have I been so afraid as when Patrick Roarke said my name. I left. If anyone left you there, with him, it was me."

"For all you know she'd gone home, or gotten away. Harder to travel with a baby on your shoulder."

Moira leaned forward. It wasn't anger he saw on her face, or impatience. It was passion. The heat of it blasted out of him, and turned cold under his skin.

"You were her heart and her soul. Her *aingeal*. And do you think I didn't check? I had, at least, the belly for that. I opened the letter. They were so relieved, so happy to hear from her. Told her to come home, to come and bring you home. Asked if she needed money to get there, or wanted her brothers, or her father to come fetch the both of you. They gave her family news. How her brother Ned had married and had a son as well, and her sister Sinead was engaged."

Overcome, she reached for the lemonade again, but this time simply rubbed the bottle between her palms. "I contacted them myself, asked them to tell me when she got there. Two weeks later, I heard from them, and they're asking me, is she coming then? When is she coming? I knew she was dead."

She sat back. "I knew in my heart when I'd been in the hovel and seen you, she was dead. Murdered by his hand. I saw her death in his eyes, when he looked at me and said my name, I saw it. Her parents, and her brother Ned, they came to Dublin when I told them what I knew. They went to the police, and were shrugged off. Ned, he was set on and beaten. Badly beaten, and rocks were thrown through the windows of my flat. I was terrified. And twice I saw him walking by there, he made sure I saw him."

She pressed her lips together. "I stepped away from it. Shameful as it is, that's what I did. Records showed Patrick and Meg Roarke were man and wife, and had been for five years. No record of your birth could be produced, but the woman said the babe was hers, and there was no one to say different. No one who dared, in any case. Girls like Siobhan came and went in Dublin town all the time. She'd turn up when she was ready, and I nodded and said that was so because I was too afraid to do otherwise."

There was a hideous weight on his chest, but he only nodded. "And you tell me this long, unsubstantiated story now, because . . ."

"I've heard of you. Made it my business to keep track of you, best I could even after I married and moved to America. I knew how you ran, much as he did. And figured those few months she was able to give you had been burned out of you, and he'd stamped himself on more than your handsome face. A bad seed, I could tell myself. You were just another bad seed, and I could comfort myself that way, and not be wakened in the middle of the night with that pretty baby crying in my dreams."

Absently, she picked up a small paperweight of clear glass shaped like a heart, and turned it over and over in her hands. "But in the last couple of years, I've heard things that made me wonder if that was so. And when Louise came to me, told me of this place, and what you meant to do with it, I took it as a sign, a sign it was time to speak of it."

She studied his face. "Maybe it's too late to make any difference to you, or to me. But I needed to say it to your face. I'll take a truth test if you want it. Or I'll resign as I said I would, and you can write me off."

He told himself he didn't believe her, not a single word. But there was pain under his heart, like a knife between the ribs. He was afraid it was truth stabbing at him. "You should understand that at least some of what you're claiming I'll be able to verify or debunk."

"I hope you'll do just that. There's one other thing. She

wore a claddaugh, a silver claddaugh on her left hand—like a wedding ring, she told me, that he'd bought her when you were born. His promise that you'd be a family, in the eyes of God and man. When she came out of the bedroom, Meg Roarke was wearing Siobhan's ring. The ring that girl wouldn't take off her finger, even after he'd beaten her. The bitch was wearing it on her pinky, as her hands were too fat for it. And when she saw my eyes land on it, when she saw that I knew . . . she smiled."

Tears began to run down her cheeks now. "He killed her—because she left, because she came back. Because he could. And kept you, I suppose, because you were the image of him. If I hadn't pushed her so hard, had given her more time to heal. To think . . ."

She wiped her face, and rose to go to her desk. From a drawer she took a small photograph. "This is all I have. I took this myself of the two of you the day before she left the shelter. You should have it," she said, and handed it to him.

He looked down, saw a young girl with red hair and green eyes still bruised from a beating. She wore a simple blue shirt with that red hair falling over its shoulders. She was smiling, though her eyes were sad and tired, she was smiling, with her cheek pressed against that of her baby. A face that was still rounded and soft with innocence, but unmistakably his own.

So he was smiling as well. A bright, happy smile. And the hand that cuddled him close had a silver claddaugh on its long, delicate finger.

Chapter 8

Portography was within easy walking distance from the college, Eve noted with some interest, and had a two-tiered parking port—shared by residents and patrons—jammed between the building and its neighbor.

"Check and see if there are any security cams for the parking facility," she told Peabody. "If there are, I want the discs for the night of Howard's murder."

The sign on the lot flashed FULL, but Eve pulled in anyway to study the setup. And flipping on her On Duty light, parked behind an aged minitruck.

"We'll run the vehicles registered to residents and staff. See if we get anything that carries the carpet fibers." She scanned the lot, counting two vans and another truck. "Could he be this careless or this arrogant?" she wondered. "Plan it all out, then get busted because of his ride?"

"They always make mistakes, right?"

"Yeah." Eve headed to the iron steps leading down to street level. "There's always something. It's doable. Get her into the vehicle over by the college, tranq her enough to keep her quiet, drive to another parking deck. Get her inside, do it, then cart her back to the vehicle, drive downtown, dump her. And your work is done.

"Risks, lots of risks," she said more to herself now. "But if you're careful, if you're driven, you factor in the risks. That's what he does. Plans it out, plots it out. Times it. Runs computer programs, maybe, on probabilities, on routes. All the details."

"It wasn't that late when he took her," Peabody pointed out. "Between nine and nine-thirty, right? Maybe somebody noticed him coming or going."

Eve studied the street, the building, the steps and glides that serviced it, and the parking tiers. "How does he get a dead girl out of the building and into his ride? Takes his time, waits until it's late, late enough that there's not much activity on the street. Not so busy in the summer, so not too late. Not so many students hitting the clubs and cafés, and those that do are already in them by nine, for the most part. Music starts cooking at nine. You're going to be exposed for a minute or two. No way around it. But if you're quick, you're careful, and willing to risk it."

"And taking her all the way downtown puts a lot of distance between the murder scene and the dump site. It's a good plan."

"Maybe" was all Eve said as she approached the door.

The first level of Portography was sales. Cameras, supplies, gadgets that were alien to Eve, and software that made no sense to her. An employee was currently demonstrating and extolling the virtues of some sort of complex-looking, multitasking imaging unit to a customer. Another was making a sale on a jumbo box of discs.

Two small screens recorded all the activity in the store from different angles, and invited customers to: CLICK HERE FOR INSTANT SELF-PORTRAIT! Try out the user-friendly Podiak Image Master. On sale! Only $225.99.

There was bright and annoying music tinkling out of the demonstrator. The proud owner of the Podiak Image Master could scroll through a menu of musical choices already loaded on, or record favorites to serve as the score to the family's home vids or stills.

Eve was idly wondering why anyone would want irritatingly happy tunes dancing all over their pictures when Peabody clicked.

"I just wanted to see," she explained. "I don't have any pictures of us." She snatched the printout. "Look. Aren't we cute?"

"Fucking adorable. Put that thing away." She pointed toward the skinny elevator, and the sign announcing the Portography Gallery on Level Two, the Studio on Three.

"Let's take a look upstairs."

"I'm going to put this in my cube," Peabody said as she tucked the printout away. "I can make you a copy. Maybe Roarke would like to have one."

"He knows what I look like." She stepped off on the second level.

There were faces and bodies lining the walls. Young, old, groups. Babies. Young girls in toe shoes, boys with sports gear. Family portraits, artsy shots of nude men and women, even several examples of family pets.

All were framed in thin silver.

To Eve, it was like having a hundred pair of eyes staring. She shook off the feeling and tried to judge if any of the images reminded her of the style used in photographing Rachel Howard.

"Good afternoon." A woman in New York black with a short, straight fringe of white hair stepped around a display wall. "Are you interested in a portrait?"

Eve took out her badge. "Who took these shots?"

"I'm sorry. Is there some sort of trouble?"

"I'm investigating the death of a Columbia student."

"Oh, yes. I heard about that. A young girl, wasn't it? Horrible. I'm afraid I don't understand how the gallery relates to your investigation."

"That's the purpose of investigating. To find out what relates. Miss?"

"Oh, Duberry. Lucia Duberry. I'm the manager here."

"Dallas, Lieutenant Eve. I'm the primary here." She drew Rachel's photo out of her bag. "Did she ever come in?"

"Pretty girl. I don't recall seeing her here. But we do get

browsers, and some of the students wander up to look around. I may not have noticed her."

"What do you think about the photograph itself?"

"Well, it's an excellent study, strong composition. You look, immediately think—as I did—pretty girl. Then you think friendly and young. Fresh is another word that comes to mind, because the pose is so easy and unstudied. Was she a photography student, or a model?"

"No. But she took an Imaging class. She might have bought supplies here."

"Well, we can certainly check on that. Would you like me to call downstairs and have one of the clerks check the receipts?"

"Yes. For Rachel Howard—let's try for over the last two months."

"It shouldn't take long." She went back around the wall, and as Eve followed she saw there was a kind of cube setup, using the display walls as barriers.

Lucia went to the 'link on a small, glossy desk, and contacted the sales floor, giving them the instructions.

"Can I get you anything while you wait? Some spring water perhaps?"

"No, thanks," Eve said before Peabody could open her mouth. "This building—commercial and residential space—has use of the parking deck next door?"

"Yes. Our building and four others."

"Security cams?"

"No. There used to be, but someone was always jamming them or zapping them, until it was more cost prohibitive to continually repair than to put up with a few parking poachers."

"The owner lives upstairs?"

"Hastings has the fourth floor for his living quarters, and his studio on three."

"Is he around today?"

"Oh yes. He has a session in studio right now."

"Any of this stuff his work?"

"All of it. Hastings is very, very talented."

"I'll need to talk to him. Peabody, come up after you've got the data from Sales."

"Oh, but—he's working," Lucia protested.

"Me, too." Eve started toward the elevator with Lucia, now animated, clipping after her. "But Hastings is in a *session*. He can't be disturbed."

"Wanna bet?" She glanced down when Lucia clamped a hand on her arm. "You really don't want to do that."

The tone, utterly flat, had Lucia snatching her hand back again. "If you could just wait until he's finished—"

"No." Eve stepped on the elevator. "Level Three," she ordered, and watched the horrified Lucia until the doors whispered closed.

She stepped off again into a blast of high-tech music that pumped, hot as summer, into the white-walled studio. Equipment—lights, filters, fans, gauzy screens—was centered around a staged area where a buck-naked model draped herself, in various athletic positions, over a huge red chair.

The model was black, and Eve's estimate put her at six feet tall. She was lean as a greyhound, and appeared to have joints made of jelly.

There were three cameras on tripods, and another held by a burly man in baggy jeans and a loose blue shirt. Two others, a tiny woman in a sleeveless black skinsuit and a young man with a tumbling crop of orange hair, looked on with expressions of concentrated concern.

Eve stepped toward the set, started to speak. The young woman turned slightly, spotted her. Shock covered her face first, and was immediately chased by horror.

If Eve hadn't seen the same look on Lucia's face, she might have drawn her weapon and spun to confront whatever terrible danger lurked at her back.

Instead, she kept moving forward, close enough to catch the guppy gulps of distress from the woman, then the choked gasp from the young man. The model met Eve's eyes with a bright glint of humor, and smirked.

"No smile!" This exploded from the man with the camera in a tone that had both assistants jumping, and the model simply relaxing her lips as she bowed her body like a long supple willow branch over the chair.

"You've got company, honey." She purred it, velvet-voiced, as she gestured with an endless and fluid arm.

He whirled, lowering his camera.

The snarl came first, and she had to admit, it was impressive. She'd never seen an actual bear, but she'd seen pictures. He had the look, and with the snarl, the sound of one.

He was a solid three inches over six feet, and a generous two-eighty, by her estimate. Wide of chest, thick of arm, with hands as big as serving platters.

And dead ugly. His eyes were small and muddy, his nose flat and spread over much of his face, his lips were flabby. At the moment, veins were bulging and pulsing in his domed-forehead, and over the shiny ball of his shaved head.

"Get out!" He banged a fist on his own bald head as he shouted as if he were trying to dislodge small demons that lived in his brain. "Get out before I *kill* you."

Eve pulled out her badge. "You want to be careful using that particular part of speech to a cop. I need to ask you some questions."

"A cop? A cop? I don't give a flying fuck if you're a cop. I don't give a flying fuck if you're God Almighty come for Judgment Day. Get out, or I'll twist your arms off your shoulders and beat you to bloody death with them."

She had to give it to him, that was a good one. As he started toward her, she shifted her weight. And when one of his beefy hands reached for her, she kicked him, full out, in the balls.

He went down like a tree, face first, bounced once. She imagined he was groaning and/or gasping, but she couldn't hear over the blasting music.

"Shut that shit off," she ordered.

"End music program." The young man sputtered it out as he danced in thin-heeled boots. "My God, my God, she's killed Hastings. She's *killed* him. Call the MTs, call somebody."

The music dropped away during his shouts, so they echoed around the room.

"Oh, pull yourself together, you asshole." The model rose, walked—graceful and naked—to a bottle of water on a high counter. "He's not dead. His balls are probably in his throat, but he's still breathing. Excellent stopping power," she said to Eve, then drank deeply.

"Thanks." She crouched down to where the felled tree was now wheezing. "Dirk Hastings? I'm Lieutenant Dallas, NYPSD. I've just spared you from an arrest for assaulting an officer. I'm happy to counteract that by hauling your idiot ass down to Central in restraints, or you can get your breath back and answer my questions here, in the comfort of your own home."

"I . . . want . . . a . . . lawyer," he managed.

"Sure, you can have that little thing. Call one up, and he can meet us at Central."

"I don't . . ." He sucked in air, expelled it. "Don't have to go anywhere with you, vicious bitch."

"Oh yeah. You do. Know why? I'm a vicious bitch with a badge and a weapon, so I'm as good as God Almighty come for Judgment Day. Here or there, pal. That's the only call you've got."

He managed to roll onto his back. His face was still sheet-white, but his breathing was steadier.

"Take your time," she told him. "Think about it." She straightened, lifted her brows at the still-naked model. "You got a robe or something?"

"Or something." She strolled over to a swatch of blue-and-white material hanging on a hook. With a few liquid moves, she shimmied it over her head where it slid down and turned itself into a microdress.

"Names," Eve said. "You first."

"Tourmaline." The model walked back to the chair, stretched herself out. "Just Tourmaline. I had it changed legally because I liked the way it sounded. Freelance artist's model."

"You do regular sessions with him?"

"This is my third this year. Personality-wise he's a jerk,

but he knows what he's doing with a camera, and he doesn't try to bang the model."

Eve turned slightly as Peabody came off the elevator. Peabody let her eyes widen at the sight of the enormous man sprawled on the floor, but walked to Eve briskly. "I have that data for you, Lieutenant."

"Hold on to it a minute. Tourmaline, give the officer your information, address, contact number. Then you can either find somewhere to wait, or take off. We'll get in touch if we need to speak with you."

"Might as well take off. He won't be shooting any more today."

"Up to you. Next." She pointed at the young man.

"Dingo Wilkens."

"Dingo?"

"Well, um, Robert Lewis Wilkens, but—"

"Fine. What's in that room?" she asked, pointing toward a door.

"Um. Dressing area. It's—"

"Good. Go there. Sit down. Wait. You." She gave the girl a come-ahead gesture. "Name?"

"Liza Blue."

"Jesus. Does everybody make up names here? Go with the dingo."

They scurried off as Eve put her hands on her hips and looked back down at Hastings. He had his camera again, and was aiming it at her. "What do you think you're doing?"

"Strong face. Good form. Lots of attitude." He lowered the camera, spread his lips in a smile. "I'll call it Bitch Cop."

"Well, you've got your breath back. You want to stay down there, or are you going to get up?"

"You going to kick me in the balls again?"

"If you need it. Take the chair," she suggested, and snagged a stool by the high counter, dragged it over. Still holding the camera, Hastings limped over to the red chair, then sprawled in it.

"You interrupted my work. I was in the zone."

"Now, you're in my zone. What kind of camera is that?"

"Rizeri 5M. What's it to you?"

"That your usual tool?"

"Depends, for Christ's sake. I use a Bornaze 6000 for some shots. Still pull out the Hasselblad Twenty-First when the spirit moves. You want a fricking imaging lesson or what?"

"How about the Hiserman DigiKing."

"Piece of shit. For amateurs. Jesus."

"So, Hastings," she said conversationally, "you like following people around? Following pretty women, taking their pictures."

"I am a portographer. It's what I do."

"You've got two stalking busts."

"Bogus! Bullshit! I'm a freaking artist." He leaned forward. "Listen, they should have been grateful I found them of interest. Does a rose file charges when its image is captured?"

"Maybe you should snap pictures of flowers."

"Faces, forms—they are my medium. And I don't *snap* pictures. I create images. I paid the fines." He dismissed this with a wave of the hand. "I did the community service, for Christ's sake. And in both cases, the portraitures I created immortalized those ridiculous and ungrateful women."

"Is that what you're looking for? Immortality?"

"It's what I have." He glanced over at Peabody, swung the camera up again, framed her in, took the shot, all in one smooth move. "Foot soldier," he said and took another before Peabody could blink. "Good face. Square and sturdy."

"I was thinking, if I had some of the pudge sucked out of the cheeks." Peabody sucked it in herself to demonstrate. "I'd get a little more cheekbone, then—"

"Leave it alone. Square is righteous."

"But—"

"Excuse me." With what she considered heroic patience, Eve raised a hand. "Can we get back to the point?"

"Sorry, sir," Peabody muttered.

"What point? Immortality?" Hastings heaved his mountainous shoulders. "It's what I have. What I give. Artist, subject. The relationship is intimate, more than sex, more than blood. It's an intimacy of spirit. Your image," he said, tapping the camera, "becomes my image. My vision, your reality in one defining moment."

"Uh-huh. And it pisses you off when people don't understand and appreciate what you're offering them."

"Well, of *course* it does. People are idiots. Morons. Every one."

"So you spend your life immortalizing idiots and morons."

"Yes, I do. And making them more than they are."

"And what do they make you?"

"Fulfilled."

"So, what's your method? You shoot here, in the studio with a professional."

"Sometimes. Or I wander the streets, until a face speaks to me. In order to live in this corrupt world, I take consignments. Portraits. Weddings, funerals, children, and so on. But I prefer a free hand."

"Where were your hands, and the rest of you, on the night of August eighth, and the morning of August ninth?"

"How the hell do I know?"

"Think about it. Night before last, starting at nine P.M."

"Working. Here, and up in my apartment. I'm creating a montage. Eyes. Eyes from birth to death."

"Interested in death, are you?"

"Of course. Without it, what's life?"

"Were you working alone?"

"Absolutely."

"Talk to anyone, see anyone after nine?"

His lips peeled back. "I said I was *working*. I don't like to be disturbed."

"So you were alone, here, alone, all evening. All night."

"I just said so. I worked until about midnight, I'd think. I don't watch the freaking clock. I probably had a drink, then took a long, hot bath to relax the body and mind. Was in bed around one."

"Do you own a vehicle, Hastings?"

"I don't understand these questions. Yes, I own a vehicle. Of course I own a vehicle. I have to get around, don't I? Do you think I'd depend on public transportation? I have a car, and a four-person van used primarily for consignments when more equipment and assistants are required."

"When did you first meet Rachel Howard?"

"I don't know anyone by that name."

She rose, walked over to Peabody. "Receipts?"

Hastily, Peabody stopped sucking in her cheeks. "Two. She used a debit card on two occasions for small purchases. June and July."

"Okay. Go check on the other two. Just peek in, look intimidating."

"One of my favorites."

Eve went back to the stool. "Rachel Howard is on record as a customer of your business."

After a long stare, Hastings let out a snort. "I don't know the idiot customers. I hire people to deal with idiot customers."

"Maybe this will refresh your memory." She pulled out the candid shot from the 24/7, and offered it.

There was a flicker, very brief, but she caught it. "A good face," he said casually. "Open, naive, young. I don't know her."

"Yes, you do. You recognize her."

"I don't know her," he repeated.

"Try this one." With her eyes on his, Eve drew out the posed photo.

"Almost brilliant," he murmured. "Very nearly brilliant." He rose with the print, moved to the window to study it. "The composition, the arrangement, the tones. Youth, sweetness, and that openness still there, even though she's dead."

"Why do you say she's dead?"

"I photograph the dead. The funerals people want preserved. And I go to the morgue now and then, pay a tech to let me photograph a body. I recognize death."

He lowered the print, glared at Eve. "You think I killed this girl? You actually think I killed her? For what?"

"You tell me. You know her."

"Her face is familiar." Now, he wet his lips as he looked back at the print. "But there are so many faces. She looks . . . I've seen her before. Somewhere. Somewhere."

He came back, sat heavily. "I've seen her face somewhere, but I don't know her. Why would I kill someone I don't know, when I know so many people who irritate me, and haven't killed any of them?"

It was a damn good question, to Eve's mind. She pressed and probed another fifteen minutes, then stashed him in a room while she pulled out the young male assistant.

"Okay, Dingo, what do you do for Hastings?"

"I-I-I-I-I-"

"Stop. Breathe. In and out, come on."

Once he'd gulped in air, he tried again. "I'm working as studio and on-site assistant. I-I-" He sucked in air when Eve pointed her finger at him. "I have the camera ready, set the lights, change the set, whatever he wants."

"How long have you worked for him?"

"Two weeks." Dingo looked cautiously at the door of the room where Hastings waited. Then leaning closer to Eve, he dropped his voice to a whisper. "Mostly his assistants don't last long. I heard the one before me was in and out in three hours. That's kind of a record. The longest was six weeks."

"And why is this?"

"He freaks, man. Complete meltdown. Nuclear. You screw up, you don't screw up, whatever, if something doesn't fly right for him, he's orbital."

"Violent?"

"He breaks shit, throws shit. I saw him beat his own head against the wall last week."

"Seen him beat anybody else's?"

"Not so far, but I heard he threatened to throw this guy in front of a maxibus during a field shoot. I don't think he actually did it, or anything."

"Have you seen this girl around here? In person, in portraits?"

Dingo took the print. "No. Not my type."

"Oh?"

"She doesn't look like she'd party."

"Would you say she's Hastings's type?"

"For party-time?"

"For any time."

"Not for partying. Don't think the dude parties much. But he'd go for the face."

"You own a vehicle, Dingo?"

He glanced up at her again. "I got an airboard."

"A vehicle, with doors?"

"Nah." He actually grinned at the idea of it. "But I can drive. That's one of the reasons I got the job, because I can drive Hastings to consignments and shit." He paused a minute, frowned down at the print. "He didn't really throw somebody in front of a maxi, did he?"

"Not that I know of. What were you doing night before last?"

"Just hanging, I guess."

"And where would this hanging have taken place?"

"Um . . . I dunno. I was just . . ." The light dawned, turning his eyes into wide, glassy saucers in a face gone dead pale. "Oh man, oh Jesus, I'm like a suspect?"

"Why don't you tell me where you were, what you were doing, who you were with?"

"I-I-I, *jeez*! Loose and Brick and Jazz and me, we hung at Brick's place for a while, then we cruised The Spot, this club we go to mostly, and Loose, he got pretty messed up, so we dumped him home about, *jeez*, about one, maybe? Then we hung a little more, and I went home and crashed."

"Do these hanging buddies have actual names?"

"Oh, oh, yeah."

"Give them to the officer, along with your address. Then you're free to go."

"I can go? Just go?" His face underwent rapid changes, from shock to suspicion, from relief to disappointment. "I don't have to, like, get a lawyer or something?"

"Just stay available, Dingo."

She had to pick her way through the same minefield of nerves with Liza Blue, who turned out to be hair and enhancement consultant. When her teeth started chattering, Eve heaved a long, long breath.

"Look, Liza, do you have anything to feel guilty about?"

"Well, I cheated on my boyfriend last week."

"I'm not going to arrest you for that. How long have you worked for Hastings?"

"Um, I freelance, you know. I work for lots of photographers, and do hair and enhancements for weddings and special occasions, like that. He likes my work, so I've been doing shoots for about a year." She looked plaintively at Eve. "Is that right?"

"Who supplies the enhancements?"

"I have my own kit, but Hastings keeps a supply. He's real fussy. Lots of them are."

"Does he have any Barrymore products?"

"Sure. That's good stuff."

"Have you ever worked on this girl?" Eve asked, handing over the print of Rachel Howard.

Liza pursed her lips. "I don't think so. I'd use a good strong pink lipdye. If I used Barrymore, like you were asking about, I'd maybe use First Blush or Spring Rose. Bring out the shape of her mouth. She's got a nice one, but it could pop a little more. And she ought to bring out her eyes some. She looks kind of familiar though. I don't know where—"

She broke off, and dropped the print as if it had burst into flames. "That's the one who's dead. I saw on the news. That's the girl they found downtown in a recycle bin."

"Where were you night before last?"

"With my boyfriend." Her voice quivered. "With Ivan. I felt real bad about cheating on him. I don't know why I did. I almost told him last night, but I clucked. We went to a vid, then back to his place."

"Peabody, get her data. You can go on home, Liza."

"You think maybe Hastings killed her? I don't want to come back here if you think he killed her."

"He's not charged with anything. I just need to ask questions."

Eve went to the room where Hastings waited. He was sitting, his arms folded over his chest, staring at himself in the dressing room mirror.

"We can do this a couple of ways," Eve began. "I can take you in, hold you, while I get warrants to search this building, including your private residence upstairs, and your vehicles. Or, you can agree now to allow this search."

"You're not going to find a fucking thing."

"Well then, it shouldn't worry you to have us look."

His eyes met hers in the mirror. "So look."

Chapter 9

She called in a team, and looked.

She found no illegals, which surprised her. She'd have pegged Hastings as the type for a taste of a little recreational Zoner, but his place was clean. None of the tranq used in subduing Rachel Howard turned up in the toss of his apartment, studio, or vehicles.

There were a number of Barrymore enhancements in the studio kit, and she matched the shades and products to those used on Rachel.

Tried to imagine Hastings carefully painting the girls lips, brushing color on her eyelids with those big hands.

There was no chair on the premises that matched the one used in Rachel's death portrait, but she did find a large spool of wire. The wire and enhancements went into evidence bags, without a peep of protest from Hastings when she gave him a receipt.

She'd leave it to the sweepers and lab techs to take samples of carpet for a comparison to the fibers in evidence while she concentrated on the massive imaging files.

Part of that concentration was to breathe down McNab's neck while he ran a disc search.

"Lieutenant." In defense, McNab hunched his bony shoulders. "This guy's got tens of thousands of images on file. It's going to take some time for me to run through them and match the victim's face, if she's here."

"She's here. He recognized her."

"Okay, but . . ." He turned his head, and all but bumped noses with Eve. "I could use a little space here."

Eve scowled at the computer screen. Half of it was filled with Rachel's smiling face, the other with a rapid blur as filed images whizzed by. Sooner or later it would stop. She knew it would stop. And a second image of Rachel would appear.

"The machine's doing all the work."

"I respectfully disagree," he replied. "The machine's only as good as its operator."

"EDD propaganda." But she backed off. She was crowding him, and knew it. "I want to know the minute you get a hit."

"You'll be the first."

She glanced over to where Hastings sat, arms folded, mouth set in a perpetual frown as he watched the small army of cops buzz through his studio. With her attention on him, she motioned to her aide. "Peabody."

"Sir."

"Pick a uniform and go interview the second name on your list."

"Sir?"

"Was there some foreign language in that order?"

"You want me to handle the interview?" Peabody's face had gone sheet pale. "Without you?"

"Is there any reason, after more than a year in Homicide, you feel unable to question a suspect without the primary holding your hand?"

"No, sir." Now her face went bright pink. "It's just that you always—I haven't—" She swallowed hard under Eve's bland stare, then squared her shoulders. "I'll take Catstevens, Lieutenant."

"Fine. When you've finished, contact me for further orders."

"Yes, sir. I appreciate you trusting me with this."

"Good. Don't screw up." She turned her back on Peabody, mentally crossing her fingers to wish her aide luck, then sauntered over to Hastings.

Her gut told her the lead was here, and Peabody would get nothing more out of the assignment than some solid field experience.

She leaned back against the windowsill, crossed her feet at the ankles. "It's a pisser, isn't it, having strangers put their fingers all over your stuff." She waited a beat while he simply stared through her. "We can cut a lot of the crap if you tell me how you know Rachel Howard."

"I never said I knew her. Seen her face somewhere. That's not a freaking crime."

"You take pictures of her?"

"Might have."

"Here, in the studio."

His brows drew together. Eve saw him struggle to think back. "No."

"She's never been up here?"

"How the hell do I know?" His voice boomed out again, ripe with frustration. "People bring people up here. Christ knows why. I hire a model or a group, and they just have to bring somebody along. Mostly I kick their asses back out, but every once in a while I'm in a good mood." He smiled thinly. "I try not to let that happen often."

"You make decent money with the imaging?"

Now he sneered. "You make decent money as a cop?"

"Hell, no. So you do it because you do it." She hooked her thumbs in her pockets, finding herself intrigued by him. "And you take images of people, even when you don't particularly like the breed." Now, she nodded. "I can relate to that. But what we have here's a pretty young girl. Men usually find a use for pretty young girls."

His color came up. "I don't muck around with the college set. For Christ's sake, I'm forty years old, what do I want with some skinny coed? I use LCs for sex. It's clean, professional, and there's no baggage. I don't like personal connections."

He's playing me, Eve thought with some amusement. "Yeah, they sure complicate things."

"I like faces." He muttered it. "I can sit here right now thinking you're a pain in the ass cop who's royally screwed up my day, but I like your face. I can hate your guts and still like your face."

"I don't know what the hell to think about yours."

Now he snorted. "Don't come much uglier. But there's a beauty in that." He looked down at his hands a moment, then blew out a windy sigh. "I never killed that girl. Never killed anyone. I like to think of ways to kill people who irritate me. Throwing them off high buildings, boiling them in oil, locking them in a dark room with live snakes, that kind of thing. It gets me through the day."

"You're a piece of work, Hastings."

"We all are. That face. That girl's face. Harmless. You know what makes people such pricks, Lieutenant Dallas?"

"They destroy the harmless."

"Yeah, they do."

"Lieutenant!" McNab waved a hand with his eyes still onscreen. "Found her."

She crossed over, studied the screen. She spotted Rachel instantly, though she was in a group of other young people. Dressed up, fussy dresses, with flowers in the background. Some sort of formal party, she imagined. Probably a wedding.

Rachel had her arm around another girl, her own head thrown back as the photo caught her in a bright, delighted laugh.

"Hastings." Eve motioned him over. "Who, what, where, and when?" she demanded.

"That's it!" His shoulder bumped McNab as he maneuvered to study the full screen, and nearly knocked the lightweight EDD man out of his chair. "I knew I'd seen that face. What is this, what is this? Yeah, the Morelli-Desoto wedding, in January. See it's labeled. There are more—"

"Don't touch the keyboard," Eve snapped. "McNab, enlarge and print the image. You've got more of her, Hastings?"

"I got the whole fricking wedding. Part of the package is I keep them for a year so people can take their time selecting. And Aunt Jane or Grandma Whoosits can come around six months later and order some. There're more of the girl there, and some I took of just her because of that face."

"McNab, run through, select any images of the victim. Enlarge and print."

He scrolled through, giving the commands. Eve saw portions of the wedding unfold—the bride and groom, the family portraits, the candids. Young people, old people, friends and relatives.

"That's the lot, Dallas."

"No. No, it's not," Hastings interrupted before Eve could speak. "I took more. I told you I took more of her, and some other faces that interested me. Subfile on this disc. Faces. They're under Faces."

McNab called it up. Eve noted Hastings hadn't bothered with the bride or groom here. There was a portrait of an old, old woman, a dreamy smile almost lost in the wrinkled map of her face. A child with icing ringing his mouth. Another, surprisingly tender, of a little girl in her party dress, fast asleep across a chair.

Faces streamed by.

"This isn't right," Hastings muttered. "She's not in here. I took them, goddamn it. Four or five candids, two posed. I took more of her than anyone else outside the freaking wedding party. I took those shots."

"I believe you." Considering, Eve tapped her fingers on her thigh. "Couple of things here, Hastings. Are you willing to take a Truth Test?"

"Fuck. Fuck. Yeah, what the hell."

"I'll set it up." She glanced at her wrist unit. Too late in the day to schedule one. "For tomorrow. Now, who worked with you on this job?"

"How the hell do I know? It was freaking January."

"You got files, records?"

"Sure, on the jobs, on the images, on the shoots. Not on assistants. I go through assistants like toilet paper, and toilet paper's a lot more useful."

"You pay them, don't you?"

"More than they're worth," he began, then blinked. "Right. Right. Lucia takes care of it. She'll know."

For the first time since he'd laid eyes on Eve, Roarke was relieved she wasn't there when he got home. Ignoring a quick tug of guilt, he went directly upstairs rather than heading back to Summerset's quarters to check on him.

He needed time. He needed privacy. He needed, for Christ's sweet sake, to think.

It could all be a hoax. It probably was, he told himself as he coded into the secured room that held his unregistered equipment. It likely was a hoax, some complicated, convoluted scheme to bilk him out of some ready cash, or to distract him from some upcoming negotiations.

But why use something so deeply buried in his past? Why, for God's sake, try to tangle him up with something he could, and bloody well would, unravel quickly enough?

It was bullshit. Bollocks.

But he wasn't quite sure.

Because he wanted a drink, a little too much, he opted for coffee, strong and black, before turning to the sleek black console.

He'd had this room built, had added all the security precautions personally. For one purpose. To get around the all-seeing eye and the sticky tendrils of CompuGuard. There was some business, even for the legitimate businessman he'd become, that was no one's concern but his.

Here, in this room with its privacy screened windows, its secured door, he could send and receive any communiqués, conduct any searches, hack into anything he had the time or skill to pursue without alerting CompuGuard.

There had been a time, not so long ago in the grand scheme of things, when he'd used the equipment in this room for purposes not quite legal—as much for fun, he could admit, as for profit. Perhaps even more out of simple habit.

He'd grown up a thief and a grifter, and such habits were difficult to break. Especially if you were good.

He'd always been good.

So good, it had been a very long time since he'd needed to steal to survive. He'd shed his criminal associations and activities, layer by layer, slicking on the polish money could bring.

He'd made something of himself, he thought now, as he looked around the room. Had begun to, in any case.

Then there'd been Eve. His cop. What could a man do when he was so utterly besotted but shed more layers?

She'd been the making of him, Roarke supposed. And still, for all they were to each other, there was a core in him even she couldn't touch.

Now someone had come along, some stranger trying to make him believe that everything up to now—everything he'd done, everything he was, everything he wanted—rested on a lie? A lie, and murder?

He crossed to a mirror. His face, his father's face. All but one and the same, and there was no getting around it. It wasn't something he thought about often, even considered. Which was why, he imagined, having it slapped hard in that face this way shook him down to that hard, cold, unreachable core.

So, he would deal with it. And be done with it.

He sat behind the glossy, U-shaped console, laid his palm on the screen against the slick black. It glowed red as it scanned his palmprint. And his face was set, like stone.

"This is Roarke," he said. "Open operations."

Lights winked on, machines began their quiet, almost human hum. And he got to work.

First, he ordered a deep-level search on Moira O'Bannion. He would know her better than she knew herself before he was done.

The first level was basic. Her date and place of birth, her parents and siblings, her husband and children. Her work record. It jibed with what she'd told him, but he'd expected that.

A good con required a good foundation, didn't it? Who knew that better than he did?

She had to be lying. Had to be, because if she wasn't . . .

Pain and panic crashed in his gut. He bore down, stared at the data on-screen. She had to be lying, and that was that. He only had to find the first chink, and the rest of her fanciful story would crumble.

As the layers peeled away, he studied her medical records, her financials, and those of her family. With a deadly calm he stripped away her privacy, and that of everyone connected to her.

It took him a full hour and he found nothing that sent up a flag.

He got more coffee, settled himself again, then spoke the command he'd hoped to avoid.

"Run search on Siobahn Brody, born County Clare, Ireland, between 2003 and 2006."

WORKING . . . THIRTY-THREE FEMALES BORN DURING THAT TIME PERIOD UNDER THIS NAME.

"Subject is proported to be one of twins."

WORKING . . . FOUR FEMALES BORN DURING THAT TIME PERIOD UNDER THIS NAME WHO WERE ONE OF TWINS.

Now his palms were damp. He was stalling, and knew it. Taking too many steps to find a single answer. "Subject is one of twin girls, sibling Sinead."

WORKING . . . MATCH FOUND, SEARCHING . . .

"Display most recent image of subject while searching. Wall Screen One."

DISPLAYING. I.D. IMAGE SIOBAHN BRODY, SEPTEMBER 5, 2023.

She shimmered onto the screen, filled it with her young, pretty face, her shy smile. Her hair was bright, bold red, drawn smoothly back from her head, her eyes a soft, soft green, her skin all roses and milk.

Younger, Roarke thought as his gut twisted, a year or two younger than the picture he'd seen in Moira O'Bannion's office. And without that deep sadness, without the wear and the bruises. But the same girl. The same.

BRODY, SIOBAHN, BORN TULLA, COUNTY CLARE, IRE-LAND, SEPTEMBER 2, 2005. PARENTS COLIN BRODY AND PATRICIA CARNEY BRODY, FARMERS. SIBLINGS EDWARD BRODY, FERGUS BRODY, SINEAD BRODY, TWIN. EDU-CATED AT MOTHER OF MERCY THROUGH GRADE TWELVE. NO FURTHER EDUCATION. EMPLOYMENT, FAMILY BUSINESS. ADDITIONAL EMPLOYMENT CAR-NEY'S PUB, TULLA, 2022 THROUGH 2023. THE WHITE HORSE, DUBLIN, NOVEMBER 2023 THROUGH OCTOBER 2024.

He stared at the screen image. "Additional data requested. Marriage, children, current status."

NO MARRIAGE ON RECORD, NO LEGAL COHABITATION ON RECORD, NO CHILD ON RECORD. CURRENT STATUS UNKNOWN. THERE IS NO DATA ON BRODY, SIOBAHN, AFTER OCTOBER 2024.

A line of icy sweat trailed down the center of his back. No record. Dropped off the face, he thought.

"Criminal investigations relating to, medical records, fin-ancials, known associates. Something for fuck's sake."

WORKING . . .

There was more, he told himself as he rose. And this time he went for whiskey. There was always more. He'd find it.

• • •

Eve walked in the door only two hours over shift. She told herself she was pleased Summerset wasn't in the foyer waiting to hassle her, and the only reason she headed back to his quarters was for the chance to hassle *him*.

She found him in his living area, propped in his chair with some sort of long-hair piano music playing while he paged through a thick, leather-bound book she imagined came from Roarke's personal library.

Galahad, perched on the arm of the chair, blinked at her.

"Where's the warden?" Eve asked.

"Taking a brisk walk around the estate, while I enjoy some much-deserved solitude." Though he pretended reluctance, he marked and closed the book, prepared to be entertained. "You're quite late this evening."

"I don't live by the clock."

"Despite my temporary difficulties, I still run this household, and require some notification of your schedule. You were expected more than an hour ago."

"You know, this is funny, I see your mouth moving but all I hear is blah, blah, blah. Maybe your little trip damaged your vocal chords. I should ask Nurse Happy Time to check it out."

He peeled his lips back in a grin. "You must have had a quiet day. There's no blood on you for a change."

"Day's not over. I'd better go see if Roarke made it home on schedule, so he doesn't get scolded."

"He's been back for some time." And hadn't come back to visit. "He's in the private office."

Her eyebrows went up, but she shrugged. "I've got work. Oh, and so you know, I left my vehicle out front to embarrass you if you have any visitors this evening."

When she strolled out, Summerset sat back, satisfied, and listened to Chopin while he scratched Galahad between the ears.

Eve went directly up to the private office, used the palm plate, gave her name and code.

ACCESS DENIED.

Baffled, she stared at the locked door, the blinking red light above it. "Well, that's bull," she grumbled and gave the door a little kick before trying again.

ACCESS DENIED.

On an oath, she yanked out her pocket-link and called Roarke's personal number. Her brows drew together when his voice slid out, but her screen remained blank.

Why the hell would he block video?

"Hey, what's up? I'm standing outside the door, but my code's not working."

"Give me a minute."

When the 'link clicked off, she stared at it. "Sure, ace, I'll give you a minute."

It took a full one, and a bit more, before she heard the security stand down. The light went green.

When she stepped in, he was seated behind the console. His sleeves were rolled up, a sign to her that he was working one or more of the keyboards manually.

But his face was as blank as the wall screens.

The door shut behind her, and locked.

"What's going on?"

"I have work."

"On the unregistered?"

Annoyance flickered over his face, and he picked up the heavy crystal glass at his elbow, watching her over the rim, coolly, dispassionately, as he drank. "Yes. On the unregistered."

There was no warmth in his voice. No smile of greeting. "Is there a problem?"

He swirled the liquid in his glass and watched her the way she'd seen him watch an adversary he intended to dispose of. "Why should there be?"

Baffled, she walked behind the console, but the screens there were also dark and blank. She caught the sharp scents of whiskey and tobacco. The ripple of unease she felt increased. "Because I was denied access, because you're sitting here drinking, because you closed down whatever you're working on so I couldn't see it."

"You were denied access because I'm working on a private matter. I'm drinking because I wanted a drink." He lifted the glass to his lips again, as if to prove it. "I closed down because what I'm doing has nothing to do with you. Does that clear it up for you, Lieutenant?"

There was a little punch of shock, dead center in her throat. Instinctively, she searched back through the day for something said or done to have caused his anger.

For it was anger, under all that cold wash. Hot and bubbling.

"If you're pissed at me about something, I'd like to know what it is. That way when I kick your ass, we'll both know why."

Get out, was all he could think. *Get out and leave me be so I can finish this nightmare.* "Not everything I do pertains to you. Not everything I feel revolves around you."

It was a quick and nasty slice in the heart, and she struggled to ignore it. "Look, something's wrong. I can see it." Worried now, she laid a hand on his shoulder, rubbed. And felt the vicious knots of tensed muscles. "If this is about Summerset, I just saw him, and he's his usual irritating self. I know you're upset about what happened to him, but—"

"He's being well seen to, isn't he? I've taken care of it. It might occur to you that I've more on my mind than you, and him, your work, your worries." He shoved away from her to get up, to get away from that supportive hand on his shoulder, to go over to pour another whiskey with the foolish hope that this time it might flood away the sickness inside him.

"Roarke—"

"Goddamn it, Eve, I'm busy here." He snapped it out, and stopped her in her tracks. "Give me some fucking space, will you? I'm not in the mood to chat or for a quick shag or a replay of your day."

Insult and anger lit her face. "Just what the hell are you in the mood for?"

"To be left alone to do what I'm set to do here."

I can't stand having you here, can't stand doing what I'm doing.

"The time I spend diddling about with your work takes away from my own, and I've got to make it up when I choose. As the bloody door was locked, it might've occurred to you that I didn't want to be interrupted. I've a great deal to do, so why don't you be about your own? I've no doubt you've plenty of the dead to keep you occupied for one evening."

"Yeah." She nodded slowly, and the temper in her eyes had faded into astonished hurt. "I've always got the dead. I'll just get the hell out of your way."

She strode for the door, heard the locks whisper open even before she reached it. The instant she was through, it shut and locked tight.

Inside, Roarke stared into the glass, then simply hurled it against the wall so the crystal showered to the floor like lethal tears.

She went to work, or tried, started by running all the names she'd been able to get from Hastings. She'd talk to each personally, but she wanted the basic background before she began.

She had Peabody's very detailed report on her foray into the field. The second pop was tidily alibied for Rachel Howard's murder. Eve expected the alibi to hold, but would have Peabody follow up.

She ran more probabilities, checked her notes, set up a board on which she pinned the images of Rachel, the class schedule, a blueprint of the parking lot, an overview of Columbia campus.

And she worried about Roarke.

At midnight, she walked into the bedroom, found it empty. The house computer told her he was where she'd left him.

He was still there when she climbed into bed alone just before one A.M.

She didn't mind a fight. The fact was, sometimes a good fight livened things up. Got the blood moving. And no matter how mad they might get at each other, they were always *involved*.

This hadn't been a fight. He'd just cut her off, cut her out, watched her with cold blue eyes, the way he might watch a stranger. Or a slightly annoying acquaintance.

She shouldn't have walked out, she told herself as she rolled to find some comfort in the big bed. She should've stayed, *made* him fight until he'd told her what was wrong.

He'd known exactly the way to get her to go. If he'd fought with her, she'd have waded in. But he'd dismissed her, flicked her away, stunning her so she'd been out the door with her tail between her legs.

Just wait, she thought. Just wait until she got hold of him again.

While she lay there, sleepless in the dark, a nineteen-year-old performing arts student named Kenby Sulu was being immortalized.

He stood tall, slim, forever young, his body carefully posed, his lifeless limbs supported by hair-thin wire so that he might look perfect in the dispassionate lens of the camera.

Such light! Such strong light. It coats me. It feeds me. He was brilliant, this clever young man with the dancer's build and the artist's soul. Now he is me. What he was lives forever in me.

I could feel him merge with Rachel, with me. We are more intimate than lovers now. We are one force of life, more than each of us could ever be without the other.

What a gift they have given me. And so I have given them eternity.

There will be no shadows in them.

Only the mad would call this madness. Only the blind will look and not see.

Soon, very soon, I think I can show the world what

I've done. But first, more light. I need two more before
I share with the world.
    But, of course, I must give them a peek.

When all was done that needed to be done, a note and an image were sent to Nadine Furst, at Channel 75.

Chapter 10

The beeping of the bedside 'link shot her out of a nightmare. From dark to dark. Shivering, groping through the panic, she dragged at the tangled sheets.

"Block video. Oh Jesus, lights, ten percent. Damn it, god-damn it."

Eve scrubbed the heels of her hands over her damp cheeks, sucked at air while her heart continued to thunder, and answered the call.

"Dallas."

DISPATCH, DALLAS, LIEUTENANT EVE.

She dragged at her hair. "Acknowledged."

REPORT IMMEDIATELY, LINCOLN CENTER, ENTRANCE TO METROPOLITAN OPERA HOUSE. POSSIBLE HOMICIDE.

"Is the scene secure?"

AFFIRMATIVE.

"Notify Peabody, Officer Delia. My ETA, twenty minutes."

ACKNOWLEDGED. DISPATCH OUT.

She rolled out of bed, the empty bed. It was nearly four in the morning, but he hadn't come to bed. Her skin was clammy from the nightmare, so she gave herself two minutes in the shower, another minute in the swirling heat of the drying tube, and felt almost steady again.

She dressed quickly in the dim light, strapped on her weapon, pocketed her badge, her field restraints, clipped on her recorder. And was halfway out the bedroom door when she cursed, stalked back, and dug a memo cube out of the drawer of the night stand.

"I caught a case," she said into it. "I don't know when I'll be back."

She thought of a dozen things she wanted to say, but they all seemed pointless. So she left it at that, tossed the memo on the bed, and went to work.

The police sensors were up, flashing red and yellow. At the curb a couple of black-and-whites nosed together, with their cones circling in cold blue, hot red.

The great fountain that graced the wide terrace was quiet, and the elegant building behind it dressed in shadows. She'd lived a decade in New York without ever having come to this cathedral of the arts. Until Roarke had taken her inside to the theater, to concerts, even the opera.

When you were hooked up with a man like Roarke, she thought, your horizons broadened whether you wanted them to or not.

What the hell was wrong with him?

"Lieutenant."

She nodded to the uniform who greeted her and pulled herself back. A cop didn't have a personal life, or personal worries on a crime scene.

"What have we got?" She skimmed his tag. "Officer Feeno."

"Male, Asian mix, about twenty. DOS. Couple of half-stewed partyers found him in the fountain. Guy pulled the kid out, woman called it in. My partner and I were first to respond and arrived about two minutes after the call. My partner's got the witnesses stashed over there."

He gestured to the steps leading up to the entrance.

"Keep them wrapped for now. Send my aide through when she arrives."

"Yes, sir. Looks like he might've fallen in and drowned. Not a mark on him, and the way he's dressed, he could be an usher for the Met or one of the other theaters in the Center. Thing is," he continued as he fell into step beside Eve, "he's about the same age as the recycle bin case. She didn't have any marks on her either."

"We'll see what we see."

There were still little rivulets and pools of wet where the body had been pulled out of the fountain. The air was already warm, but heavy enough with humidity that she imagined the water would take some time to evaporate.

She set down her field kit, engaged her recorder, and stood over the body.

Young, she thought on the first quick stir of pity. Twenty at best. Pretty face for a boy. Death had leeched his color, but she imagined his skin had been a smooth and dusky gold to go with the ink black hair and brows. Sharp facial bones, long, elegant fingers, a long trim body, mostly leg.

He was dressed in black—short jacket with a notched collar, straight pants, soft leather shoes. When she crouched, peered close, she could see the faint marks where a name tag had been removed.

Carefully removed, she thought.

"Victim is male, Asian, eighteen to twenty. No visible signs of violence. He is fully dressed in what appears to be a uniform."

She sealed up, then went through his pockets for ID. She found a wallet that held two debit cards, a student ID, and an employee card from the Lincoln Center.

"Victim is identified as Sulu, Kenby, age nineteen, Upper East Side residence, currently a registered student at Juilliard and employed by Lincoln Center."

She sealed the wallet in evidence, then examined his hands.

The skin was smooth, the nails short and well-kept. "Come from money, don't you?" she murmured. "Took care of yourself. Juilliard." She looked toward the Center. "So it was theater for you. You were working tonight. Part-time job, right? To keep close to the theater, maybe help pay your way."

She turned his right hand over, saw the faint red mark from a pressure syringe. "I'm going to find out how he got you, Kenby."

She dug into her field kit, barely glancing up when she heard the huffing breaths and rapid clap of cop shoes on pavement.

"Record on, Peabody. The body's been moved. Lifted out of the fountain, civilian found him." As she spoke, she fixed on microgoggles and examined the palm of the right hand more closely.

"Faint discoloration as is typical from pressure syringe."

"Like Howard."

"Yeah, like Howard." She unbuttoned the jacket. "He was carrying an ID, and two debit cards, got a trendy wrist unit."

"Not robbery."

"No, not robbery." She parted the jacket.

The wound was small and neat. A tidy round hole through smooth flesh, toned muscle, and into the heart. With the goggles on she could see the bits of NuSkin adhesive left around the wound. "And he didn't drown either. Primary's assessment, cause of death, heart wound induced by thin blade. Tox report will likely show opiates in bloodstream."

She sat back on her heels. "Contact Morris. I want him on this one. Run the victim's prints, Peabody, to verify ID. Get time of death, finish the scene exam. Get the names and addresses of next of kin. Then have him bagged, tagged. Homicide. I'm going to question the civilians."

She heard Peabody take a breath to steady herself as she walked away.

The couple sat close on the steps. Hip to hip in their fancy evening clothes. The woman was wearing a black-and-white speckled dress that wound around her body like the snake it mimicked. Her hair had probably started out the evening in a golden tower, but the tower had crumbled considerably, sending poofs and curls and straggles in and around her face.

The man had fared little better. His jacket was bundled in a wet ball beside him, and his snow-white ruffled shirt was transparent from his dip in the fountain. He was barefoot, with his soggy silver shoes on the steps. His pants were still dripping and clung to skinny legs.

She put them both just shy of thirty.

She motioned to the uniform to step aside, then tapped her badge. "I'm Lieutenant Dallas. Tell me what happened."

"He was in the water. I pulled him out. He was dead. I feel sick."

"I know this is difficult." She imagined he did feel sick, not only from the experience but from the crash from whatever party favors they'd been imbibing earlier in the evening. "How did you find him?"

"We went to the ballet—*Giselle*—then to a party. Friend's house on Riverside Drive."

"That's not exactly next door. What were you doing back here at four in the morning?"

"It's not against the law to walk around at four in the morning." The woman spoke up, a whiny baby-doll voice that instantly put Eve's nerves on edge.

"Nope, but sucking up illegals at a party half the night is. We can get through this quick and easy, or we can make it tough and I can take you into custody, run a tox screen."

"We were just trying to help," the man protested.

"That's why I'm not going to run the tox. Let's start again." She pulled out a notebook. "I need your names."

"I'm Maxville Drury. Look, I'm an executive at Fines and Cox, the ad agency. I don't want any trouble."

"You guys do the blimps, right, and the holoboards along the FDR?"

"Among other things."

"Do you have any idea how irritating they are?"

He managed a smile. "Yeah."

"Just wondered. Miss?"

"Loo Macabe. I'm a shoe designer."

"You design those?"

"Yes, I did."

"Interesting. Now that we're pals, why don't you tell me exactly what happened? You were here for the ballet, you went to a party. Then?"

"Okay." Maxville drew a deep breath. "We left the party. I didn't notice the time, honest to God. We were feeling good, up, you know? It's a hot night, and we were just sort of joking around about what it would be like to cool off in the fountain. One thing led to another, and we ended up back here. We were thinking we could not only cool off in the fountain, but heat up. You know?"

Eve glanced at Loo's face, caught the foolish little smile. "Must've been some party."

"I told Max how I have this contest going with some friends on who can make it at the most New York landmarks. And we thought, what the hell, let's chalk up a couple points."

"So you came back here, and . . . ?"

"I just sort of jumped in," Max continued. "Jesus, I almost landed on him. I hauled him up, dragged him out. Loo called for an ambulance. I tried to give him mouth-to-mouth, CPR. I tried. I don't know if I did it right, everything got all jumbled up. I don't know if I did it right."

Because he was looking up at her for some kind of reassurance, Eve sat beside him. "He was gone, Max. He was gone before you got here. There was nothing you could have done. But you tried, and you called for help. So you did it right."

She watched dawn come up, a hazy light in a milky sky. Street and security lights faded out, and the grand fountain spurted into life, spewing its towers of water into the heavy air.

The sounds of morning were the clank and bang of recycle bins being emptied, of maxibuses belching. Of the airtrams and buses beginning their early run across the sick white sky.

The dog walkers came out with their braces of canines,

and the joggers who preferred the sidewalks to the parks or the health clubs.

Glide-carts opened for business, and pumped out their greasy steam.

She watched the dead wagon pull away with its burden of a young man with long, graceful limbs and a minute hole in his heart.

And she watched the Channel 75 van pull up.

"I've got the next of kin, Lieutenant." Peabody stepped up beside her, and with Eve watched Nadine step out of the van. "And when I checked I learned that the victim's parents have already reported him missing."

And she would have to tell them he'd been found.

"Let me deal with this," she said and crossed to Nadine.

"I'd have contacted you," Nadine began, "but the station got the report of the body, and that cops were on scene. I had to figure one of those cops was you."

"Because?"

"Because I got another note, and more pictures. It came through my station unit at six A.M. He's a young man, Asian mix. Very slim, very attractive. Another student, I'd have to say, as the candid shot puts him at Juilliard. I recognized it. Who the hell is killing these kids, Dallas?"

Eve shook her head. "I'll give you a stand-up, here and now, Nadine. Then I'm going to ask you to send the crew away, give me the transmission, then come into Central. I have a stop to make, but I'll be in as soon as I can. I'm going to ask you not to talk to anyone about what you received this morning. I'll give you everything I can."

"Let's set it up." She signalled her crew. "Dallas, I'll do anything I can to help you stop him. But that doesn't mean I don't want the entire story, exclusive, once you have."

"I'll give you what I can when I can." A headache was waking up behind her eyes. "Let's get this done," she added with a glance at the time. "I'm on the clock."

Eve sat in the Sulu living area of their gracious uptown home at twenty after seven on a sticky summer morning, and watched two people dissolve under the shock of losing their only child.

"There could be a mistake." Lily Sulu, a tall, slender woman who'd passed her build onto her son, sat clasping her husband's hand. "Kenby hasn't come home, but there could be a mistake. He's only nineteen, you see. He's very smart, and very strong. There could be a mistake."

"I'm very sorry, Mrs. Sulu. There is no mistake. Your son was positively identified."

"But he's only nineteen."

"Lily." Chang Sulu's eyes were dark, as his son's had been dark. They glistened now as he stared at Eve, as tears slid down his cheeks. "How could this have happened to our son? Who would do this to our son? He harmed no one."

"I don't have the answers for you, but I will have. I need you to help me get those answers. When was the last time you saw Kenby?"

"Yesterday, in the morning. We had breakfast." Chang turned his head, and the look he sent his wife ripped at Eve's heart. "We had breakfast together, and you said: 'Finish your juice, Kenby. It's good for you.' "

Lily's face seemed to break apart. As tears flooded it, her body shook, and the sounds she made were more whimpers than wails.

"Is there someone I can call for you?" Eve asked.

"No. No." Chang held his wife and rocked, and now his gaze clung to Eve's face. "We had breakfast together," he repeated. "And he went to class. Early class. He is a dancer, like his mother. He left before seven. I left for work perhaps an hour later. I am an engineer with the Teckron firm. Lily is now a choreographer and is working on a play. She left home at the same time as myself."

"Where would Kenby go after his early class?"

"More classes. He had a full schedule at Juilliard. He would be there until five, then have some dinner before he went to work. He worked three nights a week at the Metropolitan Opera House, as an usher. We expected him home by midnight, perhaps twelve-thirty. We didn't worry. He's responsible. We went to bed. But Lily woke in the night, and the light we leave on for him was still lit. She checked, and when she saw he hadn't come home, woke me. We called his friends first, then we called the police."

"I'd like to have the name and addresses of his friends, his teachers, the people he worked with."

"Yes, I'll give them to you."

"Was he bothered by anyone? Did he tell you about anyone or anything that disturbed him?"

"No. He was a happy boy."

"Mr. Sulu, was Kenby photographed, professionally, in the last year?"

"You need a photograph?" Sulu continued to stroke his wife's hair. "You said you'd identified him."

"No, I don't need a photograph. It would help me to know if he was photographed."

"At the school." Lily turned her head, her ravaged face, toward Eve. "A few months ago, there were photographs taken of his ballet class. And again, there were photographs taken of the cast of the spring ballet. They performed *Firebird*."

"Do you know who took the photographs?"

"No, but I have copies of several that were taken."

"Can I have them? I'll see they're returned to you."

"If it will help. Lieutenant, we need to see our son."

"I know. I'll arrange that for you."

When Eve stepped out of the house again, she breathed in deep to try to clear the taste of grief out of her throat. And turning over the photograph of the lithe, lively Kenby with his cast mates, she tapped the name: Portography.

"Have Hastings picked up," she told Peabody.

He hadn't slept, but Roarke didn't consider sleep a current priority. Though he didn't have his wife's aversion to chemicals, he didn't feel the need for a pill to boost his energy. He was running on caffeine and nerves.

Siobahn Brody had been his mother. He didn't doubt it now. Couldn't doubt it now. Patrick Roarke had been a good hand at manipulating data, but his son was a hell of a lot better.

It had taken most of the night, but he'd dug down.

There was no marriage record, though from what he was beginning to know about Siobahn, he imagined she'd believed they'd been morally wed.

But he'd found his own birth record, something he'd never troubled himself to dig out before. It had been buried well and deep. He supposed the old man had done so to cover himself for one reason or another. But if you kept shoveling, if you had plenty of time and good reason, a man could find anything in the vast grave of data.

He was a full year younger than he'd believed. Wasn't that a fine kick in the head, he decided as he livened up the coffee with a shot of whiskey. Siobahn Margaret Mary Brody was clearly listed as mother, and Patrick Michael Roarke as father.

Sperm donor anyway, Roarke mused as he drank.

Most likely, she'd given whoever demanded such things that information. The old man wouldn't have been pleased to have his name listed on an official document. No, that wouldn't've set right with him.

Easy enough to bury it.

There was no employment record for her after his birth, but he'd uncovered both their medicals. Healthy as horses they'd been, for a bit.

Then it seemed young Siobahn had become accident prone. A broken arm here, a cracked rib there.

Fucking bastard.

He'd knocked her around, good and proper, for the next several months.

There were no police reports, but that wasn't unexpected either. None of the neighbors would have had the balls to call the cops just because a man was roughing up his wife. And if they had, Patrick Roarke would have known how to handle it. A few pounds slipped to the uniforms, and a solid beating for whoever had the bad manners to call them.

He lighted another cigarette, leaned back in his chair. Closed his eyes.

But he had found a police report, just one, on the disappearance of one Siobahn Brody, initiated by her family. After a bit of tedious cop-speak, statements from a handful of people, the conclusion was she'd taken herself off.

And that was the end of that.

So what was he supposed to do about it now? He couldn't change it, couldn't help her. He didn't know her.

She was a name, a picture in a frame. Nothing more.

Who knew better than he that you couldn't live your life joining hands with yesterday's ghosts?

He hadn't been Meg's. Meg Roarke with her wide face and hard eyes and beery breath. He hadn't come out of her after all. He'd come from that sweet-faced young girl, fresh off the farm. One who'd loved him enough to dress him in blue pajamas, and hold him close to her cheek for a picture.

He'd come from Siobahn Brody, who'd been young enough, foolish enough to go back into hell because she'd wanted to make a family. Give him a father.

God help them all.

Ill, tired, unbearably sad, Roarke sealed all the data he'd accumulated under his voice command and a password. Then he left the room, told himself he'd left the trouble of it—what else could be done—and went to prepare for the day.

He had work waiting, too much to shuffle around because he wasn't feeling quite himself. He'd built a fucking empire, a flaming universe, hadn't he, and it had to be run.

He'd have a shower, some food, make some excuse to Eve for his behavior the night before. There was no point in bringing her into it, no point in dragging out the whole sad and ugly business yet again.

But she wasn't there. The sheets were in tangles, which told him she'd spent as poor a night as he had. Guilt twisted inside him as he wondered if she'd been plagued by nightmares.

She never slept well without him. He knew that.

He saw the memo, picked it up.

"I caught a case. I don't know when I'll be back."

Feeling foolish, feeling raw, he played it back twice just to hear her voice. Then closing his fist around the little cube, he sat on the side of the bed.

Alone, he grieved for a woman he'd never known, and ached for the only one he'd ever loved.

Eve walked into her office, saw that Nadine was already inside. There was no point in tearing her hair out over the fact that Nadine ran tame in Central. For once, having her in the office rather than one of the waiting rooms suited her. It saved time.

"I need to put a tracer on your unit at 75."

Nadine crossed her legs, examined her toes in their strappy, heeled sandals. "Oh sure. Why should it be a problem to have a reporter's work unit tapped into by the cops? Why, everybody will be thrilled to pass me information that's going straight to Cop Central at the same time. I'll be deluged with tips."

"He's using you as a conduit. If he has anything more to say, he'll go through you. You authorize the tracer, or I impound the unit—and I can impound you, too, Nadine."

She waited a beat while Nadine's head snapped up. "Material witness, police protection, and so forth. I'm tempted to do it because I like you. I like you breathing."

"He's not coming after me."

"Maybe not. But psychopaths sometimes become annoyed with their tools. I'm banking on you taking care of yourself. I've got a call in to Mira. If she indicates there's a chance he'll turn on you, I'll have you wrapped up and packed away before you can freshen your lipdye for a one-on-one."

"Try it."

"Oh, I'll do it." Seated, Eve stretched out her legs. "I didn't ask you to be my friend, you know. Just worked out that way. Now you have to live with it."

"Shit." With her foxy face sulky, she drummed her fingers on the arm of the chair. Then the corner of her mouth twitched. "I like you, too, for some insane reason."

"Good, now we're all cozy. You get your picture taken lately? Professionally?"

Nadine glanced down at the photos Eve had set on the desk. "We get them taken every year at the station. Publicity shots for viewers, and for posters they have framed in the Green Room."

"Who takes them?"

"I'll find out. What's the connection between Howard and Sulu, other than the photographs?"

"I'll find out." Eve jerked a thumb at her doorway. "McNab's waiting to go to 75 with you, install the trace."

"Damn sure of yourself."

"That's right." She studied her boots as Nadine rose to leave, then she swiveled in her chair. "You're banging that suit?"

"Generally, I make him take off the suit before we bang, as you so romantically put it."

"Whatever. What I mean is, you know about men."

One perfect eyebrow lifted as Nadine turned. "Enough to be baffled, fascinated, and annoyed by the species. Why? Trouble in paradise?"

Eve opened her mouth, then firmly closed it again. "No. It's nothing." She waved Nadine away, then swiveled back to write her report. She'd let Hastings stew for a while before heading into interview. And make sure she had her own head clear before she questioned him.

She spent several minutes scrolling through the names of customers who'd registered purchases of high-end cameras over the last twelve months.

Could go back beyond that, she thought. And the killer might not have registered the equipment. Might not have worried about the whole warranty deal.

Still, she cross-referenced, looking for a link to the names on her victim and suspect list.

But her mind wouldn't stick to the point.

She hissed out a breath, kicked out with her foot, and slapped her door closed. She shut down the temptation to contact Roarke. She'd left him a memo, hadn't she? She didn't have all the rules of the marriage game aligned, but she was damned sure it was his turn to make the call.

Instead, she called someone she felt had a good handle on the rules of the road.

"Mavis."

Her friend's pixie face was slack, and naked as a child's. The hair was still streaked and decorated with bells. They jingled softly as Mavis snuggled into the pillow.

"Huh? Timezit?"

"Uh . . . I don't know. Morning."

"Ugh. Morning. Whassamatter?"

"Nothing. Sorry. Go back to sleep."

" 'Sokay." Mavis opened one eye, blue as a berry. "Summerset?"

"No, no, he's coming along." At least she figured he was. She hadn't checked. Was it her turn to check? How was she supposed to keep up, for God's sake? "Maybe you're going by there today?"

"Gonna. Poor thing. Trina and I are going by, maybe give him a face and hair treatment. Whatcha think?"

The grin spread. Maybe it was a little evil, but the image of Summerset caught in Trina's enhancement web was so beautiful. It almost brought a tear to Eve's eye. "Great. Great idea. Just what he needs."

"You okay? Something's up. I can tell."

"It's nothing."

"I'm awake." On a huge yawn, Mavis shifted, and the 'link screen showed the mountain that was Leonardo snoring softly beside her. "Tell me."

"I don't know. It's probably stupid. I'm probably stupid. Something wrong with Roarke. He won't talk about it. He shut me out, Mavis. Blasted at me out of the clear blue, then shut me out. Big-time. He didn't come to bed, and when he talked to me, he . . . Shit."

Hurt and confused all over again, she dragged a hand through her hair. "Maybe, when people are together awhile they're not all jazzed up when they see each other. That's okay, I guess. But . . ."

Screw the buts, she thought as her anger spiked again. "Damn it, usually he can't keep his hands off me, usually there's this look in his eye when I come home. It wasn't there, not even close, and he couldn't wait to get rid of me."

"You were fighting about something? You didn't do anything to piss him off?"

Aggrieved, she kicked at her desk. "How come it has to be me?"

"Doesn't." Naked, and easy with it, Mavis sat up. "I'm just eliminating possibilities. You know, marriage is a kind of mystery, just like cop stuff. So you gotta eliminate possibilities and look for clues."

"Then it oughta come with a goddamn field kit," Eve muttered.

"He's worried about Summerset."

"Yeah, but it wasn't that. I know it wasn't."

"Okay, you'd know." Mavis ticked her head back and forth, little hair bells ringing as she considered. "Maybe it's a work thing squeezing him."

"It could be, but he usually feeds on that crap. He put up this wall. It was personal."

"Okay." Mavis nodded decisively. "Then you tear it down. You don't take no for an answer. You nag and you pick and you stick until it pops out of him. Whatever it is. Girls are good at this, Dallas."

"I'm not good at being a girl."

"Sure you are. You're your own kind of girl. Think of it as kicking his ass until he cracks. At drilling him in Interview until he confesses. Dig it out of him, then, depending on what it is, you either make him suffer or comfort him. Or fuck his brains out. You'll know which."

"That doesn't sound that hard."

"It's not. Trust me. Let me know how it turns out. Since I'm awake, I think I'm going to get Leonardo revving." She blew Eve a kiss, and signed off.

"Okay, things to do: file report, interview suspect, harass ME and lab. Arrest homicidal maniac. Close case. Kick Roarke's ass. Piece of cake."

Chapter 11

Hastings hunched at the rickety table in Interview Room C, doing a pretty good job of looking bored. The dribbles of sweat along his temples were the only sign he was feeling the heat.

Eve dropped into the chair across from him, flashed a big, friendly smile. "Hey. Thanks for dropping by."

"Kiss my white, dimpled ass."

"As tempting as that is, I'm afraid I'm not allowed to make such personal contact."

"You kicked my balls, you oughta be able to kiss my ass."

"Rules are rules." She leaned back in her chair, flicked a glance at Peabody. "Peabody, why don't you get our guest some water? It's hot in here."

"I don't mind it hot."

"Me neither. People go all winter bitching and whining about the cold, right, then it heats up and they bitch and whine about that. Never satisfied."

"People bitch and whine about every damn thing." He took the water Peabody offered, downed the contents of the cup in one gulp. "That's why they're assholes."

"How can I argue with that? Well, enough of this cheery small talk. It's time for the formalities. Record on. Dallas,

Lieutenant Eve, and Peabody, Officer Delia, in Interview with Hastings, Dirk, regarding Case numbers H-23987 and H-23992." She entered the time and date, and recited the Revised Miranda. "So do you understand your rights and obligations in this matter, Hastings?"

"I get it. Just like I get you pulled me down here, screwed up my day. You screwed up my day yesterday, and I told you what I knew. I cooperated."

"You're a real cooperative individual." She pulled copies of the photos sent to Nadine, tossed them on the table so Kenby Sulu's image lay in front of Hastings. "Keep it up, and tell me what you know about this."

The chair creaked ominously as Hastings shifted his bulk. With two wide fingers he nudged first one, then the other photo closer. "I know I didn't take these. Good images, though, except I'd've cropped this candid different, and punched up the light across the eyes. Kid's got magic eyes, you want to highlight them. Had magic eyes," Hastings corrected staring down at the death photo.

"What were you up to last night, Hastings?"

He kept his gaze on the photos, staring at death posed in a dance. "I worked, I ate, I slept."

"Alone?"

"I'd had enough of people. I took shots of this kid. Dancer. Dance troupe. No, shit, not pros. Students. I took shots of him. What a face. It's the eyes. Good bones, good form, but it's all about the eyes in this face. I took shots of him," he repeated and looked at Eve. "Just like the girl. What the hell's going on?"

"Tell me."

"I don't freaking know!" He shoved back, so violently, so abruptly, that Peabody's hand went to her weapon. Lingered there even when Eve shook her head.

Hastings surged around the room, a big bear in a small cage. "This is crazy, that's what it is. Fucking lunatic. I took that kid's picture . . . where was it, where was it? Juilliard. Juilliard. Buncha puffed-up drama queens, but it pays the freaking bills. And the kid had that face. So I singled him out for a few shots. When was it? Spring. April, maybe May. How the hell do I know?"

He dropped back in the chair, squeezed his shiny bald head between his hands. "Christ. Christ."

"Did you bring him to your studio?"

"No. Gave him a card though. Told him if he wanted to earn some extra money modeling, to get in touch. He was easy in front of the lens, I remember. Not everybody is. He said maybe he would, and maybe I could do some individual pub shots for him."

"Did he get in touch?"

"No, not with me. Don't know if he called the studio. Lucia handles that crap. I never saw him again."

"Did you work with anyone on the Juilliard shoot?"

"Yeah. I don't know who. Some idiot or other."

"The same idiot or other who was with you when you did the wedding in January, the shots of Rachel Howard?"

"Not likely. They don't stick that long." He managed a thin smile. "I'm temperamental."

"You don't say? Who has access to your disc files?"

"Nobody. Nobody should, but I guess anybody who comes through and knows what they're doing." He moved his shoulders. "I don't pay attention. I never *had* to pay attention."

He shoved the photos back at Eve. "I didn't call a lawyer."

"So noted. Why is that, Hastings?"

"Because this pisses me *off*. Plus, I hate lawyers."

"You hate everybody."

"Yeah, that's true." He rubbed his hands over his face, then dropped them on the table. "I didn't kill those kids. That girl with the magic smile, this boy with the magic eyes. I'd never put those lights out." He leaned forward. "Just from an artistic standpoint—what would that smile be like in five years, or those eyes in ten. I'd want to know, to see, to capture. And personally, I don't get murder. Why kill people when you can just ignore them?"

Mirroring his move, she leaned toward him. "What about those lights? Wouldn't you want them for your own? Take them while they're young, innocent. Brilliant. Pull them in, through the lens, into yourself. Then they're always yours."

He stared, blinked twice. "You gotta be fucking kidding me. Where do you get that kind of woo-woo crap?"

Despite the horror of the situation, she let out a laugh. "I like you, Hastings. I'm not sure what that says about me. We're going through your records again, to see if we find the shots you took of Kenby Sulu."

"Why don't you just move in, bring the freaking family? Your pet dog."

"I've got a cat. I've got you scheduled for Truth Testing in about twenty minutes. I'll have an officer escort you to a waiting area."

"That's it?"

"For now, that's it. Do you have any questions or statements you wish to make at this time, on record."

"Yeah, I got a question. I got a prize-winning question for you, Dallas. Am I going to have to wonder who's next? Am I going to have to ask myself whose picture I took who's going to end up dead?"

"I don't have the answer to that. Interview end."

"You believe him." Peabody slid into the car beside Eve. "Even without the Truth Test."

"I believe him. He's connected, but not involved. And he'll know the face of the next target. He'll recognize it." And it would cost him, Eve thought. She'd seen what it was already costing him on that ugly face of his.

"The killer is someone he knows, or at least someone who knows him and his work. Someone who admires it, or envies it . . . or thinks their own is superior."

She toyed with that angle as she pulled out of the garage. "Somebody who hasn't been able to achieve the same sort of commercial or critical success."

"A competitor."

"Maybe. Or maybe someone who's too artistic, too above commercialism. He wants acknowledgment, otherwise, he'd be keeping the images for himself. But he sends them to the media."

She played back pieces of the text the killer sent to Nadine.

Such light! Such strong light. It coats me. It feeds me. He was brilliant, this clever young man with the dancer's build and the artist's soul. Now he is me. What he was lives forever in me.

Light again, Eve mused, then shadows.

There will be no shadows in them now. No shadows to smother the light. This is my gift to them. Theirs to me. And when it's done, when it's complete, our gift to humanity.

"He wants the world to know what he's doing. Artistically," Eve continued. "Hastings, or at least Hastings's work, is one of his springboards. We question everyone who's worked with or for Hastings over the last year."

Peabody pulled out her pad, keyed in, scrolled down the list. "That's going to take awhile. The guy's not kidding about going through assistants like toilet paper. Then you add in the staff, and turnover in the retail end, the models and stylists, and so on. You want to start at the top?"

"For now. But we start back at the data club. The transmission to Nadine was sent from there, both times. It's a link."

There was a lively lunch crowd jammed at tables and booths, heavy on the students, Eve decided. Lots of them gathered in groups or going solo over data and sandwiches.

She spotted Steve Audrey at the bar, working two-handed to fill orders on trendy iced drinks and coffee. He acknowledged her with a little head bob.

"Summer session has them pouring in midday." He slid something frothy and blue into waiting hands, then wiped his own on the bar rag tucked in his waistband. "Getcha something cold?"

"I wouldn't mind a Blue Meanie." Peabody spoke fast, knowing her lieutenant.

"Coming up." He pumped at levers. "What can I do for you, Lieutenant?"

"Take a break."

"I just came on an hour ago. I'm not due for a break until—"

"Take one now."

He flipped the slush machine, grabbed a glass. "Hold on. Mitz, need you to take over for five. Can't take more than five," he told Eve as he poured the blue slush into a tall, skinny glass for Peabody. "I'll get iced otherwise."

"Five'll do. Is there anyplace in here that's quiet?"

"Not this time of day." He scanned the crowd, used his chin to point. "Grab that privacy booth in the back, to the right. Give me a minute to fill these other orders."

Eve wound through, Peabody, slurping Blue Meanie, in her wake. Students, she noted, treated the club like a safari and came in loaded with bags and satchels.

There was no bag or satchel in Kenby's locker at Lincoln Center.

She stepped over, stepped around, shoved aside, and reached the booth at the same time a pair of college boys in track shirts leaped into the chairs.

They looked up at her and grinned. "You lose. We're younger and faster."

"I'm older and I've got a badge." She flipped it out and grinned back. "Maybe I should have a look through your backpacks, then brighten everyone's day with a quick cavity search."

They scrambled up and away.

"They are fast," Peabody noted.

"Yeah, but I don't need some pussy drink to be mean."

Peabody slurped again. "It's very refreshing, and contrary to its name puts me in a very amenable mood. Or maybe that has something to do with the cavity search McNab and I performed on each other last night."

Eve slapped at the cheek muscle that twitched. "Thank God I haven't had any lunch. I'd have lost it."

"I think it's nice we're both having regular sex. It keeps us in rhythm."

"Shut up, shut up."

"Can't help it. I'm happy."

"I can fix that."

With another frosty drink in his hand, Steve dropped down next to Peabody. He sucked through the straw stuck in the pale green foam. "Okay, we got five." He hit the button that closed the clear bubble around the booth. "Ah." He smiled into the silence as he drew on the straw. "Excellent."

"What do you know about the transmission sent from here this morning?"

His eyes popped open. "Huh? Again?"

"EDD's been here. They impounded the unit, talked to the day manager."

"I just came on an hour ago and had to dive right into the pool. I didn't hear about this. Is somebody else dead?"

Eve took out the photo of Kenby. "Recognize him?"

"Man. I don't know. Man. I think so, maybe. I'm not sure. Should I?"

"Take a breath, Steve."

"Yeah, right. This is brutal." After wiping his mouth with the back of his hand, he looked at the image again. "I think maybe he's been in. Is he like an actor or something?"

"Or something."

"You should ask Shirllee. She goes for the theater and artist types."

"She here?"

"Yeah, she's on. Give me a sec."

He opened the bubble. Noise poured back over them as he slid out and hurried away.

"They got curly fries," Peabody announced, and punched in an order on the menu before Eve could speak. "My blood sugar's dropping."

"That'll be the day."

Steve came back with a tall, skinny brunette. Her hair was done in multiple and equally skinny braids that fell to her waist and were joined at the tips by a black ribbon. She wore a quartet of silver spikes in her right earlobe and a trio of silver studs dripping below her left eye like sparkly tears.

She sat next to Eve and clasped her hands together so the forest of rings on her fingers clanged and clinked. "Stevie said you're a cop."

"Stevie wins a point." Eve hit the privacy button, then nudged the photo in front of Shirllee. "You know him?"

"Hey, that's Twinkletoes. I call him that 'cause he's a dancer. Sure, he comes in a couple times a week. Lunch break usually, or early dinner. But he's been here for the music a few times, weekends. He can really move. What he do?"

"He come in with anybody special?"

"Travels with a theater pack mostly. Picked one out of the herd a couple of times, but he never hung with one girl. He's straight though, 'cause I never saw him moving on another guy."

"Anybody move on him?"

"Not especially. He mostly hangs with people he knows. He tips, too." She shot a knowing look at Steve. "College kids stiff you, but Twinkles here, he always tipped. Brought up right, you ask me. Don't see him getting in trouble. He never made any trouble in here."

"When's the last time he came in?"

"That I saw him?" She pursed lips dyed dead white. "Friday night, I think. Last Friday. We had a totally mag holoband in. Hard Crash. They're completely juiced. Twinks was in here with a bunch of Juilliards on Friday. You remember, Stevie? He's a fucking dancing machine once he's revved. You were mixing him non-A Sorcerers all night."

"Yeah. Yeah, that's right." Steve looked down at the photo, ran his fingertip around the border. "Sorcerers, no punch. I remember now."

"I gotta get back on." Shirllee reached over, opened the bubble.

"Me, too." Steve looked up from the picture, met Eve's gaze. "Did that help any?"

"Maybe. Appreciate it. Let's go, Peabody."

"But my curly fries just came through."

"Life's full of hard knocks."

As Eve headed out, Peabody scooped the fries into a napkin.

She comforted herself that food eaten on the run had no calories.

When they stepped out, Eve reached over and snatched a fry. "No salt?" The first bite had her wrinkling her nose. "How can you eat these without salt?"

"I didn't have the chance for salt. Life's full of hard knocks," Peabody added in sober tones.

They started at the top of the Portography list. As Eve interviewed potentials she gained an image of Hastings. He was a maniac, he was a genius, he was impossible, he was insane yet compelling—depending on who she spoke with.

She caught one of his former assistants on a location shoot in Greenpeace Park.

The models—one man, one woman—were hyping what Eve was told was active sportswear. To her, they looked as if they were preparing to take a long hike through the desert in the buff-colored skinny tops and shorts, the clunky boots and long-billed caps.

Elsa Ramerez, a tiny woman with short, curly dark hair, tanned limbs, scooted around handing things to the photographer, signalling the rest of the crew, grabbing up bottled water or whatever other task was snapped out at her.

Seeing her day going from too long to endless, Eve stepped forward, laid a hand on the photographer's shoulder.

The thickly built blonde was no Hastings, but she delivered an impressive snarl.

"Take a break," Eve advised and held up her badge.

"We've got all the proper permits. Elsa!"

"Good for you. I'm not here about your permits. Take a break, grab some shade. Otherwise, I can hang you up for twice as long in pretty red tape while I have my trusty aide verify all the permits. Elsa?" Eve crooked a finger. "With me."

"We've only got the location for another hour." Elsa jogged over and was already dragging paperwork out of a satchel. "I've got everything right here."

"Save it. Tell me about Dirk Hastings."

Elsa's sweaty face went stony. "I'm not paying for that window. He threw the bottle at *me*. Crazy son of a bitch. He can sue me, you can lock me up, but I'm not paying for the broken window."

"You worked for him in February. From . . ." Eve perused her notes. ". . . February fourth to February eighteenth."

"Yeah, and I should put in for combat pay." She took a bottle out of the holster she wore on her hip, glugged. "I don't mind hard work—hell, I like it. I don't mind temperament, got one of my own. But life's too short to deal with crazy people."

"Do you recognize this person?" She held out the image of Sulu.

"No. Terrific face. Nice shot. Very nice. What's this about?"

"Did you have access to Hastings's disc files and records when you worked as his assistant?"

"Sure. Part of the gig was filing the shots, or locating one he wanted to finesse. What is this? Is he saying I took something of his? Took his work? That's just crap. Hell, I knew he was crazy, but he wasn't vindictive."

"No, he's not saying you took anything of his. I'm asking if you did."

"I don't take anything that's not mine. And I sure as hell don't put my name on somebody else's work. Shit, even if I was some sleazy bitch, I'd never get away with it. He's got a look. Hastings has a style, the bastard, and anybody with an eye would know."

"Is this his work?"

Elsa glanced at the photo again. "No. It's good, real good, but it's not over the edge into great. This one?" Elsa tapped a finger on her shoulder to indicate the photographer behind her. "She's good. Very competent. Gets the shot, produces the look the client's after. Straight commercial stuff. Hastings can do this blindfolded. But she'd never be able to do his artwork. Maybe you have to be crazy to cross that line. He qualifies."

"He attacked you."

She sighed, shuffled her feet. "Okay, not exactly. I didn't move fast enough when he was in the zone. Didn't anticipate, and yeah, anticipation's part of my job. He yelled, I yelled back. I got a temper, too. He threw the bottle, and okay, so he didn't actually throw it at me. He just winged it through the window. Then he says how I'm paying for it, and starts hurling insults. I walked out, didn't go back. Lucia sent me my pay, in full. She keeps things sane around there. As much as possible."

Eve detoured back to Portography to pigeonhole Lucia.

"I won't say a bad word about Hastings. I'm sure you'll find plenty who will. If he'd listened to me he'd have a lawyer and he'd be suing you for false arrest."

"He hasn't been arrested."

"All the same." She sniffed, then sat at her desk. "The man is a genius, and geniuses don't have to abide by the same rules as the rest of the world."

"Would one of those rules include murder?"

"Accusing Hastings of murder is so ridiculous I won't respond."

"He threw one of his assistants, bodily, into the elevator. Heaved a bottle at another. Threatened to pitch another out of the window. The list goes on."

Her red, red lips bowed up. "There were reasons for all of that. Artists, true artists, have temperaments."

"Okay. Putting Hastings's genius artist temper aside for the moment, what about security on his files, his records, the image discs?"

She shook her head, fluffed at her white hair. "All but nonexistent. He won't listen to me, or anyone about it. He can't remember passcodes and procedure and gets upset when he isn't able to access an image when he wants it."

"So anyone can."

"Well, they have to get up there first."

"Which narrows that down to models, clients, the revolving assistants, the staff, and employees of the retail end."

"Cleaning crew."

"Cleaning crew."

"Maintenance." She shrugged. "They're only allowed in when he's not. They make him edgy. Occasionally he allows students. They have to pay, and aren't allowed to speak."

Eve bit back a sigh. "Do you have a list of the cleaning crew, the maintenance crew, the students."

"Of course. I have a list of everyone."

Back at Central, Eve closed herself in her office. She put up a board. She hung the images of the victims, the texts Nadine had received, the lists of people she'd questioned, and had yet to question. Then she sat down, spread out her notes, and let her mind drift.

She'd re-interviewed Jackson Hooper and Diego Feliciano, and this time their stories were almost identical. Didn't know nor recognize Kenby Sulu, and had been home, alone, on the night in question.

Possible connection between Hooper and Feliciano?

Eve shook her head. She was letting her mind drift too far, she thought, and reined it back.

The killer wanted something from the victims. Their light. Hastings had said he wouldn't put that light out. Was the killer putting it out, or was he transferring it? Into himself.

For what purpose?

Glory, he wanted glory, acknowledgment, acclaim. But that wasn't all.

The victims had been chosen for specific reasons. Youth, vitality, innocence. Both had been bright, of mind, of spirit, of face.

Bright lights.

The killer used the data club to transmit. So he frequented the club. He knew how it worked, knew it drew the college crowd.

Was he one of them, or did he want to be?

Couldn't afford college? Kicked out of college? Taught at college instead of being acknowledged as an artist?

He knew imaging, was skilled in the art. Her mind wandered to Leeanne Browning. Alibied, but alibies could be manufactured.

She added to her notes: Possible connection between Browning and/or Brightstar and Hastings?

Using the computer, she called up a city map, ordered pertinent locations highlighted. The two crime scenes, the two universities, Portography, the parking port, Browning's apartment, Diego's apartment, the club, and the two victims' residences, the two dump sites.

Both victims had been dumped near their place of employment. Why was that?

Where was his place of employment? she wondered. Where did he do his work? This very personal, very important work.

Near the club? He's mobile, but why go too far afield to troll, to hunt, to observe, then to transmit?

Both victims had recognized their killer. She was sure of that. Casual acquaintance, good friend, fellow student, teacher. Someone they'd seen before. Yet they hadn't run in the same circles, known the same people.

Except for Hastings, and the club.

She did a search for imaging studios within a five-block radius of the data club. Tried a cross match with the registered owners to her lists from Lucia and came up goose egg.

She'd have Peabody get an employee list, then cross-check that.

Rubbing absently at the headache dead center of her forehead, she contacted Peabody in the bull pen. "Get me something from vending, will you? I don't have any credits on me and those damn machines won't take my code anymore."

"It's because you kick them."

"Just get me a damn sandwich."

"Dallas, you're off shift five minutes ago."

"Don't make me come out there," Eve warned and clicked off.

She worked through the change of shift, hearing the rise and fall of it through her open door. She ate at her desk, washing the lousy sandwich down with superior coffee.

She filed her updated report, harassed the lab, left two snippy messages for Morris, then turned to stare at her board again.

He'd already picked the next, and unless she found the connection, the right connection, some other bright light would be extinguished.

She gathered her things and prepared to accomplish at least one of the items on her to-do list. She'd go home and kick Roarke's ass.

The prospect didn't put a spring in her step, but she'd stalled long enough. But as she approached the elevator, she spotted Dr. Mira coming toward her.

"I thought I'd catch you."

"Just," Eve said. "We can go back to my office."

"No, no, you're on your way home, I'd like to do the same. Why don't we walk and talk. Do you mind taking the glides?"

"That's fine. You're done with Hastings?"

"Yes. Fascinating man."

Mira smiled as they stepped on one of the down glides. She managed to look fresh as morning even after a long day. Her suit was cream colored and spotless. Eve couldn't figure out how anyone could wear something that close to white in New York, particularly in or around Central and not have it go gray in an hour. Her hair, the tone and texture of rich sable, was fluffed around her face. She wore pearls.

One of the top profilers in the country, and she wore pearls to work, Eve thought. And smelled faintly, freshly floral—like the tea she liked to drink.

She stepped off the first glide in her neat, feminine pumps, then stepped on the next.

"Irascible," Mira continued. "Contentious, irritable, amusing. And brutally honest."

"So he's clear?"

"In my opinion—and I believe in yours before you sent him to me."

"I figure he might throw somebody off a roof in a tantrum, but he's not the type to sit down and plan cold-bloodedly, or execute in the same fashion."

"No, he's not. He could use some anger therapy, but it would probably be lost on him. I rather like him."

"So do I."

"Your killer has Hastings's arrogance, or its kin, but lacks his confidence, and his spontaneity. And while Hastings is more than content to be alone, the killer is lonely. He needs his images as much for companionship as for art."

"The people in them become his companions?"

"In a way. He's absorbing them—their youth and energy, and by the absorption who they are, who they know. Their friends, their families. He's taking their life force."

"He doesn't abuse them. It's all very neat and tidy. There's no rage. Because they're him or about to become him."

"Very good."

"He preserves their image, showing them at their best. Pretties them up for the camera, poses them in some flattering way. Part of that's the art, right—look what I can do, look how talented I am. But part of it's vanity. We're one now, and I want to look good."

"Interesting. Yes, very possibly. This is a complicated person, and one who sincerely believes he has a right to do what he's doing. Perhaps even an obligation. But he doesn't do it selflessly. It's not a holy mission. He wants credit. He may have been disappointed in his art in the past, feels as though his talent's been overlooked. By Hastings, or someone who preferred Hastings over him. If, as seems logical, he took the initial images of the victims from Hastings records, part of the motivation might be to outdo his competition."

"Or his mentor."

Mira raised her eyebrows as they walked into the garage. "I don't see Hastings as a mentor."

"Neither would he, but the killer might."

"I'll spend some more time on this if you like. I'd need your updated reports."

"I'll make sure you get them. I appreciate it." To buy more time, she walked Mira to her car. "Dr. Mira, you've been married a long time."

They'd come a long way together, Mira thought, for Eve to bring up something personal without prompting. "Yes, I have. Thirty-two years next month."

"Thirty-two. Years."

Mira laughed. "Longer than you've been alive."

"I guess it has its ups and downs."

"It does. Marriage isn't for the weak or the lazy. It's work, and it should be. What would be the point otherwise?"

"I don't mind work." At least, Eve thought, as she tucked her hands in her pockets, when she knew what she was doing. "People back away from each other sometimes, don't they? It doesn't mean they feel any different, just that they need a step back."

"There are times we need to be by ourselves, or work something out on our own, certainly. In any partnership, the individuals require personal time and space."

"Yeah. That makes sense."

"Eve, is something wrong with Roarke?"

"I don't know." It spilled out before she could bite it back. "I'm being stupid, that's all. He wasn't acting like himself one night, and I'm blowing it into a BFD. But, damn it, I know how he looks at me, I know the tones of his voice, his body language. And it was off. It was all off. So he was having a bad day, why can't I let it go at that?"

"Because you love him, so you worry about him."

"We didn't leave things on an easy level last night, then he never came to bed. I got called in early this morning, left him a memo. But I haven't heard from him all day. He all but threw me out of his office last night, and I haven't heard from him all day. That's not right. That's not Roarke."

"And you didn't contact him at all today?"

"No. Damn it, it was his turn."

"Agreed," Mira said with a warm smile. "And you gave him his personal time and space." She leaned forward, surprised Eve with a light kiss to the cheek. "Now go home and pry it out of him. You'll both feel better."

"Okay. Right. Thanks. I feel stupid."

"No, sweetheart. You feel married."

Chapter 12

Her puke green police issue was in front of the house when Roarke arrived, so he knew Eve was home before him.

He wasn't ready to talk to her or anyone else for that matter. But he could hardly ignore the fact that the man who'd stood in as his father for most of his life was laid up with a broken leg.

He'd check on Summerset, then try to sweat out some of the fatigue and frustration in the gym, swim a few laps. Maybe get good and drunk. Whatever worked.

Meetings hadn't. The day-to-day demands of running or overseeing his business hadn't. Nothing had been able to erase the image of a pretty redhead with a bruised face from his mind.

So he'd just try something else.

He stepped inside, relieved—and guilty for the relief—that Eve wasn't in the foyer, or the front parlor. At the moment, he was forced to admit he wasn't feeling quite equipped to go up against her again.

He couldn't remember the last time he'd been so bloody tired, and so off his stride.

Setting his briefcase aside, he glanced toward the wide curve of stairs. Likely she was up and at work in her home office, and with any luck she'd be busy with whatever case was occupying her for some time yet.

Still, he hesitated. He wasn't handling her well. Wasn't handling a bloody thing well, come to that. He just needed a bit more time to himself. A man was entitled to that, wasn't he?

Surely a man was entitled to a little time to think, for Christ's sake, when his whole life had been turned inside out.

He dragged a hand through his hair and cursed under his breath as he walked back to Summerset's quarters.

He heard the blast of music from three rooms away, and nearly turned on his heel in retreat. Mavis. God knew he adored the woman, but he didn't have the energy for her just now.

On the other hand, with her there, he could make this duty visit all the quicker.

At any other time it would have amused him to see his dignified majordomo stripped to the waist and stretched out in a sleep chair having blue goo slathered on his face. Trina, one of the few people on or off planet who actively terrified his wife, was doing the honors as she shuffled her feet to the beat of one of Mavis's music discs.

She'd chopped off her raven black hair close to the scalp and had a neon pink design of a butterfly dyed over the crown. She'd repeated the motif with temporary tattoos—or so he assumed—at the corner of her mouth, and in a running line, necklace style, over her shoulders and along the tops of her impressive breasts.

Her partner in crime was pouring some sort of pink foam into a wide pitcher. There was no way to tell whether it was intended for topical or internal use.

Mavis still had her bells on, and had donned a sunny yellow romper with a woman wearing a black g-string and leather boots painted across the butt.

The PA was wearing an eye mask and a headset while her feet soaked in bubbling blue water. Her hair was coated with something thick and green.

Pitcher in hand, Mavis turned and spotted him. "You're

home! Welcome to Summerset's Totally Iced Salon. Want a strawberry smash?"

He assumed she meant the pink foam. "Thanks, no."

"Dallas is hiding upstairs. Drag her down for us, will you? Trina wants to use this new skin product on her, and she needs—"

She broke off as she got a good look at his face. There were shadows under his eyes. She'd known him more than a year, and this was the first time she'd seen him wear shadows. "Everything okay?"

"Fine." He stepped over to Summerset. "And you?"

The eyes that peered out of the blue registered mortification, a little panic, and the faintest flicker of hope. "They really shouldn't be bothering with me. I know we have a number of things to discuss now that you're home, so—"

"Actually, I have some work to see to."

"Yes, but—" Summerset groped for Roarke's hand, gripped it like a vice. "As I explained to everyone, we need to go over the Rundale report, and the other matter."

"Can't be working the old guy when he's busted up." Trina sent Roarke a dismissive glance. "He needs to relax. What he really needs is a full week of intensive treatments. I might be able to turn his skin around. Hair's not bad." She gave it a testing tug, transferring goo. "It'll be better when I'm done."

"No doubt."

"Roarke." Summerset all but croaked it, then cleared his throat. "If I could have a moment."

"Later."

"Now." This time he snapped it out. "If you ladies would excuse us, for just a few minutes."

"No problem," Mavis said before Trina could object. "Treen, let's take these smashes into the kitchen. Don't worry about her," she added with a gesture at the PA. "She's on a relaxation and meditation program. She's zonked."

With a last worried glance at Roarke, she grabbed Trina's hand and pulled her out of the room.

"They don't mean any harm," Roarke began.

"I'm not concerned about that. I'm concerned about you. You don't look well."

"I'm busy."

"You're always busy. Are you ill?"

"For Christ's sake. No, I'm not ill. Bloody hell, music off!" The blast crashed into silence. "I've a great deal to do. More as you're incapacitated."

"I'm hardly incapacitated. I'm—"

"You broke your fucking leg. So lie back and deal with it. If you've gotten yourself into the bog here with these women, you'll have to lie back and deal with that as well. I can't help you. There's no point in whining about it."

Summerset's fingers tightened on the arms of his chair. "I don't whine, nor do I tolerate being spoken to by you in such a matter."

"Don't have much choice in that, do you? I'm not a child requiring lessons in manners any longer. As long as you're in my employ, I'll speak to you as I wish. And frankly, I'm not going to stand here wasting my time arguing with a half-naked man with God knows what all over his face."

Roarke strode out, leaving Summerset blinking after him. The twist in his gut had him doing something he'd never have considered otherwise. He reached for the in-house 'link.

"What?" Eve snarled, then grimaced at the image on her screen. "Mother of God, my eyes! Block the video for sweet Jesus' sake."

"Quiet. Something's wrong with Roarke. He's not well."

"What? What do you mean? He's sick?"

"I said he's not well. I expect you to do something about it as I'm unable to."

"Where is he?"

"He's home. Find him. Fix it."

"Done" was all she said.

She did a search, located him in the gym. Switching to video scan, she watched him strip down, drag on shorts. He looked exhausted, she thought. Not just tired, which was rare enough for him, but wiped out.

He went for the weights, and Eve bided her time. Go

ahead, she decided, sweat some of it out. That's what she'd have done.

It wasn't just the shadows under his eyes that worried her, but the cold set of his face as he pumped the weights. Cold and hard.

He was pushing himself. Punishing himself? God, what was going on?

While he worked, she paced her office, trying out a dozen possible approaches. After a brutal thirty minutes, he went into the pool house.

Lap after lap, fast, strong, hard. Too hard, she thought, and was on the point of going down to stop him when he rolled over on his back. Seeing him floating there, eyes closed, misery in every line of his face broke her heart.

"What is it?" she murmured and stroked her fingers over the screen. "Why are you so unhappy?"

Work? No, didn't compute. If it was trouble with work he might be pissed, but he'd be challenged by it. Even energized. It wouldn't make him miserable.

Summerset? Didn't play either. She'd checked, personally, with the medicals and had been told the skinny son of a bitch was healing perfectly, and already ahead of schedule.

Maybe it's me, she thought, with a slow, sick dread. Maybe his feelings for her had just . . . clicked off somehow. Everything between them had happened so fast when you thought about it. And had never made any sense, not to her. If he'd stopped loving her, wouldn't he be unhappy, guilty, tired, distraught. All the things she saw on his face now?

That was just bullshit. She kicked the desk as Roarke pulled himself out of the water. Just raging bullshit. And if it wasn't, well, he was going to be a lot more unhappy, guilty, tired, and distraught before she was done.

She marched into the kitchen, pulled out a bottle of wine and drank a glass like medicine. She'd give him a few minutes to clean himself up, then she was going in.

He was just getting out of the shower when she walked into the bath. Or swaggered, spoiling for a fight. She watched him hook a towel at his hip, met his eyes in the mirror.

"You look like shit."

"Thanks, darling."

No smile, she noted. No glimmer of warmth or amusement, not even irritation. Just nothing at all.

"I've got some things to say to you. Put some pants on."

"They'll have to wait. I've a conference call scheduled shortly." It was a lie. It passed through his mind he'd never lied to her before. And it didn't go down well.

"It's going to have to go without you." She stalked back into the bedroom, slammed the door shut.

The sound of it cut through his aching head like a laser. "Perhaps I'm not hunting down the next murdering bastard who plagues New York, but my work's important." He crossed to the closet, yanked out a pair of trousers. "I don't expect you to stop doing yours when it's inconvenient for me."

"I guess I'm not as nice and agreeable as you are."

"There's a bulletin. I'll talk to you later," he said as he yanked on the pants.

"You'll talk to me now." Her chin angled, a challenge, when he simply turned his head and stared coolly. "You've got to get through me to get out of the room. And the way you look right now, champ, I can put you down in thirty seconds."

He could feel the temper eating through the misery now, like a hot bite. "Don't bank on it."

"You want to fight?" She shifted her stance, crooked her finger. "Come on."

"You'll have to save your pissing contest for later. I'm not in the mood." He stepped toward her, intending on nudging her aside. She shoved him back.

His eyes fired, and that pleased her.

"Don't." His warning was low, and very, very calm.

"Don't what?" She shoved him again, saw his hands ball into fists. "You want to take a shot at me. Go right ahead. Get it out of your system before I knock you on your ass."

"I'm telling you to stay away from me for a bit."

She planted her hands on his bare chest and shoved him again. "No."

"Don't *push* me!" At her next move, he grabbed her

wrists, jerked her forward, back. Fury flooded him, gushing through his blood. "I don't need you crawling up my back. Leave me be. I don't want you around."

"Don't want me around." It was a slice in the gut, fast and bloodless, that she countered by running him back against a wall. "You son of a bitch, you're the one that got me into this in the first place."

He had more left in him than she'd thought, and in a ten-second sweaty grapple, reversed their positions. She countered, feinting with an elbow toward his chin as she hooked her foot around his and tossed him to the floor.

She saw the hot rage light on his face even as it flamed in her. She sprang.

He saw stars, then lost himself in the red-hazed violence as they rolled and wrestled over the floor. Something crashed, shattered.

He felt the black bloom out of that tiny core inside him. It wanted to spread. Wanted to wound. And as they grappled, breath coming fast and short, the diamond she wore on a long chain around her neck spilled out and struck his cheek.

Appalled, disgusted, he dropped his guard and let her pin him.

"Go ahead." He closed his eyes. Rage had passed, leaving him raw and empty. "I'm not going to hurt you."

"Not going to hurt me?" She lifted his head an inch by the hair, then let it thump on the floor. "You're tired of me, don't want me around, want to shake me loose, and you're not going to *hurt* me?"

"Tired of you?" He opened his eyes, and saw for the first time that hers weren't simply angry. Tears sparkled in them. "Where the hell do you get these things? I never said that. I've a great deal on my mind, that's all. Nothing that has to do with you."

He saw her face, the ripple of hurt that had her flinching as if he'd slapped her. Then she shut it down, so that her eyes went dry, went flat as she sat back on her heels.

"What a stupid thing to say," he murmured. "What a sublimely stupid thing to say." He lifted his hands, scrubbed them over his face. "I'm sorry for it. I'm sorry for last night, sorry for this. I'm bloody sorry."

"I don't want you to be sorry. I want you to tell me what the hell's going on. Are you sick?" Tears were rising in her throat when she cupped his face in her hands. "Please, *tell* me. Is there something bad wrong with you?"

"No. There's not, no, not the way you mean." Gently, he closed his hands over her wrists, over bruises he'd put there. "I've hurt you."

"Forget it. Just tell me. If you're not going to die, and you haven't fallen out of love with me—"

"I couldn't fall out of love with you if I fell all the way to hell." Emotion was storming back into his eyes, and with it some of the misery she'd seen there before. "You're everything."

"For God's sake, tell me. I can't stand seeing you like this."

"Give me a minute, will you?" He touched her cheek where a tear had spilled over. "I want a drink."

She got up, held out a hand to help him to his feet. "Is it something to do with business? Did you do something illegal?"

The faintest hint of a smile touched his mouth. "Oh, Lieutenant, all manner of things. But not for quite some time." He walked over to the panel in the wall, pressed, and opened the wide, recessed bar. He chose whiskey and had her stomach churning again.

"Okay. What, did you lose all your money?"

"No." He nearly laughed. "I'd have handled that better than I've handled this. You. All of it. Christ Jesus, I've mucked this up." He took a drink, took a breath. "It has to do with my mother."

"Oh." Of all the things that had gone through her mind, this hadn't been so much as a blip on the radar screen. "Did she contact you? Does she want something? If she's giving you grief I can help—flash the badge, whatever."

He shook his head, drank. "She didn't contact me. She's dead."

She opened her mouth, shut it again. Shaky ground, she

decided. Family deals were always shaky ground. "I'm trying to figure out what to say. I'm sorry if you are. But . . . you haven't seen her since you were a kid, right? You said she walked, and that was that."

"That's what I said, yes, and that's what I believed. All this time believed. But it happens the woman who walked wasn't my mother. I thought she was and that was that. I've learned differently."

"Okay. How did you learn about it?"

Calm, he thought. Calm and cool, his cop, when she had something to puzzle out. And how foolish he'd been not to tell her right off. He stared into the glass, then walked over to sit on the sofa.

"I met a woman at the shelter, a counselor there. She's from Dublin, and she told me a story I didn't believe at first. Didn't want to believe. About a young girl she'd tried to help. A young girl and her child."

Slowly, Eve walked over to sit beside him. "You?"

"Me. She was very young, this girl, and from the west. A farm in the west. She'd come to Dublin for the adventure, and to work. And she met Patrick Roarke."

He told her the rest.

"You've verified it? The counselor, everything she told you. You're sure it's not some scam."

"Very sure." He wanted another whiskey, but didn't have the energy to get up and pour. "This girl who was my mother tried to give me a family, to do what was right. She loved him, I imagine, and was afraid of him. He had a way of making women love, and fear him. But she loved me, Eve."

Eve's fingers linked with his, and gave him comfort. Steadied by it, he brought their joined hands to his lips. "I could see it in the picture of us. She never left me. He killed her. Another thing he was good at was destroying beauty and innocence. He killed her, and brought Meg back."

He laid his head back, looked up at the ceiling. "They were married. I found those records. Married before he met and ruined my mother, but there were no children. Maybe Meg couldn't give him a son, so he cast her out. Or she'd had enough of his whoring and scheming and left him. Hardly matters why."

He gave what passed for a shrug, keeping his eyes closed as fatigue dragged at him. "A girl like Siobahn Brody would have appealed to him. So young and malleable, so ripe for plucking. And when she had me, he'd have little use for a young girl like her, nagging at him to marry her and make a proper family."

"She was with him for, what, under two years. But wouldn't someone have told her about Meg? Wouldn't someone have told her he was already married?"

"If they did, he'd have lied his way around it. He had a quick and clever tongue, and was always ready with the credible lie."

"Or, you have a girl, not even twenty, gone over this guy and pregnant by him—maybe already a little afraid of him. Could be she just didn't hear what people said."

"True enough. Though there'd have been those back in that day, back in his prime, who'd have risked speaking of him in a way he'd dislike. But if Meg's name came to her ears, she may have pretended not to hear."

He fell silent for a moment, thinking it through. "Meg was more his match, if you understand me. Hard, with a liking for drink and a fast pound. Siobahn, she'd have irritated him eventually, simply because of what she was. But nobody walked out on Patrick Roarke—and to take his son, the symbol of his virility? No, indeed that wouldn't be permitted. So she had to be punished for trying. I can see how it was, see exactly how it would have been. He'd pull Meg back to deal with me. A man can't spend his time fussing over a baby, after all. Work to do, business to run. Get a woman to handle the dirty work. He was a right bastard, no doubt of it."

"No one ever mentioned her to you? Your mother."

"No one. I'd have found out about it myself, but I never bothered to look. It wasn't closed off in my mind, as yours was, I just never bothered. I dismissed her, you see."

He squeezed his eyes tighter, then forced them open. "Not

worth my time or trouble. I never gave her so much as a passing thought in all these years."

"You never gave Meg Roarke a passing thought," she corrected. "You didn't know."

"I never even troubled myself enough to hate her. She was nothing to me."

"You're talking about two different women."

"She deserved better, that's the point. Better all around, and better from me. I ask myself if she'd gone back to him if not for me. If not for thinking my son needs his father. Would she be alive now?"

Worried, she wanted to yank him out of this maze of guilt he was circling. But she went with instinct, with training, and spoke quietly, as she would to a victim, a survivor on the verge of shock. "You can't blame yourself for that. Or punish yourself for it."

"There should be some payment. Goddamn it, Eve, there should be *something*. I feel . . . helpless, and I don't like it. Here's something I can't fix—can't fight with my fists, can't buy or steal or talk my way around. No matter how I line it up, she's dead, and he never paid."

"Roarke, I don't know how many times—you can't keep them in your head or you go crazy—I don't know how many times I've knocked on someone's door and ripped apart the whole fabric of their life by telling them someone they loved is dead."

Hoping to comfort, she brushed her fingers over his hair. "They feel what you're feeling now. And no matter how you line it up, the one who caused it never pays enough."

"You won't like to hear it, but I'll say it anyway. There have been moments, countless moments through my life that I wished I'd been the one to do him in the end. But I've never wished it more than I do now, even knowing it means nothing, changes nothing. Maybe that's one of the reasons I didn't tell you. How can you understand that I think I'd feel more of a man right now if I had his blood on my hands."

She looked down at his hand, and the gold ring, their symbol, that shone on his finger. "You're wrong if you think

I don't understand. I understand because I've got my own father's blood on mine."

"Oh Christ." It sickened and infuriated him—he'd wallowed so deep into the mire of his own life that he'd so carelessly thrown that in her face. He drew her against him. "I'm sorry. Baby."

"It wouldn't help." She eased back so he could see her. "Take my word. And believe me, you're more of a man than any other I've known."

He rested his forehead on hers. "I can't do without you. I don't know how I ever got by before you."

"We'll just go from here. You've had a rough couple of days, so I'll try one of your favorite sports and make you eat something."

He smiled, finally, when she rose to go to the AutoChef. "Tending to me, are you?"

Glancing back she studied him. He wore nothing but the trousers. Though there were hints of amusement in his eyes now, the shadows under them still dogged them.

And he was pale yet, pale from worry and fatigue.

Well, she would damn well fix that.

"I think I can figure out how, since I've been on the receiving end often enough." She went for soup. "I don't know much about mothers—neither do you—but from everything you've just said she'd hate you blaming yourself for what happened. If she loved you, she'd want you happy. She'd like knowing you got away from him. That you grew up to be successful and important."

"However I managed it."

"Yeah." She fiddled with the soup, then brought it to him. "However you managed it."

"He's in me, you know."

She nodded, sat beside him again. "I guess it works that way, which mean she's in you, too. Gives you a big one up on me, on the DNA chart."

"I've been shuffling the past behind me all my life. It doesn't shadow me the way it does you." He ate, without much interest, because she'd gone to the trouble for him. "I didn't want to bring you into this, or anyone. I wanted to sort it out for myself, that's all. But it's eating at me. I can see her face now, and I always will. I have family I didn't know of, people who lost her. I don't know what the hell to do about it. So I find myself guilty and churned up and frustrated."

"You don't have to do anything until you feel easier about it." She lifted a hand, stroked his hair. "Give yourself a break."

"I couldn't tell you straight off." He looked at her now. "Couldn't get the words out. Shutting you out was easier. Easier yet, it seems, was taking some of that guilt and frustration out on you."

"Not so easy when I knocked you on your ass."

He leaned over, kissed her softly. "Thanks for that."

"Anytime, pal."

"I'm sorry I left you alone last night. You had a nightmare."

"I'd say we both did. We'll figure this out, Roarke."

"Not so much to . . ." Her face blurred, doubled, shimmered briefly into focus again. "Ah, fuck me. You tranq'd the soup."

"Yeah, I did." Her tone was cheerful as she took the bowl before it tipped out of his limp fingers. "You need to sleep. Let's get you into bed while you can still walk. I can't carry you the way you do me."

"You're enjoying this part."

"Well, duh." She got his arm around her shoulders, hers around his waist, and hauled him up. "And I'm beginning to see why you get such a charge out of putting me under when you think I need it. It makes me feel all righteous and gooey inside."

"Let me complete the reversal," he managed in a voice slurring with the drug, "and say, 'Bite me.' "

"Happy to, when you wake up. Step up, there you go. One more, that's the spirit."

"I should probably be pissed off at you, but I can't quite focus on it. Come sleep with me, darling Eve. Let me hold you."

"Yeah, you bet." She eased him onto the bed, lifted his

legs. His face was already going slack. "Just rest now," she whispered as she pulled the covers over him.

He murmured in Gaelic words she'd heard before. *I love you*. She sat beside him, brushed the hair back from his cheeks, then touched her lips to his.

"Same goes."

She set the lights on five percent so that if he surfaced, he wouldn't wake in the dark. Then she went down to speak to Summerset before going back to her office.

While she worked late into the night, she kept the bedroom on-screen, so she could watch over him.

Chapter 13

His hands were on her, and his mouth, heating her blood, tripping her pulse before she was fully awake.

Languidly, Eve moved under him, sighing a little. Her senses were tuned to him—the scent of her mate, his taste, his shape—and the need for him rose up even as her mind flitted around the blurred edges of sleep.

Gently, lightly, fingertips stroked over soft, warm flesh. The slide of a tongue, the brush of lips, and an erotic whisper close to her ear. She was aroused, still floating on that liquid spill where pleasure was lazy and sweet.

Then he said her name. Said her name before his mouth ravished hers, before his hand slid down to cup where she was already wet, already aching.

And he shot her from dreamy drift into urgent demand.

Now there was only sensation, the pounding of blood and shocks of heat, and the tangle of limbs as they rolled to find more. She ran her hands over him, thrilling herself with the angles, the smooth skin, the hard lines of muscle.

He was starved for her. He'd wakened wanting her, just the warm comfort of her beside him in the quiet light she'd left burning against the dark. But he'd only had to touch her, to see her face, to need.

She was his constant.

Her mouth was eager, her hands quick and greedy. Their moods matched here, he knew. *Give me more, and more. And take all you can.*

Half-mad, he dragged her up. He could see her eyes, gleaming, focused on him as she locked her legs around him, as her hips surged to take him in—into the wet heat. She watched him still as she clamped around him, already coming as she surrounded him.

His breath snagged in his throat. His heart leaped after it.

He might have spoken, or tried, but she pulled him closer, took him deeper, and banding her arms around him used those strong, narrow hips to drive him.

Just hold on, she thought. *Hold onto me this time.* And she held him while the hunger consumed them both.

They slid down together, shuddering. When his head rested between her breasts, she closed her eyes again.

"Guess you're feeling better," she managed.

"Considerably. Thanks." He brushed his lips gently over the side of her breast. "I suppose I deserved the tranq."

"Goes without saying, seeing as you've doused me too many times to count. Point is though, you needed to sleep." With her hand caught in his hair, she looked up through the sky window at the colorless morning sky. "You scared me, Roarke."

"I know it." Turning his head, he pressed his lips to her heart, then shifted so he could draw her over to him, rest her head on his shoulder. "This, all this . . . it sucker punched me. I don't seem to have my wits about me yet."

"I get that. But I think you broke a rule. The one about not sharing a personal crisis with your life partner."

"Life partner." He smiled up at the ceiling. "Is that your new, more comfortable alternative for wife?"

"Don't try to change the subject. You broke the rule. I've been collecting marriage rules over the last year."

"Always the cop," he retorted. "You're right though, and if it's not a rule it should be. I shouldn't have kept it from you. I don't know altogether why I did. I have to turn this around in my head awhile more, figure out what to do. Or not."

"Fine. But no shutting me out. Not again."

"That's a deal." He sat up as she did, then caught her face in his hands. How she could have thought, even for a moment, that he'd grown tired of her was beyond him. "Life partners," he said. "It's got a nice ring to it. But you know, I still prefer the sound of 'wife.' " He touched his lips to hers. "Mine."

"You would. I've got to get moving. I have to report to the commander this morning."

"I haven't been keeping up with you. Why don't we catch a shower together, and you can tell me about the case."

She lifted a shoulder as if it didn't matter to her one way or the other. But the fact was she'd missed, very much, being able to run through the steps and stages of an investigation with him. "Okay. But no funny business."

"And here I was, about to grab my big red nose and squirting carnation."

Naked, she turned in the bathroom doorway to stare at him. "You're a strange guy, Roarke. But there will be no clowning around—haha—in the shower."

He considered changing her mind, just on principle, but as he listened to her run through, he got caught up. And found it a relief to think about something other than his own worries.

"It shows how quick you can lock yourself into your own little world. I didn't know there'd been a second murder. Both young, both students—different universities, backgrounds, interests, social circles."

"There are connections. The club where the transmissions originate for one. Hastings and Portography."

"And their killer."

"Yeah." She scooped her hand through her wet hair as she stepped out of the shower. "And their killer."

"Maybe they both modeled for the killer at some point."

"I don't think so." She stepped into the drying tube as Roarke reached for a towel. "Why the candids?" She lifted her voice over the hum of the tube. "Why take photographs of them when they're unaware if they were modeling. Plus, they're kids, right? It seems to me a kid would get all puffed up or jazzed up about the idea of modeling and tell their friends or family. Neither victim mentioned it to anyone we've questioned."

She stepped out, and this time scooped her hand through dry hair, considered it styled for the day. "I'm starting to think this guy, or woman, isn't a professional. Or at least, not successfully. Wants to be, believes he's just aces."

"Frustrated artist."

"That's what I get. If he does commercial work, he considers it beneath him. Stews about it. Sits around in his room whining to himself that the world doesn't appreciate his genius. He has such a gift," she continued as she walked to the closet to hunt up clothes. "A light inside, but nobody sees it. Not yet. But they will. He'll *make* them see it eventually. When he's done, it'll be so bright, it'll all but blind them. Some will say he's insane, deluded, even evil. But what do they know? More, he's sure of it, more will finally recognize who and what he is—what he can do, and give. The brilliance of it. The artistry. The immortality. Then, finally, he'll get his due."

She yanked a sleeveless tank over her head, then noted Roarke was simply standing, watching her, with the faintest of smiles. "What? Jesus, what's wrong with this top? If I'm not supposed to wear the damn thing, why is it in the closet?"

"The top's fine, and that strong blue's a nice color on you, by the way. I was thinking what a marvel you are, Lieutenant. An artist in your way. You see him. Not the face and form, not yet. But you see inside him already. And that's how you stop him. Because he can't hide from someone who sees inside him."

"Long enough to kill two people, so far."

"And if you weren't standing for them, he might never pay for it. He's smart, isn't he?" He crossed to the closet, chose a jacket for her before she could do so herself. "A clever mind, and oh so organized."

He liked the pale, silvery gray jacket against the strong blue, and set it aside for her to put on after she'd strapped on her weapon. "He watches. Spends a lot of time blending rather than standing out, don't you think? Better to watch. More to see when you're not particularly noticed."

She nodded. "That's good."

"But still, if they knew him as you believe, there's something about him that made them see him as friendly, or at least unthreatening."

"They were kids. Most, at twenty, don't think anything can hurt them."

"We knew better." He stroked a fingertip over the shallow dent in her chin. "But I think you're right again. In the normal way of things, at twenty you're invulnerable. Is that something else he wants? That careless courage and innocence."

"Enough, I think, that he lets them keep it right to the end. He doesn't hurt them, mark them, rape them. He doesn't hate them for what they are. He . . . honors them for it."

It was good, she realized, really good to talk it out. She'd needed just this. "It's not envy, it's like appreciation. I think he loves them, in his twisted, selfish way. And that's what makes him so dangerous."

"Will you show me the portraits?"

She hesitated while he went to the AutoChef to program coffee. He should be studying the morning stock reports, monitoring any breaking news over breakfast, she thought. That was his routine. And she should be heading out to Central right now to prepare for her morning briefing.

"Sure." She said it casually before sitting down and calling up the file on the sitting room unit. "I'll have a couple of eggs, scrambled, and whatever else you're having."

"A very smooth way of ensuring I eat." He programmed breakfast, then studied the screen—the two images Eve had called up on it. "Different types entirely, aren't they? And yet, the same . . . vitality, I suppose."

He thought of the picture of the woman he knew to be his mother. Young, vital, alive.

"It's monsters who prey on the young," he declared.

He couldn't get the images out of his mind, even after Eve had left the house. They haunted him as he went down to make amends with Summerset. The two young people he'd never met, the mother he'd never known.

They linked together in his head, a sad and sorrowful portrait gallery. Then another joined him, and he saw Marlena in his mind's eye. Summerset's lovely young daughter. She'd been little more than a child when the monsters had taken her, Roarke thought.

Because of him.

His mother, Summerset's daughter, both dead because of him.

He stepped through the open door of Summerset's quarters. In the living area PA Spence was running a hand scanner over the skin cast to check the knitting of bone.

The wall screen played one of the morning newscasts. Summerset sat, drinking coffee, watching the news, and ignoring the PA as she cheerfully detailed the progress of his injuries.

"Coming right along," she chirped. "*Excellent* progress, particularly for a man of your age. You're going to be up and around on your own again in no time, no time at all."

"Madam, I would be up and around on my own now if you'd go away."

She clucked her tongue. "We'll just get a reading of your blood pressure and pulse for the chart. Bound to be elevated since you insisted on drinking that coffee. Black as pitch. You know perfectly well you'd do better with a nice herbal tonic."

"With you nattering in my ear I may take to starting my day with vodka. And I can take my own vital signs."

"I'll take your vital signs. And I want no trouble from you today about your vitamin boost."

"If you come near me with that syringe, you'll find it deposited in one of your own orifices."

"Excuse me." Though he'd have preferred to slink away unnoticed, Roarke stepped inside. "Sorry to interrupt. I need Summerset for a few moments, if you'd excuse us."

"I'm not quite finished. I need to update his chart, and he needs his booster."

"Ah, well." Roarke slid his hands into his pockets. "You look better today."

"I'm quite well, considering."

And angry with me, Roarke noted. "I wonder if some fresh air might be in order. Why don't I take you out through the gardens for a bit, before the day heats up."

"That's a fine idea," Spence said before Summerset could answer. And she whipped the pressure syringe from behind her back, had it pressed against his biceps and administered before he could blink. "Nothing like a nice turn around the garden to put roses in your cheeks. No more than thirty minutes," she said to Roarke. "It'll be time for his physical therapy."

"I'll have him back for it." He started to step behind Summerset's chair.

"I can navigate this bloody thing perfectly well myself." To prove it, Summerset engaged the controls and propelled himself toward the terrace doors.

Roarke managed to get there in time to open them before he whisked through.

Back poker straight, Summerset drove over the stone terrace, turned down one of the garden paths. And kept on going.

"He's in a very sour mood this morning," Spence commented. "More so than usual."

"I'll have him back for the therapy." Roarke shut the door behind him, and followed Summerset down the path.

The air was warm and close, and fragrant. He'd built this world, he thought, his world surrounded by the city he'd made his own. He'd needed the beauty. It hadn't been simply desire, but survival. With enough beauty, he could cover up all the ugliness of all the yesterdays.

So there were flowers and pools, arbors and paths. He'd married Eve out here, in this manufactured Eden. And found more than his measure of peace.

He let Summerset glide himself along for the first few minutes, understanding the man probably wanted to put some distance between himself and Spence as much as he wanted the control.

Then Roarke simply stepped up behind the chair, stopped it. Locked it in place. He walked around to sit on a bench so that he and Summerset were on the same level.

"I know you're angry with me," he began.

"You've saddled me with that creature. Locked me in with her as my warden."

Roarke shook his head. "Christ Jesus. You can be as mad as you like about that. Until you're healed you'll have the best care available. She's it. For that I won't apologize. For the things I said to you last night, for the way I behaved, I will. I'm sorry for it, very sorry."

"Did you think you couldn't tell me?" Summerset looked away, stared hard at a violently blue hydrangea. "I know the worst of you, and the best, and everything between." He looked back now, studied Roarke's face. "Well, at least I see she tended to you. You look rested."

Surprise flashed in Roarke's eyes before he narrowed them. "Eve discussed . . . she spoke to you about what I've learned?"

"However we disagree, whatever our difficulties with each other, we have one thing in common. That's you. You worried us both, needlessly."

"I did." He rose, walked a few paces down the path. Back again. "I can't get a grip on it. Any sort of a grip. It makes me sick inside in a way I haven't felt . . . in a very long time. And I wondered, I let myself wonder, if you knew."

"If I knew . . . ah." As another piece fell into place, Summerset let out a long breath. "I didn't. I had no knowledge of this girl. As far as I knew, Meg Roarke was your mother."

Roarke sat again. "I never questioned it."

"Why should you have?"

"I've spent more time, taken more care turning over the background on a low-level employee than I have on my own beginnings. I blocked them out from my mind and from data banks. Wiped most of it clean."

"You protected yourself."

"Fuck that." It was temper as much as guilt that radiated from him. "Who protected her?"

"It could hardly have been you, a babe in arms."

"And no justice for her, not by my hand. Not by her son's hand, for the bastard's been dead for years now. At least with Marlena—"

He cut himself off, drew himself in. "Marlena died to teach me a lesson. You never blamed me for it, not once have you said you blamed me."

For a long beat, Summerset looked over the garden. Those violently blue hydrangeas, the bloodred of roses, the hot pink of snapdragons. His daughter, his precious child, had been like a flower.

Beautiful, brilliant, and short-lived.

"Because you weren't to blame. Not for what happened to my girl, not for what happened to your mother." Summerset's gaze tracked back to him, held. "Boy," he said quietly, "you were never to blame."

"Neither was I ever innocent, not in my own memory anyway." With a little sigh, Roarke snapped off one of the blossoms, studied it. It occurred to him he hadn't given Eve flowers in some time. A man shouldn't forget to do such things, especially when the woman never expected them.

"You could have blamed me." He set the flower in Summerset's lap because that, too, was unexpected. A small gesture, a small symbol. "You took me in, when he'd damn near beaten me to death, and I had no one and nowhere to go. You didn't have to; I was nothing to you then."

"You were a child, and that was enough. You were a child half-beaten to death, and that was too much."

"For you." Emotion all but strangled him. "You took care of me, and you taught me. You gave me something I'd never had, never expected to. You gave me a home, and a family. And when they took part of that family away, when they took Marlena, the best of us, you could have blamed me. Cast me out. But you never did."

"You were mine by then, weren't you?"

"God." He had to take a breath, a careful one. "I suppose I was."

Needing to move, Roarke got to his feet. With his hands in his pockets he watched a small fountain gurgle to life above a riot of lilies. He watched the cool water until he was calm again.

"When I decided to come here, wanted to make my home here and asked you to come, you did. You left the home you'd made for the one I wanted to make. I don't think I've ever told you that I'm grateful."

"You have told me. Many times and in many ways." Summerset laid his hands over the strong blue flower, looked out over the garden. The peace of it, and the beauty of it.

The world within a world the boy he'd watched become a man had created. Now that world had been shaken, and needed to be put steady again.

"You'll go back to Ireland. You'll have to go back."

"I will." Roarke nodded, unspeakably grateful to be understood without having said the words. "I will, yes."

"When?"

"Right away. I think it's best to go straight away."

"Have you told the lieutenant?"

"I haven't." Unsettled again, Roarke looked down at his own hands, ran the gold band of his marriage around his finger. "She's in the middle of a difficult investigation. This will distract her from it. I'd considered telling her I had business out of town, but I can't lie to her. It'll be simpler, I think, to make the arrangements, then tell her I'm going."

"She should go with you."

"She's not only my wife. Not even always my wife first." He angled his head, smiled a little. "That's something you and I might never see quite the same way."

Summerset opened his mouth, then shut it again. Deliberately.

"People's lives depend on her," Roarke said with some exasperation. "It's something she never forgets, and something I'd never ask her to put second. I can handle this on my own, and in fact, I think it's best I do."

"You were always one for believing you had to handle everything yourself. In that area, you and she are peas in a pod."

"Maybe." Because he wanted their faces on the same level, Roarke crouched. "Once, if you remember, when I was young and things were a bit tight for me, and the hate I felt for him still hot—running like some black river inside me—I told you I was going to take another name. That I wouldn't keep his. Wanted nothing of his."

"I remember. I think you were still shy of sixteen."

"You said: Keep it, the name's yours as much as his. Keep it, and make something of it, then it'll be all of yours and none of his. Start now. Didn't tell me what to make of it, did you?"

With a short laugh, Summerset shook his head. "I didn't have to. You already knew."

"I have to go back, myself, and find whatever it is she gave me. I have to know if I've made something of it, or have something yet to make. And I have to start now."

"It's difficult to argue with my own words."

"Still, I don't like leaving you before you're on your feet again."

Summerset made a dismissive sound. "I can handle this, and that irritating woman you've chained to me, on my own."

"You'll watch after my cop while I'm gone, won't you?"

"In my way."

"Well then." He got to his feet. "If you need me for anything . . . you'll be able to reach me."

Now Summerset smiled. "I've always been able to reach you."

Eve finished her oral report to Commander Whitney standing. She preferred that kind of formality in his office. She respected him for the kind of cop he was, and had been. Respected the lines of worry and authority that scored his wide, dark face.

Riding a desk hadn't made him soft, but had only toughened the muscles of command.

"There are some media concerns," he said when she'd finished. "Let's get them out of the way."

"Yes, sir."

"There have been some complaints that Channel 75, and Nadine Furst in particular, is receiving preferential treatment in this investigation."

"Channel 75 and Nadine Furst *are* receiving preferential treatment in this investigation due to the fact that we believe the killer has sent transmissions directly to Ms. Furst at 75. She, and the station, are cooperating fully with me and my team. As the transmissions were sent to her, I have no authority to stop her, or 75, from broadcasting any and all of the contents. However, they have agreed to filter those transmissions, and any other data received, through me. As *quid pro quo*, I have agreed to filter back any information on the case I deem appropriate for broadcast to them first."

Whitney tipped his head in acknowledgment. "Then we're covered."

"Yes, sir, I believe so."

"We'll set up a media conference to keep the dogs at bay. When dealing with the media, it's best to CYA twice, whenever possible. I'll have our liaison go through your reports and cull out what we want to feed them."

Satisfied, he set the media aside, went back to the meat. "You need to work the connections, find the conduit between the victims."

"Yes, sir. I'd like to put a man, or better, a team on the club. Baxter and Trueheart. Trueheart's young enough to pass for a student. Baxter's training him, so I'd want him on board, to keep close. Trueheart hasn't had much undercover experience. McNab could cover some ground in the colleges, working the geek end of things. He's already been in the club with a badge, so I can't use him there."

"Set it up."

"Sir; my initial run of the list from Portography—Hastings's assistants. Some of the names are bogus. Some of these people just make them up, because they think they sound better. But the one who was on during the wedding where Howard was photographed rings false. I'm going to push on that. I'm also going to try some sources, see if I can narrow down the images the killer's produced to style and equipment. I've got a lot of lines to tug, which may keep my people scattered for a while, until I can pull them all in again."

"Do what's necessary to close this down. Keep me updated."

"Yes, sir." She started to step back, then stayed where she was. "Commander, there's one more thing. As I mentioned last month, I'd like to have Officer Peabody's name put in for the next detective's test."

"She's ready now?"

"She's had about eighteen months of homicide experience under me. She's worked, and closed, a cold case on her own. She's clocked more field time than some of the guys in the bull pen. She's a good cop, Commander, and deserves her shot at a gold shield."

"On your recommendation then, Lieutenant."

"Thank you."

"I'd tell her to start prepping. As I recall the exam isn't a walk on the beach."

"No, sir." This time Eve smiled. "More like a run through a war zone. She'll be prepped."

She went down to the conference room, taking the time before her team arrived to sit on the edge of the table and study the board.

The images looked back at her. She focused first on Rachel Howard. Smiling, sunny, cheerfully at work. Typical college-age job—clerking at a 24/7. Wanted to be a teacher. Studied hard, made friends, good solid family life. Middle class.

Subway shot—heading home to that solid family life, or maybe off to school. Confident, pretty. Vital.

Wedding shot. Dolled up for the event. Fussier hair, darker lips, longer eyelashes. Big, celebratory smile that just plain popped out from the rest. You noticed this girl. Couldn't help it.

Even in death, Eve thought. Sitting so neat, so pretty, with the light on her hair, her eyes staring out.

And Kenby Sulu, exotic, striking. Fairly typical job as well, particularly for the theater type. Ushering. Wanted to be a dancer, worked hard, made friends easily, good solid family life. Upper class.

Standing outside of Juilliard. Ready to go in, just coming out. Big smile for his friends.

Then the formal cast shot. Dark and intense, but still, oh yeah, still, you saw the light in him. Anticipation, health, energy.

The death shot mirrored it, she noted. The way he was posed in a dance, as if still on the move. And the light shimmering like a halo around him.

Healthy, she thought. Had to be healthy, had to be innocent, young, well-adjusted. Clean. There was something else the two victims had in common, she decided. They were clean. No history of illegals, no major illnesses on medical records. Good sharp brains, nice healthy young bodies.

She turned to the computer and started a run on any imaging business with Light in the name. She got four hits, noted them, then ran books on imaging with Light in the title. At some time, she was certain, her killer had been a student.

She hit several, and was about to print them out when one caught her eye.

Images of Light and Dark, by Dr. Leeanne Browning.

"Okay," Eve said aloud. "Time to go back to school, one more time."

When the conference door opened, she spoke without looking up. "Peabody, requisition and download a copy of a photographic text book titled *Images of Light and Dark*, by Leeanne Browning. Use the auxiliary computer. I'm not done here."

"Yes, sir. How did you know it was me?"

"You're the only one who walks like you. Find out if there's an actual book copy available while you're at it. It may be helpful."

"Okay, but what does that mean? How do I walk?"

"Quick march in cop shoes. Working here."

Eve didn't have to look up this time either to know Peabody was scowling at her shoes. She did a cross-check to locate and highlight any other book, paper, or published images by Browning, ran them through.

Sulu had gone to Juilliard, but lived only a few blocks

away from the Browning/Brightstar apartment. Could be another connection, she mused.

"I can get it in both e and print versions, Lieutenant."

"Get both. While it's downloading, you might want to check the schedule for upcoming detective exams. You've been cleared to take the next one."

"I need to wait until the requisition clears, then . . ." Her voice trailed off.

"I said get both. Screw the requisition. Order them. I'll cover it until the red tape clears."

"The detective exam." Peabody's voice was a squeak. "I'm going to take the detective exam?"

Eve swiveled in her chair, kicked out her legs. Her aide had gone ice pale, right down to the lips. Good, Eve thought. It wasn't a step any good cop should take lightly. "You're cleared for it, but it's your call. You want to stay in uniform, you stay in uniform."

"I want to make detective."

"Okay. Take the exam."

"Do you think I'm ready?"

"Do you?"

"I want to be ready."

"Then study up, take the exam."

Her color was coming back, slowly. "You put my name up, cleared it with the commander."

"You work under me. You're assigned to me. It's up to me to put your name up if I think you do good work. You do good work."

"Thanks."

"Now keep doing good work and get me what I told you to get me. I've got to go drag Baxter and Trueheart into this."

Eve walked out. She didn't have to look back to know Peabody was grinning.

Chapter 14

Eve found Leeanne Browning at her apartment. The professor wore a long red shirt over a black skinsuit, and had her hair bundled back in a braid.

"Lieutenant Dallas. Officer. You just caught me. Angie and I were about to head out." She gestured them inside as she spoke. "We're going to spend a few hours working in Central Park. The heat brings out all sorts of interesting characters."

"Including us," Angie said, hauling a large toolbox into the room.

Leeanne laughed, low and lusty. "Oh, absolutely including us. What can we do for you?"

"I have some questions."

"All right. Let's sit down and try to answer them. Is this about poor Rachel? There's a memorial service for her tomorrow evening."

"Yes, I know. I'd like you to look at these. Do you recognize the subject?"

Leeanne took the image of Kenby, standing in front of Juilliard. "No." While Eve watched her face, Leeanne pursed her lips. "No," she said again. "I don't think he's one of mine. I'd remember this face. Striking face."

"Good form," Angie added, leaning over the back of the sofa. "Nice, graceful body type."

"An excellent study. Very well done. The same, isn't it?" Leeanne asked. "It's the same portrait artist. Is this handsome young man dead?"

"How about this one?" Eve offered the picture of the dance troupe.

"Ah, a dancer. Of course. He's built like one, isn't he?" She made a small sound, a little breath of distress. "No, he's not familiar to me. None of them are. But this isn't the same photographer, is it?"

"Why do you say that?"

"Different style, technique. Such drama, and a wonderful use of shadows here. Of course, you'd want drama in this study, but . . . It seems to me that whoever took this dance study is more experienced, more trained, or simply more talented. Both, by my critique. Actually, at a guess, I'd say this was a Hastings."

Intrigued, Eve sat back. "You can look at a photo and identify the photographer."

"Certainly, if the artist has a distinct style. Of course, a clever student or fan could copy it very well, digital manipulation and so on. But this first isn't what I'd call a stylistic homage."

Setting them side-by-side, she studied them again. "No. It's very distinct and different. Two artists, interested in the same subject, and seeing it through different perspectives."

"Do you know Hastings, personally?"

"Yes. Not well, I doubt anyone does. Such a temperamental soul. But I use his work quite often in class, and he's allowed me, with some considerable persuasion, to conduct some workshops for my students in his studio over the years."

"She had to pay him out of pocket," Angie chimed in. She was still leaning over the sofa, with her chin nearly resting on Leeanne's shoulder. "Hastings likes his money."

"That's true." Leeanne's tone was cheerful. "When it comes to his art, he doesn't compromise, but he's firm on making a profit. His store, his commercial work, his time."

Eve began to play another angle in her head. "Any of your students ever work for him as models or assistants?"

"Oh yeah," Leeanne answered with a chuckle. "And most had a maxibus full of complaints afterward. He's rude, impatient, cheap, violent. But they learned, I can promise you that."

"I'd like the names."

"My God, Lieutenant, I've been sending students to Hastings for more than five years."

"I'd like the names," Eve repeated. "All you have on record, or in your memory. What about this one?" She held out the death photo.

"Oh." Her hand lifted, linked with Angie's. "Macabre, horrible. Brilliant. He's getting better at his work."

"Why do you say that?"

"So stark. It's meant to be. Death Dances. That's what I'd call it. The use of shadow and light here. The fact that he chose black-and-white, the fluid pose of the body. He could have done more with the face—yes, untapped potential there—but overall it's brilliant. And terrible."

"You often choose black-and-white. Most of your book is dedicated to the art of black-and-white photography and imaging."

With a look of surprise, Leeanne glanced up again. "You've read my book?"

"I've looked it over. There's a great deal about light—the exploitation of it, the building or taking of it, the filtering of it. The absence of it."

"Without light, there is no image and the tone of the light determines the tone of the image. How it's used, how the artist manipulates it or sees it, will be a part of his skill. Wait just a moment."

She rose and hurried out of the room.

"You suspect her." Angie straightened, studying Eve. "How can you? Leeanne would never harm anyone, much less a child. She isn't capable of evil."

"Part of my job is asking questions."

Angie nodded, and coming around the sofa sat across from Eve. "Your job weighs on you. It puts pity in your eyes when you look at death." She turned the portrait of Kenby over. "It doesn't stay there, not in your eyes. But I think it stays inside you."

"He doesn't need my pity anymore."

"No, I suppose not," Angie replied as Leeanne came back in carrying a small box.

"Hey, it's a pinhole camera." Peabody blurted it out, then flushed a little at her own outburst. "My uncle had one, showed me how to make one when I was a kid."

Eve was studying the odd little box and said simply, "Free-Ager," by way of explanation.

"Ah, yes. This is a very old technique." Leeanne set the box on a table, removed a bit of tape, then aimed the tiny hole that had been shielded beneath it toward Eve. "A handmade box, the photographic paper inside, the light outside with the pinhole as the lens that captures that light, and the image. I'd like you to keep still," she told Eve.

"That box is taking my picture."

"Yes. It's the light, you see, that creates the miracle here. I ask each of my students to make a pinhole camera like this, and to experiment with it. Those that don't understand the miracle, well, they may go on to take good pictures, but they'll never create art. It isn't all technology and tools, you see. It isn't all equipment and manipulation. The core is the light, and what it sees. What we see through it."

"What we take out of it?" Eve asked, watching her. "What we absorb from it?"

"Perhaps. While some primitive cultures feared that the camera, by reproducing their image, stole their souls, others believed that it gave them a kind of immortality. We have, in many ways, blended those two beliefs. Certainly, we immortalize with imaging, we steal moments of time and hold them. And we take something from each subject, each time. That moment again, that thought, that mood, that light. It will never be exactly the same again. Not even a second afterward. It's gone—and it's preserved, forever, in the photograph. There's power in that."

"There's no thought, no mood, no light in a photograph of the dead."

"Ah, but there is. The artist's. Death, most certainly death, would be a defining moment. Here, let's see what we've got."

She covered the hole on the box again, then slid out a sheet of paper. On it, Eve's image was reproduced, almost like a pale pencil sketch.

"The light etches the image, burns it into the paper, and preserves it. The light," she said, handing the paper to Eve, "is the tool, the magic. The soul."

"She's really interesting," Peabody commented. "I bet she's a terrific teacher."

"And as someone who knows how to manipulate images, she had the skill to dick with the security discs on her building, shift the time stamp. Her alibi, therefore, has holes. So we give her, potentially, opportunity. Means—she clicks there. Method, another click. Give me motive."

"Well, I don't . . ."

"Set aside the fact you like her." Eve merged into traffic. "What's her motive for selecting, stalking, and killing two attractive college students?"

"Art. It all deals with art."

"Deeper, Peabody."

"Okay." She wanted to take off her cap, scratch her head, but resisted. "Controlling the subject? Controlling the art in order to create?"

"On one level," Eve agreed. "Control, creation, and the accolades that result. The attention, anyway, the recognition. In this case we have a teacher. She instructs, she gives her knowledge, her skill, her experience, and others take it and go on to become what she hasn't. She's written a couple of books, published some images, but she isn't considered an artist, is she? She's considered a teacher."

"It's a very respected, and often under-appreciated vocation. You're a really good teacher, for instance."

"I don't teach anybody. Train maybe, but that's different."

"I wouldn't have the shot at a gold shield, not this soon, if you hadn't taught me."

"Trained you, and let's stay on target here. The other level is taking from the subject and seeing them as just that. A subject, not a person with a life, a family, with needs or rights. A subject, like—I don't know—a tree. If you've got to cut down the tree to get what you want, well, too bad. Plenty more trees."

"You're talking to a Free-Ager here." Peabody shuddered. "Talking about indiscriminately mowing down trees hits me in a primal area."

"The killer isn't killing just for the thrill of taking a life. It isn't done with rage, or for profit. It isn't sexual. But it is personal. It's intimate—for the killer. This person, this specific person, has what I need, so I'll take it. I'll take what they have, then it becomes mine. They become mine, and the result is art. Admire me."

"That's a pretty twisted route."

"It's a pretty twisted mind. And a smart one, a cool one."

"You think it's Professor Browning?"

"She's connected, so we line up the connections. Who knows her, and Hastings, and the two victims? Who had contact with all of them? Let's find out."

She started at Juilliard, at the theater department. At some point in their young lives, Rachel Howard and Kenby Sulu had intersected.

She sent Peabody off to make the rounds with the photograph of Rachel while she made her own.

When her 'link beeped, she was standing at the back of a rehearsal hall watching a bunch of young people pretend to be various animals.

"Dallas."

"Hello, Lieutenant." Roarke's face filled her screen, and almost immediately shifted from an easy smile to puzzlement. "Where are you? The zoo?"

"In a manner of speaking." Wanting to cut out some of the background noise, she stepped out into the hall. "Everything okay?"

"Well enough. Eve, I have to go out of town for a few days."

"Oh." It wasn't unusual for him to have to buzz around the planet, or off it. The man had interests all over the developed universe. But the timing was poor. "If you could—"

"I have to go to Ireland," he said before she could finish. "I need to go back, and deal with this."

Stupid, she thought immediately. Stupid to have this blindside her. Of course he'd need to go back. "Look, okay, I can see how you'd feel that, but I'm in the middle of things here. I need to stick with this until I close the case, then I can take some time. I'll put in for it when I get back to Central."

"I need to deal with this myself."

She opened her mouth, ordered herself to breathe before she spoke. "Right."

"Eve, it has to be done, and isn't something you need to worry about. I don't want you to worry about it, or me. I'm sorry to leave you to handle Summerset, and I'll try to make it as quick as I can."

She kept her face blank, her voice even for both their sakes. "When are you leaving?"

"Now. Immediately. Fact is, I'm on the shuttle now. I can't tell you precisely where I'll be—I don't know yet. But I'll have my personal 'link with me. You'll be able to reach me anytime."

"You knew you were going." She lowered her voice, turning her back on the corridor as students rushed by behind her. "You knew this morning."

"I had to see to some details first."

"But you'd already made up your mind to go."

"I had, yes."

"And you're telling me like this so I can't do anything to stop you."

"Eve, you wouldn't stop me. And I won't have to put your work in a holding pattern so you can come along and nurse me through this."

"Is that what you did when you went with me to Dallas? Nursed me through it?"

Frustration ran over his face. "That was a different matter."

"Oh yeah, with you being a man and all, with unbreakable balls. I keep forgetting."

"I have to go." He spoke coolly now. "I'll let you know where I am as soon as I can manage, and I'll be back in a few days. Probably sooner. You can kick my unbreakable balls then. Meanwhile, I love you. Ridiculously."

"Roarke—" But he'd already ended the transmission. "Damn it. *Damn* it." She kicked the wall, twice.

She marched back into the rehearsal room and vented her frustration by stalking through the slinking tigers and leaping chimps.

The instructor was a pencil-thin woman with a high shock of blue hair. "Ah," she said, "and here we have the lone wolf."

"Shut them down," Eve ordered.

"Class is in progress."

"Shut them down." Eve whipped out her badge. "Now."

"Oh damn it, not another Illegals sweep. Stop!" For a thin woman, she had a big voice, and her order shut off the din.

Eve stepped in front of her. "I'm Lieutenant Dallas, NYPSD." There was a communal groan at the announcement, and two students edged toward the rear doors. "Hold it! I'm not interested in what you've got in your pockets or your bloodstream, but anybody goes out those doors, I will be."

Movement stopped.

"I have a picture. I want you to come up here, one at a time, and look at it. I want to know if you know this girl, have seen her, or have any information on her. You." She pointed at a boy in a black unitard and baggy shorts. "Here."

He swaggered up. "Nope."

"Look at the picture, smart-ass, or this is going to turn into an Illegals sweep."

He smirked at her, but he looked. "Don't know her, never seen her. Can I go, Officer?"

"Lieutenant. No. Stand over there." She pointed to the right wall, then gestured to a girl, also in black.

She started up, flicking a toothy grin at the boy now lounging against the wall, as though they shared a private joke. But when she looked at the photo, the humor drained out of her face.

"On the news. I saw her on the news. It's that girl from Columbia who was killed. Like Kenby."

The murmuring started from the crowd of students, and Eve let it roll. "That's right. Did you know Kenby?"

"Sure. Sure I did. Everybody did. Man, oh man, this sucks so large."

"Have you seen this girl before?"

Even as she shook her head, someone called out. "I have. I think."

Eve shifted, looked at the boy who stood with his hand raised. "Come up here. Go stand over there," she told the girl.

"I sort of think I saw her." The boy wore the black uniform, and a forest of silver loops along the curve of his ear. He had a trio of matching hoops at the peak of his left eyebrow.

"What's your name?"

"Mica, Mica Constantine. Kenby and I had a lot of classes together, and we hung out sometimes. We weren't real tight, but sometimes we partied with the same group."

"Where did you see her?"

"I *think* I saw her. When I saw her on the news reports, she looked sort of familiar. And when Kenby—when I heard about what happened to him, like with her, I thought, hey, isn't that the chick from the club?"

Eve felt the vibe at the base of her spine. "What club?"

"Make The Scene. Some of us go there sometimes, and I think I've seen her there. I think I remember seeing her and Kenby dancing a couple of times. I'm not absolute about it, just it seems to me."

"When do you think you saw them together?"

"Not together. I mean they weren't like a thing. I think I saw them dancing a couple of times, like last month maybe. I haven't been to the club in a while. Only reason I remember is they looked good, you know. I'm taking this class to learn how to free up my body, how to move it. So I was watching the dancing especially, and they really moved."

"I bet other people noticed them."

"I guess."

When she reconnected with Peabody, they had three witnesses between them who'd seen Rachel and Kenby dancing at the club.

"They didn't come in together, sit together, leave together," Eve summed up as she headed back downtown. "A few casual dances, over a few weeks in the summer, from what we have so far. No way it's a coincidence."

"Someone saw them there, and that cemented it?"

"Saw them there, or saw them at some point, somewhere else. Individually or together. They both liked to dance, so maybe they hooked up elsewhere. Both college kids. She might've gone to see one of his performances. Diego and Hooper both frequent the club. Odds are either or both of them saw these two together. We'll sweep Columbia again, see if any of Rachel's friends or classmates remembers seeing her with Kenby. Or mentioning him."

While Eve tugged on the next line, Roarke walked down the streets of South Dublin. The area had once been as familiar to him as his own face. There'd been changes since his youth, plenty for the good.

The Urban Wars had crushed this part of the city, turned the projects into slums, and the streets into a battlefield. He remembered the aftermath only dimly. Most of it had been over and done before he'd been born.

But the consequences had lasted a generation.

Poverty and the thieves it bred still haunted this area. Hunger and the anger it fed lived here, day by day.

But it was coming back, slowly. The Irish knew all about wars, conflicts, hunger, and poverty. And they dealt with it, sang of it, wrote of it. And drank around it of an evening.

So, there was the Penny Pig. It had been a neighborhood pub when he'd been a boy and most of his neighbors were villains of one sort or the other.

He supposed it wouldn't be inaccurate to name him one of the villains.

It had been a haunt for him, and those he ran with. A place to go and have a pint and not worry about the cops coming in to roust you. There'd been a girl there he'd loved as much as he was able, and friends he'd valued.

All of them, dead and gone now, he thought as he stood outside the door. All but one. He'd come back to the Penny Pig, and the one friend alive from his boyhood. Maybe he'd find some of the answers.

He stepped inside, to the dark wood, the smokey light, the smell of beer and whiskey and cigarettes, and the sounds of rebel songs played low.

Brian was behind the bar, building a Guinness and holding a conversation with a man who looked to be older than dirt. There were a few at the low tables, drinking or having a sandwich. A miniscreen playing some Brit soap opera sat over the bar with the sound muted.

It was early in the day yet, but never too early to stop by a pub. If you wanted conversation, information, or just a sociable drink, where else would you go?

Roarke stepped up to the bar and waited for Brian to glance over.

And when he did, Brian's wide face creased in smiles. "Well now, here's himself come to grace my humble establishment once more. We'd break out the French champagne had we any."

"A pint of that'll do well enough."

"Do you see here, Mister O'Leary, sir, who we have among us today?"

The old man turned his head, and his rheumy eyes stared at Roarke out of a face as flat and thin as a plank. He lifted the pint Brian had just passed him, drank slow and deep.

"It's Roarke, is it, all grown up and fancy as a prince. Bit rougher around the edges, you were, when you came around to pinch wares from my shop down the street."

"You chased me out with a broom more than once."

"Aye, and it's no doubt your pockets were heavier when you lit out than when you came in."

"True enough. It's good to see you again, Mr. O'Leary."

"Got rich, didn't you?"

"I did, yes."

"So he'll pay for your pint as well as his own," Brian said and slid a pint down to Roarke.

"Happy to." Roarke took out a bill large enough to pay for a dozen pints, set it on the bar. "I need to speak with you, Brian, on a private matter."

Friends or not, the note disappeared into Brian's pocket. "Come back to the snug then." As he turned, he pounded a fist on the door behind the bar. "Johnny, get off your lazy arse and mind the bar."

He walked down to a small room at the end, opened the door for Roarke. "And where's Lieutenant Darling?"

"She's home."

"And well, is she?"

"She's well, thanks. Busy."

"Rounding up criminals, no doubt. You give her a kiss for me, and remind her when she's done with you, I'm waiting to make her mine."

He sat at one of the spindly chairs at the single table gracing the little room. Then grinned. "I'll be damned to hell and back, it's good to see you. Happier circumstances I hope, than the last."

"I haven't come to bury another friend."

"God bless him." Brian clicked the glass he'd brought with him against Roarke's. "To Mick then."

"To Mick, and the rest of them that's gone." He drank, then just stared into the foam.

"What's troubling your mind?"

"Long story."

"Since when haven't I had the time and the inclination to hear a long one? And when you're buying?"

"Do you remember when Meg Roarke left?"

Brian's eyebrows lowered, his lips pursed. "I remember she was here, then she was gone, and nobody was sorry to see the back of her."

"Do you have any recollection of . . . of someone else living with him—before she came. Do you remember anyone speaking of a young girl who was with him?"

"Seems to me there were a number of women who came

and went. But before Meg? Can't say. Christ, Roarke, I'd've been in nappies, same as you."

"Your father knew him, and well. Did you never hear the name Siobahn Brody mentioned in your house, or around the neighborhood?"

"I don't remember, no. What's this about then?"

"She was my mother, Bri." It still caught in his throat. "I've learned Meg wasn't, and this young girl from Clare was." Roarke lifted his eyes. "The bastard killed her, Brian. He murdered her."

"Sweet singing Jesus. I don't know of this. I swear to you."

"I don't think he could have managed it alone. Not without a bit of help, or not without someone knowing what he'd done."

"My father ran with him off and on, and did things—all of us did—that weren't right along the clean side of the law. But murder a girl?" Looking Roarke dead in the eye, Brian shook his head. "My da wouldn't have had any of that."

"No. He wasn't one I thought of for this."

"But you're thinking." Brian nodded, and put his mind to it himself. "It was an ugly time. There were still petty little wars raging. Death was everywhere and cheaper in many ways than living."

"He had mates. Two I remember especially. Donal Grogin and Jimmy Bennigan. They would have known."

"Maybe. That may be," Brian said slowly. "But Bennigan died in a cage sometime back, and would be no help to you."

"I know." He'd done his research. "Grogin's still around, and not far from here come to that."

"That's true. He doesn't come in here much, and hasn't for the last years. Frequents a place a bit closer to the river, known as Thief's Haven. Tourists think it's a colorful name until they step inside. Then most step out again quick."

"He might be there now, but more likely at home this time of the day."

"More like." Brian kept his gaze on Roarke's face.

"I can do this myself, and there's no hardship between us

if you'd rather not come along with me. But it'd go faster and cleaner with a friend."

"Now?"

"I'd as soon move fast."

"Then we'd best be going," Brian replied.

"Is this why you came without your cop?" Brian asked him as they walked one of the meaner streets.

"One of the reasons." Absently, Roarke fingered the mini-blaster in his pocket. "We have different methods of interviewing a witness."

Brian patted his own pocket, and the leather sap inside. "I recall getting my face busted a time or two by the cops."

"She can bust faces herself, but she tends to let the other throw the first punch. Her way's effective, believe me, but it takes longer, and I want this done."

He worried the wedding ring on his finger as he walked along a street his cop would have recognized. She couldn't have read the graffiti as most of it was in the Gaelic that had come into fashion with street toughs when he'd been a boy. But she'd have understood the meaning where it smeared the pocked sides of buildings, and have understood the faces of the men who loitered in doorways.

Here a child would learn how to pinch a wallet from an unguarded pocket before he learned to read. And that child would be put to bed at night more often with a backhand rather than a kiss.

He knew this street, too. It had spawned him.

"She's irritated with me," Roarke said at length. "Hell, she's right pissed, and I deserve it. But I couldn't have her with me for this, Bri. I'll kill him if it comes to it. I couldn't have her in the middle of that."

"Well now, how could you? No place for a wife or a cop, is it?"

It wasn't. No, it wasn't. But if he dealt death today, he'd have to tell her of it. And he wasn't sure what it would do to what they'd become. He wasn't sure if she would ever look at him the same way again.

They went inside one of the ugly concrete boxes on the

hard edge of the district. The stink of urine took him back
to his own childhood. The sharp sting of it, the softer stench
of vomit. It was the kind of place where rats didn't wait until
dark to come hunting, and where violence was so thick it
clogged the corners like greased grime.

Roarke looked toward the stairs. There were twenty units
in the building, he knew, twelve of them officially occupied,
with squatters in some of the rest. Few who lived in such a
place worked by day, so there was likely forty or fifty people
at home or within earshot of a shout.

He doubted any would interfere. In such circumstances,
people minded their own, unless it was to their advantage to
do otherwise.

He had money in his pocket along with the blaster, and
would use whichever came most easily into play to convince
anyone who needed convincing that he was conducting private business.

"Ground floor for Grogin," Roarke said. "Easy in and
out."

"You want me to go outside, round to the window in case
he gets past you?"

"He won't get past me." Roarke knocked, then stepped to
the side so Brian was in view of the Judas hole.

"What the fucking hell do you want?"

"A moment of your time, if you will, Mr. Grogin. I have
a business opportunity I believe could be mutually profitable
for both of us."

"Is that so?" There was a snorting laugh. "Well then,
come right into my office."

He opened the door, and Roarke stepped through.

The man looked old. Not so old as O'Leary, but much
more used. His face hung in sags at the jaw, and his cheeks
were an explosion of broken blood vessels. But his reflexes
remained sharp. A knife appeared in his hand, a hand that
moved as quick and smooth as a magician's. But even as he
started to sneer his eyes widened on Roarke's face.

"You're dead. Saw you myself. How'd you climb out of
hell, Paddy?"

"Wrong Roarke." Roarke bared his teeth. And rammed his fist into Grogin's face.

He had the knife in his own hand now, and crouching, held it to Grogin's throat before Brian could finish shutting the door.

Not a soul had stirred into the hallway beyond.

"Still as quick as ever you were," Brian said.

"What's this about? What the fucking hell is this about?"

"Remember me, Mr. Grogin, sir?" Roarke spoke softly, a voice smooth as satin as he let Grogin feel the point of the blade. "You used to backhand me for sport."

"Paddy's boy." He licked his lips. "Now, come, you're not holding a grudge all these years, are ya? A boy needs the back of a hand from time to time to help him grow to a man. I never meant you any harm."

Roarke nicked Grogin, just under the jaw. "Let's say I don't mean you any more harm now then you meant me then. I'm going to ask you some questions. If I don't like your answers, I'm going to slit your throat and leave you for the rats. But I'll let Brian have a go at you first."

Smiling cheerfully, Brian took the sap out of his pocket, slapped it on his palm. "You knocked me about plenty as well. I'd like a bit of my own back, so I wouldn't mind if your answers don't suit my mate here."

"I don't have anything." Grogin's eye ticked back and forth, from face to face. "I don't know anything."

"Better hope you do." Roarke hauled him up, heaved him toward a filthy sofa. "You can try it," he said, kicking a chair around when Grogin's eyes flicked toward the rear window. "We'll be on you like jackals, of course. But I'll just hunt up someone else for the answers I need."

"What do you want?" he whined. "There's no need for all this, lad. Why, I'm practically an uncle to you."

"You're nothing to me but a bad memory." Sitting down, Roarke ran the tip of the knife over his thumb, watched the thin line of blood bead. "Keep it honed, I see. That's fine. I'll start with your balls, if you've still got them. Siobahn Brody."

Grogin's gaze stayed locked on the knife. "What?"

"You'd best remember the name, if you want to live so long as another hour. Siobahn Brody. Young and pretty, fresh. Red-haired, green-eyed."

"Lad, now be reasonable. How many young girls such as that might I have known in my life?"

"I'm only interested in this one." Stone-faced, Roarke sucked blood from his thumb. "The one who lived with him more than two years. The one he planted a child in, and she gave birth to me. Ah there now." Roarke nodded as he saw Grogin's pupils widen. "That's stirred the juices some."

"I don't know what you're talking about."

Before Brian could move in, Roarke simply reached over, and snapped the bone in Grogin's index finger. "There's one for Siobahn. I'm told he broke three of hers, so I've two more to even that score."

Grogin went deathly white and let out a long, thin scream.

"I'm feeling superfluous here," Brian complained and settled himself on the ratty arm of the sofa.

"He beat her," Roarke said flatly. "Blackened her eyes, broke her bones. She was all of nineteen. He let you have a go at her, Grogin? Or did he keep her to himself?"

"I never laid a hand on her. Not a hand." Tears leaked from Grogin's eyes as he cradled his injured hand. "She was Patrick's woman. Nothing to do with me."

"You knew he beat her."

"A man, well, a man's liable to need to teach his woman a lesson now and then. Paddy, he had a heavy hand, you've cause to know yourself. It's not my doing."

"She left him for a while, took me and left him."

"I can't say." He jerked when Roarke leaned forward again, and yelping, cupped his hands at his own throat. "For God's sake, have pity. It wasn't me! How am I to know what went on behind Patrick's door? I didn't live in the man's pocket, for Christ's sake."

"Brian," Roarke said smoothly. "Have a go here."

"All right, all right!" Grogin was shouting before Brian so much as shifted his weight. "She might've gone off for a bit. Seems I recall him saying something."

When Roarke's hand snaked out, took a hold of Grogin's

wrist, the man curled into a ball, weeping as his bladder let go. "Yes! I'll tell you. She took off with you, and he was mad to get her back. A woman didn't walk out on a man, take his son that way. Had to be shown her place, you know? Had to be disciplined, so he said. She came back."

"And was shown her place?"

"I don't know what happened." Grogin began to sob now, fat tears, snotty sobs. "Could I have a drink? God's pity, let me have a drink. My hand's broken."

"One bleeding finger, and he's crying like a lass." On a huff of disgust, Brian heaved himself up and fetched the bottle of whiskey from a table, poured some into a cloudy glass.

"Here then. Fucking *slainte* to you."

Wrapping his good hand around it, Grogin brought the glass to his lips, gulped down the whiskey. "He's dead now, you know. Paddy's dead, so what does it matter? It's him that done it," he said to Roarke. "You know how he was."

"Aye. I know just how he was."

"And this night, well, he was drunk when he called me. Stinking. I heard the boy—heard you wailing away in the background, and him saying I was to come straight away, to cop a car and come. Well, you did what Paddy said you were to do in those days. You did it or you paid dear. So I boosted a car and came straight away. When I got there . . . I had nothing to do with it. I can't be blamed for it."

"When you got there?"

"Another drink, then? Just to ease my throat."

"Tell me the rest," Roarke demanded. "Or you won't have a throat to ease."

Grogin's breath wheezed. "She was dead already. Dead when I got there. It was a bloody mess. He'd gone crazy on her, and there was nothing to be done about it. Nothing I could've done. I thought he'd killed you, too, as you were quiet. But he'd given you something to put you to sleep, a bit of a tranq, is all. You were on the couch sleeping. He'd called Jimmy, too. Jimmy Bennigan."

"Give him another drink, Bri."

"Thanks for that." Grogin held out his glass. "So you see,

you understand, the deed was done when I got there."

"What did you do with her? You and Jimmy and the one who murdered her."

"We, ah, we rolled her up in the rug, and carried her out to the car." He gulped at the whiskey, licked his lips. "As Paddy said. We drove along the river, as far as we could. We weighed the body down with stones, and dumped her in. There was nothing else to be done. She was dead, after all."

"And then?"

"We went back and cleaned things up, in case, and we put 'round that she'd dumped the boy and taken off. And how if anyone spoke of it, of her, they'd pay. No one lived in the neighborhood that wasn't scared of Roarke. He got Meg to come back, don't know how. Paid her I think, promised her more. And called her your mam, so everyone did."

He swiped his good hand under his dripping nose. "He could've killed you as well. Nothing to it. Bashed your brains in, smothered you."

"Why didn't he?"

"You had his face, didn't you?" Grogin continued. "Spitting image. A man wants a legacy, doesn't he? A man wants a son. If you'd been a girl, he might have tossed you in the river with your mam, but a man wants a son."

Roarke got to his feet, and whatever was on his face had Grogin cringing back. "His pocket cops went along with it?"

"Wasn't nothing to them, was it?"

"No, it was nothing to them." Just a girl, beaten to death and tossed aside. "They came looking for her, her family, some time after. Her brother, I'm told, was set on and laid into. Who'd have done that?"

"Ah . . . Of course, Paddy would've wanted to see to that matter himself."

A lie, Roarke thought. "As I recall, that was the sort of petty business he had you for."

In a lightning flash, Roarke had the man's head jerked back by a hank of dirty hair. And the knife at his throat.

"How do I know?" Spittle slid out of Grogin's trembling lips. "For pity, how do I know? I bashed heads for him. Too many to count. You can't do me for it now. You can't. It was years back."

One easy move of the wrist, Roarke thought. That was all it would take to have the man's blood flooding out on his hands. He could feel his own muscles trembling for that single, simple action.

He could hear ugly shouting on the street. A brawl brewing. He could smell Grogin's terror in stale sweat, fresh blood, in the urine spreading a new stain over the crotch of his pants. For a heartbeat, for eternity, the keen edge of the blade bit against flesh. Then he stepped back, slid the knife into his boot.

"You're not worth killing."

They left Grogin sitting in his own piss and sobbing.

"There was a time," Brian said as they walked, "back in the day, when you'd have done more than break his finger."

"There was a time." Roarke fisted his hand, imagined the satisfaction of pummelling it, again and again, into Grogin's face. "Not worth it, as I said. He was nothing but Patrick Roarke's pet cur. Still, he'll wonder for a while, a long while, if I might come back and do more. And that'll keep him cold at night."

"You knew already most of what he told you."

"I had to hear it said." It was cooler in Dublin than in New York. And he could see the river. The River Liffey, with its lovely bridges shining in the summer sun. The river where they'd tossed the broken shell of her. "I had to see it, how it was, before I can go on to the next."

"What's the next?"

"She had family. They're in Clare. They need to be told what happened to her, and why. Oh, Christ, Brian. I need to go and tell them, but I need a night's drunk first."

"You've come to the right place." Brian draped an arm over Roarke's shoulder, steered him away from the river. "You'll come home and stay with me tonight."

Chapter 15

It was probably cowardice, but Eve wasn't going to worry about it.

"We need to sort through all these interviews, coordinate the time lines, run these names." She checked her wrist unit as if concerned with the time. "We're coming up on end of shift. I'll run you by your place so you can pick up what you need. It'll be easier to work out of my home office, and bring the rest of the team in there in the morning."

"You want me to spend the night at your place?"

"It'll be easier."

"Uh-huh." Peabody folded her hands neatly in her lap while Eve drove out of Columbia's parking port. "One of the things I need to pick up is McNab."

"Fine."

"Fine," Peabody echoed, pressing her lips together to hold back a grin. "So that means both of us will be bunking at your place."

Eve stared straight ahead. "We need to put in some time on this, so it'll be easier this way."

"And you'll have a Summerset buffer."

"What's your point?"

"You have less trouble with the idea of me and McNab

bouncing on the gel bed in the guest room than you do with dealing one-on-one with Summerset. It's kind of sweet."

"Don't make me stop this vehicle, Peabody."

"Did you have a chance to ask Roarke if he's got any apartments up for grabs?"

"No. He's been busy. He's got stuff on his mind."

Peabody sobered. "So I gathered. Dallas, is he in trouble?"

"Yeah. It's a big mess, personal mess. He's working it out. It's a family thing."

"I didn't think he had any family."

"Neither did he." She couldn't talk about it. Didn't know how to talk about it. Didn't know if she was supposed to talk about it. "He'll work it out. He'll be back in a couple of days."

Meanwhile you're off, Peabody thought, because he's off. "McNab and I can hang at your place until he's back if you want."

"Let's take it a day at a time."

She didn't complain about waiting while Peabody packed a bag. Instead, she sat in her vehicle and began streamlining her notes into a report. She didn't complain about swinging by Central to pick up McNab. Anything was better than going home alone.

So it had come to that, she thought, tuning out the chatter Peabody and McNab insisted on making. She didn't want to go home alone. A couple of years before she'd have thought nothing of it. In fact, she'd have preferred it. Closing herself into her own space and spending the bulk of any evening on her caseload.

Of course, she hadn't had Summerset hovering around somewhere. Broken leg or not, he was still in the house. Still breathing the same air as she was.

But that wasn't the whole reason she was dragging Peabody and McNab home with her. She wanted the company, the noise, the distraction. Something, anything, to keep her mind focused on the work so she'd stop worrying about Roarke for a while.

Where the hell was he now, and what was he doing?

Deliberately, she blocked that train of thought and tuned back in to the conversation.

"Crimson Rocket is totally juiced," McNab claimed. "They're completely iced."

"Oh please. They blow."

"You don't jive with rocking tunes, She-Body. Catch this."

He turned on his pocket player and had something screaming out. It sounded, to Eve's ear, like a train wreck. "Off!" she ordered. "Turn that shit off."

"You gotta give it a chance, Dallas. Open up to the energy and irony."

"Two seconds, and I'm opening up the window and throwing you and your energy out on the street."

Peabody's face settled into smug lines. "Told you they suck."

"You've got no musical taste."

"You don't."

"You don't."

Eve hunched her shoulders, trying to lift them over her ears. "What have I done?" she asked herself as she drove through the gates of home. "What have I done?"

They argued all the way up the drive, taking jabs at each other's musical preference with terms like Free-Ager pap, and retro-rock ripoff. She slammed on the brakes, all but leaped out of the car to escape it, but they were right behind her, bickering their way to the door.

"Go. Go back there." Eve stabbed a finger in the general direction of Summerset's quarters. "Take the insanity back there. Maybe his head will explode, and I'll have one less problem. Visit the patient, argue until your tongues turn black and fall out, have dinner, have monkey sex. Go away."

"But, sir, you wanted to work on the case," Peabody reminded her.

"I don't want to see either of you for an hour. One full hour. I must have gone mad," she mumbled as she started upstairs. "I went mad and didn't know it, and now I need a nice, quiet padded room."

"What's with her?" McNab wanted to know.

"Roarke's got some problems. It messes her up. Let's go back and see how Summerset's doing. Crimson Rocket still blows," she added.

"Man, how can I be in love with a woman who doesn't recognize true musical genius?" He gave her butt a squeeze. "Oh yeah, that's one reason." He leaned down to her ear. "Think we can fit Summerset, chow, and monkey sex into an hour?"

"Bet we can."

Eve went directly to her office, directly to the kitchen, directly to the AutoChef. "Coffee. Coffee will keep me sane." She ordered a pot, considered drinking it straight down where she stood, but restrained herself. Taking it and a mug to her desk she sat, poured. Took a long, long breath.

"Computer on." She sat back and sipped the first mug. Cleared her head. "Dallas, Lieutenant Eve, primary, case numbers H-23987 and H-23992 connected. Additional notes. Connection between victims Howard and Sulu is established through various witness statements. Both frequented Make The Scene data club, and had interaction there. Both were photographed by Hastings. Connection between Hastings and Browning, one of Howard's professors, one of the last people to see Howard alive, established. They know each other professionally and personally. Through her recommendation some of Browning's students have served as photographic assistants for Hastings, giving them access to his files, and the images of the victims removed from said files. Browning also had access when escorting classes to Hastings's studio for workshops."

She let that stand while she turned the known facts over in her head. "Browning's alibi is loose and verified by her spouse. Suspect has capability to manipulate security discs. EDD will study discs for any sign of tampering.

"It's not her," Eve said quietly. "Just doesn't fit, but you've got to do what you've got to do. Considering Angela Brightstar, Browning's spouse. Loose alibi also applies, giving her means and opportunity. Motive? Jealousy and/or artistic expression."

She picked up her coffee so she could pace and drink.

"Computer, run probability. Given method of crimes and current profile, is perpetrator of the same age bracket as victims?"

WORKING . . . WITH KNOWN DATA, PROBABILITY PERPETRATOR AND VICTIMS SHARE AGE BRACKET—18 TO 22—IS THIRTY-TWO POINT TWO PERCENT.

"Yeah, that's my take. Not impossible we've got a kid working here, some twisted wunderkind with a lot of patience, but it feels more adult.

"Computer, run list noted in casefile of Hastings's assistants. Give me the age span."

WORKING . . . AGE SPAN IS 18 TO 32.

"Okay, display, wall screen, all names from age 25 up."

WORKING . . . DISPLAY ON.

She scanned them, saw two of the names Peabody had listed as bogus. "All right, Brady, Adams, Olsen, Luis Javert. Cross check those names with students sent to Hastings from Browning. Search for match with family names, street addresses. Also run combinations. Run combinations for match to photographic or imaging artists of any note."

WORKING . . . ESTIMATED TIME TO COMPLETE ALL TASKS IS TWENTY-THREE POINT FIVE MINUTES.

"Whatever. Switch display to map on file while working.

SWITCHING DISPLAY . . .

She moved forward, studying the routes and locations she'd already highlighted. Nothing matched the names she was running. In her mind, she ran those routes, trying to see what he'd seen.

"Where do you work?" she queried aloud. "Where do you

store your vehicle? Who are you? *Why* are you?"

Light, she thought. Light equals energy, life. Light equals soul. There's no image without light. No life without light.

Something stirred in her brain. She tilted her head as if to bring it to the surface.

And her 'link beeped.

"Damn it." She crossed over to answer. "Dallas."

"There she is. Hello, darlin'."

"Roarke." Every other thought flew out of her head, slapped away by love and worry. "Where are you?"

"In Dublin's fair city." He grinned at her.

"Are you . . . Are you *drunk*?"

"Well and truly pissed, that I am. We're well into the second bottle now. Or maybe it's the third. Who's counting?"

"Who's we?"

"Me and my old boyhood mate, Brian Kelly. He sends all his love and devotion."

"Right." They'd gotten plowed before, foolishly buzzed on wine while on holiday. But she'd never seen Roarke stupidly drunk. His beautiful eyes were blurry, and his wonderful voice so thick with Ireland and slurred from drink, she could barely understand him. "You're at the Penny Pig."

"We're not, no. I don't believe. No," he verified after glancing around. "Don't appear to be in the pub. This much whiskey deserves a more private setting. We're drunk in Bri's flat. Come quite some ways from the shanties, Bri has. Nice cozy flat here. That's him you hear singing now about Molly Malone."

"Uh-huh." So he was safe then, she thought, and wouldn't go stumbling out of the pub and in front of a maxibus. "I guess it's after midnight there. You should go lie down now, get some sleep."

"Not ready to sleep, don't want the dreams. You'd understand that, wouldn't you, my one true love?"

"Yeah, I would. Roarke—"

"Found out some things today that I don't want to think about quite yet. Drowning them for the night. Found out some things from one of my father's old mates. Bastard. Didn't kill him, you'll be pleased to know. But I wanted to."

"Don't go anywhere tonight. Promise me you'll stay in Brian's flat. Drink yourself unconscious, but don't go anywhere."

"Not going anywhere till tomorrow. Heading west tomorrow."

"West?" She got an image of cattle ranches and mountains and long, empty fields. "Where? What, Montana?"

He laughed until she thought he'd burst. "Christ, is it any wonder I'm besotted with you? West in Ireland, my darling, darling Eve. I'm bound for Clare tomorrow. Odds are they'll kill me the minute they see my face—his face. But it has to be done."

"Roarke, why don't you stay with Brian another day. Let things settle down some. Then . . . What the hell was that?" she demanded when she heard a violent crash.

"Ah, Brian's down, and appears to have taken a table and lamp with him. Passed out flat on his face, poor sod. I'd best go try to haul his ass up and into bed. I'll ring you up tomorrow. See that you take care of my cop. I can't live without her."

"Take care of my drunk Irishman. I can't live without him either."

He blinked those blurry eyes in confusion. "What, Brian?"

"No, you idiot. You."

"Oh." He grinned at her again, so foolishly her throat burned. "That's good then. Makes us even. 'Night now."

"Good night." She stared at the blank screen, wishing she could just reach through it and haul him back to where he belonged.

The computer was just detailing her matches when Peabody and McNab strolled in. "Summerset's fine," Peabody told her. "He gets the skin cast off tomorrow and can start walking for short periods."

"Picture me doing handsprings. Matthew Brady, Ansel Adams, Jimmy Olsen, Luis Javert. Who are these guys?"

"Jimmy Olsen, cub reporter, the *Daily Planet*," McNab supplied.

"You know him?"

"Superman, Dallas. You've got to get more exposure to pop culture. Comics, graphic novels, vids, games, toys. See, Superman's this superhero from the planet Krypton who's sent to Earth as a baby, and—"

"Just the highlights, McNab."

"He disguises himself as mild-mannered reporter Clark Kent and comes to Metropolis to work at the *Daily Planet*, a newspaper. Jimmy Olsen's one of the characters, a young reporter and photographer."

"Photographer, check. And the other two?"

McNab shrugged his bony shoulders. "Got me."

"Ansel Adams was a photographer," Peabody supplied. "My father's got some of his prints. Nature stuff, powerful."

"And Matthew Brady." She went to the computer for that one. "Another photographer. Three for three. No other matches in family names, street address. And behind door number two?"

Her eyes went flat and hard. "We've got a winner. Not Luis but Henri Javert, photographer, primarily known for his portraits of the dead. Came to popularity early this century in Paris. Though Shadow Imagery, as this art form was termed, went quickly out of fashion, his work is considered the best of the style. Examples of his work can be viewed at the Louvre in Paris, the Image Museum in London, and the International Center of Photography in New York.

"McNab, get me everything you can on Henri Javert."

"On it."

"Peabody, there's a couple dozen matches here for Luis. Trim it down. Children," she said with a fierce grin, "we've got his scent."

She worked until she thought her eyes would bleed, worked long after she'd sent Peabody and McNab off to do whatever they were going to do on the gel bed.

When her thoughts began to blur as well as her vision, she crawled into the sleep chair for a few hours down. She didn't want another night alone in the big bed.

And still the dreams found her, and tugged her with icy hands from exhaustion to nightmare.

The room was familiar. Terrifyingly so. That hideous room in Dallas where the air was brutally cold and the light was washed with dirty red. She knew it was a dream and fought to will herself out of it. But she could already smell the blood—on her hands, on the knife clutched in them, splattered on the floor, seeping out of him.

She could smell his death, and the vision of it—of what she'd done, what she'd become to save herself—was etched on her mind.

Her arm screamed with pain. The child's arm in the dream, the woman's who was trapped in it. It was burning hot where he'd snapped the bone, burning cold up to the shoulder, down to the fingertips that dripped with red.

She would wash it off. That's what she had done then, that's what she would do now. Wash off the blood, wash away the death in the cold water.

She moved slowly, like an old woman, wincing at the sting between her legs, blocking out the reason for it.

It smelled metallic—the water, the blood—how could she know? She was only eight.

He'd beaten her again. He'd come home, not quite drunk enough to leave her be. So he'd beaten her again, raped her again, broken her again. But this time she'd stopped him.

The knife had stopped him.

She could go now, away from the cold, away from this room, away from him.

"You never get away, and you know it."

She looked up. There was a mirror over the sink. She could see her face in it—thin, white, eyes dark with shock and pain—and the face behind it.

So beautiful, with those magic blue eyes, the silky black hair, that full mouth. Like a picture in a book.

Roarke. She knew him. She loved him. He'd come with her to Dallas, and now he'd take her away. When she turned to him she wasn't a child anymore, but a woman. And still, the man who'd been her father lay bloody between them.

"I don't want to stay here. I need to go home now. I'm so glad you're here to take me home."

"You've done Richie in, haven't you?"

"He hurt me. He wouldn't stop hurting me."

"Well now, a father has to hurt the child now and again to teach them some respect." He crouched, and taking a grip on her father's hair, lifted the head to examine it. "I knew him, you know. Wheeled some deals. We're two of a kind."

"No, you're nothing like him. You never met him."

Those blue eyes sparked with something that made her stomach clutch like a fist. "I don't like being called a liar by a woman."

"Roarke—"

He picked up the knife, rose slowly. "You've got the wrong Roarke. I'm Patrick Roarke." Smiling, smiling, he turned the knife in his hand as he stepped toward her. "And I think it's time you learned a little respect for fatherhood."

She woke with the scream trapped in her throat, and sweat pouring off her like blood.

By the time her team arrived, she was steady. Bad dreams, worries about Roarke, even the conversation she knew she needed to have with Summerset were all locked away.

"We're looking for this Luis Javert, listed as Hastings's assistant during the period in January the photographs of Rachel Howard were taken at a wedding. Going off profile, we're going to assume he's between twenty-five and sixty years of age. Highly functional, artistic, intelligent. Odds are he lives alone and owns or has access to imaging equipment. I'm saying owns. These are his tools, his work, his art.

"Feeney, I want you to work Browning on this angle. The name doesn't appear on her list of students sent to Hastings, but he might have changed it. I'm banking that he studied under her, and that she covered Javert in some of the class-work at one time or another. She's tired of looking at me at this point, and maybe a fresh face will jog something loose."

"First time I've been called a fresh face in two decades." Feeney munched on a danish.

"McNab, I want you at Columbia. Work on students, play up the Javert angle. Who's interested in that kind of work."

"Cops are." His mouth was full of scrambled eggs. "Homicide cops are always photographing the dead."

"They don't generally take pictures of them before they're dead."

"How about doctors?" He scooped up bacon. "They take imaging records of patients, right? Then there's the before and after records. Mostly it's to cover their asses in case somebody decides to sue, but—"

"You may not be as stupid as you look." Eve snitched one of his slices of bacon. "Hard to believe, but you may not be. Light. Energy, health, vitality. I was playing with it last night, and got distracted. Maybe our boy's sick. What if he's convinced himself that by absorbing vital life through photography, he can be cured?"

"It's out there."

"Yeah, well, so is he. Peabody and I will follow this up. Baxter and Trueheart stick with the clubs."

"It's a tough job." Baxter drained his coffee. "Hanging out in clubs, watching all the nubile young bodies." He winked at Trueheart. "Right, kid."

Trueheart's blush turned his young, smooth face rosy pink. "There's a lot going on there. The dancing, the music, the bar scene, the data flood."

"He got hit on three times," Baxter added. "Two were girls."

"Talk photography," Eve told him. "Bone up some on this Henri Javert and work the conversation around to him when you're being hit on."

"It wasn't like that, Lieutenant. They were just talking to me."

"I love this guy." Baxter wiped an imaginary tear away. "Just fucking love him."

"If Baxter hits on you, Trueheart, you have permission to kick his ass. Moving on. Memorial service this evening for Rachel Howard. Baxter and Trueheart will be dancing among the nubiles, but I want the rest of us there. Our boy may show. Let's move out. Peabody, I have a personal matter to deal with downstairs. Be ready in ten."

Eve went downstairs, and found Summerset in the middle of a fight with the PA.

"If you want the cast off, you will cooperate and let me transport you to the health center. You require a doctor's authorization and supervision for its removal."

"I can have this irritant off in two minutes. Move aside." He started to haul himself up. She shoved him back down.

Fascinated, Eve watched the show. "Madam, I have yet to strike a woman, despite considerable provocation. You are about to be my first."

"You piss him off even more than I do," Eve commented and had two furious faces turning toward her. "I think we may have to keep you."

"I expect some cooperation," Spence began, lifting her chin so high her curls bounced.

"I will not have this person drag me to a health center for a simple procedure."

"It requires a doctor."

"Then bring the doctor here," Eve suggested. "And get it done."

"I'm hardly going to request a doctor make a home call for something as minor as a skin cast removal."

"If it's so minor, why do we need a doctor?"

"Ah!" Summerset raised one long, bony finger. "Exactly."

"I bet I can zap it off with my weapon." Thoughtfully, Eve drew it. "Why don't you stand back, Spence, and I'll just—"

"Put that thing away," Summerset snapped. "You lunatic."

"Might've been fun." With a shrug, Eve holstered it. "Tag the doctor," she ordered Spence. "Tell him Roarke wants him to come here and remove the cast, and do whatever the hell else is necessary to get this pain in my ass on his feet, and out of the house."

"I fail to see why—"

"You're not required to see, you're required to do it. If the doctor has a problem with this," Eve added, "he can speak to me."

Spence huffed off, and Eve stuck her hands in her pockets. "Sooner you're on your feet, sooner you're on vacation somewhere that's not here. And I can start turning cartwheels."

"Nothing would please me more."

With a nod, she nudged at Galahad who left Summerset's lap long enough to wind around her feet. "Roarke called last night. From Brian Kelly's place in Dublin. He was drunk. Seriously drunk."

"Playfully so, or dangerously so?"

"The first mostly. I guess." Frustrated, she dragged a hand through her hair. "But not in control of himself, and that's dangerous enough. He said something about getting some information out of one of his father's old friends. You know who that might be?"

"I didn't know Patrick Roarke well. I tended to avoid him, and his like. I had a child to look after." He paused a moment. "For a time, I had two to look after."

She said nothing to that. There was nothing to be said. "He said he's going to Clare today. That's in the west. That's where she was from, his mother. He's not looking for a warm welcome."

"If they blame him, it's their loss. The father couldn't break the child, nor could he turn the child into a monster. Though he tried." He studied Eve, and wondered if she understood he wasn't referring only to Roarke now.

But her eyes showed him nothing as she stepped forward, leaned down, spoke quietly. "Did you kill Patrick Roarke?"

Like hers, his face stayed blank. "There is no statute of limitations on murder."

"It's not the cop who's asking you."

"I had children to protect."

She let out a short breath. "Roarke doesn't know, does he? You never told him."

"There's nothing to tell. That's old business, Lieutenant. Shouldn't you be off, taking care of new?"

Their eyes held another moment. "Yeah." She straightened, turned. "Just remember, you won't be sitting around on your flat ass much longer, and this house will be Summerset-free for three glorious weeks."

He smirked, then lifted a hand to stroke down Galahad's back when the cat leaped back into his lap. "I believe she'll miss me."

Chapter 16

When you had connections, you used them. Doctors, as a breed, were one of Eve's least favorite species, yet somehow she'd managed to develop personal relationships with two of them.

For this line of the investigation, she'd tug on Louise Dimatto.

Knowing Louise's scattershot schedule, she tagged her by 'link first, pinned down her location, then wheedled an appointment.

The Canal Street Clinic was Louise's baby. She might have gone against her family's uptown grain to establish and run a free clinic on the verges of Sidewalk City where sidewalk sleepers made their beds in packing crates and unlicensed beggars trolled for marks, but she'd dug in with her manicured fingers.

She'd put her own time and money on the line, and then had launched a campaign to drag more time, more money from every source at her disposal. Louise, Eve knew, had a lot of sources.

She'd ended up being one herself. Or more accurately, Roarke had, she thought as she double-parked beside an ancient, rusted two-seater that had been stripped of its tires, seats, and one of its doors. It was his money, even if the sneaky bastard had dumped it into her account.

Whatever the sources, it was money well spent. The clinic was a steady beam of light in a very dark world.

The building was unimposing, unless you considered the fact it was the only one on the block with windows that were clean, and walls that were graffiti-free.

Across the street a funky-junkie wearing thick black sunshades sat with her muscles jerking to whatever tune she crooned. A couple of badasses stood hip-shot in a doorway looking for trouble that was never far away in this sector.

Behind their riot bars most of the upper-story windows were thrown open in the doomed hope that a lost breeze might stumble in on its way uptown. Out of them vomited the wail of babies, the burn of trash rock, and voices already raised in petty furies.

Gauging her ground, Eve flipped on her On Duty sign, then strolled over to the badasses. They straightened and fixed appropriate sneers on their tough guy faces.

"You know Dr. Dimatto?"

"Everybody knows the doc. Whatiz to you?"

"Anybody comes around here to hassle the doc," his companion warned, "they gonna *get* hassled."

"Good to know, because the doc's a friend of mine. I'm going in to talk with her. See that police vehicle?"

One of them snorted. "Piece of shit cop car."

"My piece of shit cop car," Eve acknowledged. "I want it in the same shitty condition it is now when I come out. If it's not, well, the hassling will begin, starting with each of you fine gentlemen. Clear?"

"Ooh, Rico, I'm shaking." The first elbowed the second as he cracked up. "This skinny girl cop here, she's gonna slap my face if somebody pisses on her tires."

"I prefer the term 'bitch cop from hell.' Isn't that right, Peabody?"

"Yes, sir," Peabody called back from her stance by the vehicle. "It is absolutely correct."

With her eyes shifting from one badass face to the other, Eve asked, "And why is that, Peabody?"

"Because, sir, you're so damn mean. And rather than slap someone's face for relieving his bladder on your official tires, you are more likely to twist off said reliever's balls, then use them to strangle him."

"Yes. Yes, I am. And what would I do then, Peabody?"

"Then, sir? Then you would laugh."

"I haven't had a good laugh today, so keep that in mind." Satisfied her vehicle would remain untouched, Eve sauntered back across the street and into the clinic.

"The laugh was a good touch, Peabody."

"Thanks. I thought it added just the right tone. Boy." She scanned the waiting area. It was full, jammed with people in varying forms of distress. A good many of them made the badasses across the street look like boy scouts, but they sat, and they waited.

The room was clean. Fresh paint, spotless rug, thriving plants. A portion was sectioned off and held child-sized chairs and toys. In it she saw a boy of about four rhythmically bashing a boy of about two over the head with a foam mallet. He punctuated each bash with a cheerful: "Bang!"

"Shouldn't somebody make him stop doing that?" Eve wondered.

"Huh? Oh, no sir. He's just doing his job. Older siblings have to beat on younger ones. Zeke used to just about drill a hole in my ribs with his finger. I really miss him."

"Whatever." Baffled, Eve walked to the reception desk.

They were shown into Louise's office. However much the clinic had evolved, Louise's space was still small, still cramped. The clinic's benefactors needn't worry that the doctor was using their contributions to plump her own work nest.

Eve used the wait time to check on any voice or e-mail that had come into her unit at Central, stewing when she found one, very brief transmission from Roarke.

Louise dashed in, a pale green lab coat over jeans and a white T-shirt. Something that looked like curdled milk dribbled down the breast of the lab coat.

"Hi, gang. Coffee! I've got ten minutes. Spill it."

"You've already spilled it." Eve gestured to the dribble.

"Oh, I'm running peds today. Just a little baby puke."

"Oh. Bleck."

With a chuckle, Louise grabbed coffee from the Auto-Chef. "I imagine you come home some days with a lot more interesting bodily fluids on your clothes than a little harmless baby puke. So?" She sat on the edge of the desk, then sighed. "Ah, I'm off my feet. Feels almost better than sex. What can I do for you?"

"Are you up on the story about the two murdered college kids?"

"I've caught the media reports. Nadine's particularly." She blew on her coffee, drank. "Why?"

"I'm working on a theory that the individual who killed them may be sick, even dying. Some disease, some condition."

"Why?"

"It's a complicated theory."

"I've got ten minutes." She dug in her lab coat pocket and came up with a red lollipop to go with her coffee. "You'll have to simplify it."

"There's an old superstition about absorbing the soul through the camera. I think he may be taking it to another level. He talks about their light—pure light. And how they belong to him now. It could be reaching, but what if he thinks he needs their light to live?"

"Mmm." Louise sucked on the lollipop. "Interesting."

"If he does, then it may follow he got some bad news regarding his life expectancy at some point. Don't you guys call tumors and masses, the bad stuff, shadows?"

"A tumor, a mass, would show as a kind of shadow—a dark spot—on an X ray or ultrasound."

"Those are like images, right? Like pictures?"

"Yes, exactly. I see where you're going, but I'm not sure how I can help."

"You know doctors, and they know other doctors. You know hospitals and health centers. I need to know who's gotten bad news in the last twelve months. I can fine-tune that to male patients between the ages of twenty-five and sixty."

"Oh well then, piece of cake." Louise shook her head,

and drained her coffee. "Dallas, even with cancer vaccines, early diagnosis, the success rates of treatments, there are quite a number of people who fall to incurable or inoperable conditions. Add to those, the ones who for whatever reason refuse treatment—religious reasons, fear factor, stubbornness, ignorance—and you've got hundreds just in Manhattan. Maybe thousands."

"I can cull through that."

"Maybe you can, but there's one big problem. It's called doctor–patient confidentiality. I can't give you names, and neither can any other reputable doctor or health care provider."

"He's a killer, Louise."

"Yes, but the others aren't, and are entitled to their privacy. I'll ask around, but no one's going to give me names and I couldn't, in good conscience, give them to you."

Irritated, Eve paced the limited confines of the office while Louise pulled another lollipop out of her pocket and offered it to Peabody.

"Lime. Thanks."

"Sugar-free."

"Bummer," Peabody replied, but ripped off the clear wrapping.

Eve huffed out a breath, settled herself. "Tell me this. What kind of shadow is most usually a death sentence?"

"You don't ask easy ones. Assuming the patient took the recommended vaccines, went in for routine annual exams so early detection was a factor, I'd go for the brain. Providing the mass hasn't spread, we can remove, kill, or shrink most bad cells, or if necessary, replace the involved organ. We can't replace the brain. And," she added, setting her empty cup aside, "this is ridiculously hypothetical."

"Gotta start somewhere. Maybe you can talk to your brain doctor pals. The individual remains highly functional, able to plan and execute complicated acts. He's articulate and he's mobile."

"I'll do what I can. It's going to be very little. Now I've got to get back to my own front lines. By the way, I'm

thinking of having a little dinner party. Just friends. Both of
you, Roarke and McNab, me and Charles."

"Um," Eve managed.

"Sounds great. Just let us know when. How's Charles?"
Peabody added. "I haven't had a chance to talk to him in a
while."

"He's great. Busy, but who isn't. I'll be in touch."

"Hey. Give me a damn sucker."

With a laugh, Louise tossed Eve one, then bolted out of
the room.

Outside, Eve walked around her vehicle. Crouched as if
to examine the tires. Then sent the two men still in the doorway a big, toothy smile before popping the lollipop into her
mouth. She didn't speak until she and Peabody were pulling
away.

"Okay, none of my business, but why aren't you weirded
out by the idea of a cozy little dinner party with Louise and
Charles?"

"Why should I be?"

"Oh, I don't know, let me think." As if contemplating,
Eve rolled the round of candy in her mouth. Grape, she
thought. Not bad. "Could it be that at one time you were
dating Charles, and the fact that you were hanging around
with our favorite licensed companion made your current bed-
mate swing so far out of orbit he knocked Charles on his
undeniably adorable ass?"

"Kind of spices up the stew, doesn't it. Anyway, Charles,
of the undeniably adorable ass, is a friend. He loves Louise.
I like Louise. I wasn't sleeping with Charles, and even if I
had been, it shouldn't matter."

Playing mattress tag always mattered, no matter what anyone said. But Eve kept that opinion to herself. "Okay. If it
shouldn't matter, why haven't you told McNab that you and
Charles never did the mattress mambo?"

Peabody hunched her shoulders. "He acted like such a
moron."

"Peabody, McNab *is* a moron."

"Yeah, but he's my moron now. I guess I should tell him.

I hate to give him the satisfaction though. It gives him the hand."

"What hand?"

"The upper hand. See, now I have the hand because he thinks I was sleeping with Charles and I stopped sleeping with Charles because of him. McNab. But if I tell him I never did the deed with Charles anyway, I lose the hand."

"Now my head hurts. I should never have asked."

She went back to the beginning. Rachel Howard.

Carpet fibers. They'd identified the make and models of the vehicles that came standard with the type found on both victims, and the list of registered owners. Diego Feliciano's uncle's work van didn't match, nor did Hastings's.

So far, this had been a dead end, but she'd push harder against the wall.

There was the tranq. A prescription opiate, not street buzz. If her theory about the killer held, odds are it was his prescription. Something recommended to help him sleep, calm his nerves, block whatever pain he might have due to his condition.

She'd cross-check the vehicle owners with local pharmacies. Cross-check both against imaging equipment purchases over the last twelve months.

A tedious proposition, and time consuming. More so as she had to wait for the authorization to do some of the searches.

Would she have cut through that if Roarke had been around? she wondered. Would she have used him, let him talk her into involving himself in the case, let him man his far superior equipment with his far superior skill, and his habit of bypassing the standard security and privacy codes?

Probably.

But he wasn't around, so it wasn't an option. Time was weighing on her. The killer had taken two lives within a week, and he wasn't finished.

He wouldn't wait much longer to seek out the next light.

Eve began her first level of cross-checks while she waited for the authorization to go deeper. And she worried about some faceless college kid already caught in the crosshairs of a camera lens.

And she worried about Roarke, trapped in the cage of his own past.

He hadn't traveled often to the west of the country where he'd been born. Most of his business was centered in Dublin, or south in Cork, north in Belfast.

He had some property in Galway, but he'd never stepped foot on it, and had spent only a handful of days in the castle hotel he'd bought in Kerry.

Though he didn't share his wife's ingrained suspicion of the countryside, he usually preferred the city. He doubted he'd know what do to with himself for long in this place of rolling green hills and flower-strewn yards.

The pace would be too slow to suit him for more than a short holiday, but there was a piece of him that was glad it had been left much as it had been, century by century.

Green, velvet green, and quiet.

His Ireland, the one he'd fled from, had been gray, dank, mean, and bitter. This curve of Clare wasn't simply another part of the country, but a world away from what he'd known.

Farmers still farmed here, men still walked with their dogs across a field, and ruins of what had been castles and forts and towers in another age stood gray and indomitable in those fields.

Tourists, he supposed, would take pictures of those ruins, and scramble around in them—then drive for miles on the twisting roads to find more. And the locals would glance at them now and again.

There, you see, they might say, they tried to beat us down. Vikings and Brits. But they never could. They never will.

He rarely thought of his heritage, and had never held the grand and weepy sentiment of Ireland so many did whose ancestors had left those green fields behind. But driving alone now, under a sky layered with clouds that turned the light into a gleaming pearl, seeing the shadows dance over the endless roll of green and the lush red blooms of wild fuschia rise taller than a man to form hedgerows, he felt a tug.

For it was beautiful, and in a way he'd never known, it was his.

He'd flown from Dublin to Shannon to save time, and because the night's dip into whiskey had given him a miserable head. Conversely, he'd opted to drive through Clare, to *take* his time now.

What the hell was he going to say to them? Nothing that had run through his brain seemed right. He'd never be able to make it right, and could find no logical reason for trying.

He didn't know them, nor they him. Going to them now would do no more than open old wounds.

He had his family, and he had nothing in common with these strangers but a ghost.

But he could see that ghost in his mind's eye, see her walking across the fields, or standing in a yard amongst the flowers.

She hadn't left him, Roarke thought. How could he leave her?

So when the route map he'd programmed into the in-dash 'link told him to turn just before entering the village of Tulla, he turned.

The road wound through a forest, much of it new growth, no more than fifty years old. Then the trees gave way to the fields, to the hills where the sun was sliding through the clouds in a lovely, hazy way.

Cows and horses cropped, close to the fenceline. It made him smile. His cop wouldn't be pleased with the proximity of the animals, and she'd be baffled by the little old man, neatly dressed in cap and tie and white shirt, puttering toward him on a skinny tractor.

Why? she'd wonder in an aggrieved voice he could hear even now, does anyone want to do that? And when the old man lifted his hand in a wave as if they were old friends, she'd be only more puzzled.

He missed her the way he would miss one of his own limbs.

She'd have come if he'd asked her. So he hadn't asked. Couldn't. This was a part of his life that was apart from her, and needed to be. When he was done with it, he'd go back. Go home, and that would be that.

DESTINATION, the 'link informed him, ONE-HALF KIL-OMETER, ON LEFT.

"All right then," he said. "Let's do what needs to be done."

So, this was their land—his mother's land—these hills, these fields, and the cattle that grazed over them. The gray barn, the stone sheds and fences.

The stone house with its blossoming garden and white gate.

His heart tripped a little, and his mouth went dry. He wanted, more than he wanted anything, to simply drive straight by.

She'd have lived here. It was the family home, so she'd have lived here. Slept here. Eaten here. Laughed and cried here.

Oh Christ.

He forced himself to turn the car into the drive—what the locals would call the street—behind a small sedan and a well-worn truck. He could hear birdsong, and the distant bark of a dog, the vague sound of a puttering motor.

Country sounds, he noted. She'd have heard them every day of life here, until she didn't really hear them at all. Is that why she'd left? Because she'd needed to hear something new? The bright sounds of the city? The voices, the music, the traffic in the streets?

Did it matter why?

He stepped out of the car. He'd faced death more times than he could count. At times he'd fought his way around it until his hands ran with blood. He'd killed—in blood both hot and cold.

And there was nothing in his life he could remember fearing as much as he feared knocking on the bright blue door of that old stone house.

He went through the pretty white gate onto the narrow

path between banks of cheerful flowers. And standing on a short stoop, he knocked on the blue door.

When it opened, the woman stared back at him. His mother's face. Older, some thirty years older than the image that was carved into his brain. But her hair was red, with just a hint of gold, her eyes green, her skin like milk tinted with rose petals.

She barely reached his shoulder, and for some reason, that nearly broke his heart.

She was neat, in her blue pants and white shirt, and white canvas shoes. Such little feet. He took it all in, down to the tiny gold hoops in her ears, and the scent of vanilla that wafted out the door.

She was lovely, with that soft and contented look some women carried. In her hand was a red-and-white dishcloth.

He said the only words he could think of. "My name is Roarke."

"I know who you are." Her voice held a strong west county accent. Running the cloth from one hand to the other, she studied him as he studied her. "I suppose you'd best be coming in."

"I'm sorry to disturb you."

"Do you plan on disturbing me?" She stepped back. "I'm in the kitchen. There's still tea from breakfast."

Before she closed the door, she took a look at his car, lifting her brows at the dark elegance of it. "So, the claims you've money coming out of your ears, among other places, are true then."

His blood chilled, but he nodded. If they wanted money from him, he'd give them money. "I'm well set."

"Well set's a variable term, isn't it? Depending on where you're standing."

She walked back toward the kitchen, past what he assumed was the company parlor, then the family living area. The rooms were crowded with furniture and whatnots, and fresh flowers. And all as neat as she.

The table in the big family kitchen could have fit twelve, and he imagined it had. There was a huge stove that appeared to be well-used, an enormous refrigerator, miles of butter yellow counters.

The windows over the sink looked out over garden and field and hill, and there were little pots he supposed were herbs sitting on the sill. It was a working room, and a cheerful one. He could still smell breakfast in the air.

"Have a seat then, Roarke. Will you have biscuits with your tea?"

"No, thank you. I'm fine."

"Well, I will. Don't get much of a reason to eat a biscuit in the middle of the day, might as well take advantage of it when I do."

She dealt with the homey chores, and had him wondering if she was giving them both time to settle. The tea was in a plain white pot, and the biscuits she put on a pretty blue plate.

"Yours is a face I never expected to see at my door." With the chores done, she sat, chose a biscuit. "So, why have you come?"

"I thought I . . . felt I . . . Ah, well." He sipped the tea. Apparently, she hadn't given him time enough to settle. "I didn't know about you—about Siobhan—until a few days ago."

Her eyebrow lifted. "Know what?"

"That you—she—existed. I'd been told, I believed, that my mother . . . the woman I thought was my mother, had left. Left me when I was a child."

"Did you?"

"Ma'am—"

"I'm Sinead. Sinead Lannigan."

"Mrs. Lannigan, until a few days ago, I'd never heard the name Siobahn Brody. I thought my mother's name was Meg, and I don't remember her particularly well except she had a hard hand and she walked out, leaving me with him."

"Your mother, your true mother, wouldn't have left you if there'd been breath in her body."

So she knows already, he thought. Knows her sister's long dead. "I know it now. He killed her. I don't know what to say to you."

She set her cup down, very carefully. "Tell me the story as you know it now. That's what I want to hear."

He told her, while she sat in silence, watching him. And when he'd told her all he knew, she rose, filled a kettle, put it on the stove.

"I've known it, all these years. We could never prove it, of course. The police, they didn't help, didn't seem to care. She was just one more girl gone astray."

"He had a few cops in his pocket back then. One or two is all it takes when you want something covered. You could never have proved it, however you tried."

Her shoulders trembled once on a long breath, then she turned. "We tried to find you, at first. For her sake. For Siobahn. My brother, Ned, nearly died trying. They beat him half to death, left him in a Dublin alley. He had a wife, and a babe of his own. Much as it pained us, we had to let you go. I'm sorry."

He only stared, and said, very slowly. "My father killed her."

"Yes." Tears swam into her eyes. "And I hope the murdering son of a whore's burning in hell. I won't ask God to forgive me for saying it, for hoping it." Carefully, she folded the red-and-white dishcloth, then sat back down while the kettle heated for more tea.

"I felt, when I learned all this, what had happened to her, I felt you—her family—deserved to be told. That it was only right that I tell you, face-to-face. I realize it's no easier hearing it from me, maybe harder at that, but it was the only way I knew."

Watching his face, she leaned back. "Come from America, did you, for this?"

"I did, yes."

"We heard of you—your exploits, young Roarke. His father's son, I thought. An operator, a dangerous man. Heartless man. I think you may be a dangerous man, but it's not a heartless one sitting in my kitchen waiting for me to slap him for something he had no part in."

"I didn't look for her, never thought of her. I did nothing to put it right."

"What are you doing now? Sitting here with me while your tea goes cold?"

"I don't know. Christ Jesus, I don't know. Because there's nothing I *can* do."

"She loved you. We didn't hear from her much. I think he wouldn't let her, and she only managed to sneak a few calls or letters off now and then. But she loved you, heart and soul. It's right that you should grieve for her, but not that you should pay."

She rose when the kettle sputtered. "She was my twin."

"I know."

"I'd be your aunt. You have two uncles, grandparents, any number of cousins if you're interested."

"I . . . it's difficult to take it in."

"I imagine it is. Aye, I imagine it is. You have her eyes," she said quietly.

Baffled, he shook his head. "Hers were green. Her eyes were green, like yours. I saw her picture."

"Not the color, but the shape." She turned around. "The shape of your eyes is hers. And like mine, don't you see?" She stepped to him, laid a hand over his. "It seems to me that the shape of something is important, more important than the color."

When emotion stormed through him, Sinead did what came naturally. She drew his head to her breast, stroked his hair. "There now," she murmured, holding her sister's boy. "There now. She'd be glad you've come. She'd be happy you're here, at last."

Later, she took him out to where the edge of the yard met the first field. "We planted that for her." She gestured to a tall, many-branched tree. "We made no grave for her. I knew she was gone, but it didn't seem right to make a grave for her. So we planted a cherry tree. It blooms fine every spring. And when I see it bloom, it gives me some comfort."

"It's beautiful. It's a beautiful place."

"Your people are farmers, Roarke, generations back." She smiled when he looked at her. "We held on to the land, no matter what. We're stubborn, hotheaded, and we'll work till we drop. You come from that."

"I've spent years trying to shake off where I came from. Not looking back."

"You can look back on this with pride. He couldn't break you, could he? I bet he tried."

"Maybe if he hadn't tried so bloody hard I wouldn't have gotten away. I wouldn't have made myself. I'll . . . I'll plant a cherry tree back home for her."

"There's a good thought. You're a married man, aren't you, married to one of the New York guarda."

"She's my miracle," he told her. "My Eve."

His tone stirred her. "No children though."

"Not yet, no."

"Well, there's plenty of time for them yet. I've seen pictures of her, of course. I've kept tabs on you over the years. Couldn't help myself. She looks strong. I suppose she'd have to be."

"She is."

"Bring her with you next time you come. But for now, we should get you settled in."

"I'm sorry?"

"You don't expect to get away so easy, do you? You'll stay at least the night, meet the rest of your family. Give them a chance to meet you. It would mean a great deal to my parents, to my brothers," she added before he could speak.

"Mrs. Lannigan."

"That's Aunt Sinead to you."

He let out a half-laugh. "I'm out of my depth."

"Well then," she said cheerfully, and took his hand, "sink or swim, for you're about to be tossed into the deep end of the pool."

Chapter 17

She questioned over two dozen registered owners of vehicles with carpet matching the fibers found on the victims. Including a little old lady who used hers to transport other little old ladies to church on Sundays.

Eve found herself trapped inside a two-room apartment that smelled of cats and lavender sachet. She wasn't sure which was worse. She drank weak, tepid iced tea because Mrs. Ernestine Macnamara gave her no other choice.

"It's so exciting—terrible of me, but I can't help myself. So exciting to be questioned by the *police* at my age. I'm a hundred and six, you know."

And looked it, Eve thought sourly.

Ernestine was tiny and dry and colorless, as though the years had leached her. But she shuffled around the room with some energy in her faded pink slippers, shooing or cooing at cats. There appeared to be a full dozen of them, and from some of the sounds Eve heard, some were very busy making more cats.

She supposed Ernestine would be considered spry.

Her face was a tiny wrinkled ball set off by oversized teeth. Her wig—Eve hoped it was a wig—sat crookedly on top and was the color of bleached wheat. She wore some sort of tracksuit that bagged over what was left of her body.

Note to God, Eve thought: Please, if you're up there, don't let me live this long. It's too scary.

"Mrs. Macnamara—"

"Oh, you just call me Ernestine. Everybody does. Can I see your gun?"

Eve ignored Peabody's muffled snort. "We don't carry guns, Mrs. . . . Ernestine. Guns are banned. My weapon is a police issue hand laser. About your van."

"It still shoots and knocks people on their butts, whatever you call it. Is it heavy?"

"No, not really. The van, Ernestine. Your van. When's the last time you used it?"

"Sunday. Every Sunday I take a group to St. Ignatious for ten o'clock Mass. Hard for most of us to walk that far, and the buses, well, it isn't easy for people my age to remember the schedule. Anyway, it's more fun this way. I was a flower child, you know."

Eve blinked. "You were a flower?"

"Flower child." Ernestine gave a hoarse little chuckle. The sixties—the *nineteen* sixties. Then I was a New-Ager, and Free-Ager. And oh, whatever came along that looked like fun. Gone back to being a Catholic now. It's comforting."

"I'm sure. Does anyone else have access to your van?"

"Well, there's the nice boy in the parking garage. He keeps it for me. Only charges me half the going rate, too. He's a good boy."

"I'd like his name, and the name and location of the garage."

"He's Billy, and it's the place on West Eighteenth, right off Seventh. Just a block from here, so that's easy for me. I pick it up and drop it off on Sundays. Oh, and the third Wednesday of the month when we have the planning meetings for church."

"Is there anyone else who drives it or has access? A friend, a relative, a neighbor?"

"Not that I can think. My son has his own car. He lives in Utah. He's a Mormon now. And my daughter's in New Orleans, she's Wiccan. Then there's my sister, Marian, but she doesn't drive anymore. Then there's the grandchildren."

Dutifully, Eve wrote down the names—grandchildren, great-grandchildren, and God help her, the great-greats.

"Ernestine, I'd like your permission to run tests on your van."

"Oh my goodness! Do you think it could be involved in a *crime*?" Her little wrinkled face flushed with pleasure. "Wouldn't that be something?"

"Wouldn't it?" Eve agreed.

She escaped, drawing in the humid, clogged air like spring water. "I think I swallowed a hair ball," she said to Peabody.

"You've got enough cat hair on you to make a rug." Peabody brushed at her uniform pants. "Me, too. What is it with old women and cats?"

"Cats are okay. I have a cat. But if I ever start collecting them like stamps, you have permission to blast me in the heart."

"Can I get that on record, sir?"

"Shut up. Let's go talk to Billy, the good Samaritan parking attendant."

Good Samaritan, my ass, was Eve's first thought.

Billy was a long, loose-limbed black man with doe-brown eyes behind amber sunshades, and nimble feet inside five hundred dollar airboots.

The shades, the boots, and the glint of gold she noticed shining in his ears were hardly in the range of budget for a vehicle jockey in a small parking garage in Lower Manhattan.

"Miss Ernestine!" His smile lit up like Christmas morning, full of joy and innocence. "Isn't she something? I hope I get around like that when I hit her age. She's in here Sunday mornings like clockwork. Churchgoing."

"So I hear. I have her written authorization to search her van, and, if I deem it necessary, to impound it for testing."

"She wasn't in an accident." He took the authorization Eve offered. "I'd've noticed if there were any dings on the van. She drives careful."

"I'm sure she does. Where's the van?"

"I keep it down on the first level. Makes it easier for her."

And you, Eve thought, as she followed him back into the shadows and harsh lights of the garage.

"There aren't too many parking facilities with attendants in the city," she commented. "Most that do have attendants use droids."

"Nope, not too many of us left. But my uncle, he owns this one, he likes the personal touch."

"Who doesn't? Miss Ernestine mentioned that you give her a nice discount."

"We do what we can," he said cheerfully. "Nice, elderly lady. Keeps her slot year round. Gotta give her a break, you know."

"And she only uses it five times a month."

"Like clockwork."

"Tell me, Billy, how much do you make, any average month, renting out vehicles."

He stopped by a small gray van. "What's that?"

"Somebody needs a ride, they drop in and see Billy, and he fixes them up. You get the codes, pocket the fee, vehicle comes back, you put it in its slot. Owner's none the wiser, and a nice sideline for you."

"You've got no proof of something like that."

Eve leaned on the van. "You know, as soon as somebody tells me I've got no proof, it just makes me want to dig down and get it. I'm just that perverse."

He pokered up. "This van stays in this slot except on Sundays and every third Wednesday. I park and I fetch, and that's all I do."

"You're independently wealthy then, and provide this service to the community out of a spirit of altruism and benevolence. Nice boots, Bill."

"Man likes nice shoes, it's no crime."

"Uh-huh. I'm going to run tests on this van. If I find this van was used in the case I'm investigating, your ass is in a sling. It's homicide, Billy. I got two bodies so far. I'll be taking you into Interview and holding you as an accessory."

"Murder? Are you crazy?" He took a stumbling step back,

and Eve shifted to the balls of her feet in case he decided to run.

"Peabody," she said mildly, catching her aide's movement to box Billy in. "Am I crazy?"

"No, sir. Billy does have nice shoes, and appears to be in big trouble."

"I didn't kill anybody!" Billy's voice spiked. "I got a job. I pay rent. I pay *taxes*."

"And I bet when I do a run of your financials—income, outlay, and so on, I'm going to find some interesting discrepancies."

"I get good tips."

"Billy, Billy, Billy." On a windy sigh, Eve shook her head. "You're making this harder than it has to be. Peabody, call in a black-and-white. We'll need our friend here transported down to Central and held for questioning."

"I'm not going anywhere. I want a lawyer."

"Oh, you're going somewhere, Billy. But you can have a lawyer."

Eve went with instinct and called in a team of sweepers.

"You think this is the vehicle."

"Nondescript gray, no fancy touches. Who's going to notice it? It's parked and largely unused, only a good healthy walk from the data club. Quick subway ride or a longer but still healthy walk from there to the 24/7 where Rachel Howard worked. Same with Columbia. Drive it uptown to Juilliard, to Lincoln Center. Hey, you can take it out basically whenever you want. Safer than using your own, if you have one. Safer than officially renting anything. Slip friendly Billy the fee, drive off."

She stood back as the sweepers arrived and got to work. "It fits him. You don't steal a vehicle. That's makes the vehicle a target. Borrow a friend's? What if the friend mentions it to another friend? What if you run into trouble, have a fender bender? Friend's going to be pissed. But something happens to this, you just ditch it, and leave Billy holding the bag."

"But Billy knows him."

"Unlikely. Just another side customer. If he used it, he used it twice, and made certain he didn't do anything to make him memorable. He's smart," Eve continued. "And he plans. He'd scoped out Ernestine, this place, the van, Billy, well in advance. He lives or works in this sector."

She tucked her hands in her back pockets and looked toward the garage entrance, toward the street. "But he didn't kill them here. Don't piss in your own pool."

"Should I run imaging and photographic businesses in this sector?"

"Yeah." Eve replied. "We're closing in."

One of the sweepers popped out. "Getting a lot of human and feline hair, Lieutenant. And some synthetic. Plenty of prints."

"I want everything you get taken directly to Berenski at the lab. I'll clear it."

"Shouldn't take long. Vehicle's pretty clean."

"Appreciate it. Peabody." She headed back to her own vehicle, pulling out her pocket-link as she walked. "Berenski."

"Yeah, yeah, busy. Go away."

"Dickie. I've got a sweeper haul heading your way within the hour. Sucked up from what I believe is the van used to transport the vics in the two college homicides."

"Tell them to take their time. Won't get to it till tomorrow, maybe the day after."

"You get to them before end of shift, give me verification, I've got two seats, owner's box, for the Yankees. You pick the game."

He rubbed his chin with his long, long fingers. "You're not even going to argue and threaten me first. Just the bribe?"

"I'm kind of pressed for time myself, so let's just cut to it."

"Four seats."

"For four, I want the results wrapped in a pink ribbon and delivered to me within two hours—from now."

"Done. Go away."

"Dickhead," she spewed as she stuffed the 'link back in her pocket.

"How come you never offer me seats in the owner's box?" Peabody complained.

"How come my ass has only managed to plop down in one twice this season? Life's a bitch, Peabody."

Billy probably thought so as he sat in an Interview room with his prune-faced public defender and waited for Eve to question him.

She'd put him on ice for an hour, and was stalling a bit longer, waiting for Dickie to come through. While she waited, she watched Billy through the one-way glass.

"No priors," she said to Peabody. "Not on his adult record. A couple of minor brushes as a juvenile. He's careful. Slick operator."

"You don't think he's involved."

"Not directly. He's a scam artist with a nice, easy scam. His uncle probably taught it to him. I'm going to go get started on him. When Dickhead sends the lab results, bring them in."

Billy glowered at her. The PD pursed her thin lips.

"Lieutenant Dallas, you've held my client for more than an hour. Unless you're prepared to charge him—"

"Don't tempt me. I'm well under the legal time frame, so don't pull the 'poor schmoe' routine on me. Record on. Dallas, Lieutenant Eve, conducting a formal interview with Billy Johnson regarding case files H-23987 and H-23992. Your client, Billy Johnson, has been advised of his rights and obligations, and has opted to take advantage of his rights and avail himself of the services of a public defender. Correct?"

"That is correct. At this point, neither my client nor I are clear on why he was forcibly brought in for questioning in—"

"Forcibly? Anyone use force on you, Billy? Did you sustain any injuries during your transport to this facility?"

"Took me off my job. Didn't give me much choice."

"Let it be on record that the subject was remanded into police custody and transported to Interview at Central, without force. He has been read the Revised Miranda. He has availed himself of counsel. You want to muddy the waters, sister, I'll muddy them right back. Now you and I can continue to play pushy-shovey, or I can question your client and get this done."

"My client was not given the opportunity to voluntarily—"

"Oh, zip it," Billy snapped and rubbed the crop of cornrows covering his head. "What the hell do you want?" he demanded of Eve. "I don't know anything about anybody getting dead. What the hell do you want?"

"We've swept Ernestine Macnamara's van, Billy. Lots of prints, lots of trace evidence. We both know we're going to find some of that trace evidence doesn't go back to Ernestine or her faithful Sunday group."

"I park the car for her, so my prints—"

"We're going to find more than yours, too. And that puts you in the wringer." She kept her focus on him. "Rachel Howard. Kenby Sulu."

She watched his mouth tremble. "Oh my Jesus. Those college kids. Oh my God. I watched the reports on the news. Those are the dead college kids."

"Mr. Johnson, I advise you to say nothing—"

"Shut the hell up." His breath came fast as he stared at Eve. "Look, maybe I make a little extra on the side, but I never hurt anybody."

"Tell me about the money on the side."

"Just a minute." The PA rapped a fist on the table with enough force that Eve glanced at her with some admiration. "Just a damn minute. My client will cooperate, will answer your questions only on the condition of immunity. No charges will be forthcoming against him on this or any other matter."

"Why don't I just give him one of our platinum get-out-of-jail-free cards?"

"He will make no statement without guarantees. Cooperation is contingent on immunity from any charges regarding the parking facility and/or the homicides."

"I'll just go ask Rachel Howard and Kenby Sulu how they feel about immunity from homicide," Eve said coldly. "Oh wait, I can't. They're dead."

"I don't need immunity from any homicides. I didn't hurt anybody." He leaned forward, grabbed Eve's hand. "I swear to God. I swear on my son. I got a little boy. He's three. I swear on his life I didn't kill anybody. I'll tell you anything I can."

He drew a little breath, sat back. "But, well, I could use that immunity when it comes to the parking garage. I got a little boy. I gotta think about him."

"I'm not interested in rousting you over the sideline, Billy. As long as the sideline is shut down. And believe me, I'll know if it starts up again."

"It's closed."

"Lieutenant." Peabody stepped in, passed Eve a file. "Lab results."

"Thank you, Officer. Stand by." She opened the file, did her best to smother the laugh when she spotted the pink ribbon tucked inside. At least Peabody had had the foresight to remove it.

She skimmed the data. Not only did the carpet fibers match, but the sweepers had removed hair identified as Rachel Howard's and Kenby Sulu's from the van.

No longer amused, Eve lifted cool, flat eyes to Billy's face. "I want to know who took the van out on the nights of August eighth and August tenth."

"Okay, see here's how it works. Somebody comes by, says to me, 'I need a ride.' Maybe they want a nice little two-seater to drive their girl someplace, or a cushy sedan to take their grandma to a wedding, or something."

"Or a set of wheels to drive away in after they've hit a liquor store. Maybe a nice sturdy all-terrain to bop around in when they're making an illegals deal over in Jersey. This way they don't have to jack it, or bother with any pesky paperwork."

"Maybe." He gave her a slow nod. "I don't ask. Don't want to know, particularly. What I do is tell them what's available, and for how long. Fee's stiff and you gotta pay double up front. Get the deposit back when you return the vehicle in good condition. Still, we're cheaper than standard rental, and there's no paper."

"Everybody loves a bargain."

"See we got a lot of slots taken up on a yearly basis. We keep the rates down. Give regulars a good break. Some of these people, like Miss Ernestine, wouldn't be able to keep a ride 'cause the slot rent's so steep."

"Just your little community service. You're going to have a long wait for your medal, Billy."

"Didn't figure how it hurt anybody. The customer gets a good deal, and I get the bonus. It's put my kid in a classy pre-school. You know what those cost?"

"Who rented the van?"

"See, that's the thing. People come and they go. Repeaters, you get to know, get to figure what ride they like best. This guy, I just don't remember too much. Only came by the two times, I'm pretty sure. Knew what he wanted, paid the fee, brought it back. I didn't think anything of it. White guy," he said quickly.

"Go on."

"Average-looking white guy, I don't know. Who pays attention?"

"Old, young?"

"Ah, twenty-five, thirty. 'Round there. Shorter than me, but not much. Maybe a little under six feet? Dressed neat. I mean not sloppy. Looked like an average working white guy. Could be I'd seen him around the neighborhood before. Could be. He didn't look like anybody special."

"What did he say to you?"

"Ah. Shit. Something like: 'I need to rent a van. A nice, clean one.' Probably I said something about does this look like a rental port to you—nice and polite though. Then he . . . yeah, yeah, I sort of remember. He pulled out the fee and deposit. All cash. And he said he'd take the gray van on the first level. I took the money, he took the code, and drove off. Brought it back about three A.M. My cousin logged it in."

His gaze shot back down, and he winced. "Damn. Damn. Is my cousin gonna get in trouble?"

"Give me your cousin's name, Billy."

"Shit. Fucking shit. Manny Johnson. He just logged it back in, Lieutenant Dallas. That's all."

"Let's go back to the guy who rented the van. See what else you remember?"

"I didn't pay enough attention. Ah, he had shades on. Dark shades, I'm thinking. And a ball cap. Maybe a ball cap? Me, I'm looking at the cash money and the threads more than anything else. He dressed neat, he had the fee. Maybe if you showed me his picture or something, I'd remember him, but I don't see how. He had on the shades and the cap, and we're doing the thing inside the port, where it's shady. He just looked like an average white guy to me."

"Average white guy," Eve repeated after the interview. "One who's killed two people. Who knew how to access a nearly untraceable vehicle to transport them, knew how to get them into said vehicle with minimal fuss, and when and where to dump the bodies without anyone noticing."

"But you did trace the vehicle," Peabody reminded her. "We can start doing a canvass, maybe we'll find someone who saw it around the universities, or the dumping sites."

"And maybe the Tooth Fairy's going to come knocking on your door tonight. We'll go there, Peabody, but first we take the van back to the garage. Average white guy lets Diego off the hook, at least for the pickup."

Too skinny, too slicked up, Billy had said when he'd looked at the printout of Diego's ID shot.

"We still got a maybe out of Billy on Hooper."

"Maybe. Maybe he was shorter, maybe he was older. Maybe he wasn't. He's not done yet, so maybe he'll come back for it. The van and the garage go under surveillance."

She checked the time. "And now, we've got a memorial to attend."

She hated memorials, that formal acknowledgment of grief. She hated the flowers and the music, the murmur of voices, the sudden bursts of weeping or laughter.

It was probably worse when the dead were young, and

the end was violent. She'd been to too many memorials for violent death.

They'd laid Rachel in a glass-sided coffin—one of the trends of mourning Eve found particularly creepy. They'd put her in a dress, a blue one and probably her best, and fixed a little spray of pink roses in her hands.

She watched people file by. The parents, both looking shell-shocked and too calm. Tranq'd to get through the event. And the younger sister who simply looked ravaged and lost.

She saw students she'd questioned, the merchants from the shops near where she'd worked. Teachers, neighbors, friends.

Leeanne Browning was there, with Angela at her side. They spoke to the family, and whatever Leeanne said had tears breaking through the drugs and trickling slowly down the mother's face.

She saw faces she'd already filed away; and new ones, as she stood by searching for an average white guy. There were plenty of them that fit into the age span. Rachel, a friendly girl, had met a lot of people in her short life.

There was Hooper, neatly dressed in a suit and tie, his face somber, his shoulders straight as a soldier's. A group of what Eve assumed was his peers surrounded him the way groups tend to surround the attractive.

But when he looked around, his eyes were empty. Whatever they said didn't reach him, and he turned and walked away, through those young bodies as if they were ghosts.

He didn't look at the people, nor, she noted, did he look at the box, the clear box that held the girl he'd said he thought he might have loved.

She lifted her chin, a kind of reverse nod signal to McNab. "See where he goes," she ordered when McNab moved into place beside her. "See what he does."

"Got him."

She went back to studying the crowd, though she wished she could have been the one to step outside after Hooper, into the night. Into the air. Despite the overworked climate control the room was too warm, too close, and the smell of the flowers cloying.

She spotted Hastings across the room. As though he felt her eyes on him, he glanced toward her, then lumbered over.

"Thought I should come, that's all. Hate this kind of shit. I'm not staying."

He was embarrassed, she realized. And a little guilty.

"They shouldn't have dressed her up that way," he said after a moment. "Looks false. I'd've put her in her favorite shirt. Some old shirt she liked, given her a couple of yellow daisies to hold. Face like that, it's for daisies. Anyway . . ." He downed his glass of sparkling water. "Nobody asked me."

He shifted from foot to foot. "You'd better catch whoever put that kid in that glass box."

"Working on it."

She watched him go. Watched others come and go.

"He went outside," McNab reported. "Walked down to the corner and back a couple times." McNab hunched his shoulders, stuck his hands in his pockets. "Crying. Just walking up and down and crying. A group came out, gathered him up, into a car. I got the make and tag if you want me to run and pick them up."

"No." She shook her head. "No, not tonight. Pack it in. Get Peabody, and tell her she's off the clock."

"Don't have to tell me twice. I want to go somewhere people are talking about something stupid and eating lousy food. Always do after a memorial. You want to come along?"

"I'll pass. We'll pick this up again in the morning."

As the crowd thinned out, she made her way over to Feeney. "Would he come, Feeney? Would he need to see her again, like this? Or are his images enough for him?"

"I don't know. You look at it from his perspective, he got what he wanted from her, so he's done."

"Maybe, but it's like a circle, and this closes it. Something tells me he'd want to see her like this. Still, if he was here, I couldn't make him."

"Fucking average white guy." He puffed out his cheeks. She looked beat, he thought. Beat and worried and under the gun. He patted her shoulder. "What do you say we go get a beer?"

"I say, that's a damn fine idea."

• • •

"Been a while since we did this," Feeney commented.

"Guess it has." Eve sampled her beer.

By tacit agreement, they'd avoided the known cop bars. Kicking back in one of them meant somebody would stop by to shoot the shit or talk shop. Instead, they'd caught a booth in a place called The Leprechaun, a dim little bar with aspirations of simulating an Irish pub.

There was piped in music with someone singing about drinking and war, and a lot of signs written in Gaelic, and framed pictures of what Eve assumed were famous Irish people. The waitstaff all talked with Irish accents, though their server's accent had a definite Brooklyn edge to it.

Since she'd had occasion to spend some time in an actual Irish pub, she could tell the owner—who she imagined was somebody named Greenburg—wasn't even close to being Irish.

And thinking it made her think of the Penny Pig. And Roarke.

"Why don't you tell me what's on your mind, kid?"

"I think he's going to move within the next forty-eight hours, so—"

"No, not about the case." There was a bowl of peanuts in the shell between them, but he shoved it aside, got out his bag of candied almonds. "You got trouble at home?"

"Shit, Feeney." Because it was there, she dug into the bag. "I've got Summerset at home. Isn't that enough?"

"And Roarke off somewhere while his man's at home with a busted pin. Must've been important to pull him away just now."

"It was. It is. God." She braced her elbows on the table, then dropped her head into her hands. "I don't know what I'm supposed to do. I don't know if I should tell you. I don't know if he'd want me to tell you."

"He doesn't have to know you did. It doesn't go beyond here."

"I know that." He'd trained her, Eve thought. Taken her green from the Academy. And she'd trusted him. He'd partnered with her, gone through every door. And she'd trusted him.

"I'll have to tell him I told you. I think that's one of those marriage rules. There are too fricking many of them."

Feeney didn't interrupt her, and when he'd finished his beer, ordered another.

"It's got to mess him up, you know? You go your whole life thinking one thing, dealing with what you believe is truth, then you get slammed in the gut, and it all changes around on you." She sipped her beer. "He doesn't get drunk. He'll dance up to the line, should the occasion call for it. But even when it's just the two of us off somewhere, he doesn't go over the line. He's going to stay aware, in control. That's core Roarke."

"You shouldn't worry because a man ties one on."

"I wouldn't, if the man wasn't Roarke. He did it because he's hurting and needed to get away from the pain. Feeney, he can take a hell of a lot of pain."

So can you, Feeney thought. "Where is he now?"

"In Clare. He left me a message—damn time difference. He said I shouldn't worry, he was fine. He was probably going to stay there, another day at least, and he'd be in touch."

"Did you tag him back?"

She shook her head. "I started to, then I started second-guessing myself. Is it like nagging? I don't know. He said he wanted to handle this himself. He's made it pretty clear he doesn't want me involved."

"And you're letting him get away with that." He sighed, heavy, and his basset hound eyes seemed to droop lower. "You disappoint me."

"What am I supposed to *do*? I'm in the middle of this investigation, and he says he's going to Ireland. He won't wait, won't give me time to figure things out. Okay, he can't wait—I can get that. He's got a problem, and he'd want to deal, straight off."

"One of those marriage rules is if one of you's in pain or trouble, you're not in it alone. You suffering here, him there. That doesn't work for either of you."

"Well, he left. He was on his way out when he told me, for Christ's sake. I'm still pissed about that."

"So you should be out the door behind him."

She drew her brows together. "I'm supposed to go to Ireland? Now? He said he didn't want me there."

"If he did, he's lying. That's a man for you, kid. We can't help it."

"You think he needs me to be there?"

"I do."

"But the case. I can't just—"

"What am I, a rookie?" Feeney had the wit to look insulted. "You don't think I can manage as temporary primary for a couple days? Or do you just want the collar yourself?"

"No. No! But I'm working all these angles, and the odds of him hitting again in the next couple of days are—"

"If you got word Roarke was hurt, bleeding from the ears, would you worry about the case or get your ass moving?"

"I'd get my ass moving."

"He's bleeding from the heart. So you go."

It was so simple. A no-brainer when put just that way. "I'll have to clear it, and set up some schedules for tomorrow. Get a report in."

"Then let's go do it." Feeney pocketed his nuts.

"Thanks. Really."

"No problem. You buy the beer."

Chapter 18

It took some doing, asking for favors, fighting the urge to triple check every detail she'd already double checked.

It took blocking every natural instinct and putting her travel arrangements into Summerset's hands.

She went home to pack a light bag, reminding herself she could be reached anywhere, at any time. That she could, if necessary, fly home as quickly as she was flying away. And that she could run an op by remote control. She had a capable team.

She wasn't the only cop on the NYPSD. But she was Roarke's only wife.

Still, she paced the plush confines of his fastest jet shuttle as it careened across the Atlantic in the dark. She reviewed her notes, reread the files and witness statements.

Everything that could be done was being done. She'd ordered round-the-clock surveillance on the garage and the van. EDD had installed a homer on the van as backup.

If he came for it, they'd move in and have him in custody before he could finish keying in the ignition code.

All the trace evidence was being matched. Within twenty-four hours, forensics would have eliminated anything from

Ernestine and her church group, the garage employees, the victims. What was left would be the killer's.

They'd have DNA, and a solid case.

She had men in the data club, men at the universities, Louise on the medical front. Something would break, and soon.

She tried to sit, relax. But couldn't.

That was all cop stuff. She knew what she was doing as a cop.

But where she was headed was wife territory. She'd learned some of the ground, and considered she'd figured how to negotiate it fairly well. But this sector was uncharted.

If he didn't want her there, was she going to make things worse?

She plugged a disc into her PPC and played back the message he'd left on her home office 'link while she'd still been at Central clearing the way to leave.

"Well, I hope you're sleeping." He smiled, but he looked so tired, she thought. Worn out tired. "I should've called before. Things got . . . complicated. I'm about to go to bed myself. It's late here. Early, more like. I can't seem to remember the time change—imagine that. I'm sorry I haven't spoken with you today—yesterday. What the hell."

He gave a half-laugh, pinched the bridge of his nose as if to relieve some pressure. "I'm punchy, need a couple hours down, is all. I'm fine, no need to worry. Things aren't what I expected here. Can't say what I expected. I'll call you after I've slept a bit. Don't work too hard, Lieutenant. I love you."

He wasn't supposed to look so tired, she thought on a sudden spurt of anger. He wasn't supposed to look so befuddled, so damn vulnerable.

Maybe he didn't want her there, but he was just going to have to deal with it.

Dawn was shimmering over the hills when Roarke stepped outside. He hadn't slept long, but he'd slept well, tucked up into a pretty, slanted-ceiling bedroom on the top floor, one with old lace curtains on the windows and a lovely handmade quilt on the wide, iron bed.

They'd treated him like family. Almost like a prodigal son returned home, and they'd served roast kid and pandy as the Irish version of fatted calf.

They'd had a *ceili*, packed with food and music and stories. People, so many people gathering around to talk of his mother, to ask of him, to laugh. To weep.

He hadn't been quite sure what to make of it all, or them, the uncles and aunts and cousins—grandparents for God's sake—that had so suddenly come into his life.

The welcome had humbled him.

He was still unsteady. This life they lived, and the world in which they lived it, was more foreign to him than the moon. And yet he'd carried a part of it, unknowing, in his blood throughout his life.

How could he resolve, in a matter of days, something so enormous? How did he understand the truths buried more than thirty years under lies? And death?

With his hands in his pockets, he walked beyond the back gardens with their tidy rows of vegetables, their tangled cheer of flowers, and fingered the little gray button he carried.

Eve's button. One that had fallen off the jacket of a particularly unattractive suit the first time he'd seen her. One he'd carried like a talisman ever since.

He'd be steadier if she were here, he was sure. Christ, he wished she were here.

He looked across a field where a tractor hummed along. One of his uncles or cousins would be manning it, he supposed. Farmers. He sprang from farmers, and wasn't that a kick in the ass?

Simple, honest, hard-working, God-fearing—and everything the other half of him wasn't. Was it that conflict, that contradiction, that went into the making up of what he was?

It was early enough that the mists snaked up from the green, softening the air, softening the light. A snippet of Yeats ran through his head—*where hill is heaped upon hill*. And so it was here. He could see those hills rolling back to forever, and smell the damp of dew on grass, the loamy earth beneath it, the wild rambling roses above.

And hear the birds singing as though life was a singular joy.

All of his life—certainly all of it after he'd escaped the bastard who'd sired him—he'd done as he wanted. Pursued the goal of success and wealth and comfort. He didn't need a session with Mira to tell him he'd done so to compensate, even defeat, the years of misery, poverty, and pain. And so what?

So the fuck what?

A man who didn't do what he could to live well instead of wallowing was a fool.

He'd taken what he needed, or simply wanted. He'd fought for, or bought, or in some way acquired what made him content. And the fight itself, the hunt, the pursuit were all part of the game that entertained him.

Now he was being given something, freely, something he'd never considered, never allowed himself to want. And he didn't know what the hell to do with it.

He needed to call Eve.

He looked across the field, across the silvered mists and gentle rise of aching green. Rather than pull out his pocket-link he continued to toy with the button. He didn't want to call her. He wanted to touch her. To hold her, just hold her and anchor himself again.

"Why did I come without you?" he murmured, "when I need you so bloody much?"

He heard the muscular hum, recognized it for what it was an instant before the jet-copter broke through the mists like a great black bird breaks through a thin net.

And recognized it as one of his own as it skimmed over the field, startling cows, and causing his uncle—cousin—they were all a blur of faces and names to him yet—to stop the tractor and lean out to watch the flight.

His first reaction was a quick clutch in the gut. Eve, something had happened to Eve. His knees went weak at the thought as the copter arrowed down for a landing.

Then he saw her, the shape of her in the cockpit beside the pilot. The choppy cap of hair, the curve of her cheek. Pale, naturally. She hated riding in those machines.

The grass of the field went swimming in the displaced air as the copter set down. Then the sound died, the air was still.

She jumped down, a light pack slung over her arm. And his world righted again.

He didn't move, couldn't seem to as he was so struck by the sight of her. Striding across the green, casting a wary look at the cows over her shoulder before her eyes met his. Held his.

His heart rolled over in his chest; the most lovely sensation he'd ever known.

He walked forward to meet her.

"I was just wishing for you," he said. "And here you are."

"Must be your lucky day, Ace."

"Eve." He lifted a hand, not quite steady, skimmed his fingers along her jaw. "Eve," he said again, and his arms were around her, banded like steel as he lifted her off her feet. "Oh God. Eve."

She felt the shudder run through him as he buried his face in her hair, against the curve of her neck. And knew she'd been right to come. Whatever else there was, she'd been right to come.

"Everything's okay now." To soothe, she ran her hands over his back. "It's okay."

"You landed in a field of cows, in a jet-copter."

"You're telling me?"

He rubbed his hands up and down her arms before linking them with hers and easing back to look at her face. "You must love me madly."

"I must."

His eyes were wild and beautiful, his lips warm and tender as he pressed them to her cheeks. "Thank you."

"You're welcome, but you missed a spot." She found his mouth with hers and let him sink in. When she felt the heat, the punch, her lips curved against his. "That's better."

"Much. Eve—"

"We've got an audience."

"The cows don't mind."

"Don't talk about the cows, they creep me out." When he

laughed, she nodded over his shoulder. "Two-legged audience."

He kept an arm around her waist, possessively, drawing her close to his side as he turned. He saw Sinead standing by the rambling roses, an eyebrow cocked.

"This is my wife," he told her. "This is my Eve."

"Well, I hope she's yours, the way you've got a hold of her. A tall girl, isn't she, quite handsome, too. Looks like she suits you."

"She does." He lifted Eve's free hand to his lips. "She does indeed. Eve, this is Sinead Lannigan. This is . . . my aunt."

Eve took the woman's measure in a slow, careful study. Hurt him, her face said clearly, deal with me. She watched Sinead's eyebrow wing higher, and a faint smile ghost around her mouth.

"It's nice to meet you, Mrs. Lannigan."

"Sinead will do. Did you come all the way from New York City in that little thing?"

"Just the last leg."

"Still, you must be a brave and adventurous soul. Have you had breakfast then?"

"She wouldn't have, no," Roarke said before Eve could respond. "Brave and adventurous, she is, but a weak stomach for heights."

"I can speak for myself."

"I'll wager you can." Sinead nodded. "Come in then, and welcome. I'll fix you breakfast. Your man hasn't eaten either."

She walked back toward the house. Understanding his wife, Roarke gave Eve's hand a quick squeeze. "She's been nothing but kind. I'm staggered by the kindness I've found here."

"Okay. I could eat."

Still, she held her opinion in reserve as she found herself seated at the enormous kitchen table with Sinead manning the stove and the pots and skillets on it like a conductor mans an orchestra.

She was given tea, nearly as black as coffee and so strong

she was surprised it didn't melt the enamel on her teeth. But it settled her as yet uneasy stomach.

"So you're a cop. One who hunts murderers." Sinead glanced back over her shoulder as she wielded a spatula. "Roarke says you're brilliant, and dogged as a terrier, with a heart big as the moon."

"He's got a soft spot for me."

"That he does. We're told you're in the middle of a difficult case now."

"They're all difficult, because someone's dead who shouldn't be."

"Of course, you're right." Intrigued, Sinead watched her as meat sizzled in the pan. "And you solve the thing."

"No. You never solve anything, because someone's dead who shouldn't be," Eve repeated. "They can't get up out of the grave, so it can't be solved. All you can do is close the case, and trust the system for justice."

"And is there justice?"

"If you keep at it long enough."

"You closed this one quickly," Roarke began, then stopped when he saw her face. "You didn't close it."

"Not yet."

For a moment, there was only the sound of the meat frying in the skillet. "Lieutenant, I wouldn't have pulled you away from your work."

"You didn't. I pulled myself away."

"Eve—"

"Why are you badgering the girl, and here she's not even had her breakfast." To settle a matter that looked to her would heat up as quickly as the bacon, Sinead heaped food on plates, set them down. "If she's as brilliant as you say, she ought to know what she's about."

"Thanks." Eve picked up a fork, exchanged her first comfortable look with Sinead. "Looks great."

"I'll leave you to it then, as I've some things to see to upstairs. Don't worry about the dishes when you're done."

"I think I like her," Eve commented when they were alone, then poked a fat sausage with her fork. "Is this from pig?"

"Most likely. Eve, I want to be sorry you felt it necessary to leave in the middle of an investigation, but I'm so bloody glad you're here. I haven't been able to find my balance, haven't been able to settle myself since I found out about my mother. I've handled the entire business badly. Bungled it, top to bottom."

"Guess you did." She tried a bite of sausage, approved. "It's nice to know you can screw up now and again, like the rest of us mortals."

"I couldn't find my balance," he repeated, "until I stood out there in the mist of the morning and saw you. Simple as that for me, it seems. There she is, so my life's where it should be, whatever's going on around it. You know the worst of me, but you came. I think what's here, though I don't understand it all yet, haven't taken it all in, may be the best of me. I want you to be part of that."

"You went to Dallas with me. You saw me through that, even though it was about as rough on you as it was on me. You've shuffled your work and your schedule around more times than I can count to help me out—even when I didn't want you to."

He smiled now. "Especially when you didn't."

"You're part of my life, even the parts I wanted you clear of. So, same goes, Roarke. For better or worse, or all the crap that's in between, I love you." She scooped up eggs. "We straight on that?"

"As an arrow."

"Good." And so were the eggs, she discovered. "Why don't you tell me about these people?"

"There's a lot of them to start. There's Sinead, who was my mother's twin. Her husband, Robbie, who works the farm here with Sinead's brother Ned. Sinead and Robbie have three grown children, who would be my cousins, and between them, there are five more children, and two more on the way."

"Good God."

"Haven't even gotten started," he said with a laugh. "Ned, he's married to Mary Katherine, or maybe it's Ailish. I'm good at names, you know, but all these names and faces and bodies were coming down like a flood. They've four children, cousins of mine, and they've managed to make five—no I think it might be six more. Then there's Sinead's younger brother, that's Fergus, who lives in Ennis and works in his wife's family's restaurant business. I think her name's Meghan, but I'm not entirely sure."

"Doesn't matter." Already feeling crowded, Eve waved her fork.

"But there's so many more." He grinned now, and ate as he hadn't been able to do for days. "My grandparents. Imagine having grandparents."

"I can't," she said after a moment.

"Neither can I, though I appear to have them. They've been married nearly sixty years now, and they're hearty. They live now in a cottage over the hill to the west. They didn't want the big house, I'm told, when their children were grown and married, so it came to Sinead as she was the one who wanted it most."

He paused, and she said nothing. Just waited for him to finish.

"They don't want anything from me." Still puzzled by it, he broke a slice of toasted brown bread in two. "Nothing that I expected them to want. There's none of this, 'Well now, we could use a bit of the ready since you've so much and we're in the way of being family.' Or 'You owe us for all the years that've gone by.' Not even the 'Who the hell do you think you are, coming around here, you son of a murdering bastard.' I'd expected any of those things, would have understood that. Instead it's 'Ah, there you are, it's Siobahn's boy. We're glad to see you.' "

With a shake of his head, he set the toast down again. "What do you do with that?"

"I don't know. I never know how to act, or feel, when somebody loves me. I always feel inadequate, or just stupid."

"We never had much practice at it, did we, you and I?" He covered her hand with his, rubbed it as though he needed the feel of her skin against his. "Two lost souls. If you're done there, I'd like to show you something."

"I'm overdone." She pushed the plate away. "She made

enough food for half the residents of Sidewalk City."

"We'll walk some of it off," he said and took her hand.

"I'm not going back with the cows. I don't love you that much."

"We'll leave the cows to their cow business."

"Which is what, exactly? No, I don't want to know," she decided as he pulled her out the door. "I get these weird and scary pictures in my head. What's that thing out there?" she asked, pointing.

"It's called a tractor."

"Why's that guy riding around with the cows? Don't they have remotes, or droids, or something?"

He laughed.

"You laugh"—and it was good to hear it—"but there are more cows than people around here. What if the cows got tired of hanging around in the field and decided, hey, *we* want to drive the tractor, or live in the house, or wear clothes for a while. What then?"

"Remind me to dig out *Animal Farm* from the library when we get home, and you'll find out. Here now." He took her hand in his once more, wanting the link. "They planted this for her. For my mother."

Eve studied the tree, the lush green leaves and sturdy trunk and branches. "It's . . . a nice tree."

"They knew, in their hearts, she was dead. Lost to them. But there was no proof. Trying to find it, to find me when I was a baby, one of my uncles was almost killed. They had to let go. So they planted this for her, not wanting to put up a stone or marker. Just the cherry tree, that blooms in the spring."

Looking at it again, Eve felt something click inside her. "I went to a memorial for one of the victims last night. This job, you go to too many memorials and funerals. The flowers and the music, the bodies laid out on display. People seem to need that, the ritual, I guess. But it always seems off to me. This seems right. This is better."

He watched her now as she studied his mother's tree. "Is it?"

"The flowers just die, you know? And the body gets buried or burned. But you plant a tree and it grows, and it lives. It says something."

"I can't remember her. I've searched back, making myself half-mad trying, somehow thinking if I could remember something, some small thing, it would make it better. But I can't. And that's that. So this tree here, it's something solid, and more comforting to me than a stone marker. If there's more than whatever time we have bumbling around here, then she knows I came. That you came with me. And that's enough."

When they went back in, Sinead was in the kitchen clearing breakfast away. Roarke walked to her, touched a hand to her shoulder.

"Eve needs to go back. I need to go with her."

"Of course." She lifted her hand, touched his lightly. "Well then, you'd best go up and get your things. I'll have just a moment here with your wife, if she doesn't mind."

Trapped, Eve slid her hands into her pockets. "Sure. No problem."

"I'll only be a minute."

"Ah . . ." Eve searched for something appropriate to say when she was alone with Sinead. "It means a lot to him that you let him stay."

"It means a lot to me, to us, to have had this time with him, however short. It was difficult for him to come, to tell us what he'd learned."

"Roarke's no stranger to doing the difficult."

"So I gather, and neither would you be, if I'm a judge." She wiped her hands on a cloth, set it aside. "I was watching him from the window before, sort of gathering up pictures of him you might say. Ones I can share with Siobahn when I speak with her. I talk to her in my head," Sinead explained at Eve's blank look. "And right out loud now and then when no one's about. So I'm gathering up my pictures, and there's one I'll never forget. The way he looked—the change in his face, in his body, in the whole of him when he saw it was you. The love was naked on him when he saw it was you, and it's one of the loveliest things I've ever seen. It's a fine picture to have in my head, for he's my sister's child, grown man or no, and I want what's good for him. You seem to be."

"We seem to be good for each other, God knows why."

She smiled now, bright and pretty. "Sometimes it's best not to know all the reasons. I'm glad you came, so I had a chance to look at you, and see the two of you together. I want more chances with him, and you'll be a large part of letting that happen, or preventing it."

"Nobody prevents Roarke."

"Nobody," Sinead said with a nod, "but you."

"I wouldn't do anything to get in the way of something he needed. He needed to come here. He'll need to come back. Maybe you weren't looking in the right place when he introduced me to you, when he looked at you. He already loves you."

"Oh." Her eyes filled up before she could stop them, and she blinked, wiping at them quickly when she heard him coming back in. "I'll fix you some food for the journey."

"Don't trouble." Roarke touched her shoulder again. "There's plenty of it on the shuttle. I've made arrangements to have the car I drove here picked up."

"Well that'll be sad news for my Liam, who thinks it's as fine and fancy a machine as ever built. I've something for you." She reached in her pocket, closing her fingers over the treasure as she turned to him. "Siobahn didn't take all her things when she went to Dublin. She was going to come back and get them, or send for them, but, well, one thing and another."

She pulled out a thin chain and the rectangle of silver that dangled from it. "It's just a trinket, but she wore it often. You see this is her name, in Ogham script. I know she'd want you to have it."

Sinead pressed it into Roarke's hand, closed his fingers around it. "Safe journey then, and . . . ah, damn it."

The tears beat her, plopped onto her cheeks as she wrapped her arms around him. "Come back, will you? Come back sometime, and keep well until you do."

"I will." He closed his eyes, breathed her in. Vanilla and

wild roses. He murmured in Gaelic as he pressed his lips to her hair.

She gave a watery laugh, pulled back to swipe at her cheeks. "I don't have that much of the Gaelic."

"I said thank you for showing me my mother's heart. I won't forget her, or you."

"See that you don't. Well, be off then before I start blubbering all over you. Good-bye to you, Eve, keep yourself safe."

"It was a pleasure to meet you." She took Sinead's hand in a firm grip. "A genuine pleasure. The shuttle runs both ways, if you decide to come to New York."

Roarke pressed a kiss to her temple as they walked to the field, and the waiting copter. "That was well done."

"She's a stand-up."

"That she is." He looked back toward the house, and the woman who stood in the back doorway to wave them off.

"You should get some sleep," he said to her when they were settled on the shuttle.

"Don't start poking at me, pal. You're the one who looks like he's been on a week's bender."

"Might stem from the fact that I've consumed more whiskey in the past two days than I have in the past two years, altogether. Why don't we both stretch out for a bit?"

She jiggled her foot, checked the time, did the math. "Too early to call Central and check in. I'll be back in a couple hours anyway, won't even have missed any time."

"Just missed sleep." He engaged the mechanism that turned the wide sofa into a wide bed.

"Too revved to sleep."

"Is that so?" Some of the light she loved was back in his eyes. "Well, what can we do to pass the time, help you relax? Cribbage, perhaps?"

Her eyes narrowed. "Cribbage? Is that some perverted sexual activity?"

He laughed, and grabbing her, tossed her onto the bed. "Why not?"

But he was gentle, and so was she. Tender, as she was.

They watched each other as they touched. So she could see the shadows that had haunted him these last days lift away, and leave that deep and vivid blue clear again.

Love, she thought, the act of it, could chase away ghosts for a while, tuck the dead away. Here was life, with him filling her, life as she surrounded the hard length of him, and their fingers linked, their mouths meeting.

Life, he thought, while she rose to him so he could only sink into her. Their life.

She was definitely relaxed, and not particularly sleepy when they arrived at the transport dock in New York. Then again, she figured, if a woman wasn't relaxed after an energetic session of cribbage with Roarke, something was wrong with her.

She let him take the wheel of the city vehicle she'd left in his personal parking slot for the drive home so she could use her energies to alert Central she was back, and on duty.

"No point in mentioning you could have taken a couple of hours personal time before diving back in."

"I've had more than my quota of personal time. I'm fine." She looked over at him. "We're fine now."

He closed a hand over hers as he maneuvered through the early morning traffic. "We are, yes. My head's clearer than it's been in days. I guess I'm a bit anxious to get back to things myself."

"Good deal. So before we both get back to things, is there anything else you should tell me?"

He thought of Grogin, and how close he'd come to crossing a line. Eve's line. "No. Oh wait, there is one thing. It turns out I'm a year younger than I thought I was."

"No kidding. Huh. Does it feel weird?"

"A bit, actually."

"I guess you'll get used to it." She snuck a look at the time. "Listen, I'll dump you home, then head straight downtown to . . . Damn." Her communicator signaled.

DISPATCH, DALLAS, LIEUTENANT EVE.

"Dallas, acknowledged."

REPORT EAST SIDE HEALTH CENTER, SECOND LEVEL
UNDERGROUND PARKING FACILITY. HOMICIDE VERIFIED
BY FEENEY, CAPTAIN RYAN, ON SCENE.

"On my way. Dallas out. Goddamn it, goddamn it. I
thought I had more time. I have to dump you now, Roarke."

"I'll take you. Let me do this," he said before she could
object. "Let me do whatever I can."

Chapter 19

Sirens were screaming, and the lights from the emergency vehicle whirled as it sped by. Someone was in trouble.

But Alicia Dilbert had no more need for sirens or whirling lights; her trouble was over.

The scene was already cordoned off, with cops doing their busy work. The morning was beginning to steam, with the hot breath from the subway belching up through the sidewalk vent adding another layer.

On the corner, an enterprising glide-cart operator was set up and doing a brisk business selling coffee and fried egg sandwiches to cops and health workers—both of whom should have known better.

Eve smelled the stink of fake eggs sizzling on the grill, the body odor from men who'd been at work too long, and the medicinal scent of hospital that clung to the crowded air.

If the dog days of August didn't take a breather soon, the city was going to parboil in its own sweat.

She sealed up, and crouched with Feeney by the body.

"Got word you were back, so I held off having her bagged." He nodded toward Roarke who stood at the edge of the barricade. "Quick trip."

"Yeah. We're fine. He's fine. Shit, Feeney. *Shit*. I should've been here."

"Wouldn't have made a damn, and you know it. He didn't get past us. Van hasn't been touched. Nobody approached it."

"She's still dead, so he got past us one way or another." She fixed on microgoggles and studied the neat heart wound. "He keeps things orderly, stays on pattern." With the goggles in place, she could see the thin, faint line of bruises around the wrists.

"He posed her. When Morris gets her in, he'll find other marks from the wires he uses."

"Yeah. Dallas. He went a little off pattern this time around." Though his face was cold and set, there was a little flare of fury in his eyes as he reached in his evidence bag and took out a sealed note.

"She was holding this. He had it taped to her fingers." He turned the bag to show Eve the envelope, and her name printed on it.

Eve took the evidence bag, turned the note to read.

Lieutenant Dallas. You don't understand. How could you? Your scope is limited. Mine is expanded. You see here a victim, but you're wrong. She has been given a gift, a great gift, and by a small sacrifice offers that gift to others.

You think I'm a monster, I know. There will be those who agree with you and curse my name. But there will be more, many more, who will see, and finally understand the art, and the beauty, and the power I've discovered.

What I do is not simply for myself, but for all mankind.

Her light was brilliant, and is brilliant still. I hope one day you will know it.

You see too much death. One day there will only be life. And light.

It is almost done.

"Yeah, it's almost done," she muttered. She slid the note into her bag. "My scope's limited, Feeney, but what I see here is a pretty black girl, around twenty years of age, dressed in a medical uniform. About five-five, a hundred and thirty. No defensive wounds."

She bent close again, turned the girl's right palm up. "Slight round mark, consistent with pressure syringe, on her right palm. Hi, how you doing, nice to see you again. And the bastard tranqs her with a handshake. Dressed for work, so she was coming or going. We know which?"

"Med student, doing rotation here. Off shift at ten. We got statements from some of the staff who saw her clock out."

"Mmm." She continued to study the girl. Pretty face, high, sharp cheekbones. Glossy black hair, curly and drawn tidily back with a band at the nape of her neck. A trio of studs along the lobes of each ear.

"Pretty busy around here. Big risk to scoop her up right outside a health center at ten at night. You got her home address?"

"Got that, and the rest." Though he remembered, he pulled out his e-pad. "Alicia Dilbert, twenty. Student at NYU, Medicine. Residence on East Sixth, puts her place three blocks north of here. Next of kin's a brother, Wilson Buckley."

"What?" Her head came up. "What did you say?"

"Buckley, Wilson, next of kin."

"Damn." She massaged the back of her neck. "Goddamn, Feeney, we know him."

When she'd done all she could on scene, she walked to where Roarke stood beside Nadine. "Don't ask me now," she said before Nadine could speak. "I'll give you what I can when I can."

Something in Eve's expression had Nadine harnessing her natural instincts and nodding. "Okay. By ten, Dallas. I need something by ten, something more than the official line."

"When I can," Eve snapped back. "He sent you the transmission at oh-six hundred."

"My usual wake-up call, yeah. I did my civic duty, Dallas. Feeney's got everything."

"So he told me. I can't give you more now, Nadine." Eve combed a hand through her hair.

Something's here, Nadine thought. Something bad. "What is it?" In a gesture of friendship, she touched Eve's tensed shoulder. "Off record, Dallas. What is it."

But Eve only shook her head. "Not now. I have to notify next of kin. I don't want her name out until I do. You can get the official line from Feeney. He'll be on scene for a while yet. I have to go. Roarke?"

"What is it you won't tell her?" he asked as they walked through the crowds and noise to her car. "What's different about this one?"

"Degrees of separation, I guess. I know her brother. So do you." She looked back at the scene before climbing behind the wheel. "You said you wanted to do what you could, so I'm using you. I want Peabody with Feeney, talking to the staff here, interviewing people at her residence. I'm going to need some help with the next of kin."

"Who is it?"

He'd kept himself close to his baby sister, Eve noted. Not in the same building, not even in the same block, but close. And had kept her distant from his business. The simple geography spoke to her.

Give her some room, let her spread her wings, but don't let her fly too far. And don't let the dregs that frequented the club smear her.

His building had good security. He'd be careful about such matters. Her badge got her through it, and up to the fifth floor where she took a long breath before pressing the buzzer.

Minutes passed before she saw the light blink on the scanner, and knew he was checking his security panel, seeing her standing there.

It blinked green, and he opened the door.

"Hey there, white girl. Why you gotta roust me during my sleeping time?"

He was huge, a huge black man naked but for a purple loincloth and many tattoos.

"I need to talk to you. Crack, we need to come in."

Puzzlement ran over his face, but he grinned. "Now, you ain't hassling me 'bout some trouble down to the D&D. No more going on there than the usual."

"It's not about the club." The Down and Dirty was his baby, a sex and music club in the bowels of the city where the drinks were the next thing to lethal.

She'd had what had passed for her bridal shower there.

"Shit. Gonna need coffee if I gonna be talking to some skinny-assed cop this time of day. Roarke, can't you keep this white girl busy enough so she leave me be?"

She stepped inside. The place didn't surprise her, nothing about Crack did. It was spacious and tidy, tastefully decorated in what she supposed was African art, the masks, the bright colors, the lush fabrics.

As a testament to his preference for the night, the wide windows were covered with long thick drapes that blocked out the morning in shades of crimson and sapphire.

"Guess you be wanting coffee, too," he began, but Eve laid a hand on his arm before he could move toward what she assumed was the kitchen.

"Not now. We need to sit down. I want you to sit down."

The first hints of irritation snapped into his voice. "What the hell's this about that I can't have me a hit of coffee when you get me out of bed before the crack of noon?"

"It's bad. It's bad, Crack. Let's sit down."

"Somebody hit my place? Sumbitch, somebody mess with the D&D? I locked up myself a couple hours ago. What the hell?"

"No. It's about your sister. It's about Alicia."

"Alicia? Get out." He snorted, waved one of his platter-sized hands in dismissal, but she saw the leap of fear in his eyes. "That girl's not in any trouble. That girl's good as gold. You messing with my baby girl, Dallas, you gonna mess with Crack."

No other way to do it, Eve thought. No other way. "I'm

sorry to have to tell you, but your sister's dead. She was killed some time early this morning."

"That is bull*shit*!" He erupted, grabbing her by the arms, hauling her to her toes. Even as Roarke stepped forward, Eve shook her head to hold him back. "That's a goddamn lie. She's in medical school. She's going to be a doctor. She's in class right now. What's wrong with you, coming in here telling me lies about my baby?"

"I wish it was a lie." She spoke quietly. "I wish to God it was a lie. I'm so sorry, Wilson." She said his given name, gently. "I'm so sorry for your loss, sorry to be the one to tell you. She's gone."

"I'm going to call her right now. Right now, and get her out of class." The jive vanished from his speech. "I'm going to get her out of class so you can see this is a lie. What you did, is you made a mistake. You make a mistake about this."

She let him go, resisted the urge to rub her throbbing arms where his fingers had dug into flesh. She waited while he barked into his 'link, waited while a musical female voice cheerfully told him she wasn't able to take the call, to leave a message.

"She's just busy in class." His voice, so big, so sure, was beginning to shake. "We'll just go down to the college, get her out of class. You'll see."

"I rechecked the ID personally," Eve told him. "I rechecked it when I saw your name. Get dressed now, and I'll take you to her."

"It won't be her. It won't be my baby."

Roarke stepped forward. "I'll give you a hand. Bedroom through here?" He led Crack along as if the big man were a small child.

Eve took a deep breath when the bedroom door shut.

Then another as she called the morgue.

"This is Dallas. I'm bringing next of kin in to Dilbert, Alicia. I want her presented as cleanly as possible. I want her draped, and I want the viewing room cleared. No civilians or personnel in the area when I come in."

She clicked off. She could give him that, she thought. It was little enough.

• • •

He didn't speak on the way to the morgue, but hulked in the back of the car with his arms folded over his chest and dark sunshades wrapped around the top half of his face.

But she felt him there—the blasts of cold that was his fear, the pumping heat that was his hope.

He kept his face averted from hers, on the drive, on the walk down the chilly white corridors of the morgue. It was her fault now, she understood that. Her fault because there was no one else to blame for his terrible fear, his terrible hope.

She took him into a private viewing room where she and Roarke could flank him.

"If you'll watch the monitor," Eve began.

"I ain't watching no monitor. I don't believe nothing I see on no screen."

"All right." She'd expected this, prepared for this. The glass in front of them was still dark, the privacy screen engaged. She pressed a button under it.

"Dallas, Lieutenant Eve, escorting Buckley, Wilson, next of kin. Request viewing for personal identification of Dilbert, Alicia. Remove privacy shield."

The black faded slowly to gray, then cleared. Beyond the glass she lay on a narrow table, covered to the chin with a white sheet.

"No." Crack lifted his fists to the glass, pounded once, twice. "No, no, no." Then he rounded on Eve, would have leaped on her if Roarke hadn't anticipated and muscled Crack back, slapped him against the glass.

"This isn't what Alicia would want." Roarke spoke quietly. "This won't help her."

"I'm sorry" was all Eve could say.

Though his face was murderous now, he made no move. "You let me in there. You let me in there with her right now, or I'll throw him through this glass and you after him. You know I can do it."

He could, and she could stun him. But the grief was already raging up to smother the fury on his face.

"I'll take you in," she said calmly. "I have to be with you, and the cameras have to stay on. That's procedure."

"Fuck you, and your procedure."

She signaled Roarke back, spoke into the speaker again. "I'm bringing in the next of kin. Please vacate the area. Come with me." She motioned with the hand low at her side for Roarke to stay where he was.

She moved through the doors, down a short corridor, and through another set.

There were other tables here, other victims waiting to be viewed. And more, she knew, in the refrigerated drawers lined in a steel wall along the back. She couldn't shield him from them, could only walk directly to Alicia, and rest her hand on the butt of her weapon in case he lost control.

But he stepped to the table, looked down at the pretty face with its sharp cheekbones. He stroked the glossy black hair gently, so gently.

"This is my baby. My baby girl. My heart and my soul." He leaned over, touched his lips to her forehead.

Then he simply slid down, nearly seven feet of solid mass, into a weeping puddle on the floor.

Eve knelt beside him, put her arms around him.

Through the glass, Roarke watched as the huge man curled into her like a baby wanting comfort. And she rocked him while he wept.

She pulled more strings and commandeered an office, got him water, and sat, holding his hand while he drank.

"I was twelve when Mama came up pregnant again. Some bastard made her all kinds of promises, and she believed them. He didn't stay around long after the baby came. Mama did domestic work, and whored some on the side. She put food on the table, a roof over our heads, didn't have time for much more. Alicia, she was the prettiest baby you'd ever seen in your life. Good as gold, too."

"And you took care of her," Eve prompted.

"Didn't mind it. Guess I wanted to. Alicia was about four when Mama died. Wasn't the whoring that did it. Some asshole she was cleaning for got hold of a bad batch of Zeus and chucked her out a ten-story window. I was working in clubs already, picking up change. Got some breaks, got some money. I took care of my baby. Just because I run clubs and crack heads doesn't mean I didn't take care of my girl."

"I know that. I know you took good care of her. You saw she got into college. She was going to be a doctor."

"Smart as a whip, my girl. Always wanted to be a doctor. Wanted to help people. Why would anybody hurt that sweet girl?"

"I'm going to find out. I'm promising you. I'm giving you my word that I'm going to take care of her now. You have to trust me to do that."

"If I find him before you—"

"Don't." To cut off the words, she tightened her grip on his hand. "If you think I don't know how you feel, you're wrong. But it won't help Alicia. She loved you as much as you loved her, didn't she?"

"Called me her big, bad brother." Another tear slid down his cheek. "She was the best thing in my life."

"Then you help me help her. I want names of people she knew. People she worked with, played with. Did she have a boyfriend, anyone special?"

"No. She'd've told me. She liked boys all right, wasn't any prissy thing, but she studied hard, worked all she could at the health center. She'd go out with friends, let off steam. Not in my place," he said with what passed for a smile. "Didn't want her in my place."

"Other clubs, though. Did she mention any specifically? Did she ever mention spending time at a place called Make The Scene?"

"Data place, sure. Lots of the college crowd go there. And she liked this little joint near the health center. Coffee bar called Zing."

"Crack, did she have her picture taken, professionally, any time recently. For any reason. Work maybe, or something at school. Maybe at a wedding or a party."

"For my birthday last month. She asked what I wanted, and I said I wanted a picture of her, in a gold frame. Not just one of those snap-it-yourself jobs, but a real portrait where she was all dressed up fine, and the photographer knew what he was up to."

She kept her voice cool as she noted it down. "Do you know where she had the portrait done?"

"Someplace called Portography, uptown. Classy. I—" He broke off as his brain started to work through the grief. "I've been hearing this on the news. This is that son of a bitch who's killing college kids. Taking their picture and killing them. He killed my baby."

"Yes, he did. I'm going to find him, Crack. I'm going to stop him and see he's put in a cage. If I think you're going to get in my way on this, I'll have you put in one until I do."

"You can try."

"I won't just try," she said evenly. "You know me, and you know I'll stand for her now, no matter what it takes. Even if it means locking you away until I do what's right for her. She's mine now, too. Mine as much as yours."

He tried to hold back the tears. "Any other cop said that to me, I wouldn't believe it. Any other cop said that to me, I'd say whatever I needed to say to shake him loose so I could do what I wanted to do. But you're not any other cop, white girl. You take care of my baby sister. You're the only one I'd give her to."

"What can I do?" Roarke asked her when they stood at her car outside the morgue.

"You got any pull at the East Side Health Center?"

"Money, Lieutenant, always has pull."

"Here's what I'm thinking. Maybe he tagged her from the files at Portography. That's a link. Maybe he tagged her from the data club. It pops every time. But, if he's sick, and I think he's sick, she might have recognized him from the health center. If he uses it, or has used it, the staff might not notice him hanging around. If he took her out there, it was because people are used to seeing him, or recognized his face and didn't think anything of it. I've got Louise asking around, but she's going at it from the doctor angle—no names, patient privacy, and blah blah."

"And you'd like someone who isn't so particular about privacy."

"Three dead kids. Yeah. I don't give a flying fuck about privacy. Grease whatever palms you need to grease and see if you can find me somebody—male, twenty-five to sixty—no, forty. He's younger. That age span, with a serious, perhaps fatal neurological condition. Get me a name."

"Done. What else?"

"Isn't that enough for you?"

"No, I'd like to keep busy right now."

"Summerset—"

"I've spoken to him via 'link. What else?"

"You could use that twisty brain and those clever fingers to dig me up all you can on Javert. Any combination with Henri or Luis. Anything that pops around the dump sites, the data club, the colleges, Portography and the suspect names I'm going to give you that I shouldn't be giving you."

"Smells like drone work."

She smiled. "So?"

"Happy to be of assistance, Lieutenant."

"Question. You own parking ports, garages, lots, undergrounds."

"I believe I have a few in my vast empire, why?"

"Get me the ones that do sidelines?"

His brow lifted. "I'm afraid I don't understand what you're insinuating."

He was back, she thought. Slick as ever. "Save it, pal. I especially want ones within a ten-block radius of Eighteenth and Seventh. He saw us roust Billy. He knew we were there, watching the van, so he found alternate transpo. He plans, so he had a backup already earmarked, and I'm betting he had it close. I'm looking for a backdoor rental, nondescript vehicle in good condition, probably another van. You pop me something good, and you'll get a reward."

"You, naked, and a large quantity of chocolate sauce?"

"Pervert. Round up your own transpo, pal. I've got to scoop up Peabody and get into the field."

He grabbed her for one hot kiss first. Oh yeah, she thought as the top of her head flew off, he was definitely back.

"Nice being in tandem with you again, Lieutenant."

"Is that what we are?" She paused, studying him as he

stood on the sidewalk. "You get Summerset on his feet and out of the country, and I'll bring the chocolate sauce."

"There's a date," he murmured as she slid into her vehicle and drove away.

"I'm sorry about Crack, Dallas."

"So am I."

Seated in the passenger seat, Peabody lifted her hands. "I didn't even know he had a sister. It feels like I should've."

"She'd still be dead," Eve said flatly.

"Yeah, she'd still be dead. Do you think we should, I don't know, send flowers? Something."

"No, not flowers." She thought of Siobahn's cherry tree. "Put it away, Peabody. We do the job."

"Yes, sir." Peabody struggled against the resentment. Crack was a friend. You did *something* for a friend. "I just want him to know we're thinking about him, that's all."

"The best thing to do for him is to close the case, see that the person who did his sister is locked away. Flowers aren't going to comfort him, Peabody. Justice might, at least a little."

"You're right, it's just hard when it hits this close."

"It's supposed to be hard. When you start thinking it's easy, turn in your badge."

Peabody opened her mouth, insulted by the tone, then saw the fatigue, and the anger just under the shield. "Where are we going? I should know, I should be able to figure it out." The detective's exam loomed over her head like an ax. "But I can't."

"How did he transport her?"

"We don't know. Yet," she added.

"Why don't we know?"

"Because he didn't use the van we had under surveillance."

"Why didn't he use the van we had under surveillance?"

"Because . . . because he knew we were watching it." At the last minute she managed to change the tone from a question to a statement. "Do you think Billy tipped him?"

"Do you?"

She struggled with it for a moment, worked it through. "No, sir. At least not deliberately. Billy's small-time. He's not holding hands with a serial killer. He copped to the sideline, he cooperated. He's got a kid and the kid matters. He doesn't want this kind of trouble."

"So, how did our guy know to steer clear of Billy's garage?"

"Somebody else could have tipped him." But that didn't gel for her. "He might've gotten nervous, using the same van. But no," she continued, working it out, "he sticks to pattern. He likes his routine. So he had to know we'd made the van and were waiting. He had to see us there. He saw you. Recognized you from the screen, knew you were primary on this case, spotted my uniform. Jig's up on the gray van."

"And how did he see us?"

"Because . . . shit. Because he lives or works in the area! You already said you figured he did, and this adds weight. He spotted us from the street, or a window."

"Gold star for you."

"I'd settle for a gold shield."

Eve pulled up a half-block from the parking port. She'd wanted to see the area firsthand rather than on a computer screen. She wanted the feel of it, the rhythm of the sector, the viewpoints.

Not too close, she mused. He'd be careful about picking his transpo from a port right next door. But close enough so he could watch it, see the deals being made, the operation. Scope it out, choose his mark.

Yeah, the nice gray van driven by the old lady. Runs like a top, no special features. Blends. Plenty of space if things start going south and he has to muscle his mark into the back.

"He lives here," Eve said. "Not his work space. He sees the van go out on Sundays. He watches the port at night to see how the deals go through. He lives around here, keeps to himself, doesn't bother his neighbors. Low profile. Blends, just like his vehicle of choice."

She climbed back in her unit and prayed the climate control would hold back the heat while she worked. "Start running the buildings for residents. I want single males first."

"Which buildings?"

"All of them. The whole block."

"Going to take some time."

"Then you'd better get started." Eve scanned the buildings a block west, and zeroed in on the upper floors. Guy with image equipment probably had some nice long-range lenses, she speculated.

Using her 'link, she began a run of her own.

Chapter 20

Nothing popped for her, and when the climate control began to waffle, she ignored it and kept working. Ugly clouds rolled in, shooting the street into a sludgy gloom. Fat, mean splats of rain began to pound the windshield, heralded by a long growl of thunder.

"Storm looks nasty." Peabody mopped at the back of her neck and shot a glance at her lieutenant's profile. There was a light dew of sweat on Eve's face, but it could have been the result of that vicious concentration as much as the heat. "Maybe it'll cool things off."

"We'll just have wet heat. Fucking August." But she said it absently, almost affectionately. "He's here, Peabody, but where's his bolt-hole? Someplace nice and safe, where everything's tidy, everything's in its place.

"Pictures," she muttered, staring through the rain-washed window into the gloom. "Images tacked up all over the walls. He needs to see his work. Judge it, admire it, critique it. His work is his life. His work is life."

"Matted and framed."

"What?"

"Not tacked up," Peabody said. "Matted and framed. He'd want the best of it well presented, right?"

With a considering frown, Eve turned her head. "Good. That's damn good. Matted and framed. Where does he get the material? Local? Online? He'd want good stuff, wouldn't he? The best he could afford. Lots of frames. Probably unified. He's got a specific style, so he'd want them framed in a specific style. Get me the top ten outlets in the city to start."

"Yes, sir. Where are we going?" she asked as Eve pulled away from the curb.

"Home office. Better equipment."

"Woo-hoo. Sorry." But Peabody didn't bother to suppress the grin. "Better food, too. Jesus." She jumped when lightning lashed through the sky. "Serious stuff. Did you ever hide under the covers during a storm when you were a kid and count the seconds between the flash and boom?"

She'd been lucky if she'd *had* covers as a kid, Eve thought. And storms weren't the scary part of her life. "No."

"We did. I still do sometimes—habit. Like . . ." She watched the next flash and began to count out loud. "One, two, three. Pow." She gave a quick shudder at the boom. "Pretty close."

"If you hear it, it's not close enough to worry about. Outlets, Peabody."

"Sorry, coming up. I got three uptown, one midtown, two in Soho, one Tribeca—"

"Cull it to ones near the parking port or the universities. Five-block radius." While Peabody worked, Eve followed the next hunch and called Portography. "Give me Hastings."

"He's in session," Lucia said primly, and with a dislike not quite veiled. "I'd be happy to take a message."

"He gets out of session, or I come in and pull him out of session. Choose."

Lucia scowled, but switched the 'link to Hold where Eve was treated to shifting images of Hastings's work and a musical accompaniment. He came on looking sweaty and red-faced.

"What? What? Do I have to murder you in your sleep?"

"Dumbass thing to say to a cop, pal. Where do you get your frames?"

"What? What?"

"Stop saying that. Frames? Where do you get the frames for your photographs. Your personal work?"

"How the hell do I know? Freaking hell. Don't we carry them downstairs? Lucia! Don't we carry fricking frames downstairs?"

"You know, Hastings, I'm starting to like you. Do you use the fricking frames you carry downstairs for your work in the gallery?"

"I don't know. I don't know." If he'd had hair, Eve was sure he'd have been pulling it out. "If I find out, will you leave me the hell alone?"

"I might."

"I'll get back to you," he snapped, and rudely shut off.

"Yeah, I like him."

She was driving through the gates when he buzzed her back.

"We got all kinds of fricking frames. We're lousy with them. We don't carry what I use because, Lucia tells me, then everybody'd use them and they'd no longer be unique or some happy horseshit. I get them from goddamn Helsinki."

"Helsinki," Eve repeated, amazed.

"Clean, simple, Scandinavian." His mouth twisted in a rare smile. "Asinine, but there you go. Special order from some place called *Kehys*. Means Framework. *Har de har.* That it?"

"Yeah, for now."

"Good." He cut her off again.

"Man after my own heart. Peabody?"

"Already on it. Data on *Kehys* coming through."

"Follow it up."

"Me, sir?"

"It's your line. Tug it." With this, Eve rolled out of the car and made a beeline for the house.

She shook herself like a wet dog when she hit the foyer, started to strip off the jacket that had gotten soaked on the short run. And the voice, like God's coldest wrath, rolled down the pristine hall.

"Stop that immediately! This is a home, not a bathhouse."

With her jacket dripping in her hand, she watched Summerset come forward. He used a cane, and limped rather heavily, but his face was set in its usual pruney and disapproving lines. He carried towels over his arm.

"If you're able to walk on those ugly sticks you call legs, why are you still in my universe?"

He handed her a towel, then adroitly snatched the jacket from her. "I will be leaving on my postponed holiday in the morning. Meanwhile, you're making a puddle on the floor."

"Meanwhile you're making a buzzing in my ears." She turned toward the stairs just as Peabody rushed in.

"Summerset!" The delight in her voice had Eve rolling her eyes heavenward. "Hey, it's great to see you up and around. How're you feeling?"

"Quite well all in all, thank you." He offered her a towel. "Your uniform's damp, Officer. I'd be happy to get you something dry to wear and have your uniform laundered."

"I'd really appreciate that." She broke off at the sound Eve made—a kind of guttural snarl. "I'll be in her office," Peabody whispered, then jogged up the stairs behind Eve. "It is damp," she began. "I could catch a chill or something. Don't want to get sick during an investigation, especially when I'm studying like mad during my off time."

"Did I say anything?"

"Oh yeah. You said plenty."

Eve merely sent Peabody a long, bland stare that made the hair on the back of her aide's neck stand at attention. "I'm going to change into something nice and comfy and dry."

She veered off and strode into the bedroom.

Just for spite, she let her wet clothes fall into a soggy pile. That would burn his bony ass, she thought. She dragged on a T-shirt, jeans, strapped her weapon back into place, and considered herself done.

To give Peabody extra time, she headed into Roarke's office rather than her own.

When he glanced up, when he smiled, she felt a number of the rocky areas of her life go smooth again.

"Hello, Lieutenant."

"Hello, civilian." Maybe she could take just a minute of extra time herself. She walked around his console, leaned down, and caught his face in her hands, pressed her mouth to his.

"Well then," he remarked, and started to yank her onto his lap.

"Uh-uh, that's all you get."

"So, you just came in to torture and torment me?"

"There you go. What have you got for me?"

"A very crude answer to that question springs to mind, but I take it you're referring to my little homework assignment rather than my—"

"Affirmative." But relieved, she sat on the edge of his console to face him. It was good to see the tension gone from his face, from the set of his shoulders. "I've got Peabody working an angle, one she came up with. I've just spent a good hour stewing over one of my own without getting a bump."

"I don't know how much I can add to that. Though spreading the grease around, per your request, has netted me a few names, none fit your profile."

"Maybe I'm off." She pushed away from the console, paced over to the window to stare out at the storm. "I've been off since the get-go on this."

"If you have, I'll take the blame for it."

"You don't live inside my brain."

Don't I? he wondered. "I haven't been any help to you."

"Funny," she said without turning. "I managed to be a pretty good cop for a full decade before you came waltzing along."

"I don't believe I waltzed along. And I've no doubt you'd continue to be a great deal more than a pretty good cop without me. But the fact is I've distracted you. Worrying about me has split both your concentration and your priorities. I'm sorry for it."

"I guess you've never had them split because you were worried about me."

"I'd like to say something to you. Look at me, will you?" He waited until she'd turned. "I'm caught between pride and terror every time you put on that weapon and walk out the door. Every time. But I wouldn't have it any other way, Eve. Wouldn't have you any other way, as that's who you are and who we are together."

"It's not easy being married to a cop. You do a good job of it."

"Thanks for that." He smiled again. "You do a good one being married to a former criminal."

"Hooray for us."

"It's important to me to have a connection with what you do. Even if it's only to listen, though I enjoy doing more than that."

"Tell me."

"I'm annoyed with myself for scattering your focus on this case because I didn't do what I'd have demanded you do. I didn't dump on you. If I had, we'd have pulled this all together sooner. Next time I'm troubled like this, be sure I'll drag you into my worries straight off."

Her lips twitched. "Sounds good. And if you don't drag me quick enough, I'll just smack you around until you spill."

"Fair enough."

"Now, let's take a look at the names."

He put them on a wall screen. "There's nothing on any male in your age group. Not with a serious neurological problem."

"Maybe it's not the brain. Maybe it's some other part gone dinky."

"Well, I took that into consideration. There's still no patient out of that particular health center with a life-threatening condition in that profile. I can expand it, by spreading more grease as it were, or simply saving time and money by sliding into records in other facilities."

She considered it. It wouldn't be the first time she'd let him slither around the line. But even with his skills, it was bound to take hours, potentially days, to hack through the numerous medical facilities in the city.

And it was just a hunch. Just a gut thing.

"Let's play it by the book, more or less, for now."

She scanned the names. People were dying, she noted, but

there was no killer to hunt and cage. The killer was their own body, or fate, or just bad luck. Tumors sprouting up in inconvenient places, spreading, propagating, brewing inside the brain.

Science could locate them, and if it was early enough, if the patient had the right insurance or bank account, treatment could and did eradicate. But it was often too late, she mused, reading the list of names. She'd had no idea death was so prevalent from inside the body.

Most were elderly, it was true. Most had already celebrated their centennial. But there was a scattering of younger victims.

Darryn Joy, age seventy-three. Marilynn Kobowski, age forty-one. Lawrence T. Kettering, age eighty-eight.

Already dead or dying, she noted.

Corrine A. Stevenson, age fifty. Mitchell B.—

"Wait. Wait. Stevenson, Corrine A., full data."

"Get a bump, did you?"

"Yeah, oh yeah." She yanked out her PPC, pulled up the resident information on one of the buildings she'd run, the one a block west of the parking port.

"Stevenson just happened to live within walking distance of the parking port. Twelfth floor—giving a nice view of the area, an excellent view if you happen to have long-range lenses."

"As a photographer would."

"Yeah." She looked back on-screen. "She died, despite what—two years of treatments—last September. No spouse on record. One child, surviving son, Gerald Stevenson. Born September 13, 2028. There's a goddamn bump. Run the son."

"Already on it," Roarke said from behind her as Peabody burst through the adjoining door.

"Dallas, I got something. Javert, Luis Javert." Her face was flushed with the discovery. "Ordered frames—the same style as Hastings's standing order, from the Helsinki outlet. One size—16 by 20. He's had 50 of them shipped to a mail drop in New York, West Broadway Shipping, in Tribeca."

"How'd he pay?"

"Direct transfer. I need authorization to request a warrant for the financials."

"You've got it. Use my badge number. Roarke."

"A bit of time here, Lieutenant. There's more than one Gerald Stevenson in the flaming city. But none with that DOB," he said after a moment. "None at that residence. He's not using that name. If he's changed it legally, I'll have to . . . dig around a bit."

"Then get a shovel. Her name's still listed as resident on the apartment. Somebody's living there and wouldn't it be Corrine Stevenson's son Gerald? Peabody! With me."

"Yes, sir. One minute."

"Tag Feeney," she called to Roarke as she strode out. "Give him what you've got. The more e-drones on this, the better."

"E-men, Lieutenant," he corrected. "E-men." Then he wiggled his fingers like a pianist about to play a complex sonata.

It was good to be back.

She had to wait for Peabody to get back in uniform, so used the time to contact the commander and brief him.

"Do you want uniform backup?"

"No, sir. If he spots uniforms, it might spook him. I'd like Baxter and Trueheart, soft clothes, just to watch the egresses of the building. The suspect has not, to date, demonstrated any violent tendencies, but he may do if and when cornered. The apartment where I believe he resides is twelve floors up. Only way out is through the front door, or out the window and onto the emergency evac route. Peabody and I will have the door. Baxter and Trueheart can man the evac route."

"You've got a nice pile of circumstantial, Lieutenant, but having a mother die of brain cancer isn't going to be enough for a warrant."

"Then I'll have to be persuasive, sir, and convince him to let me inside." She looked over her shoulder as Peabody came down the steps, in her freshly laundered, meticulously pressed summer blues. "We're ready to go here, Commander."

"I'll have your backup in place within fifteen minutes. Move softly, Dallas."

"Yes, sir." She ended the communication.

"Nothing like a clean uniform." Peabody sniffed her own sleeve. "He uses something with just the faintest hint of lemon. Nice. I'll have to ask him what it is when he gets back from his vacation."

"I'm sure the two of you will have a fine time exchanging household hints, but maybe we could focus on our pesky little op for the moment."

Peabody shifted her expression to somber. "Yes, sir." But she admired the knife-edge crease of her uniform trousers as Eve filled her in.

The building had twelve floors, and she considered the advantage of placing one of her backup on the roof. Waste of manpower, she decided. If her target bolted out the window, she could bolt right after him, and head up if that was his tact. He was more likely to shoot for the street, if he bolted at all.

Would he have an escape route mapped out? He was a planner, so it was probable he'd considered the possibility of being cornered in his nest.

She called Roarke. "I need a blueprint display of the target building. I want to see the setup on the twelfth floor, the layout of the target apartment. How fast can you transmit—" She broke off when the diagram filled her screen. "Pretty damn fast," she replied.

"I'd decided to take a look at it myself. As you can see, it's a nice layout. Roomy living space, efficiently sized kitchen, two bedrooms."

"I got eyes. Later."

One bedroom for mom, one for son? She wondered. Did he work in the extra bedroom now? If he worked out of the apartment, why have the frames delivered so far downtown?

If he worked there, how the hell did he get four tranq'd people through building security and up to the twelfth floor?

She was hoping to be able to ask him directly, very soon.

She met up with Baxter and Trueheart in the lobby. It was a small space, very quiet, very clean. Security cams swept the entrance and the two silver-doored elevators. It didn't boast a doorman, live or droid, but it had required a scan of her badge to gain entrance.

"The target is apartment 1208, east-facing unit, third in from the south corner. Windows are, from south to north, numbers six, seven, and eight."

She glanced at Trueheart—couldn't help it. It was so rare to see him in civilian clothes. If possible he looked even younger in the sports shirt and jeans than he did in uniform.

"Where's your weapon, Trueheart?"

He patted the base of his spine, under the long tail of his baby blue shirt. "I thought I'd attract more attention wearing a jacket in this heat. I know it looks a little sloppy, Lieutenant, but it's more usual street wear."

"That wasn't a fashion question."

"She'd be the last to ask one of those," Baxter put in, and looked cool and casual in summer khakis and a faded green tee. "Not that she doesn't always look hot. Especially since somebody with taste's buying her threads these days."

"I'll remind you to bite me later. Right now, we're going to try to pinpoint and apprehend a serial killer, so maybe we can talk about how cute we all look some other time.

"Communicators on," she continued. "Weapons low stun. You two take the sidewalk across the street. Spread out. You see anybody at any of the target windows, I want a heads-up. Anybody fitting profile enters or exits the building while I'm inside, I want to know about it. Let's pin him down."

She walked to the elevators, scooping up a fake potted fern on the way.

"I didn't know you liked houseplants, Dallas."

"Home decorating is always on my mind. He sees my face through his security peep, he's not going to open the door. He knows me."

"Oh, camouflage."

"Stay out of the line of sight," she ordered Peabody. "We need him to open the door, establish he's in there, get a look at his face. Record on."

"So if he panics, slams the door again, we've got probable cause and a face."

"And he's bolted in until we get a warrant. Nobody dies tonight," she stated as she stepped out on twelve.

She hitched the fern up, looking through the fronds as she approached the apartment. It had a security peep, full screen, a palm plate, and voice box.

Taking no chances, are you, she thought. You're a careful bastard. Don't want some casual burglar lifting your locks and finding your goodies.

She rang the bell, waited.

The red locked light stayed steady.

She rang again. "Delivery for 1208," she called out.

Hearing the door behind her open, Eve shifted her weight and put her free hand on her weapon.

A young woman stepped out of 1207, eyes widening when she spotted Peabody's uniform. "Is there some sort of trouble? Is anything wrong? Is Gerry okay?"

"Gerald Stevenson." Eve set the fern down. "Does he live here?"

"Sure. Haven't seen him for, I don't know, a few days anyway. But that's his place. Who are you?"

"Dallas. NYPSD." She took out her badge. "So, Gerry's not home."

"No. Like I said, I haven't seen him for a while. He's probably out on assignment."

"Assignment."

"Yeah, you know, taking pictures."

Eve felt the quick leap in her blood. "He's a photographer."

"Image artist. That's what he calls it. He's good, too. He took some of my husband and me last year. Of course, he hasn't been doing much work since his mother died. What's this about, anyway?"

"When his mother died," Eve prompted. "What happened?"

"What you'd expect. He fell apart. They were really close. He took care of her through the whole thing, and believe me, some of it had to be horrible. She just died by inches. Mark and I did what we could, but really, what can you do? Has something happened to Gerry? God, has he been in an accident?"

"Not that I know of. Mrs?"

"Ms. Ms. Fryburn. Jessie. Listen, I've knocked a couple times in the last week, and I've tried to reach him on his 'link, just to check. He seemed better lately, a lot better, and said he was working pretty steady. If something's happened, I'd like to help. He's a nice guy, and Ms. Stevenson, well, she was a jewel. One in a million."

"You might be able to help. Can we come inside, talk to you?"

"I . . ." She glanced at the time on a slim silver wrist unit. "Yes. Sure. I just have to call in, reschedule a few meetings." She looked at Eve again, at Peabody, then at the fern Eve sat beside the door. And began to put some of it together. "Is Gerry in trouble?"

"Yes. Yes, he's in trouble."

It took more time than Eve wanted to spend, but she wanted Jessie Fryburn's cooperation. It took precious time to batter back the woman's instinctive defense of Gerald Stevenson. Her refusal to believe he could be involved in anything illegal, much less murderous.

She dug in on it until Eve wanted to take her loyal spine and twist it into a pretzel.

"If, as you continue to insist, Gerry's innocent, it'll only be to his benefit for me to find him and clear all this up." *I'm just about through screwing around with you in any polite manner,* Eve thought.

"Oh, like an innocent man isn't ever arrested and dragged through the mud until his life is ruined." Jessie was so focused on the heat of her own outrage, she missed the warning flare of Eve's. "You're just doing your job, I understand that perfectly well, but it is a *job*. And people make mistakes on the job every day."

"You're right. And it would probably be a mistake for me to slap restraints on you right now, haul your ass down to Central, and into lockup for impeding an investigation, for obstruction of justice, for just being a complete pain in the ass. But you know what?" She rose and tugged her restraints off her belt. "People make mistakes on the job every day."

"You wouldn't dare."

"Peabody?"

"She would dare, Ms. Fryburn. She would absolutely dare. And lockup isn't very pleasant."

A flush from insult and temper stained Jessie's cheeks. "I'm calling my lawyer. I'm not saying another word until I do. If she advises me to talk to you, fine. Otherwise." She lifted her chin so that Eve had to resist taking the invitation to rap it with her fist. "You can do your worst."

"She really doesn't understand just how good your worst is. Or how bad—depending on your point of view." Peabody said this out of the corner of her mouth as Jessie stalked to a 'link.

"The only reason she's still standing is because I respect loyalty, and she's clueless. He's a nice guy, he took care of his dying mother. He didn't cause any trouble. A nice, neat, quiet neighbor. Fits profile."

"Where do we go from here?"

"Haul her in, if we need to. Plow through the lawyer and talk her into working with an Ident artist. I want a goddamn image. And I want a warrant to get through that door across the hall."

She yanked out her communicator. "Commander," she began when he came on. "I need some pressure."

Time leaked out of the day, and the gloom edged into an early twilight. More storms circled, threatened, shot out heat lightning and threatening blasts of thunder.

She danced with the lawyer, until she thought her ears might bleed, but in the end a reluctant Jessie agreed to a session with an Ident artist. As long as it took place in her own apartment.

"You think I'm being stubborn." Jessie sat, arms folded and frowned at Eve. "But I consider Gerry a friend. I watched what he went through with his mom, and it was heart-breaking. I've never seen anyone die before. She fought so hard, and he was right there, in the trenches with her. And when she was too weak to fight, he kept right on."

Obviously moved, she bit her lip to keep her voice steady. "He cleaned up after. He bathed her, fed her, sat with her. He wouldn't let anyone else do the dirty work. I've never seen that kind of devotion. I don't know if I have it in me."

"That kind of experience might push a person over the edge."

"Maybe. Maybe, but . . . God, I *hate* this. He's already suffered so much. Whenever I saw him after, after it was over, he looked like a ghost. Just getting through, just getting by. He lost weight, looked nearly as sick as she had. Then he seemed to come back. The last few months, he seemed to find his feet again. You want me to think he's crazy, some sort of insane monster. But I've lived across the hall from him for two and a half years, and he's not."

"There are three young people dead who looked at him, who I believe looked right into his face. They didn't think he was a monster either."

"He's just out on assignment, you'll see. He's just out working, trying to get his life back on track. You'll see."

"One of us will," Eve replied.

Chapter 21

Eve peered at the door of apartment 1208 as if some of the heat of her impatience would gather and bore holes through the panel so she could *see*.

One simple authorization was keeping her out, one simple go-in-and-look was all she needed.

Circumstantial, her ass. She *knew*.

She believed in the working of law. The rules, the checkpoints. Cops had no right to break into a private home like stormtroopers. On hunches, on whims, on personal vendettas.

Probable cause. She needed it. And she had it. Why in the hell didn't a judge have enough working brain cells to see she had it?

Patience, she ordered herself. The warrant would come through, and she'd go through the door.

But waiting made her imagine how it might have run if she'd come here with Roarke. Would she have used her master to gain entrance? Hell, he'd have finessed the locks before she'd pulled it out of her pocket.

And then, of course, whatever she'd found inside would be inadmissible. Going in the easy way would have presented Stevenson with a walk.

Checks and balances, she reminded herself. The rules of law.

God, what was taking so long?

Peabody stepped out of Jessie's apartment where Eve had stationed her. "She's still stalling," Peabody reported under her breath. "Yancy's good, and he's building up a rapport with her, gaining trust, but it's not going to be quick."

Straining against impotence, Eve glanced in the apartment. Yancy, the Ident artist, kept up a cheerful banter as he worked with his kit. He was young, but he was good, he was solid.

She had to leave him alone, Eve thought. Had to stay out of the mix. The witness already had a resentment against her, and if she went in, pressed, it would only gum up the works.

"She keeps changing her mind on the details," Peabody went on. "Jawline, nose, even skin tone. But he's bringing her around."

"I'd like to plant my boot up her ass," Eve commented. "That would bring her around."

Instead, she pulled out her communicator and tagged Baxter. She wasn't going to leave her men out on the street, twiddling their thumbs and waiting for Stevenson to show.

"Yo, baby" was Baxter's response.

"Yo, baby?"

"Just making sure you haven't forgotten me."

"I never forget irritants. I'm bringing in a couple of replacements. You and Trueheart take the club for a few hours."

"Ah, a cool libation would go down fine right now. Hear that, kid?"

"You and the kid stick to nonalcoholic libations." She considered how long they'd been on duty that day. "Give it an hour, just do a sweep. You want in if we locate this prick?"

"Damn straight."

"I'll let you know. If we don't pin him tonight, consider yourselves sprung at twenty-one hundred."

"Copy that. Come on, Trueheart, let's go raise a glass to

our illustrious lieutenant." He winked at Eve. "By the way, hubby's on his way in."

"Hubby? Hubby who?"

"Ah, I think he means Roarke," Peabody said when Baxter clicked off on a bark of laughter. "Hubby—husband?"

"Oh, Christ." Annoyed all over again, she marched down to the elevator to wait for him.

"I didn't send for you." She jabbed a finger at him the instant he stepped out.

"And my heart aches at the lack. I've got some data you wanted, Lieutenant, and preferred giving it to you face-to-face." He cocked his eyebrow, smiling down the hall at Peabody who hovered between apartments. "How's it going here?"

"Slow. What've you got?"

"Bits and pieces. A few parking facilities that, and this shocks me, run sidelines. Then it happens I had a chat with Stevenson's neurologist. I know, you didn't ask me to, specifically, but I took my own initiative." The smile flashed into a grin. "I'm banking on a raise."

"Yeah, you keep banking on that. What was the content of this chat?"

"I'm told the patient was an extraordinary woman. Brave, optimistic, a classy woman who was dealt a very bad hand. She was, as it happens, a health care worker herself. A nurse, at—"

"The East Side Health Center," Eve finished.

"There you are. Her son was completely devoted to her, and a bit more fanciful than optimistic. He simply refused to believe she would die, and when she did, took it very hard. He blamed the doctors, the health center, God, and whoever else was handy. Refused any and all grief counseling. The doctor was concerned the son might do something rash. Self-termination being top of his list."

"Too bad he wasn't right. He'll ID him?"

"He's willing, and anxious to cooperate."

She nodded, and pulled out her communicator. "I've got an Ident man in there with a neighbor who's neither willing nor anxious to cooperate. He'll get our image, but it's taking too long. I'm going to arrange to have another artist work with the doctor. Give me his name and location."

When she'd completed the arrangements, she started to pocket her communicator again. It beeped in her hand.

"Dallas."

"Lieutenant, your warrant's coming through."

About damn time, she thought, but bit back the words. "Thank you, sir. Officer Yancy is still working with the neighbor. I've called in replacements for Baxter and Trueheart, so the building's still covered, and ordered them to do an hour's surveillance at the data club before clocking out. Peabody and I will enter subject's apartment as soon as the warrant's in hand. Am I clear to call in the sweepers I have on alert?"

"Call them in, get it done. Let's put this away tonight."

"Nothing I'd like better," she agreed as she watched his face blink off.

"Darling." Roarke skimmed a hand down Eve's hair while Peabody pretended to look elsewhere. "You needed to get into an apartment, and you didn't call me?"

"Thought about it." She spoke under her breath, then turned to face him while she willed the warrant to come through. "I won't deny I thought about just going in. But it wouldn't wash clean, and it has to. I'm not giving this bastard any legal way out."

"You're right, of course. Your patience—"

He broke off as her communicator beeped again, signalling the authorization.

"Son of a bitch, bite my *ass*! It's about fucking *time*!" She spun around and strode down the hall. "Peabody, we're going in."

"Perhaps patience wasn't precisely the right word," Roarke considered as he followed her.

She shot him one brief look, and considered. Argue with him, give in. Or make it her idea. "You're going in with us. Seal up." She tossed him a can of Seal-It and enjoyed the quick wince on his face as he studied it. "It'll come off your fancy shoes, Ace."

"But they'll never be quite the same. Ah well, being a good citizen requires some sacrifice."

"Like you don't have two hundred other pairs. He's got a good eye," she said to Peabody. "We can use him."

"Yes, sir. I often think of uses for your hubby." And because Roarke was between them, the safety factor, she grinned.

"That's really amusing, Peabody. I'll be chuckling when I tie your tongue into a knot later. Straighten up," she ordered. "Record on."

Behind her back, Roarke passed the Seal-It to Peabody and added a wink.

"Dallas, Lieutenant Eve, Peabody, Officer Delia, and civilian consultant Roarke are duly authorized with warrant, signed by Judge Marcia B. Brigstone to enter apartment 1208 of this location on full search and seizure. All pertinent data regarding this procedure are listed in said warrant. Sweeper unit is en route. Using police master to disengage locks and security."

She inserted it, keyed in her code. And the access was denied.

"Damn it. Subject has installed secondary security that repels standard master." Deliberately she turned away from the door so the record showed the apartment across the hall. And she looked coolly at Roarke. "It will be necessary to send for and utilize a battering ram in order to gain entrance and fulfill the authorization of the warrant."

Understanding, Roarke slipped behind her and taking a slim device from his pocket went to work on the locks.

"Officer," Eve began, noting that Peabody was watching Roarke with obvious fascination.

"Yes, sir, Lieutenant." But her eyes never left Roarke, and her mouth formed a silent "wow" as she watched his fingers move, and okay, wondered if they were just that skilled in other, more personal activities.

Imagining they were, she felt her heart give a quick, hard knock against her ribs.

"Officer!" Eve repeated. "We're going to try the master

again momentarily. Contact Dispatch and request a unit with battering ram."

"Uh-huh. I mean, yes, sir."

"Perhaps you should try your master again, Lieutenant." Expression bland, Roarke stepped away from the door. "Before your aide fulfills that order. Sometimes these things jam a bit."

"Affirmative. Belay that order, Peabody. Retrying master."

He'd done whatever magic he could do, and this time her code had the security flashing to green.

"Locks are disengaged. Must've just been a jam," she said, turning to Peabody.

"Yes, sir." Peabody gave her a sober nod. "Happens all the time."

"Entering Stevenson apartment."

Though she believed it to be empty, she drew her weapon. "This is the police," she called out as she opened the door, swept the room. "We are duly authorized to enter. Stay where you are, with your hands above your head and in clear sight. Lights on."

Like the Fryburn apartment across the hall, it was spacious. It was clean, ruthlessly so, and appointed in such a way that made Eve think: female.

Color, texture, thriving, live plants, pretty dust-catchers set around. The windows were privacy screened, and through them she could see a new storm boiling in the dark sky.

The lights, on bright and full, illuminated the framed photographs lining the walls.

Gotcha, Eve thought, but her face was set and cold as she gestured Peabody to the left, Roarke to the right.

They'd check the entire apartment for Stevenson, or anyone else, before beginning the search.

"This is an official NYPSD operation," she said clearly, though she knew the place was empty. She closed the door at her back. If she was wrong, she didn't want to give him an escape route.

She moved through the living area with its homey floral sofa and deep, welcoming chairs. She checked closets—

noted that a woman's coat, a woman's jacket, winter boots, a bright pink umbrella were still mixed in with a man's outer gear.

She moved into the kitchen, saw a bowl of glossy red apples on the counter and a quartet of oversized coffee mugs in the same flashy color.

"Dallas?" Peabody stepped to the doorway. "Nobody home."

"He plans to come back." She picked up an apple, tossed it lightly. "This is still home. Let's get started."

She called Feeney, wanting him and McNab on the apartment's 'links and electronics as soon as possible. But with Roarke already there, she didn't see the point in waiting for them to arrive.

"I want all incoming, all outgoings. Any communications that give us a line on his whereabouts, his place of employment, where he hangs, what he does. I want to know if he made any contact with any of the victims from this location."

"I know what to do."

"Yeah, you usually do. Peabody, start in his mother's bedroom. We want anything that ties him to the vics, but we're also looking for anything that points to his location. I'll take his room."

But first she walked along his gallery, studying faces, images, trying to see him in them.

There were several of his mother. An attractive woman, soft eyes, soft hair, soft smile. There was always a light around her. Had he done that deliberately, or was it just chance?

He left nothing to chance.

There were other faces, other themes. Children at play, a man in a ball cap hoisting a loaded soy dog. A young woman stretched out on a blanket by a pool of flowers.

But none of the images that played in her head, none of the dead, graced these walls.

Did he? she wondered. Were any of these faces his?

She'd have Feeney run an image check for ID. It would take time, more precious time, but they might get lucky.

She moved into his bedroom.

It was neat and orderly, like the rest of the apartment. The bed tidily made, pillows fluffed. In his closet, the clothes were arranged by type, and by color.

Obsessive/compulsive, she decided, though it ran through her mind that Roarke's department store of a closet was similarly arranged.

Young. She studied the wardrobe choices. Trendy shirts, airboots, gel sandals, plenty of jeans, lots of styling pants. Nothing too cheap, nothing too pricey. Lived within his means, but liked his clothes. Liked to look good.

Image.

She started on his desk first.

In his organized files she found an orientation disc for Columbia University, another marked class notes from a course titled Exploring the Image, Professor Leeanne Browning, from the previous year.

Piling up on you, Ger, she thought as she labeled them and sealed them into evidence.

She moved to his dresser, began to search through the neatly folded socks and underwear. Tucked among them was a small, cloth-covered box, and inside some of his treasures.

A dried rosebud, a shiny rock, an old ticket stub from Yankee Stadium, a scrap of cloth that might have been from a blanket.

One of the toss-away coasters often found in clubs. This one had Make The Scene scrolled across it in electric blue letters. She sealed that and a business card for Portography into her evidence bag.

She stepped back, took stock. Live here, but you don't work here. This isn't your work space. Got to keep that separate. This is your mother's place, the place you come for a nice, quiet meal, for a good night's sleep. But it's not where you create.

Haven't been here in awhile. She ran a fingertip through the light layer of dust on the dresser. So much work to do. Too much to do to come home and relax. To come home and not find your mother waiting for you.

"Eve."

She looked over at the doorway where Roarke stood. "Finished already?"

"Not much there. He has a thirty-day clearing system. If you take the units in, you could dig out the deleted transmissions, but from here, without any tools, you'll only get the month. And he wasn't the chatty sort. He ordered pizza about three weeks ago, and fresh flowers for his mother's grave—"

"Location of cemetery?" she interrupted.

"I've got it for you, yes. There aren't any transmissions to or from friends, relatives, acquaintances. He's left his mother's voice announcement on the unit."

"But his voice is on there. We'll get a clear voice print."

Something moved in his eyes before the shutter came down. "Yes, that's no problem."

"You want me to feel sorry for him because he lost his mother? Because you're still close enough to your own grief to relate in some way. Sorry, fresh out of sympathy here. People die. It sucks. You don't deal with grief by murdering three innocent people."

"No, you don't." He sighed. "There's just something pathetic about this place, about the way he's living here with his mother's things. Her clothes still in the closets, her voice still on the machine. I've been working out there and found myself looking up, time and again, at her face. Do you see what he's done?"

"No, what has he done?"

"He's made her into an angel. From all reports, she was a good woman, maybe a special one at that. But human, mortal. It's that he hasn't accepted, you see. She isn't allowed to be human, so he deifies her. He's killing for her, and God knows, it doesn't seem she deserves it."

"It's her you feel sorry for."

"A great deal. She would have loved him, wouldn't she? Loved him very much by all accounts. Wouldn't she love him still, even after all he's done?"

"I don't know."

"Well, I don't suppose we ever will. Here's Feeney now," he added, and stepped out.

Had he been talking about Gerald Stevenson's mother, Eve wondered, or his own?

She cleared the bedroom for the sweepers and huddled with Feeney. "Where's McNab?"

"Ah, he nipped into the other bedroom there. Said he'd give Peabody a hand."

"I bet it's not his hand he's hoping to give her."

Feeney could only wince. "Please. Don't put such pictures in my head."

"I like to share, since they keep getting jammed into mine. Pictures," she repeated and gestured to the wall. "I don't think he's here. No nice little photos sitting around his mother's room. There would've been. She'd have had some of him in there, or sitting around."

"Mothers tend to," Feeney agreed.

"Figures, especially given his line of work or interest. So he cleared out any images of himself, just in case."

Trying to ignore what may or may not be going on in the bedroom, she tapped an evidence bag. "The mother liked Barrymore products. He left her enhancements in her room."

She jerked her head toward the open hallway door. "Yancy's still working on the witness—stubborn twit. Hopefully, he'll have it done soon, but I figure you should start an image search on the faces here anyway, see if anything pops."

"Take awhile." He brightened. "I'll have McNab do it. Keep his hands, and everything else on him, where it belongs."

"Works for me. I'm going to goose Yancy in a minute. If he's making progress I'm taking Roarke and checking out the parking facilities he tagged for us. Be easier if we have the guy's face to show around.

"He's coming back here, Feeney. His mother's things are here, this gallery of photos, some of his clothes, his mom's girl stuff. There's still food in the kitchen, and he's too compulsive and well-trained to let it spoil. But he's got work to do. I think he wants to finish his work before he comes home. The neighbor was right. He's on assignment."

"How close is he?"

"Pretty close to done. He knows we're moving in. He's had to move to backup plans. It's not that he planned to kill until he got caught." Face set, she dropped the bag of enhancements back onto a table. "He planned to kill until he was finished. It's not the thrill that drives him, it's the work, so he has an endgame. He wants us to see it, wants us to see the finished work. He may have to move a little quicker now to get it done, so he can show it off before we stop him. He'll have the next target in sight by now."

"Lieutenant." Pretty-faced Yancy leaned against the doorway. "I think we've got it. Sorry it took so long. It's tougher when the witness figures we're, you know, full of shit."

"Are you confident she's not stringing you?"

"Oh yeah. I explained, really politely and apologetically, that she could be charged with obstruction and so forth if she knowingly gave me a false image. Her lawyer made lots of lawyer noises, then verified—that's another thing that delayed the result."

"Let's see what we've got."

He pulled out his Identi-pad, turned it so she could view the finished image.

"Jesus Christ." Her heart did a quick leap into her throat. "Transmit that image to Central. I want every black-and-white, every on-duty officer to have that image ASAP. Suspect is identified as Gerald Stevenson, aka Steve Audrey, employed as bartender at Make The Scene. Get it out, Yancy, now!"

She yanked her communicator out of her pocket and tried to raise Baxter.

He'd given it the hour, and saw nothing more than the usual scene. A crowd of mostly kids, preening and parading, sipping ridiculously named drinks and heating up the keyboards when they weren't jamming onto the dance floor.

Not that he didn't enjoy watching young, agile female bodies gyrate in skimpy summer clothes, but the music was too loud, too brash.

It gave him a mild headache, and worse—much worse— made him feel old.

He wanted to go home, prop up his feet, suck down a beer, and watch some screen.

Christ, when had he become his father?

What he needed was to get cozy with a woman again. A noncop type female with long lines and soft curves. The job had been eating up too much of his recreational time—which went to show what happened when you transferred to Homicide from Anti-Crime, ended up under Dallas—and not in a sexual way—and took on a green rookie.

Nothing wrong with Trueheart, though, he had to admit it as he tracked his gaze across the room and saw his boy sipping a soda water and chatting up some fresh-faced young thing.

Kid was bright as a polished star, eager as a puppy, and would work until he dropped. He'd never figured on taking on the responsibility of trainer, but by damn, he was enjoying it.

Made him feel good the way the kid looked to him for advice, listened to his stories, believed his bullshit.

Oh yeah, he was turning into his old man right in front of his own eyes.

Time to clock out and go home.

He paid his tab, noting the change of shift at the bar. He wasn't the only one calling it a night.

Casually, he made a circle, around the tables, scanning faces one last time, watching the data hounds, eyeballing the staff. He waited until Trueheart shifted his gaze, then Baxter tapped his wrist unit in the signal they were packing it in.

Trueheart nodded, turned his glass on the bar to indicate he'd just finish up, then head on home himself.

Working well together, Baxter decided as he walked out into the heavy air. *Kid's coming along fine.* He glanced up once at the storm-tossed sky, and hoped to hell he made it home before it broke.

He was in his car, and ten full blocks uptown, when his communicator signalled.

"Ah, shit, Dallas. Can't a guy go home once in a damn while?" Grumbling to himself, he pulled out his communicator. "Baxter. What the hell do you want now?"

"Suspect's ID'd. Gerald Stevenson is Steve Audrey, your friendly, fucking bartender."

He shot a look at his rearview, his sideview mirrors, then cut across a lane of traffic before he was pinned in by a maxibus and a streamline of Rapid Cabs. "I'm ten blocks away, heading north. I'll double back. Suspect clocked off shift at twenty-one hundred. Trueheart's still in there."

"Contacting him now. Keep your communicator open and active. Get back there, Baxter. I don't want the kid handling this alone. I'm already on my way."

Baxter tried to squeeze between cabs, listening as Eve called for Trueheart.

He'd finished his drink, and was feeling a little flattered, a little nervous as the girl who'd come over to talk to him had asked for his number.

She'd wanted to dance, too, but he was a terrible dancer. And he really had to get home, get a good night's sleep. You never knew when the case was going to break.

He knew he was blushing when he gave the girl, Marley, his private 'link number. He hated that color so easily washed into his face, and prayed he'd grow out of it. Soon.

Cops didn't blush. Dallas sure as hell didn't. Baxter didn't.

Maybe there was some sort of medical treatment to prevent it.

Amused at himself, he walked out of the club. Storm's coming up, he thought, and found himself pleased. He loved a good booming storm. He debated whether to jump into the subway, head straight home underground, or walk a few blocks while the air turned electric.

He wondered if—after the case was closed and he could tell Marley he was a cop—she would want to go out with him.

Just pizza and a vid, maybe. Something really casual. You just couldn't get to know somebody very well in a club when the music was loud and everybody was talking at once.

He watched a snake of lightning uncoil overhead, and decided the subway was best. If he got home quick enough, he could watch the storm from his window. He started to walk south, still looking up at the sky.

His communicator beeped. He pulled it out, engaged.

"Hey! It's gonna rain in a minute. Need a lift?"

Trueheart looked over, felt the blush work up his throat again at being caught staring up at the sky like some kid in a planetarium. Automatically he palmed the unit, switched it to hold so it went silent and didn't blow his cover.

"Just about to catch the subway." He gave the man he knew as Steve a friendly smile. "Done for the night?"

"Actually, I'm heading to my other job. Did I see you talking to Marley?"

"Yeah." The color worked into his cheeks. "She's nice."

"She's very nice." Gerry winked, chuckled, then stuck out a hand. "Good luck."

Without thinking, Trueheart took the offered hand. He didn't need the quick prick in his palm to tell him he'd made a terrible mistake.

It was in the eyes.

He yanked his hand free, tried to reach for the weapon at the small of his back, but his balance was already gone. He stumbled, had the wit to close his fingers over the communicator even as they began to tingle.

"Steve Audrey," he mumbled as his tongue went thick. "Block south of Make The Scene."

"That's right." Gerry already had his arm and was leading him away. "Feeling a little dizzy? Don't worry. I've got a car nearby."

Trueheart tried to pull away, tried to remember basic hand-to-hand, but his head was spinning, spinning. Gerry had an arm banded around his shoulder blades now.

His vision was fading in and out, and all the lights, the headlights were blurring, haloing, speeding by him like comets.

"Tranq'd," Trueheart managed.

"Don't worry." Gerry took his weight, like a brother-in-arms. "I'm going to take good care of you. You've got such a wonderful light, and it's going to shine forever."

Chapter 22

Fear wanted to ice her gut, her brain, her throat. She shut it down.

"Baxter?"

"I copy. I'm going the wrong fucking way." She heard the clashing chorus of horns as he maneuvered. "Shit. Fuck. Heading back. I'm better than ten blocks away, Dallas. Goddamn it."

"Parking port," she snapped at Roarke. "Closest to the data club, on the south."

"Getting it." He already had his book out, keying in for the data.

"Feeney! He's got Trueheart. Let's move, let's move. Yancy, get that image out. Now!"

"E-Z Park, on Twelfth, between Third and Fourth," Roarke told her as cops bolted for the door en masse.

"All units, all units, officer in distress. Code Red." She relayed the location. "Suspect ID's as Gerald Stevenson aka Steve Audrey. Image forthcoming. Subject is believed to be responsible for multiple murders. May be armed."

Her communicator squawked with responses as units began to roll. She paused only to bore one long look at Jessie as the woman rushed into the hallway.

"He's got one of my men. Anything happens to my officer. Anything, I'm coming back for you."

Still snapping out orders and data, she dived into the elevator.

"Quiet." She tossed up a hand to stop the chatter, heard Gerry's voice, light and cheerful.

Nope, no problem. My friend here's been partying pretty hard. Just going to take him home.

Parking . . . facil . . . level . . .

She closed down another leap of fear as she heard Trueheart's weak, slurred voice.

That's right. Got a ride parked. Let's get you in. Maybe you should just lie down in the back. Don't worry about a thing, I'm going to take care of you. Just relax.

"He's got him in the vehicle. Baxter?"

"Six blocks from the port. Got some jams on Third, breaking through."

"Tell me what kind of vehicle, Trueheart. Tell me."

"Itza van," he muttered as if he'd heard the order. *It's . . . dark. Tired.*

"Stay with me." Eve raced out of the building. "You stay with me."

She jumped into the passenger seat. It never occurred to her to drive—not with Roarke there. He was better at it, faster and slicker. Without a word, Peabody leaped into the back while Feeney and McNab ran to another car.

"He's thinking, he's still thinking like a cop." She swiped at the sweat on her face as Roarke screamed away from the curb. "He's left his communicator open. Peabody, monitor his transmissions. That's all I want you to do? Understood?"

"Yes, sir. I'm on him. They're on the move, Lieutenant. I can hear the engine, some traffic sounds. He's got the radio on. Sirens. I hear sirens."

Come on, come on, come on, Eve chanted in her head while she continued to relay orders. "Subject is driving a van. Exiting parking facility."

Roarke punched into vertical, pushing the clunky police issue into a stomach pitching lift to skim over a clump of Rapid Cabs, and simultaneously wrenching to the left to take a corner at a speed that had Peabody bouncing in the back like dice in a cup.

The tires kissed the top of an umbrella on the corner glide-cart, then hit the street again.

"Holy God," Peabody managed as buildings whizzed by.

He was threading through traffic like a snake sliding around rocks. She didn't have the courage to check out the speed.

"Black van, Dallas. Trueheart said black van, no windows in the back. He's fading."

"He's not going to fade."

She wasn't going to lose him. She wasn't going to lose that young, fresh-faced, quietly dedicated cop who could still blush.

"He needs to switch the communicator to homing pattern. That's all he needs to do." Her hand balled into a fist, bumped on her thigh. "Baxter, goddamn it!"

"Block and a half. No van sighted."

Pizza and a vid, Trueheart thought as he rolled helplessly in the back of the van. Wished he could dance better. Woulda asked her to dance if he wasn't such a klutzo.

No, no, in a van. Black panel van. In trouble. Oh boy, in trouble. Steve. Bartender. Brown and brown, five-ten, a hundred and . . . what was it?

Tranq'd me. Gotta think. Do something. Something . . .

She was so pretty. Marley. Really pretty.

But it was Eve's face that blurred in his brain. *Straighten up, Officer Trueheart. Report.*

Report, report. Officer down. I'm really down. Supposed to do something. He tried to reach the weapon at the small of his back, but his arm wouldn't cooperate. Communicator, he thought. He was supposed to do something with the communicator.

The procedure floated in and out of his brain as the music played and the van drove smoothly through the night.

Eve leaped out of the car at the parking port, sprang at Baxter who already had the operator in a choke hold against the kiosk.

A half dozen cop cars and twice that many cops were blocking crosstown traffic. The air was full of sirens, shouts, threats, and the rolling boom of thunder.

"Don't know what you're talking about. Don't know." The operator gasped out the words as his eyes bulged from a face going a dangerous shade of puce.

"Stand down, Detective." Eve grabbed Baxter's arm.

"My ass. You're going to tell me, you flat-nose little shit-faced weasel, or I'm going to wring your neck like a Thanksgiving turkey."

"Stand down!" Eve boomed it out, knocked Baxter back two steps. Anticipating them both, Roarke locked Baxter's arms behind his back as Eve stepped in to drill a finger into the operator's heaving chest. "You got ten seconds, or I let him have you. Then I let the rest of these cops finish the job. I want the make, model, license number of the van you just sidelined."

"I don't know what—"

She leaned in, spoke very softly. "I will give you more pain than you can imagine. Your brains will leak out of your ears, and your bowels out of your ass. I will cause that to happen without leaving a mark, and every cop here will swear you died of natural causes."

He'd been afraid of Baxter, but it wasn't fear he felt now. It was jittering, jelly-filled terror. The man cop had been all heat, and heat could give you a few bruises. But cold, this kind of cold killed.

"Chevy Mini-Mule. 2051 model. Black, panel style. I gotta look up the license. I don't want any trouble. Hey, the owners are out of town for two weeks. Guy just wanted a ride."

"Look it up, you pus-ball. You've got twenty seconds."

She pointed at a uniform to go with the operator into the kiosk. Baxter had stopped struggling against Roarke. He stood now, pale as ice, with grief already creeping into his eyes.

"I was going the wrong way, Dallas. The wrong goddamn way. I left the kid in the club. Wanted to go home, put my feet up, have a beer. I left him there."

"What are you Psychic Cop now? You should've known this was coming down." There was a sneer in her voice, a brutal one she knew would snap him out of it. "I didn't know that about you, Baxter. We'll have to have you transferred to Special Ops. They could use your talents."

"Dallas. He's mine."

"We're going to get him." She let herself go long enough to take Baxter's arm. "Pull yourself together, or you won't be able to help him."

Her head was buzzing with the fear that wanted to sneak back, with the anger, with a sense of being just one step too late. Taking the license number, she drew it all in.

"All units. All units. Subject vehicle is identified as a black Chevrolet Mini-Mule, 2051, panel style. License is NY 5504 Baker Zulo. Repeat. New York, 5504 Baker Zulo. City-wide APB on vehicle and on suspect Stevenson, Gerald, aka Steven Audrey. This is Code Red."

She slapped the communicator back in her pocket. "Peabody?"

"Nothing for the last couple minutes, sir. They're still in motion. I heard a tourist blimp. Pretty sure. Couldn't catch much, but there was something about Chinatown."

"Downtown. He's headed south. All units, sweep area south of Canal. Let's move out. Baxter, you're with me."

"I've got my ride—"

"Leave it." She didn't trust him to drive, or to be on his own. "You're with me. I'll take the wheel," she told Roarke. "You, Feeney, McNab, start working on finding residents below Canal. Look for something near West Broadway. Anything that pops. Javert, Stevenson, Audrey, Gerald. Single residents. It'll be someplace that has parking close. Upper floors. He'll want space, light, and a view."

She climbed into the car. She'd wasted time with Fryburn. Ten minutes sooner, five, and they'd have moved on him before he'd laid a hand on Trueheart.

Minutes. It was coming down to minutes now.

"Peabody?"

"He's still conscious, sir. He mumbles every once in a while. I can't make much of it out." But she'd made notes of every word. "Communicator. Bartender. Pizza and vid. Officer down. Report."

While she headed downtown Eve called in, requesting that Traffic give her the location of the tourist blimp.

"You get any sense of the street, Peabody?"

"It's quieted down. I don't hear many horns. I'm catching sirens, but nothing too close. Not yet. There's some bumps. I think I'm getting them because the communicator's on the floor of the van. I can hear the tires go over potholes. I think—"

"Hold it. Wait." Eyes straight ahead, Eve strained her ears. "Street crew. That's an airjack."

"Ears like a cat," Roarke murmured. "I'll relay it to Feeney."

It took minutes, precious minutes, before Feeney's voice punched through. "Street crews scheduled on West Broadway and Worth, Beekman and Fulton at Williams."

"We've got the blimp passing over Bayard." She drew the map in her head even as Roarke brought it up on her 'link screen. "We split to all locations." But she had to go with her gut. "Head west," she told Roarke.

"Lieutenant," Peabody said from the back. "They've stopped."

As the van stopped, Trueheart closed his numb fingers over his communicator. Something he needed to do. Switch to homing. Thank God, thank God, he remembered. Finally remembered. But his fingers felt so fat, so *gone*. He couldn't quite make them work. Struggling to stay awake, he tucked the unit into his palm as the doors opened.

Gerry was very gentle. He didn't want to cause bruises. He didn't want to give pain. He explained that in comforting tones as he pulled Trueheart out of the back.

"This is the most important thing either of us will ever do," Gerry told him, supporting Trueheart's weight, moving steadily forward as Trueheart's civilian shoes bumped over the sidewalk.

"Murder," Trueheart mumbled. "You have the right to . . ."

"No, no." Patiently, Gerry drew out his key card, used it, then the palm screen to gain access to the building. "You've been listening to the news reports. I'm pretty disappointed with the angle they're taking, but I expected it. It'll all change once they understand."

Trueheart struggled to pay attention to the scene. The lights were dim, or maybe it was his eyes. "White walls, mail chutes, secured entrance, two elevators."

"Observant, aren't you?" Gerry laughed lightly as he called the elevator. "Me, too. My mother always said I noticed everything, and saw things other people didn't. That's why I became an image artist. I wanted to show people what they didn't see."

Inside the car, he requested the fifth floor.

"I noticed you right away," he went on.

"Fifth floor."

"Yeah, that's right. As soon as you walked into the club, I knew. You've got such strong light. Not everyone does. Not strong and pure, anyway, like yours. It's what makes you special."

"Five . . . B," Trueheart mumbled as his vision faded in and out on the apartment door.

"Yep, just A and B up here, and A works nights. Makes it easier. Come on in. You can lie down while I set things up."

"Loft. Village? Soho? Where?"

"Here now, just stretch out here."

He wanted to fight, but with arms and legs weak as a baby, his struggles were more petulant than defensive.

"Relax, relax. I don't want to give you any more soother just now. You have a right to know what you're about to do. About to become. Just give me a few minutes."

He had to save his strength, Trueheart thought dimly. What there was of it. Save it and observe. Observe and report. "Converted loft. Big space. Windows. Ah, God. Three large windows front, sky windows above. Top floor? Walls. Oh jeez, oh God. Walls . . . portraits. See the victims. I'm the victim. There's me. I'm on the wall. Am I dead?"

• • •

"He's losing it, Dallas."

"He's not." Eve clenched her fist, rapped once against the wheel. "He's doing the job. Roarke, give me something. Goddamn it."

"I'm working it." His hair fell like a black curtain over his face as he raced his fingers over a minipad. "I've got five possibles so far, more coming. These are popular sectors for singles."

"Five-story building, lofts."

"I heard him, Lieutenant." His voice was calm as a lake. "I need a few minutes."

She wasn't sure Trueheart had a few minutes.

Going with her gut, she drove across Broadway to skim along the cross streets. It was funkier, she thought. More welcoming to artists, Free-Agers, the young bohemians, and the well-heeled urbanites who enjoyed them.

He was young enough to want that sort of scene, and he had a solid financial backing. Nobody would think twice about seeing a guy help another guy—or girl—into a building. Quiet neighborhood. Young residents. Nobody would question that someone had been partying, was drunk or blissed out. Half of them would be the same.

Sirens and thunder rocked the night, and she watched lightning slice like a jagged-edge knife through the sky. The rain gushed out.

"Let me explain," Gerry said as he tested the lights and filters he'd set up. "My mother was an amazing woman. Pure and kind. She raised me on her own. She couldn't afford to be a professional mother, but she never neglected me. She was a nurse, and she spent her life helping people. Then she got sick."

He stepped back, studied the stage he was setting. "It shouldn't have happened. It's wrong for someone so selfless and bright to have a shadow take her. They call them shadows, the medicals call tumors shadows. She had shadows in her brain. We did everything right, everything they said. But she didn't get better. More shadows, deeper ones. It's just wrong."

He nodded. "Just about ready here. Sorry to take so long, but I want this to be perfect. It's the last one. You're the one who'll finish the work, so I don't want to make a mistake. Light is so important to image. You can finesse it on the computer, and that's an art, too, but the *real* art is in getting it right in the first place. I've studied for years, in school, on my own. Couldn't get a showing in New York. It's a tough town."

He didn't sound resentful. But patient. As Trueheart struggled to make his fingers work, he watched Gerry step back to study his own work, the work that lined his walls.

Rachel Howard. Kenby Sulu. Alicia Dilbert. All posed and perfected. All dead in their thin silver frames.

There were other images of them, Trueheart saw dimly. The candid shots. He'd framed them as well, and grouped them on the wall.

"I had a little showing in Philadelphia a year ago," Gerry went on. "Just a little gallery, but still. It's a good start. I was going places, just as I was meant to. But after Mom got sick, I had to put that on hold. Drop out of grad school, concentrate on her. She didn't want me to, but how could I worry about fame and fortune when she was sick? What kind of a son would that make me?

"I watched her die," he said softly. "I watched the light go out of her. I couldn't stop it. I didn't know how. Then. But I figured it out. I wish . . . I only wish I'd known before it was too late for her."

He turned back, smiled kindly. "Well, we need to get started."

As he crossed the room, sweat ran down Trueheart's face from the effort to key in his homer.

"Where's the van?" Despite the storm, Baxter had the window open, his head stuck through as he scanned the streets. "Where's the goddamn van?" He swiped his dripping hair out of his face. "Every cop in the city out looking, and we can't find one stinking van?"

He could have taken it underground, Eve thought. Into another port. But she didn't think so. Not from the scene she'd heard through her communicator. Street parking, first level. They hadn't clanged down steps.

She was close. She *knew* she was close. But if they were even a block off . . .

"Greenwich Street. 207, apartment 5-B." Roarke lifted his head now, and his eyes were no longer cool. "Javert Stevens."

"All units," Eve began, and ignoring all traffic codes, swung her vehicle into a hard, sliding U-turn. Cars parted for her like the Red Sea as she bulleted the wrong way up a one-way street.

"Homer's engaged!" Peabody lurched in her seat, grabbing Baxter's arm. "He did it! We're two blocks away."

Beside her, Baxter pulled his head in. Even as he began to pray, he checked his weapon.

He wasn't sure he'd managed it, couldn't be sure, but Trueheart let the communicator slide into the cushions on the sofa where Gerry had laid him.

He tried to push the hands away as they reached for him, but only flailed once before his arms dropped weakly.

"It's going to be all right, I promise. It's not going to hurt. I'm going to take care of that. Then you'll see. It's the most amazing thing. I want you posed standing. Very straight. Like a soldier. That's what I see in you, a soldier—brave and true. But not stiff, so we have to work that a little."

He leaned Trueheart against a waist-high stand, drew wires he'd already attached around his ankles. "You want music? I'll put some on in just a minute. I think I'm going to try this as—what do they call it? Parade rest? Let's see how it looks."

He brought Trueheart's arms back, hooking them by more wire to the post.

"This is going to look good. See, I'll take the post and wires out of the image with the computer. Maybe I should tuck your shirt in."

Another line of sweat dribbled down Trueheart's back. If he found the weapon, it would all be over. Maybe it was over anyway.

But Gerry stepped back, angled his head. "No, you know I like it out. Shows you're relaxed, a little casual, but still on alert. You struck me as being on alert in the club. Looking around, watching people. That's why I thought of the solider pose."

He picked up a pressure syringe. "I'm going to give you a little more now, so you won't be afraid, so you won't feel any discomfort. And when I'm finished. When I have the image, you'll understand everything. You'll be part of everything."

"Don't." Trueheart's head lolled on his neck.

"Ssh. Ssh, don't worry."

He felt the light push against his arm, felt himself going under—soft waves, gentle breezes. Lights out.

Eve roared up to the curb, and over it as her tires fought to find purchase on the wet street. The black van was parked just ahead.

Even as the car shimmied, Baxter was out. Eve was steps behind him. "Hold it together," she ordered.

"I'm together. I'm so fucking together there are two of me in here."

He yanked out his master.

"Palm plate—this is faster." Roarke shoved him aside, and went quickly to work with illegal tools.

"You didn't see this," Eve snapped out.

"I don't see a damn thing."

"You listen to me. Detective Baxter, you listen to me now. I am in command." She nodded briskly when Feeney and McNab, then a trio of black-and-whites braked in front of the building. "We go in fast, but we go in organized."

She shoved through the door Roarke opened. "Stairs. Uniforms, elevator. Peabody with me." She continued to toss orders as she pounded up. "Baxter, Trueheart is your priority."

"You don't have to tell me that."

"You will find and safely secure Officer Trueheart. I want a medic up here," she barked into her communicator. "I want a medi-van on site. Now. Leave the suspect to me unless directly engaged. Is that clear?"

"I got it."

"He's put music on, Lieutenant," Peabody reported, huffing a bit as they hit the fourth level. "I can't hear anything else now."

"Roarke, on the door. Give me two units on emergency evac. He isn't going to rabbit on us. Get this building surrounded. Two men stationed on each floor at stairway. Disengage the elevators."

The next boom of thunder shook the floor under her feet as she rushed to 5-B.

Her weapon was in her hand, her blood cold, her head clear.

"I go in low," she stated, rocking onto her toes as Roarke finessed the locks.

He worked fast, elegant fingers flying. She kept her eyes on them, focused, focused, and watched them lift clear.

"Go."

She kicked it open, surged through, and had her weapon trained dead between Gerry's startled eyes.

"Police. Drop it. Drop it now and step back, or I will shut your lights down permanently."

"You don't understand." His voice remained reasonable as he clutched the long, thin knife. "I'm going to make him live forever."

"Drop your weapon," she repeated, and refused to let herself be distracted by the sight of Trueheart, shirt open, as he stood unconscious, at parade rest.

"But—"

"Screw this." Baxter was already rushing across the room. To save them all the trouble, Eve lowered her weapon. And shot a stunning stream into Gerry, mid-body.

The knife hit the floor seconds before he did. The clever lights and shadows streamed over him on the white floor.

"Okay, kid, okay." Baxter's hands trembled visibly as he pressed his fingers to the pulse in Trueheart's throat. "He's breathing. We're going to get you down from here." His voice thickened as he fought with the wires. "I need some wire clippers. Goddamn it—"

"Here." Roarke handed him a tool. "Let me help you."

"Scene and suspect secure," Eve announced into her communicator and set her boot on Gerry's back in case he came out of it before she had him restrained. "Officer Trueheart appears to be unharmed. Where's my medic?"

She turned, found the loft full of cops. She gave it a minute, catching her breath, letting the adrenaline rush dissipate. She understood their need, wanted to give them this moment.

But . . .

"Too many cops in here. This scene is now secure, Code Red is ended. I need this area cleared. Officers, I imagine there's some crime somewhere in the city that needs dealing with. Good job," she added. "Thank you."

"Damn good job," Feeney told her and laid a hand on her shoulder as they watched Roarke and Baxter lay Trueheart on the floor. "You okay, kid?"

"A little shaky in the knees now. That was awful damn close."

"Close don't mean shit." He swiped at his forehead with his arm. "I'm getting too old to run up five flights of stairs. Want me to take this asshole in for you, book him?"

"Yeah. Appreciate it. I want first crack at him, though. So put him in one of the cages, and if he says anything about lawyers—"

"I've been having a little trouble with my ears. Gotta get them checked." He grinned viciously, then crouched down and pulled out his restraints.

She walked over to kneel by the medic.

"Just buzz juice," she was told. "Pulse is strong, bp's low, but not dangerously. He's going to need a lot of fluids, and he'll have one bitch of a headache, but he's young, strong, and fit."

"He's coming around." Baxter pushed a hand through his still dripping hair. "Look at that. Hey, kid, come on back. Can't have you lying down on the job, making me look bad."

Trueheart's lashes fluttered. His vision was blurry and his

mind confused. "Sir." He tried to swallow, coughed a little. "Lieutenant? Am I dead?"

"Not even close." She couldn't resist, and took his hand. Baxter already had his other one. "You did the job, Officer Trueheart. You did good. Suspect is in custody."

" 'Kay. Pretty tired now," he said, then conked out again.

"He'll go in and out for a while," the medic said cheerfully. "We'll get some fluids in him, take him overnight for observation. He'll be good as new by morning."

"Dallas, I want to stick with him."

"Affirmative," she said to Baxter. "Update me on his condition. Contact his mother. Make sure she knows he's okay first, then let her know he did the job."

She straightened up, and prepared to do hers.

Epilogue

"You see," Gerry explained. "They're inside me now. Not my body—the body's just a shell. My mother explained all that to me. They're in my soul. Light to light."

"Did your mother tell you to take their light, Gerry?"

"No." He shook his head, leaned forward earnestly. "I wish we'd understood it all before she died. It didn't have to happen. It *never* has to happen. We'll all live forever, we have the capacity. It's just the body that needs to be shed off."

"So," Eve said, just as reasonably. "You shed off Rachel Howard's, Kenby Sulu's, and Alicia Dilbert's bodies for them?"

"Yes. Their light was so strong, you see. If you really looked, really understood my portraits of them, you'd see that. My mother told me about the light, how as a nurse, she'd see the light in the eyes of the patients. It would be so strong in some, even when medically it seemed as though there wasn't a chance for them. But she'd see that light, she said, and knew they were going to beat the odds. Others, well, you'd think they were going to be fine, but the light wasn't there. And they'd die. Just slip away."

"Your mother's light was strong."

"Yes, but not strong enough." Grief shuddered over his face, and for a moment his eyes weren't mad. They were young and shattered. "Too many shadows. The shadows smothered the light. You see . . ." He shifted in his chair again. When his face cleared of sorrow, the madness was back over it. "I studied the work of Henri Javert. He was—"

"I know. He photographed the dead."

"It's a fascinating art. I could see what my mother meant about the light. In the dead, once the light's been taken, the shell is empty. Javert's work was brilliant, and helped show me the way. Preserve the light, shed the body."

"Take the light into yourself, through the camera."

"The lens is magic. It's not all technology, you know. It's art and magic. Through it you can see the soul. You can look into a subject and see their soul through the lens. It's amazing. I have the gift."

"Why did you use Hastings?"

"I don't understand the question."

"You took file images from him."

"Oh. I really admire his work. He's a difficult man, but an incredible artist. I learned a lot from him, in a very short time. He also photographs the dead, but for commission. Not for pure art. This is art."

"Did you assist him in photographing the dead?"

"Only once, but it was amazing. I'd been so down, you know, after my mother. Professor Browning helped get me back on track. She understood I was going through a rough patch and suggested I take the job as Hastings's assistant. Keep busy. I only worked with him for a week or so, but it brought me back. When I saw Rachel Howard at that wedding, saw the light just spilling out of her . . . it was an epiphany. Hastings saw it, too. I had to stop myself from just grabbing the camera from him to take her portrait, but he saw it, too. So I realized he was part of the path. Like a guide."

"And you took the discs."

"I guess it wasn't right, and I'm sorry. I'll pay the fine," he told her with an apologetic smile. "But it was for something so important—I'm sure Hastings will understand that.

I went back later, once I had it all worked out. He's a little careless and disorganized about his files. I just went through them to see. And the light—the faces—just jumped out at me."

"Trueheart wasn't there."

"Trueheart?"

"My officer. The one you had in your studio tonight."

"Trueheart. It's a perfect name for him. I hadn't completed my research on him because I had someone else in mind for the last. But as soon as I saw him in the club, I knew. I just knew, and tonight it fell into place."

"About the club. Why did you change your name?"

"You have to be careful. I knew people wouldn't understand, would try to stop me. I thought I'd set up an alter ego, just as a cushion."

"You'd already changed it once, as Hastings's assistant. Were you already planning your . . . gallery?"

"I think, somewhere in the back of my mind, I was. But lots of artists take a professional name, and I was just trying that one on. I took Javert's name because I really admired him."

"When you took the job at the club," she prompted, "you had your plan in place."

"Oh yeah. But for the club, I thought I'd just keep it simple—my name, I mean. Audrey is Mom's middle name, so it was kind of an homage to her. I'm kinda thirsty? Can I get a drink?"

"Sure." She gestured to Peabody. "How'd you pick the data club?"

"Oh, I used to hang there sometimes. A lot of the college kids come into the club. Almost all of them pass through sooner or later, so taking a job tending bar was a good way to observe and select. And the data club made sense. I could get the word out on my work efficiently, privately."

"How?"

"I'd just slip back in after I'd done the portraits and discarded the shell. Slip the data disc to the dj, or dump it into an in-basket. Nobody pays attention. I knew Nadine Furst would get the story out. She's really good, you know?"

When Peabody offered him water, he took it gratefully. "And 75 has the best ratings in the city. I did my research."

"Bet you did."

Drinking, he nodded. "You've seen my work now. My studio, my gallery." Dressed in the ugly orange NYPSD jumpsuit, his ankle chained to the table, the harsh lights from the overhead in Interview Room A spilling over him, he looked proud.

"Yes, Gerry, I've seen it."

"So, you understand now. I did research on you, too. You're smart and creative. You have strong light. It's not pure, but it's strong. You'll let me finish, right? You have to let me finish the work. One more portrait and I'll be immortal. People will see. We never have to die. No one ever has to lose someone they love, ever again. No one has to suffer or have pain."

"Gerry, I'm going to ask you again, just so we're really clear. Do you understand your rights and obligations?"

"Oh yeah. Sure."

"And you've waived your right to legal representation during this interview."

"I just want to tell you what it all means. I don't want people to think I'm some kind of monster. I'm not. I'm a savior."

"And you did willingly take the lives of Rachel Howard, Kenby Sulu, and Alicia Dilbert?"

"I preserved their light," he corrected. "Forever."

"To do so, you took the aforementioned individuals to your studio on Greenwich, took them there in a drugged state that you induced, and there caused the death of their mortal bodies by inserting a knife into their hearts."

"I didn't want to hurt them, that's why I gave them the medicine they gave my mom. It made her sleep easy, took away the pain."

"You also took Officer Troy Trueheart to that same location tonight, in the same condition with the same purpose in mind."

"Yes, to shed their mortal bodies." Relief washed over her face as he nodded. "Their shells. And by taking their portrait so near the instant of death, I took their light into myself, joining it to mine, preserving it, and giving them immortality. They live in me," he told her. "With the last light joined, the work will be done. I'll know all they knew. They'll know me. Always."

"Understood. Record off."

"So I can go now?"

"No, I'm sorry. There are some other people you'll need to talk to. Explain things to."

"Oh, okay." He glanced around, blankly. "But I really need to get back to work soon."

Sanity, Eve thought, was a thin and slippery line. Gerry had tipped over it. If he could still function, still plan, still make images, he'd be doing it all in a secured room in a mental health facility for the rest of his life.

"I hope it won't take very long," he added as a uniform entered to take him back to a cage.

When Eve didn't rise, Peabody walked over, poured two cups of water. "My dad used to love these old cartoon vids. I remember this one, where this talking cat was crazy. Totally bonked. Anyway, to show it, they had these little birds flying around his head and chirping."

She drank her water while Eve stared at her own. "Anyway, that's what I'd see with him. Little birds flying around his head, except it's too sad and too awful for little birds."

"Sometimes, you do the job, you close the case, but the door just doesn't shut for you. I guess this is going to be one of those. Roarke was right. He's just pathetic. It's easier when they're vicious or greedy or just downright evil. Pathetic leaves the door open a crack."

"You should go home, Dallas. We should all go home now."

"You're right." She rubbed her eyes like a tired child.

But she wrote up the report first, and filed it, hoping to close the door a little more. The department shrinks, and whatever private ones Gerry might eventually engage, would have a field day with him.

But he would never step out of that secured room again.

She detoured by the hospital to look in on Trueheart. He

was sleeping like a baby, with the monitors recording the steady beat of his pulse. In the chair beside the bed, Baxter was slumped and snoring.

Quietly, she moved into the room, stood beside the bed for a moment just looking at Trueheart. His color was good, she decided, his breathing even.

Tied to the bed guard was some sort of novelty balloon that looked like giant female breasts.

Leaning down she gave Baxter's shoulder a quick shake and his snoring cut off with a shocked snort. He jerked awake and his hand went automatically to his weapon.

"Stand down, Detective," she whispered.

"Kid okay?" He pushed up in the chair. "Shit. I was out."

"Tell me. The rhinoceros snoring's going to wake Trueheart up. Go home, Baxter."

"I was just going to sit with him awhile, make sure . . . Guess I conked."

"Go home," she repeated. "Catch a few hours horizontal. They're going to release him mid-morning. You can come back and take him home. I'll clear your personal time."

"Yeah." He sighed. "Appreciate it. He did good, Dallas."

"He did good."

"Stevenson?"

"He's away."

"Well." Baxter got to his feet. "I guess that's that."

"That's that," she agreed, but when Baxter was gone, she sat and kept watch another hour herself.

She drove home as the sun came up. The storm had passed, and the light was almost gentle, almost pretty over the city. She supposed there was a metaphor in there somewhere, but she was too damn tired to dig it out.

But the light grew stronger as she turned toward home, and stronger yet as she passed through the gates. It showered over the house, the great house out of a sky that decided to be bright and summer blue.

It was cooler, she noted as she stepped out of the car. Cooler than it had been in days. Weeks. Maybe years. Damn if there wasn't a nice little breeze kicking up.

She walked inside, peeled off her jacket, and just let it drop.

Roarke came out of the parlor. "Good morning, Lieutenant."

"Pretty nice day out there."

"It is." He crossed to her, skimmed a finger down the dent in her chin, studied her tired eyes. "How are you?"

"Been better, but I've been a hell of a lot worse. Trueheart came out of it—they'll release him today. He's none the worse for wear, and Baxter was hovering over him like a mother duck. It's kind of cute."

"Did you put him in for commendation?"

She laughed a little. "What am I, transparent?"

"To me." He put his arms around her, drew her in.

"How was he doing when you went by the hospital to see him?"

He smiled into her hair. "Apparently you see through me, too. He looked young and eager, if a bit tired. Baxter bought him an obscene balloon in the shape of enormous breasts. With obvious embarrassment and delight, Trueheart tied it to his bed guard."

"Yeah, I saw it when I went by. All's right with the world again. Or as close as it gets."

"You're sorry for him."

She knew he didn't speak of Trueheart now. "More than I want to be. He's twisted. Maybe his mother's death turned him, or maybe he'd have ended up that way anyhow. That's for the head guys to figure out. I'm done. Guess I should go up and fall on my face for a few hours."

"I imagine so. We'll have to keep our date later."

"What date?"

He slipped an arm around her waist, turned for the stairs. "The date we outlined for when Summerset left for holiday."

"Wait a minute, wait a minute." She jerked back, scanning the foyer. "He's gone? The house is Summerset-free?"

"Left not twenty minutes ago, still limping a bit, but—"

"I must be slipping. I should've known. I should've felt it."

She kicked her jacket into the air, wiggled her hips, did

what might have been a cha-cha down the hall.

"You seem to have found a stored pocket of energy."

"I am reborn!" Cackling, she whirled around, pushed off with her toes and leaped on him. "Let's have monkey sex," she said as she wrapped her legs around Roarke's waist.

"Well, if you insist. It so happens I have a pint of very nice chocolate sauce in the parlor."

"You're kidding."

"One never kids about monkey sex with chocolate sauce."

She laughed like a loon, then crushed her mouth to his—hot and hard enough to make him stagger. And when they tumbled onto the floor, she thought she heard the door close, just a little more.

If you enjoyed

Portrait in Death

you won't want to miss

IMITATION IN DEATH

Here is a special excerpt from this provocative
novel by J. D. Robb.

Available from Berkley Books!

You never saw it all. No matter how many times you walked through the blood and the gore, no matter how often you looked at the horror man inflicted on man, you never saw it all.

There was always something worse, something meaner, or crazier, more vicious, more cruel.

As Lieutenant Eve Dallas stood over what had once been a woman, she wondered when she would see worse than this.

Two of the uniform cops on scene were still retching at the mouth of the alley. The sound of their sickness echoed back to her. She stood where she was, hands and boots already sealed, and waited for her own shuddering stomach to settle.

Had she seen this much blood before? It was hard to remember. It was best not to.

She crouched, opened her field kit, and took out her ID pad to run the victim's fingerprints. She couldn't avoid the blood, so she stopped thinking about it. Lifting the limp hand she pressed the thumb to her pad.

"Victim is female, Caucasian. The body was discovered at approximately oh-three-thirty by officers responding to anonymous nine-one-one, and is herewith identified through

fingerprint check as Wooton, Jacie, age forty-one, licensed
companion, residing 375 Doyers."

She took a shallow breath, then another. "Victim's throat
has been cut. Spatter pattern indicates wound was inflicted
while victim stood against the north-facing wall of the alley.
Blood pattern and trail would indicate victim fell or was laid
across alley floor by assailant or assailants who then . . ."

Jesus. Oh Jesus.

"Who then mutilated the victim by removing the pelvic
area. Both the throat and pelvic wounds indicate the use of
a sharp implement and some precision."

Despite the heat her skin prickled, cold and clammy as
she took out gauges, recorded data.

"I'm sorry." Peabody, her aide, spoke from behind her.
Eve didn't have to look around to know Peabody's face
would still be pale and glossy from shock and nausea. "I'm
sorry, Lieutenant, I couldn't maintain."

"Don't worry about it. You okay now?"

"I . . . Yes, sir."

Eve nodded and continued to work. Stalwart, steady, and
as dependable as the tide, Peabody had taken one look at
what laid in the alley, turned sheet white, and had stumbled
back toward the street at Eve's sharp order to puke elsewhere.

"I've got an ID on her. Jacie Wooton, Doyers. An LC.
Do a run for me."

"I've never seen anything like this. Just never seen . . ."

"Get the data. Do it down there. You're in my light here."

She wasn't, Peabody knew. Her lieutenant was cutting her
a break, and because her head wanted to spin again, she took
it, moving toward the mouth of the alley.

She'd sweated through her uniform shirt, and her dark
bowl of hair was damp at the temples under her cap. Her
throat was raw, her voice weak, but she initiated the run.
And watched Eve work.

Efficient, thorough, and some would say cold. But Peabody had seen the leap of shock and horror, and of pity, on

Eve's face before her own vision had blurred. Cold wasn't the word, but driven was.

She was pale now, Peabody noted, and it wasn't just the work lights that bleached the color from her narrow face. Her brown eyes were focused and flat, and unwavering as they examined the atrocity. Her hands were steady, and her boots smeared with blood.

There was a line of sweat down the middle back of her shirt, but she wouldn't stumble away. She would stay until it was done.

When Eve straightened, Peabody saw a tall, lean woman in stained boots, worn jeans, and a gorgeous linen jacket, a fine-boned face with a wide mouth, wide eyes of gilded brown, and a short and disordered cap of hair nearly the same color.

More, she saw a cop who never turned away from death.

"Dallas—"

"Peabody, I don't care if you puke as long as you don't contaminate the scene. Give me the data."

"Parents listed as next of kin. They live in Idaho."

"The potato place, right?"

"Yeah." Peabody managed a shaky smile. "Spud central. Victim's lived in New York for twenty-two years. Previous residence on Central Park West. She's resided down here for eighteen months."

"That's quite a change of venue. What she get popped for?"

"Illegals. Three strikes. Lost her top drawer license, did six months in, rehab, counseling, and was given a probationary street license about a year ago."

"She roll on her dealer?"

"No, sir."

"We'll see what the tox screen tells us once she's in the morgue, but I don't think Jack's her dealer." Eve lifted the envelope that had been left, sealed to prevent blood stains, on the body.

LIEUTENANT EVE DALLAS, NYPSD

Computer generated, she guessed, in a fancy font on elegant cream colored paper. Thick, weighty, and expensive.
The sort of thing used for high-class invites. She should
know, she mused, as her husband was big on sending and
receiving high-class invites.

She took out the second evidence bag and read the note
again.

> Hello, Lieutenant Dallas,
>   Hot enough for ya? I know you've had a busy
> summer, and I've been admiring your work. I can think
> of no one on the police force of our fair city I'd rather
> have involved with me on what I hope will be a very
> intimate level.
>   Here is a sample of my work. What do you think?
> Looking forward to our continued association.
>   Jack.

"I'll tell you what I think, Jack. I think you're a very sick
fuck. Tag and bag," she ordered with a last glance down the
alley. "Homicide."

Connect with Berkley Publishing Online!

For sneak peeks into the newest releases, news on all your favorite authors, book giveaways, and a central place to connect with fellow fans—

"Like" and follow Berkley Publishing!

facebook.com/BerkleyPub
twitter.com/BerkleyPub
instagram.com/BerkleyPub

From #1 *New York Times* Bestselling Author

J. D. ROBB

THE IN DEATH SERIES

NAKED IN DEATH

GLORY IN DEATH

IMMORTAL IN DEATH

RAPTURE IN DEATH

CEREMONY IN DEATH

VENGEANCE IN DEATH

HOLIDAY IN DEATH

CONSPIRACY IN DEATH

LOYALTY IN DEATH

WITNESS IN DEATH

JUDGMENT IN DEATH

BETRAYAL IN DEATH

SEDUCTION IN DEATH

REUNION IN DEATH

PURITY IN DEATH

PORTRAIT IN DEATH

IMITATION IN DEATH

DIVIDED IN DEATH

VISIONS IN DEATH

SURVIVOR IN DEATH

ORIGIN IN DEATH

MEMORY IN DEATH

BORN IN DEATH

INNOCENT IN DEATH

CREATION IN DEATH

STRANGERS IN DEATH

SALVATION IN DEATH

PROMISES IN DEATH

KINDRED IN DEATH

FANTASY IN DEATH

INDULGENCE IN DEATH

TREACHERY IN DEATH

NEW YORK TO DALLAS

CELEBRITY IN DEATH

DELUSION IN DEATH

CALCULATED IN DEATH

THANKLESS IN DEATH

CONCEALED IN DEATH

FESTIVE IN DEATH

OBSESSION IN DEATH

DEVOTED IN DEATH

BROTHERHOOD IN DEATH

jdrobb.com
facebook.com/jdrobbauthor
penguin.com

M1732AS1015